SPECIAL MESSAGE TO

THE ULVERSCROFT FO~~UNDATION~~
(registered UK charity number 264873)
was established in 1972 to provide funds for
research, diagnosis and treatment of eye diseases.
Exampl~~e o~~f major projects funded by the
~~Ulve~~rscroft Foundation are:-

- Th~~e Childr~~en's Eye Unit at Moorfelds Eye
  H~~ospital, L~~ondon
- T~~he Ulvers~~croft Children's Eye Unit at Great
  O~~rmond S~~treet Hospital for Sick Children
- F~~unding re~~search into eye diseases and
  ~~treatment~~ at the Department of
  ~~Ophthalmo~~logy, University of Leicester
- ~~The Ulve~~rscroft Vision Research Group,
  ~~Institute o~~f Child Health
  ~~Operat~~ing theatres at the Western
  ~~Eye~~ Hospital, London
- ~~Chair~~ of Ophthalmology at the Royal
  ~~Australia~~n College of Ophthalmologists

You c~~an h~~elp f~~u~~rther the work of the Foundation
by making a d~~o~~nation or leaving a legacy. Every
contributio~~n is~~ gratefully received. If you would
like to he~~lp su~~pport the Foundation or require
fur~~ther i~~nformation, please contact:

THE ULVERSCROFT FOUNDATION
The Green, Bradgate Road, Anstey,
Leicester LE7 7FU, England
Tel: (0116) 236 4325

website: www.ulverscroft-foundation.org.uk

THE WOMEN OF WATERLOO BRIDGE

London, 1940. After her fiancé breaks off their engagement, Evelyn decides to do her part for the war effort by signing up for construction work on Waterloo Bridge. Grieving after her little boy dies in an air raid, Gwen is completely lost when her husband sends their younger children to the countryside for safety. Enlisting as a construction worker, she is partnered with cheerful Evelyn. The two women strike up a heartwarming friendship. Musical prodigy Joan's life has always been dictated by her controlling mother. When an affair nearly ends in scandal, Joan finally takes her life into her own hands. She soon finds work at Waterloo Bridge. Yet there are other troubles for her to overcome . . .

JAN CASEY

THE WOMEN OF WATERLOO BRIDGE

Complete and Unabridged

MAGNA
Leicester

First published in Great Britain in 2020 by
Aria
an imprint of Head of Zeus Ltd
London

First Ulverscroft Edition
published 2021
by arrangement with
Head of Zeus Ltd
London

This is a work of fiction. All characters,
organisations, and events portrayed in this novel
are either products of the author's imagination or
are used fictitiously.

A catalogue record for this book is available
from the British Library.

ISBN 978–0–7505–4879–3

Published by
Ulverscroft Limited
Anstey, Leicestershire

Printed and bound in Great Britain by
TJ Books Ltd., Padstow, Cornwall

This book is printed on acid-free paper

For my lovely Mum and Dad who
always said I could do it.

Note from the Author

As we passed under Waterloo Bridge, the pilot of the Thames River cruiser said, 'This bridge is known as the Ladies' Bridge because there's an urban myth that it was built by women during the Second World War. Careful it doesn't fall on top of you!'

The urban myth turned out to be fact that had been whitewashed by history. This book is a tribute to the women who turned their hands to the tools to construct Waterloo Bridge, and other structures, during WW2 and then went back to their daily lives when peace was declared, as if nothing extraordinary had happened.

Contents

Contents

1

December 1940

Evelyn

Evelyn sat on a thin blanket, chin on her knees, unable to take her eyes off the stairs leading down from the street. Hordes were pushing in even though they were packed down here already. There was never a lot of room, but tonight they kept moving along under the Wood Green sign and rearranging themselves to make way for others who, like them, didn't want to take their chances up there.

'Budge up,' Dad said, nudging Evelyn's shoulder. 'We're over here now.'

Evelyn looked around and her neck caught, stiff from holding it at an angle for so long. Dad cocked his thumb to a spot behind him and Evelyn could see now that her family had moved on and another set up camp around her. Blinking, she gathered her things and apologised to a woman who was passing bread and dripping to her children, their grubby hands still white and shivery from the cold.

Settling her bedding next to his, Dad indicated the woman organising her children's tea. 'That'll be you in no time,' he said.

Evelyn pulled a face. 'Mine won't be that mucky.'

1

'Oh, won't they?' Dad smiled as if he knew something Evelyn didn't. 'You were. So was that sister of yours. Your mother used to despair.'

'We haven't even set a date yet,' Evelyn said.

Dad twisted the ring round Evelyn's finger until the minuscule gem was facing the right way. He tapped it and said, 'Won't be long though and then . . .' They both looked over at the children again in time to see the oldest girl cram the last of her tea in her mouth.

Dad chuckled and picked up his paper. 'Let's have a cup of tea, shall we?'

'In a minute,' Evelyn answered. She turned back to the entrance, searching again for her sister's burgundy heels amongst the endless pairs of shoes that descended.

'Give her a chance, she'll barely have finished her shift. Then she might be meeting someone.' Dad made a show of turning the page with studied nonchalance. 'You know what she's like.'

Evelyn was as worried about Sylvie's safety as her dad, but not in the way he presumed. She wanted her here in one piece so she could kill the silly mare herself. 'We all know what Sylvie's like. Nothing puts her off.' Not even a night like this, Evelyn thought. If conditions were bad when she'd made her way down, a couple of hours ago, things must be dreadful out there now. She knew that by the looks on the faces pressing in around her, the snippets of news she caught passed on from the newcomers. When Uncle Bert made his way towards them, hair ruffled, cap in hand, Evelyn saw him catch Dad's eye and shake his head. He didn't need to elaborate for them to understand

2

the seriousness of what was happening above them.

Evelyn gathered their cups together and negotiated her way over to the makeshift kitchen. The queue for tea was long and orderly, none of them having the energy to do anything other than shuffle their way closer to the urn. Evelyn turned several times and glanced over the heads of the women behind her to scan the platform for Sylvie. Then the line snaked around the wall and her view was obscured. She gazed down at her brown lace-ups and thought about the words she'd had with Sylvie that morning, needles of heat prickling through her as she recalled the argument.

* * *

Her weekly letter from Ron had been delivered and she'd managed to grab a couple of minutes to herself after breakfast to sit and read it. She was about to slit the envelope when a movement at the front gate had cast a shadow over the sitting room. She'd moved closer to the window and craned her neck to see what had distracted her. 'Sylvie,' she'd fumed when she'd glimpsed the flash of her sister's camel coat swinging out of sight. Stuffing the letter behind a cushion, she'd rammed her feet into her shoes and run out onto the pavement. She was determined that Sylvie wouldn't get away with it this time.

The wiggle her sister had recently cultivated made it easy to gain on her and when Evelyn could almost touch her Sylvie had turned, a puzzled look on her face.

'Where is it?' demanded Evelyn.

'What?' Sylvie said with exaggerated innocence.

'It can't be in *there*.' Evelyn snatched at the minute black clutch bag, exquisitely embroidered with tiny sequins and perfect for a night on the town after work, which Sylvie carried under her arm.

Sylvie dangled the shiny bag from its strap and said, 'Of course it's not. Don't be daft. Besides, that old gas mask doesn't match what I'm wearing, does it?' She swept her arms wide, encouraging Evelyn to take in her outfit from hat to shoes and she smiled, her Max Factor red lips framing her even white teeth. She looked lovely, as she always did. Evelyn knew she could look like that, if and when she wanted to. But she wasn't going anywhere so there was no need. Except back to the all-pervasive housework and her letter, after she'd knocked some sense into Sylvie.

'Stop behaving like this. You're being irresponsible.'

Sylvie let her arms drop to her sides and exhaled through puffed cheeks, like a deflated party balloon. 'There's nothing wrong with having a bit of fun, is there? Or have you forgotten all about that?'

'All you ever talk about is fun and it's getting boring. I'm talking about something much more important.'

'Me? Boring?' Sylvie put her hands on her hips. 'The word was invented for you. And that fiancé of yours.'

'Don't start all that again, Sylvie. I'm asking you. No, I'm telling you. Come back to the house

4

and get your mask, then you can go and have fun.'

'No.' Sylvie shook her head. 'And don't forget, I am older and therefore wiser.'

'Then try acting it.'

'Oh, I *am*. It's you who's got it wrong. Twenty-two going on fifty if you ask me. Besides, Mum told *me* to look out for *you*, not the other way around.'

'Don't bring Mum into it,' Evelyn said, her voice catching. 'She's not here. But Dad is, and he'd be gutted if he found out about this.'

'Well, *I'm* not going to tell him. Are you?'

Evelyn knew when she was defeated. They stood looking at each other until Sylvie walked a few steps backwards, blowing Evelyn a kiss. 'I do know what I'm talking about when it comes to Ron. He's nice enough, but a bit dry. Like toast without the butter and jam. When you want it, the offer of fun's still there.' Then she turned, and Evelyn watched her run towards the bus stop, her skirt revealing the perfect amount of leg with each stride.

★ ★ ★

The line reached the sink. Evelyn swilled the cups around in an inch of brown water and dried them on a soggy tea towel. Three women, about the same age as Mum would have been, hadn't stopped gossiping since they joined the queue and were now throwing out remarks to others closer to the tea. She wondered if they recognised her and if they did, whether they would still feel sorry for her like they had after Mum died, when they

5

would stop to stroke her hair or search their pockets for a toffee, one for her and one for Sylvie.

'Squeeze one more out, dear sister.' Sylvie spoke right into Evelyn's ear, almost causing her to scald herself. 'Steady.' Sylvie laughed and took the pot from Evelyn. 'You see to the milk and sugar — I've got this.'

Relief overwhelmed Evelyn but she checked it with a stern glare. 'Your mask is in my satchel,' she said. 'Dig it out when Dad's not looking and he'll think you had it with you all along.'

Sylvie set the pot on the small, ring-stained table to brew, and put her arms around Evelyn, kissing her cheek with a loud smacking noise. 'Thank you,' she said. 'I'll do the same for you some time.'

Evelyn looked away and busied herself with the cups. 'Let's take these back to Dad and Uncle Bert,' she said.

'No, let's be friends first,' Sylvie said, rubbing at the red stain her mouth had left on Evelyn's face. 'Please? I have so much to tell you and I want to hear about your letter from Ron.'

Evelyn was reluctant to be drawn in so quickly. A sense of restlessness could be felt from the women in the queue behind. 'Hurry up with the pot,' Evelyn said, holding the cups out for Sylvie to pour.

'Say it,' Sylvie said, her grinning face pressed close to Evelyn's. 'Say friends.'

'Alright,' Evelyn conceded, laughing out loud. 'Alright. Friends.'

The talk in their camp was all about the war. Evelyn expected that was the case everywhere. Sylvie, though, wanted to tell her about dancing. Or, as it

6

had turned out that night, the lack of it. She and a girl from work had tried two or three of their usual haunts, then walked to Regent Street where they'd heard that nothing stopped the 'prancing at the Paradise'.

Evelyn opened her mouth to chastise Sylvie for roaming so far, but stopped herself because she didn't want to start another quarrel. More to the point, she was enjoying Sylvie's retelling of her evening. She could picture the clubs and pubs they'd called in on and how she and her friend had escaped to the lav to repaint their faces and laugh at a couple of blokes they'd met along the way.

'So you managed to fight them off?' Evelyn asked.

Sylvie rolled her eyes. 'It didn't take much. They were all over the place, the soppy sods. The Paradise was a dead loss, too. Packing up like everywhere else.'

'Well, everyone needed to get to a shelter, or home if they could.'

'I know.' Sylvie sighed and smoothed her stockings over her calves. 'Don't matter. Tomorrow's another day.'

'And the day after that? New Year's Eve.'

'Got to be something happening then. Dancing and a . . .'

'. . . bit of fun,' Evelyn finished for her.

'And you're coming out with me that night. With me and Helen. No arguing with your big sister.'

Quiet supplanted the earlier commotion. A few kids who'd been chasing around with battered paper

7

crowns on their heads, holding tight to Christmas for as long as possible, stopped their games and settled down. Some men nearby played a muted hand of cards and, from close to the tunnel, underneath faded red and green garlands working their way loose from slimy walls, a group of women started to sing a song. No one joined in, perhaps because what was happening up there made it impossible to muster the energy.

A number of people were still coming down but — sure that no trains would pass through until dawn — wardens were guiding them on to the tracks, something Evelyn hadn't seen happen before.

'This is horrible,' Sylvie said, looking around. 'Would you choose to sleep with any of these people?'

'Trust you to think of that.'

'No, I mean just sleep. If any one of them suggested such a thing in normal circumstances you'd be appalled, wouldn't you? I would.'

Evelyn nodded and flared her nostrils, a vile smell hitting the back of her throat. She waved her hand in front of her face and said, 'The stench. It's okay when I don't think about it.'

'But when you do . . . ' Sylvie gagged. 'Here.' She tapped a few drops of 4711 onto one of Dad's big hankies and they sat side by side with it pressed to their faces.

Sylvie unclasped her ear clips and nestled them in the toes of her shoes. They punched their coats into pillow shapes and lay down close together. 'Now,' Sylvie said, her hands under her head, 'tell me about Ron. Anything exciting to report from

Colchester?'

Evelyn was hoping Sylvie had forgotten about the letter from Ron. She felt the same wound reopening as it had done earlier when Sylvie had said Ron was dull. And the times before when she'd called him boring and dreary and tedious. She was left in no doubt about what Sylvie thought of Ron.

'Well?' Sylvie propped herself up on her elbow. 'What did lover boy have to say for himself?'

'Well, the truth is . . .' Evelyn picked a bit of fluff off her blanket and rolled it into a ball. 'I was so upset after our set-to that I didn't read Ron's letter after all.'

'Oh.' Sylvie slumped down. 'Sorry. I really am.'

'Never mind,' Evelyn said, although that wasn't the truth. Sylvie would be unshakeable if she knew what Evelyn had felt when she'd opened the envelope and unfolded the sheets of writing. The letter was dated Monday 23rd December 1940. Ron always wrote on a Monday. *My dearest fiancée Evelyn*, it started. Evelyn had searched through all the other letters from Ron she kept in Mum's old writing box and she was right; the greeting was the same on every single one. Then he went on to tell her what he'd had for tea in the canteen that evening and hoped he wasn't making her tummy rumble with hunger. She could probably write a book about the meals served in training camps.

She hadn't needed to read the rest of the letter to know that there would be a bit about the weather, something that witty Chalky White had said to make the lads laugh, details of pressing his uniform and how his ingrown toenail was healing

9

— or not. Huge tears had boiled over the rims of her eyes then and scorched her cheeks as they ran down her face. She'd balled up the letter and thrown it in with the others, kicking the box back under her bed.

'Perhaps . . .' Sylvie's voice was teasing now. 'Perhaps your Ron's a dark horse and the letter is just too, too saucy to share. Was it?' Sylvie leaned closer. 'Go on, tell all.'

'*Oh* . . .' Evelyn groaned and turned away from Sylvie. She'd given herself a firm telling-off as the day had worn on, reminding herself what a decent, steady chap Ron was and that was why she was going to marry him. All she needed to do was concentrate on Ron's good points — and there were plenty of them. She wouldn't be drawn into Sylvie's cataloguing of the qualities he lacked.

But Sylvie never could stand silence for long. 'Do you think people have a quick dash up the channel under the blankets?' Sylvie said.

Evelyn laughed out loud. 'I don't like to think about it, but I expect they do,' she said.

'You can hear them sometimes, trying hard to be clever and quiet.'

They were still for a minute — then both realised at the same time they'd been listening for the sounds of stifled moans and grunts. Dad wound his way towards them and bent to kiss them both on their foreheads. They watched him crawl under his bedding and cover his face with yesterday's paper. 'Good job he didn't hear us,' Sylvie said.

'He would have been shocked.'

'And said something about Mum wanting us to be nice girls.' They tried to muffle their laughter,

10

stuffing their knuckles into their mouths.

'Are you, Sylvie? Nice?'

Sylvie folded her hands and lowered her eyes, as if she was in church. 'I'm trying. I say to my admirers, ''Dancing's one thing but there'll be none of the other.'' You're more likely, though, so close to being Mrs Ron.' Sylvie opened her eyes and looked eagerly at Evelyn. 'Is it hard to keep saying no?'

Evelyn lay back and looked up at the sloping tiled roof. She wished it was. When Ron had walked her home after their engagement party, last June, he'd pushed his hand up her skirt and found the top of her thigh. There he drew feeble circles round and round with shaking fingers until her flesh felt numb. He kissed her neck and the top of her breasts, but never dared push her vest aside to expose them to his mouth and no matter how she moved against him, that was it. It became a pattern, that and his tongue limp against hers, and every time they were alone together it was the same, until she cringed when he started his fiddling.

'Well?' Sylvie said. 'We were just getting to the good bit.'

'You wear me out.' Evelyn turned on her side and pulled her engagement ring over her knuckle, then shoved it back down on her finger with force. She closed her eyes, longing for sleep.

★ ★ ★

Standing at the sink, Evelyn lifted up the grey dishcloth and studied the holes in the threadbare

11

material. She watched as a stream of greasy water dripped into the washing-up bowl, leaving bits of carrot and potato clinging to the loose fibres. She wrung it out and sighed. The last thing she felt like was a night on the town, but upstairs in their bedroom Sylvie was organising clothes and make-up like a military operation, telling her they would get ready together when everything was set out. She shook the rag and dropped it into a bowl of bleach. Perhaps she'd feel better in a couple of hours when she was fresh and clean, rejuvenated like the cloth when she fished it out.

After gathering the coal scuttles together, she carried them towards the shed. The fireplaces still needed to be set for the morning, the dishes were waiting to be dried and there were Dad's sandwiches to cut and wrap ready for his night in the Underground. A currant loaf in the oven would soon be ready, and she always made sure the blackouts were secure. It hadn't been like this before her engagement. Both she and Sylvie had worked then, so they shared the chores and, to be fair, it had been she who'd changed the routine. She'd been in her first year of teaching and loved it, but Ron said there was no point in her carrying on. 'You might as well leave now,' he'd said, 'as wait until after we're married and then feel as though you're being forced out.'

There was some sense in his logic, but his certainty about how she would feel had niggled at her. When she tried to explain to him that she was more than capable of putting across her own point of view, he wouldn't have any of it. 'Don't be so silly,' he'd said, dismissing the subject with a wave of his hand. 'It was a misunderstanding. That's all.'

Once at home all day, there was no reason for her not to take over the running of the household, as she had to do something with her time. 'In training to be Mrs Ron,' Sylvie said, in a chirping tone of voice that made it sound as though Evelyn should be grateful for finding her calling. But it didn't feel as though being a wife and taking care of the domestic side of life would be enough for her. Or was she allowing herself to think in a selfish and indulgent manner when dissatisfaction nudged its way in around the endless tasks of polishing, wiping down, scrubbing and dusting?

From what little she could remember of Mum, she had never seemed disgruntled or displeased about the endless cycle of shopping, cooking and cleaning, nor did other women she had a chance to observe going about their daily business. Perhaps having children to care about made for a difference in perspective. Or maybe most women accepted their lot and got on with it and she would have to learn to do the same, but that made her heart sink down towards her practical and inelegant house slippers.

She thought about Rosie Harris with her crooked teeth and the coat that was two sizes too small and her endless questions. 'Why do lady teachers have to leave when they get married?' she'd asked — and Evelyn hadn't been able to give her an answer that satisfied either of them. Rosie had cried when the school said goodbye during morning prayers, and so had Evelyn when she left for the last time. Sometimes she saw one or two of

13

the children who hadn't gone to the country and they always shouted after her, 'Are you coming back to school, Miss Draper?'

She would flash her ring and say, 'You know I can't. I'm getting married.' Then she would smile so they could see how happy she was.

She felt for her ring now, but her fingers stroked an empty space. For a moment she was unsettled until she remembered she'd put it on the shelf, safe from the washing-up and the coal. She studied her hand without it, tracing the indentation where the ring usually settled, and rubbing the small callous that had appeared where the band pressed down into the flesh of her palm. In twenty years' time, she thought, the imprint of the ring on her finger would be indelible, as if she had been branded. She must remember to put it on before she went out later. It was time to get a move on; Sylvie would soon be ready to transform her.

Everything Sylvie owned was spread around the bedroom. Dresses and jackets laid out on the bed, necklaces hanging over them to maximise their effect; make-up and scent bottles in rows on the dresser; shoes against the wall; a bowl of sugar water on the bedside table. Sylvie was busy inspecting items of clothing for marks or loose threads. 'Now.' Sylvie was business-like. 'You've seen all of these before.' She pointed to the bed. 'So has everyone in London. But we can make anything look a bit different if we mix and match. See anything you fancy?'

Evelyn looked through the outfits, touching the material and holding one or two up against herself for Sylvie's reaction. Anything she borrowed would have to be adjusted in some way, a pin at the neckline or a fold at the waist. 'I think I'll wear my turquoise dress.'

'Your engagement dress?' Sylvie looked up, a bottle of scarlet nail varnish suspended mid-shake. 'I thought you were keeping that wrapped in tissue paper.'

'Well, that seems a shame, doesn't it?'

'*I* always thought so.'

'Just to wear it the once.' Evelyn remembered how it accentuated her neck and cleavage and made her legs seem longer. 'And it fits so well.'

'You'll look lovely,' Sylvie said. 'Now, let's get our hair set.'

Evelyn sat down in a chair facing the mottled mirror that showed their faces back to them as distorted pieces of mosaic. Sylvie tipped it so they could both see what she was doing. Evelyn watched her pick up swathes of her thick, fair hair and twist it around strips of fabric, tie the ends of the rags together and leave the waves to set. They swapped places and Evelyn pushed Sylvie's darker hair into finger curls with the syrupy water. They finished dressing, let their hair down, turned around as far as they could to scrutinise themselves in the mirror. Pleased with their reflections, they turned off the lights and gas and stepped out into the cold night.

Helen was waiting for them outside Piccadilly Tube. They linked arms, Evelyn in the middle so she could be guided along by Sylvie and Helen, who seemed to know the route like automatons. As they walked along Shaftesbury Avenue they chatted over Evelyn about work. Sylvie had recently left her job with Lyons and signed up as a labourer on a building site.

'Are you doing that, too?' Evelyn asked Helen.

'I might,' said Helen. 'It's either that or the telephone exchange next to St Paul's.'

'You could get another job now, Evelyn,' Sylvie said.

Not this again. 'But Ron . . .'

'Ron couldn't object to war work. Or shouldn't, anyway.'

They hurried down Greek Street and cut across Soho Square, then they turned right and went down a few steps. A narrow doorway led to a dark corridor that smelled of carpets stained with spirits and Craven A. They checked their coats in at the cloakroom, and Evelyn followed Sylvie and Helen towards the contagious noise of laughter and chatter on the opposite side of the swing doors. The band must have been on a break, as the light hit her first. Nowhere had been this bright for more than a year, and she shaded her face with her hand while she adapted. Helen was saying something to her and she had to lean close to hear. 'Your ring. Sylvie told me you're engaged. I was going to ask to see your ring.' Helen looked at Sylvie, worried she might have said the wrong thing.

Sylvie grabbed at Evelyn's hand. 'Why you little minx,' she said.

'I left it on the side. Near the sink.'

'And there I was, thinking I'd have to force you to have a good time, when you had this planned all along.'

'It was a genuine mistake.' Evelyn could feel

16

her face glowing; she was desperate to make them believe her. 'Perhaps I should go back.'

'Don't be so daft,' Sylvie said. 'You're out and you'll stay out and enjoy yourself.' Evelyn saw her look over at Helen and raise her eyebrow. 'Much more without that ring on. Look, I think there's room over there.'

Sylvie nodded her head towards everyone she recognised around the table and Evelyn repeated their names. A man with oily hair said he'd get them a drink. Evelyn sat down next to a woman wearing the most authentic-looking string of costume pearls she had ever seen, with a bracelet to match, her long, elegant fingers playing languidly with the Gin and It on the table in front of her.

The lights dimmed, the band took their places and Sylvie and Helen were soon in the thick of it. Evelyn caught sight of them as they swept past and then lost them amongst the turning crowd. Reaching for the drink she thought must be hers, she sat and tapped her foot in time to the music. The table was quiet now, only one couple sitting close together and a young man with a disappointed look on his face, drawing circles in a patch of sticky residue.

Evelyn felt a touch on her shoulder and looked up to see a man in an immaculate navy uniform leaning towards her. 'Can you foxtrot?' he enquired anxiously, a deep crease running along his forehead as if he'd been scored with a paring knife. Evelyn wondered if he was working his way around the club, hoping each time he asked a girl to dance that the answer wouldn't be another rejection. He didn't look as though he would lurch at her or try to pin her too close. He was tame, she decided, but when she stood, she was surprised at how tall he was, and when he led her to the floor his hand on her elbow was firm.

'I took lessons at home,' he said, after a few minutes spent watching his feet and counting time under his breath. 'How'm I doing?' He looked up and grinned, the groove across his brow disappearing.

'They've paid off,' she said. He was more relaxed now, although his hands were a bit damp and he kept looking down to study his footwork. Evelyn noticed his neat ears and liked the smell of what he used to tame his thick, wavy hair. 'Where's home,' she said. 'Scotland?'

'Belfast. I'm an engineer at Chatham. You know, in Kent. What do you do?'

Evelyn looked at her hand, resting on this strange man's lapel. The depression left by her engagement ring had lifted, that finger now as plump and filled out as the others. 'I'm a teacher.'

'Oh, really? How do you stand it? I feel sorry for you if your class is anything like mine was. Joe's the name, by the way.'

'Evelyn.' The band shifted to a quickstep. They readjusted their hands, Joe counted a few bars and they glided around the floor with everyone else. She felt a nudge and when she turned, Sylvie winked at her. 'My sister,' she explained. 'This was her idea. She thinks I need to go out more often.'

'Too busy marking copybooks? That's no good.'

'No,' Evelyn said. 'I don't suppose it is.'

The dance ended and Joe walked her back to

18

the table. 'Would you like a drink?' he asked.

'I've got one here somewhere, thanks.'

He produced a pack of cigarettes, lit hers and one for himself. He handed her the drink she'd pointed to, and then they stood against a pillar, watching the dancers and commenting on their techniques. 'Wasn't that your sister?' Joe asked.

'Probably,' said Evelyn.

'She's with another different lad.'

'Then there's no probably about it.' Evelyn laughed. 'That was Sylvie.'

'Shall we, again?'

But before he could put her glass on the table, the bandleader turned to the floor and said, 'Ladies' Request.'

Evelyn hesitated. That felt less innocent some-how, asking Joe to dance with her instead of the other way around. A flush spread up from his collar as he waited and Evelyn remembered his anxiety from earlier. *Where's the harm in it?* she thought — and was about to take his hand when a pretty girl in a lavender blouse spun him around and pulled at his sleeve. Looking over his shoulder at Evelyn, he was led away through the tables and into the middle of a waltz. Then she lost sight of him.

Two other nice, polite men asked Evelyn to dance. She hoped she'd see Joe again, at least to mouth sorry to him, but the crowd thickened and became more raucous and she eventually gave up. Around eleven, there was some talk of moving on to the Astoria to see in the New Year. 'What shall we do?' Helen asked. 'Go on or stick to what we know?'

'Let's try Hatchetts,' Sylvie said. 'Evelyn wants to see more than one place on her only night out this year. Evelyn?'

'Yes, let's,' Evelyn said. 'That way we won't have far to go to the Tube after midnight.'

The streets were busy. So many people determined to suspend everyday reality for a few hours of revelry. Hoping that to say the words 'Happy New Year' would make it come true. They were waiting to cross at the bottom of the road when Evelyn heard someone shout her name. All three of them turned and saw Joe dodging his way towards them.

'I must have forgotten something,' Evelyn said, searching herself to see what it might be.

'I'm glad I caught you.' Joe was out of breath. 'You're a fine dancer. I didn't trip up once with you.'

Evelyn laughed and said, 'That's not what my feet are telling me.'

For a moment Joe looked hurt, the rut reappearing along his forehead, then he laughed, too. 'Here's how you can get in touch with me. If you'd like to.' He pressed the torn corner of a beer mat into her hand, an address scrawled on it in pencil.

Sylvie and Helen were watching for her response, amused looks on their faces.

'Joe.' They heard a shout from a crowd of men. 'We're going this way.'

Evelyn tried to pass the scrap of paper back to Joe but he closed her fingers around it. Then he pressed his mouth to hers with a solid hand on the back of her head. She was startled and made a small noise of protest, but his lips were cool and

20

his tongue, when it found hers, was hot and full of energy.

'Joe.' Another shout from further away and he ran towards his friends without looking back.

After a few seconds of silence, during which Sylvie and Helen looked stunned, they both began whooping and cheering with delight.

'Stop it,' said Evelyn, wiping her mouth on the back of her hand. She felt mortified at what she'd allowed to happen.

'It's alright,' Sylvie said. 'You've probably had too much to drink.'

Let them think that. Then they might not keep on at her.

They carried on to Hatchetts, but Evelyn couldn't think about anything else except that kiss and how it had made her feel. A tide of disloyalty washed over her in waves, but she hadn't thought about Ron then, not while it was happening. Now each time she replayed the scene, her remorse became more raw. She refused to dance and wouldn't have a drink. Someone pulled her from her seat for 'Auld Lang Syne', but as soon as it was over, she told Sylvie and Helen she was going home. Well, down to Wood Green Tube. Dad was expecting them. 'Sorry to put a damper on the evening,' she said, 'but I've had enough for one night.'

Helen stayed on with some other girls she knew and Sylvie decided to leave with Evelyn. They walked to the Tube in silence, but on the way down Sylvie said, 'Don't worry about this. Ron will never know.'

Evelyn turned to her sister sharply. 'No. He

21

won't. No one will. And don't goad me to go out with you again. I know you mean well, but . . . just don't.'

'I won't,' said Sylvie. And she kept her promise.

* * *

By the middle of March, Evelyn was pleased to realise that when she thought about Joe she couldn't quite picture his face. The kiss, however, was taking a bit longer to blot out.

Working her way through a pile of potatoes, peeler in hand, she heard the post land on the doormat. Late again; but these days it was a wonder it arrived at all. She dried her hands and was surprised to see a letter from Ron. It was Monday. How could he write a letter and it be delivered on the same day? She tore it open. One sheet of paper; there'd always been two. *Dear Evelyn*, it began. Not the usual reference to her being his fiancée. She felt as if she'd been demoted. *You're a lovely girl*, the letter went on.

> *That is why I cannot continue to string you along. The fact is I have met someone else. Please do not think badly of me and I swear to you that nothing has happened, in that way, between us yet. But I am afraid that I do like this girl and it has made me think that you and I are not really very well suited. I find your independent attitude a bit overpowering and I also get the feeling that you want more fun out of life than I can give you. That makes me feel on edge.*

22

I know you will find someone who deserves
you and who will love and take care of you. I
hope in time you can think fondly of me as I
do of you.
Ron

Evelyn was stunned. How *dare* he? Boring Ron
Clarke had jilted her, or as good as. 'Met someone else'. And 'nothing had happened, yet'. She
was outraged. Well it won't, she thought. *Jane or*
Daisy or Anne or whatever your name is. Nothing
except a cold lump of tongue pushed like a dead
slug against yours. Well, you're welcome to that.
She marched back to the kitchen and attacked
the vegetables, scraping and chopping and tunnel-
ling eyes out with a vengeance. Then she changed
the beds and put the sheets in the copper to boil.
She polished the mantelpiece, washed the kitchen
floor, blacked the front doorstep. At half past five
she put the kettle on the gas ready for Sylvie's
arrival home, and wondered why she hadn't cried.
She stood still for a minute, watching the flames
lick and twist around the pot. 'Thank you, Ron,'
she whispered. She looked at the letter again and
kissed it. 'Thank you very much.'
When Evelyn heard the gate click she flopped
into a chair, pulled off her ring and placed it on
top of the letter. Then she curled up and covered
her face with her hands.
'Whatever's the matter?' Sylvie said when she
walked in.
Evelyn sniffled and pointed to the letter that
Sylvie at once snatched up and read aloud. 'This
is rich.' Sylvie read it again. 'Ron giving you the

elbow.' She flung the letter aside and put her arms around Evelyn. 'Oh, you poor thing. You poor little lamb. What will you do now?'

In a feeble, quavering voice, Evelyn said, 'I have a couple of ideas, but I'm going to need your help.'

'Anything,' Sylvie said. 'And I hope one of them is wringing his scrawny neck.'

Unable to keep up the pretence, Evelyn spread her hands, like shutters opening on a spring day and laughed aloud. 'Visit the Labour Exchange in the morning,' she said. 'And how do you fancy a dance tonight?'

★ ★ ★

The waiting room was stuffy and crowded. Evelyn's feet throbbed to the rhythm of one of last night's dance numbers; her eyes felt dry, and she had to keep blinking to keep them open. She was sure she'd had, at most, two or three hours' sleep. Sylvie, sitting next to her on a hard, wooden bench looked for all the world as if she'd gone to bed at nine with a boring book and a mug of Horlicks.

'What time did we get home?' she asked Sylvie.

'Hmmm.' Sylvie looked up from examining her nails. 'About three. Quarter to, I think.'

The wall clock read ten-thirty. 'That's terrible,' Evelyn said.

'I know.' Sylvie beamed with delight. 'But we had a great time, didn't we?'

Evelyn managed a smile. 'Yes. I think so,' she said. 'But I don't think I could make a habit of it.'

The signage above one row of windows at the counter read 'Men', the other 'Women'. But the women in the Labour Exchange this morning far outnumbered the men. *This is what it's going to be like, Evelyn thought, most of the men away and women holding the fort.* For a fleeting moment dread passed through her, like the aftershock of a bomb exploding somewhere close by. War was a ghastly way of making it possible for women to do something else besides the drudgery of housework, no matter how exciting that prospect seemed.

Posters on the walls depicted some of the things that women could sign up to do. They could replace postmen, farmers, bus conductors, ambulance drivers. There were women in smart suits carrying briefcases and walking towards offices, women in white coats doling out ladlesful of soup, women holding spanners, blowing whistles through a fog of steam on a train platform, measuring milk into churns. They were all smiling and looked the picture of health.

'Someone told me that soon girls will be *told* where to work. A bit like conscripted men. But I think you can ask for what you want to do for now,' Sylvie said. 'Given it any thought?'

'It would be a shame not to use what I learned when I was teaching. Do you suppose there's any need for someone to instruct the armed forces in reading and writing?'

'I suppose it's possible,' Sylvie said.

'Although it might be interesting to try something completely different. Something I wouldn't have a chance to do otherwise. Is that why you went for building work?'

'No.' Sylvie shook her head. 'I thought I should

do something that was considered war work rather than serving food in a restaurant, so I let them place me where the labour was most needed.'

'Miss Evelyn Draper. Window 6, please.'

When Evelyn stood, the floor beneath her seemed to wobble. She made her way to the counter by pulling herself along unsteadily from one chair to another. When she sat down, she could feel the heat rising off the women at the windows next to her. From behind, she was certain she could feel the breath of others who were pressing forward. The interviewer was an older woman with a topknot and powder caked around her nose. She filled in a form on Evelyn's behalf with a pencil she licked between each of her questions. The counter heaved one way then the other, tiny coloured stars sparked in front of her eyes, sweat pooled behind her knees.

'Any preference for your war work, Miss Draper?' the woman asked.

All Evelyn could think about was being outside in the fresh air. 'The bridge,' she managed at last. She pointed towards Sylvie for help. 'My sister,' she said.

Sylvie caught Evelyn under her arms and propped her up. 'I'm sorry,' she said to the woman behind the counter. 'My sister isn't feeling herself today.'

'Oh dear. Yes, I can see that. We've almost finished here. She said she would like to work on a bridge, then she mentioned her sister.'

'Oh,' Sylvie said. 'That's me.' Evelyn could tell by her tone of voice that Sylvie felt proud. 'She wants to work with me. Construction work on Waterloo Bridge.'

26

2
December 1940

Gwen

The world was ending. Every night Gwen thought the same thing, but tonight she was certain. The first blast hit seconds after the siren began to wail and she was caught running with the kids to the shelter. The explosion that followed was so terrific it lit up the sky with an orange flash that stretched across the horizon and seeped in to every crack in the skyline. For a second she stood mesmerised, watching the colour spread like a vile spillage on a masterpiece.

'Mum,' Johnny shouted.

'In you go,' she ordered, pushing him and Will through the door. Setting Ruth down, she pressed her towards her brothers in the dark.

When she turned to pull the door closed there was a barrage to the left, or was it the right? Or left again? Fires blazed here, there, the flames licking out towards each other and flaring upwards when they met. Rubble fell, and through it all, she heard the rise and fall of muffled voices. She forced herself to bang the door shut, knowing that the muted, distorted noises would be harder to bear than being in the middle of the chaos outside.

She rested her head on her arms and willed it to stop. Just stop or let the whole world end now.

27

Instead, the world shuddered and heaved sickeningly with what she was sure must be a direct hit to the house. Had she remembered to turn off the gas? She saw herself closing the tap after tea. Or was that the night before?

Another series of strikes ricocheted around the shelter, each more powerful than the last. She bit down hard on a healing whitlow to stifle the sobs that racked her chest. Her fingers fumbled backwards and forwards along the shelf above the door for the torch; it wasn't there, where she always kept it. Pushing her spectacles closer to her eyes, she peered into the gloom. It must be indoors. She thought it needed a new battery and she'd meant to check. But there was a candle. Grasping it, she took a deep breath and steadied herself, desperate for the kids not to pick up on the state she was in.

'It's a candle for us tonight.' She tried to sound jolly, to make it seem like a treat.

'Ain't we got the torch?' Johnny asked. 'What's happened to it?'

'It's in the kitchen. Now, stay right where you are. Don't move. Johnny, keep hold of Ruthie but let go of Will's hand.' In the darkness she sensed Will reaching out towards the candle then felt his hands around it. 'Good work.'

Gwen groped again and found the matches, picking them up with care. She didn't trust her nerves to hold out if she had to look for the spare box in the trunk with the other supplies against the back wall. *What a ridiculous place to keep them,* she thought; how could she find them there without slipping and knocking herself out on the way?

28

'Have you got them, Mum?' Ruth whispered.

'Got them.'

'Good work,' said Johnny, lowering his voice and mimicking his mother's turn of phrase.

Gwen and all three children giggled, the tension broken for a moment. 'Let's get some light. Ready, Will?'

'Ready, Sergeant Major,' Will said, eager to match Johnny's witty success.

At the instant Gwen scratched the match along the striking edge, illuminating the three waiting faces as if caught in a harsh spotlight, another volley of fire hit from every direction. It felt as if the shelter would be rent apart, as fragile against the force as the wooden matchbox. Covering her ears with her hands, Gwen let loose a guttural sound she didn't recognise. The match fell from her fingers and fizzed in the rainwater sloshing around their feet, the darkness swallowing them up again. Ruth started to cry and Will joined in.

One brutal round followed another, each more powerful than the last. Gwen reached out towards the children but lost her footing, landing with one leg beneath her and grazing her knee. The kids piled around and their trembling calmed her. Keeping them safe was her priority. George was scornful when she said that, quick to remind her that everyone felt the same but most people had more sense than to allow their kids to go through this every night.

Her arms around the children, she twisted a loose shard of cuticle she'd missed earlier and tore it off her fingernail. There couldn't be any more scenes like this, she told herself firmly, no more blundering about and scaring the kids. What would George say when he came in if he found them all wet and shivering on the floor, no candle flickering and no blankets on the bunks? She knew what he would say: he'd drag up the same old argument about packing them off to the country, and finding them in this turmoil would only add fuel to his fire.

'Have you still got that candle, Will?'

'I've got it now, Mum,' Johnny said.

Gwen ruffled his fine, floppy hair and Johnny squeezed his arms tighter around her middle.

'Well, you've managed better than silly old me,' Gwen said, flinching at another hit somewhere close by. 'I've only gone and dropped the box of matches in this mucky old puddle.'

Will whimpered. 'Now we'll have to stay in the dark till Dad comes home.'

'I don't like the dark,' Ruth said. 'I can't look at my book in the dark.'

Gwen began to nudge them up. They were shivering and she knew she would have to get them into dry things quickly. 'We ain't had a candle for such a long time I do believe I can see in the dark now, like an owl.'

Ruth began flapping her arms and hooting. Johnny and Will laughed and egged her on.

Gwen picked herself up and guided the kids to their bunks. It was easy; she should have done it ages ago and not given in to her nerves. She felt her way to the storage box and dug to the bottom to find more matches. Johnny held the candle out and when it was lit, they cheered. It was then she saw the torch, standing on the shelf above her mattress. She felt foolish and looked away, not wanting to draw the children's attention to it but Johnny spotted it and grabbed it down.

'It was here all along, Mum,' he said. He played the beam across the wall.

'Lots of silly things are happening tonight.' She turned away from him. 'Don't waste the battery now you've found it. Come and get yourself into dry things.'

'Silly Mum,' Will said. 'I'm very cold.' Gwen threw a pile of clothes next to him and told him to start changing; she would be over to rub him with a towel when she'd taken care of Ruth. Minutes later they were in warm things, blankets wrapped around them, looking through their Christmas annuals. The resounding din jarred and jolted through her, but for now she was in tenuous control, the ragged skin around her nails the only sign of her earlier panic.

By half past eight the boys were head to foot in the top bunk, Ruth tucked up underneath. They were quiet but not asleep. When there was a lull — and surely there must be at some stage — they might drop off. Gwen swept the flooded rainwater towards the sump and watched it swirl away, then sat on the storage box and swapped her wet slippers for a dry pair.

'When will Dad be home?' Ruth asked. 'I want to kiss him night-night.'

'Yeah,' Johnny said. 'Where is Dad? It must be late.'

Gwen had been thinking the same thing. She picked up the clock and, turning away from them, shone the torch on its face. It was late for George;

31

very late. But she said, 'Oh, it ain't as late as it seems.'

Will rolled over and leaned on one elbow. 'Show it to us,' he said.

She flicked off the torch. 'No need. He'll be home soon.' Will groaned and flopped back on the pillow. 'The best thing you can do is go to sleep. Dad will be tired when he gets in and he'll want to go straight to bed himself. He won't want to have you up adding to the commotion.'

'Dad likes seeing us,' Ruth said.

'Of course he does, love. But close your eyes now and he'll kiss you when he comes in. Then you can see him in the morning. Promise.'

Gwen listened to them fidgeting and making themselves comfortable.

'Johnny,' Will hissed, prodding his brother with his foot. 'Johnny. There'll be lots of shrapnel tomorrow, won't there?'

Johnny replied with a sleepy grunt.

'Probably some of it will still be warm. Hot maybe. Red hot. Will you help me find some? Please?'

'I ain't going to help you with anything ever again if you don't leave off your kicking.'

'That's enough, boys. And we'll see what things are like in the morning before anyone goes anywhere.' When they seemed to have settled a bit, she carried the candle to the small table wedged next to her bunk and thumbed through a notebook, meaning to write her list for tomorrow. She listened hard to pick out the familiar sounds of George coming home. A couple of times she thought she heard his whistle or his boots on the path and she watched the door, willing it to open a crack and see him edge his bulk in around it.

She pushed her glasses up and peered again at the clock, shaking it to prove it wasn't fast. George was on the day shift this week. He should have been home hours ago — and he watched last night, which meant he should have tonight off. Schedules and shifts were of no use now though, she knew that; they couldn't be relied on and that made waiting worse. But George was good, and on the nights when he wasn't going to be home as predicted, he tried to send word. She didn't care if he started on about the kids again — she might even agree with him after tonight. She just wanted to know he was safe. She bit through the remedy varnish on her right thumbnail, and as it didn't taste too ghastly, worked her way along the fingers, then started on the other hand.

A blast seemed to wrench the door open and Gwen flew towards it to make sure it was secure, petrified yet desperate at the same time to see what was happening outside. But there was George. He pulled the door closed and stood, his uniform torn and his head and face covered in a greasy film of sweat and grey dust. Gwen could see his hands were scratched and bleeding and there was a swollen bruise above his right eye. 'Bloody, bloody hell,' he said.

Gwen rushed towards him and for a second he held her. She could feel his arms and shoulders twitching beneath his coat, but when she started to rub at them he moved her to one side. 'I've only come in to make sure you're alright. Betty's taken a packet, so have the Smiths.'

'No. Not Betty.'

'Shhh. She's fine. But Len's not so good. They've been taken to hospital.' He rubbed hard at his face. 'Is there a bowl of water?'

'I'll clean the worst off for you.'

She turned to pull the first-aid box out and saw all three kids awake and watching. George bent and murmured to them, tucking the blankets around the boys and rescuing Ruth's doll from the floor. 'Hurry.' He sat next to her on the bed. 'I can't be long.'

'The trains ain't still running, are they?'

He shook his head and talked in a low voice. 'We were told to leave the engines in a depot and get to our other posts. I left the train at Waterloo and made my way to the station. Bloody hell, Gwennie. It's an inferno, the whole damn place.'

She made a small noise but kept her tears in check. 'I know. Well, I can imagine although I don't want to.'

'There are hundreds of people out there and still there ain't enough. Directly you start digging through some wreckage or beating at a fire you turn and there's something more urgent to see to. And the noise . . . ' He hung his head and his voice cracked. 'The screaming and shouting . . . '

He snatched his hands away and stood up. 'I'll take the torch and some of these bits and pieces,' he said, grabbing at bandages and cotton wool.

In amongst the supplies Gwen found a scarf and wrapped it around his neck. She didn't plead with him to stay because she knew he wouldn't. Besides, she wouldn't be able to live with herself if he did. He kissed the top of her head and said he'd

34

be back soon. He looked at the kids and mouthed, 'They'll have to go.'

She could feel the quiver in her lips. 'I know,' she whispered.

From the crack in the door Gwen followed the light of his low torch. He made his way across the garden and around what looked like a crater where the fence joining them to number fifty-one had been. To the right was Betty's house, what was left of the kitchen and sitting room gaping and exposed. Above, like props on a stage, two German bombers were caught in the interweave of searchlight beams, a sentry line of barrage balloons floating beneath them. When she looked back for George's light it was gone. She closed the door and blocked out the sight.

Sitting on the edge of his bunk, Johnny was searching amongst his things. He had one shoe on as well as his trousers and a thick jumper.

'What do you think you're doing, young man? You can use the pot. I'll get it for you.'

'I'm going with Dad,' he said, tugging his other shoe out and pulling it on. Gwen was taken aback.

'Oh, Johnny.' She sat beside him. 'You're very brave but you can't — you know that. You're too young.' She went to put an arm around him but he pulled away.

'I'm ten. And big for my age — you're always saying that.'

'That's right, love, you are. And that's why I need you here, especially when Dad ain't at home.'

He ignored her, still piling on his hat and coat. 'I heard him say there ain't enough helpers.'

'That's enough now, Johnny.' She meant this to

35

be the last word. 'Back into bed this instant. You'll wake Will and Ruth and then we won't be able to have a biscuit and put a puzzle together, just the two of us, will we?'

But the others were sitting up, frightened looks on their faces, watching Johnny dress himself for the outdoors.

Then she could not grasp what happened next. Johnny ran to the door and opened it with a clean blow to the latch. Gwen lunged at him and had his coat in her fist but he twisted from her grip and bolted in the same direction his dad had taken. 'Johnny!' she shouted, his name vanishing amidst all the others being screamed for in the night. Will and Ruth were crying and Gwen turned back to them, then spun again and shrieked for Johnny. Will was getting out of bed. Gwen pushed him back then plucked Ruth from her bunk and shoved her in with her brother. 'I'll be back in five minutes,' she said. 'Stay here together.'

'Don't leave us, Mum,' Will said.

'I have to — just for a bit. Be good and *do not go anywhere*. We'll be back very soon.'

She lurched through the same hole in the fence that George and then Johnny had run through, calling Johnny's name until her throat burned. Would he have turned left or right, run straight through the bomb site on the opposite side of the road, or doubled back towards the river? Nothing looked the same; all landmarks were gone, obliterated. Black holes where windows had been, odd bits of cutlery and chairs strewn along the pavement, a lamp post twisted and fizzing across the bar of The Builders Arms. If *she* couldn't get her

36

bearings, then how could a small boy?

She gulped down his name then screeched it out again. She flew across the road, tunnel vision blurring the flames and debris around her. When she reached the corner of Pier Street her heart was pounding so hard it felt as though it was moving up through her chest to where she would heave it from her mouth. She had to stop and try to force it back down. Behind her, a handful of people were picking through the wreckage of Price's little grocery shop. She ran towards them shouting, 'Johnny. *Johnny*.'

A few dirt-streaked faces looked up, the others too intent on their own miserable searches. 'Mrs Gregson.' Gwen recognised the voice of Evans and scrabbled her way towards him. He kept his torch down but she could make him out, his badge glinting in the dark. He left what he was doing and caught her as she stumbled. 'What's happened to your Johnny? And to you?' Gwen saw him look her up and down, taking in the soaking slippers on her feet, the torn stockings stuck to her knees with blood, the apron still tied round her waist.

'Have you taken a hit?' Evans asked, fumbling through his satchel for his notebook.

'Have you seen Johnny?' Gwen's voice rose to a shrill, piercing pitch. 'Has he run past here?'

'Now, now, Gwen,' said Mrs Price. 'That won't help.' The older woman put an arm around Gwen and tried to get her to sit on an upturned bucket.

Gwen backed away from them and spun round. 'He's trying to follow George.' She sniffed at the tears and snot running down her face. 'To help him.'

A boom. A blinding flash so close it distracted them and for a moment they stood, arms covering their heads, backs hunched against the onslaught. Evans took her by the elbow. 'I spoke to George not five minutes ago,' he said. 'He was heading back to his station and asked me to keep an eye on all of you.'

'And Johnny?' Gwen sobbed. 'You must have seen him. Which way did he go?'

Evans shook his head. 'Best thing you can do, my dear, is get back to the other two.'

'They're still indoors, are they?' Mrs Price asked.

'In the shelter.'

'With a neighbour?' Evans waited for Gwen to answer.

Gwen shook her head. 'On their own.' Then she remembered. 'With a candle.'

'Come along now.' Evans began to march her back the way she'd come.

'But Johnny . . .'

'Johnny will be safe and sound by now, drinking tea with George in the station. Let's get you home.'

With a prod of her elbow, Gwen escaped him. 'Can't you send someone to check on Will and Ruth?' She swiped at the air. 'My Johnny's out here by himself.'

'I'll go,' said Mrs Price. 'I'll walk round.'

'No,' Evans shouted as she staggered over the rubble. 'Mrs Gregson, be sensible.'

From there, Gwen had meant to cross Mud-chute Park towards George's station, but she stumbled into Manchester Road, caught up in the

38

surge of people rushing towards that terrific crash from a few moments ago. She could see that the whole bottom end of the thoroughfare was alight: flames consuming the school, the sweet shop, the row of houses, the ropeworks, the post office. Every building was nothing more than a smouldering shell — and still the bombs exploded.

Backwards and forwards she veered along the road. A wheel cracked and fell off a cart, narrowly missing her foot. She ran in front of a fire engine, then jumped out of the way of an ambulance manoeuvring around a lorry parked with both doors open.

He wouldn't have come this way, not Johnny. Not unless he was very muddled or something had compelled him. This was the opposite direction from where his dad had been headed. But if she had come this way, moved along by the crowds and the noise, why wouldn't he have done the same? As she got closer, she could feel the heat from the fire and had to shield her face from the ashy soot that settled on her clothes like dirty grey sludge. She thought she saw a small figure darting towards the back of a blackened shed but when she screamed out Johnny's name, she saw it was an elderly woman, round-shouldered in a huge dark coat.

A good few people had formed a column and were shouting orders to each other as they passed buckets and hoses along the line. No one was allowed through the makeshift cordon and Gwen found herself standing with a pitiful crowd, watching and waiting. She convinced herself that she wouldn't find Johnny here and turned to make her way back through the side streets and alleys to George's station. Shivering, she stopped to draw her cardigan together and heard voices in the crowd behind her call out; then there was a hush.

She looked to where their attention was drawn and there, emerging through a charred doorway, was George. He walked as though he had a metal rod in his spine, his coat wrapped around a small body pressed hard against his chest. It must be someone else's kid, surely? Countless children wore the same shoes, had a scab above the dimple in their knee. Then she *knew*, and at once her retching sobs pierced the lull.

Calling out their names, she threw herself towards them but George looked straight ahead and continued to walk through the crowd with the same measured pace, leaving Gwen to cling to his sleeve so she wouldn't fall to the ground. When she reached round to hold Johnny's hand, she found a tiny piece of shrapnel in his fist. They buried it in the coffin with him.

★ ★ ★

During the long days and nights after the funeral, Gwen wondered how things could be so different and yet carry on around her in the same way. So many people had lost someone — she knew that. George's work pal lost two sons at Dunkirk. The woman at the end lost her baby early when her house caught a packet. But everyone else could blame their loss on the Germans, the government, the war in general, a loved one's bravery or stupidity. She alone was responsible for her

40

own son's death, as sure as if she had murdered him. How she wished she had done something to him that was accountable in law, so that then she could shout, 'Guilty, guilty,' on every count and find relief in the punishment.

After the initial retelling, no one questioned her again or asked her to justify herself, not even George. But she tortured herself without respite, reliving every detail. She forced herself to think about what would have happened if . . . and in every imaginary outcome Johnny was still there, rushing around with his football, working his tongue at the corner of his mouth as he frowned over his problems, swinging his legs under the chair while he ate his tea; breathing, laughing, teasing his brother. Alive and warm beside her. If she hadn't hesitated at the end of the garden, if she hadn't stopped at Price's, if she'd let Evans resolve matters his way. She could feel Johnny's coat in her fist and she was sure now that if she had just tightened her grip on it then . . .

Over and over she twisted and turned through those last hours until she reached the thought that gave her the most pain. Johnny should not have been in London. He should have been in Wales with his school pals. And that, too, had been her decision.

George sat still in his chair for hours on end, an unopened paper on his lap. When he shuffled to the table for a meal or stared, unblinking, out of the window, Gwen found the stoop he'd developed unbearable and she had to turn away. She thought he'd be angry with her or more. She waited for him to fly into a rage, shake her and call

41

her names. Perhaps he would leave her and take a room somewhere close to the station or shout that from then on, he would be in sole charge of Will and Ruth.

None of those things happened. But the slumping quiet was not characteristic either and she thought his staged politeness was the only way he could control the hate he must have for her. One dismal afternoon, while the kids were upstairs, she went outside and heaved a wall of broken bricks and concrete against the door of the Anderson. She let the sharp edges tear at her hands, opening up the bitten sores until her fingers were bleeding and raw. She would never go in there again. George came out and stood watching, then turned away without saying a word and shut the door behind him.

Weeks passed, each grey day indistinguishable from the last. The war raged on with cruel insensitivity. George returned to work and to his fire-watching duties, speaking but not really talking to her when he was at home. Gwen kept her eyes lowered, sure others in the shop queues must be talking about her. The food she cooked was flavourless; buttons went unsewn on shirts and trousers. A bright, hopeful snowdrop dared to appear under the front window and she kicked at it until it broke off at the root.

One Sunday morning, Ruth helped her mother by putting slices of bread on a plate for breakfast as Gwen cut them off the loaf. 'Two for Mum, two for Dad.' She piled the slices on top of each other. When Gwen stopped cutting the loaf at eight, Ruth, still warm and puffy from sleep, looked around and said, 'Ain't Johnny having toast?'

Will tightened his mouth and nudged her under the table.

'I forgot,' she said, and buried her face in Gwen's neck. Gwen wished she could forget. She would gladly have abandoned everything were it not for Ruth and Will. She kept them close and made sure she was holding on to them whenever possible. At night, they sat under the stairs until the all-clear, then she put them into bed with her, entwining her arms and legs around theirs. Without protesting, George slept in Ruth's bed — unable, Gwen thought, to face Johnny's empty place behind the curtain on the boys' side of the room.

By the end of February Will was restless and took any opportunity to go to his room, with Ruth trailing behind more often than not. *They can't wait to get away from me*, Gwen thought, *and I don't blame them*. Sometimes she listened at the door to catch what they might be saying, but all she could make out were the sounds of play.

Will stopped talking about Johnny and started asking questions about himself. 'When am I going back to school, Mum?'

Gwen felt the knot in her stomach tighten. 'We think you should both stay home for a while, love,' she said.

'Then can I play out? Marty plays football every day before tea. With Richard and some of the others. Why can't I?'

'You know why.'

He shook his head crossly. 'They think I'm a baby. Always stuck in with you.'

'It ain't forever, Will,' she said. 'Just until . . . '

43

'When?'

The end of the war. When the bombing stops. If I can ever trust my judgement again. Never. Those were the answers she wanted to give. Instead she knelt next to him on the floor and rocked him.

'Please, Mum,' Will said. With the heel of his hand he wiped at her tears. 'I ain't going to run off like Johnny. Promise.'

'Let me talk to Dad,' Gwen said. 'And if he gives his permission, I'll take you back to school on Monday morning.'

Will let out a cheer and called up the stairs to Ruth.

An hour after the raid ended, George came in and kicked off his boots. Gwen lay in bed and listened to the hiss of the gas under the kettle, the clatter as he took his plate from the oven. When she thought he'd be sitting down to eat, she put her dressing gown around her shoulders and went downstairs, creeping on her toes across the sitting room in the light from the kitchen. Not wanting to startle him, she put her head around the door and called softly.

But his chair was empty, his food growing cold on the table. 'George,' she whispered again. She followed a noise from the pantry where she discovered him standing with his back to her, clutching the salt cellar in one hand, holding onto a shelf with the other. When he turned, she saw the rings under his eyes, the creases around his mouth, the swollen nose, chapped from crying. She took the salt from his hand and led him back to the kitchen.

'Talk to me, George,' she said, pulling a chair close to his.

44

He looked away.

'I don't care what you say. Nothing can make this any worse. Tell me you hate me. Say you wish it had been me.' She grabbed his arm. 'Say it.'

George shook his head. He unpeeled her fingers from his shirt and placed her hand on the table. He looked down at his knees and into the corner above the meat safe; anywhere but at her. He hacked as if something was caught in his windpipe. Then he said, 'That night. After I left you in the shelter . . . ' The clock ticked and from a distance came the early sounds of clearing up.

'I can hear everything, see it all again. Do you know what I mean, Gwen?'

She nodded.

'I . . . I can't . . . ' He swiped at the tears caught in the black and grey of his unshaven chin. 'It was . . . '

A bed creaked in the room above and George turned his face towards the noise.

'Go on, George. Please.'

'It don't matter now.' George stared, as if studying her after a long absence. Then his eyes narrowed. 'It won't bring him back.'

It did matter, though. To her it did. But all she could say was, 'Nothing will.'

'As for *them*,' George said, pointing upwards. 'They're going to Wales.' She opened her mouth to tell him he was right, even though the idea petrified her, but he stopped her short. 'No discussion. No arguing. That's the end of it.'

★ ★ ★

45

Gwen had been mortified when it seemed that Betty wouldn't be able to move back into number forty-seven and there had been talk of her and Len staying with their daughter-in-law in Clapham. But the rubble was cleared and when the side door and two windows were bricked over, the inspector gave permission for them to return. Gwen was so grateful for Betty, who split her time between seeing to Len and helping her organise the clothes and books the kids would need to take with them. They had a week to get things ready, but a year wouldn't have been long enough for Gwen to prepare herself to let the children go. Together they darned socks and scrubbed collars, folded a change of clothes and pyjamas into two small suitcases. Soap and toothbrushes were rolled up in towels. Gwen wanted them to wear their best, so used some money she'd put aside to buy them each a coat and shoes.

Will was wild with excitement, choosing first one book, then swapping it for another and trying to wedge in his beloved tin Spitfire without denting the wings. Marty and Richard were the last of his schoolmates to leave for Wales and he couldn't wait to meet up with them and the other boys he hadn't seen for weeks. Ruth was less happy. Sometimes she copied Will's boisterous preparations, but most days she wanted to sit on Gwen's lap or trail along after her, clutching her knitted doll. There was no question of exchanging Susie for a game or a puzzle, so Betty dressed the doll in a new outfit for the occasion, sewn together from the scraps of her old armchair, which had been salvaged from the hit.

On the Saturday afternoon before they were due to leave, Gwen put on a special tea. Even though the thought of eating anything turned her stomach, she wanted the children to have something nice to remember about their last day at home. George was late on the trains and couldn't change his shift, at least that was what he said, so Betty came in and tried to jolly them along. The custard was burnt, the tea was weak and Will did most of the talking. 'Will they ask about Johnny?' he blurted out.

Gwen had no idea what, if anything, the children from Johnny's class had been told.

'What will I tell them?' he asked.

Ruth looked at Gwen, her lips trembling. 'I don't want to talk about Johnny. It makes Mum cry. And Dad.'

Gwen knew that Betty was waiting for her to come up with an answer, but she couldn't lift her eyes from her plate.

'You tell them your Johnny was a very brave boy,' Betty said at last. 'A proper little hero and it was all Hitler's fault. Ain't that right? Gwen?'

Gwen pushed a bit of greasy sausage around her plate, then stabbed it with her fork.

A horrible couple of hours passed before Betty scraped her chair back and said, 'Well, my dears. I best get back to Len. Make sure he's behaving himself — you know what a terror he can be.' She held her arms out to the children. 'Give us a hug, then.'

Ruth wrapped her arms around Betty, but Will stood back, holding his hand out to shake hers when Ruth released her grip.

'Is that all I get, young sir?' Betty asked, forcing his head into her chest. 'You're almost up to my shoulder, ain't you? Look at him, Gwen.'

Will stood tall and measured himself against Betty. 'Almost,' he said.

'Next time I see you I expect you'll be up here somewhere.' She marked an imaginary height inches above her head.

'And I'll be just there.' Ruth stood on her toes and touched Betty's nose.

'Don't forget your promise,' Betty said. 'Write to me and I'll write back.'

Gwen followed Betty into the kitchen; she wanted to get the bath out and filled before the siren. At the door, Betty looked down at the cases and masks ready for the morning. 'Are you alright now, Gwen?' she asked. 'Is there anything else I can do for you tonight?'

'You've been a great help, Betty,' Gwen said, the tears starting again. 'There ain't nothing more you or anyone else can do.'

'Maybe you could think about getting some kind of work. You know, to keep yourself busy.'

'Oh, Betty.' Gwen dragged her hands through her hair, pulling out a pin and putting it in her apron pocket. 'That's the last thing I can think about right now.'

'I don't mean this minute.' Betty stopped Gwen's fingers short of her sharp teeth and cupped them in her hands. 'But soon you might have to. Len's mate left his paper when he came to visit and in it there was a list of jobs for ladies. I couldn't believe it. Might as well choose something you like the sound of before you get given the dregs.'

48

'I've got enough to be getting on with right now,' Gwen said.

'You can't sit around here all day and night brooding. You'll make yourself ill.'

Gwen unwound her hands from Betty's and folded her arms, standing away from the door to let Betty pass. 'Ta, Bet,' she said. 'I'll get tomorrow over and done with first.'

The blackouts were drawn and the copper full of water was heating on the stove. Gwen dragged the bath in front of the fire and draped nightclothes and towels over the guard. Will was racing around the sitting room, acting out the flight of a plane from take-off to landing with all the stages and noises in between. She moved in slow motion, fussing over details, trying to hold back the clock. This would be the last time for ages that she would be helping Will and Ruth get ready for their baths. She hated the thought that tomorrow someone else would be in charge of her kids, but she despised herself for not having done this for Johnny.

'What was that noise, Mum?' Ruth asked.

'Wasn't it just Will, being a plane?'

'A different noise,' Will said. 'From the kitchen.'

Perhaps George had leave to come home after all, Gwen hoped. But no one was there, although it was obvious Betty had been back because, spread open at the page she had been talking about, was a copy of the *Labour Gazette*. Ambulance drivers, land army, builders, postwomen; the list went on. Betty meant well, Gwen was sure of that, and she couldn't want for a better friend so would hate to offend her. She would read the article next week

49

and then be able to tell Betty she had done so. But for now, she folded the paper, tucked it behind a vase on the sideboard and made sure the towels were warm enough to wrap around her children.

★ ★ ★

Coming back to an empty house, with rations for two, was one of the hardest things Gwen had to endure. The silence screamed at her. The walls ranted about Johnny and what she should or shouldn't have done for him, questioned the decision she had made about Will and Ruth, chided her about the lack of kindness between her and George. When she reached the point where she thought she would wail aloud, her hands pinned to her ears, she would escape to Betty's, or the library, or the park. Then she would have to once more steel herself to unlock the door and step into the abyss of her family home.

It took two weeks to clean almost every inch of the house and Gwen knew that when she'd finished, she would start all over again. She left the children's room as it stood, unable to face the toys, books and clothes that lay in the exact positions the kids had placed them. If she moved things, the children's fingerprints on them would be lost forever; if she left them to gather dust, they would remind her of their last days at home. So best to leave the door closed tight against her eyes, her nose and the touch of her hands.

Despite that, she came across evidence of them in the least likely places. Right at the back of a cupboard under the sink, she found a jam jar full of brown river water, a couple of inches of green scum on the surface. Will had been sure it was populated with tadpoles, but none had materialised. A button from Susie's dress appeared in the corner of the stairs on the landing; she tore down and ripped up the football chart that Johnny and Will had filled in without fail every Saturday afternoon; a couple of pieces of Meccano Johnny had searched for to complete an intricate model of a crane were behind the clock on the mantelpiece.

She sat with each item she found, nursing it in her hands and remembering when she had last seen her child using it, or the outing they had been on when they gathered the stone or stick or leaf. Their faces came back to her in detail. She could picture the way they moved their mouths, their hands, their eyes. Will had a way of blowing upwards so his hair fluttered away from his forehead; Ruth would rub her eyes with her knuckles when she tried too hard; Johnny would tap his fingers while he thought about his arithmetic or drawing or what to make with his construction set.

One dull afternoon, Gwen could feel her arms and legs heavy with fatigue, as if concrete had replaced muscle and bone; but she could not stop. Moving a bowl, some knitting patterns and a vase from the sideboard, she saw a newspaper fall to the floor. At first, she didn't recognise it as George's daily; then she could see it was that *Labour Gazette* Betty thought she was doing her a favour by bringing round. The sight of it brought back the memory of the day before Will and Ruth went away and Gwen scrunched it hard to use on the fire later. But then the tears began again. Weariness flooded through her and she thought that she would have to sit for ten minutes.

In George's chair, she closed and opened her eyes, needing rest but frightened of the nightmares that marred her sleep. She unfolded the paper on her lap and found the page Betty had asked her to read. The list of jobs women could do now spread out over four pages. She took up a pencil from the side table and tried to imagine herself in each of the advertised jobs.

She put a cross through every job except one: construction. Not that she was keen on that either, but Johnny would be proud to think of her amongst the cranes and spanners and scaffolding. And it was either that or sit here where the quiet could not get any louder, the skirting boards cleaner, or the absent children more vivid.

3
December 1940

Joan

In the limbo between unconsciousness and waking, Joan imagined her mother nursing her through chicken pox, scarlet fever or some other childhood illness. Mother checking her pulse, Mother stroking her hands, Mother wiping her forehead, Mother stroking her hands, stroking her hands, always worrying about her hands. She was no longer that child, but she sensed that Mother was nearby, assuring herself that Joan's hands were in perfect order above anything else.

Then she drifted away again to a picture of herself in Ralph's study. There, by the window, she saw the three-legged table on which he threw his watch, cufflinks, loose change and other paraphernalia when he had finished his duties for the day. A lavishly inlaid bureau stood against the wall on the left, and Joan could make out the documents waiting to be filed on its open-hinged jaw.

One afternoon she'd wrenched the door open in her eagerness to see him after a week's absence and sent the whole lot up into the stratosphere of the high ceiling. Afraid to look at the reaction on Ralph's face, she'd clamped her hands over her mouth and watched as pages fluttered down around them like sycamore pods. Ralph laughed then and held out his arms to her. In her relief at not having spoiled the reunion, she'd stomped all over the reports and lists settling on the maroon and green patterned carpet.

He'd patted his lap and she'd nestled into him, her hands tracing the lines of his face: the imperceptibly receding hairline; high, curved cheekbones; his asymmetrical nose, thickened on one nostril by a childhood scar; the dark, coarse moustache above the mouth that she'd heard others in the orchestra describe as malevolent. Snorting, he'd snatched her fingers between his teeth, slobbering over them, teasing them between biting and sucking.

Acting coy, she'd withdrawn her hands and buried them between her thighs and his. 'Now, now,' she'd said. 'Can't you hear Mother?' And she'd aped her mother's mantra. 'Joan. Please, dear. Mind your hands.'

He'd laughed at that, the warmth of his chest and belly rising and falling against hers. 'I'd love to tell your mother what those hands of yours get up to,' he'd said. 'But shall I help you to be ever such a good girl this time and do as she says?' And as he'd manoeuvred her to the leather sofa, he'd circled both her wrists with one of his hands and held them stretched out above her head.

But when she came to, she was in the bedroom that had been hers since childhood and which could not have been more different from Ralph's study. Mother's favourite pastels were prominent here on the cushion covers and vanity table skirt, reclaimed from curtains taken down to make way for the blackouts. Putting aside her embroidery, Mother rose from the chair where she had been keeping watch, and Joan felt acrid disappointment rise from her stomach like bile when she saw Mother's face, rather than Ralph's, hover into view. Mother reached for her hand, but Joan turned away and let her fingers wilt on the outstretched palm.

Then pictures of Mother administering the orange juice and castor oil, three days earlier, came creeping back. They broke through the flimsy lines of defence sleep had contrived. Mother had lifted the concoction of tepid syrup to Joan's lips and instructed her to hold her nose as she gulped it down so the cloying mixture could begin its lethal task before she could taste it and spit it out. 'Now this, dear,' Mother had said, encouraging a tumbler of gin to Joan's mouth as if she were offering her a pre-dinner cocktail. Twenty-four hours later, enfeebled by merciless cramps, Joan hung her limp head over an old pail, clutching it in order to give her a sense of stability. 'Your hands, Joan,' Mother ordered. 'Relax your fingers.' If she'd had the strength, she would have delighted in hurling the bucket and its contents over Mother's pristine facade.

Of course, when Joan had admitted the pregnancy to Mother, the details of her love affair with Ralph had been bullied out of her, too. Joan had expected Mother to be angry; she and Father had, after all, invested hundreds of pounds in her career. Not to mention, which Mother often did, the time and energy and sacrifices at the altar of pursuits, holidays and assets of their own. When Joan reminded Mother that at seven years old, she'd had the violin foisted on her, Mother

55

retorted that Joan had begged to learn to play.

'Of course I did,' Joan shouted. 'Little girls always want to mimic their mothers. But you . . . you never let it go. Not for one minute.'

'No, I didn't because I have diligence and dedication. Pity you didn't copy those assets. If I'd had your chances, I would never have given them up for a sordid little entanglement.'

They'd spent their days arguing. 'You will be ruined,' Mother would say over and over, like a scratched seventy-eight record. Mother was petrified for Joan's reputation, but there was no doubt in Joan's mind that Mother's main dread was not for her standing as a young woman, but for her musical career. According to Mother, the only possible thing Joan could do was get rid of the baby. 'We can put it behind us,' she said. 'Look at your hands, Joan. They're still perfect, aren't they? That's all you need worry about.'

If only that was the case. The absurdity of Mother's thinking and the dilemma Joan battled with, reduced her mind to a mushy pulp. She hadn't yet told Ralph about the baby and could not decide if she should. If he knew, he might break off their affair and she would have to revert to her life before him; inconceivable. If she got rid of the baby, with the help Mother persistently offered, then at least she and Ralph would continue as before. That was some comfort — but there was one other possibility. One she almost dare not imagine even though the picture of it would not leave her alone. If she told Ralph now, before it was too late, he might leave his wife for her and the child.

As each night fell, she and Mother called a

truce. They huddled on opposite ends of the sofa in the drawing room, the bickering and squabbles put on hold as they tried to drown out the wailing of sirens and bombing strikes with Mozart or Beethoven on the gramophone. It was war, inside and out. So acute was the feeling of entrapment that Joan often found it difficult to move or take a proper breath. Ralph would have found the indignity of the situation insufferable.

★ ★ ★

Sir Ralph Myers' induction speech to the newly appointed musicians, sitting at the back of the Hall, intimated that he would never tolerate a spectacle. Joan felt childish pride as she imagined his praise was meant solely for her. 'You've done well to get here. Do you know how many talented musicians auditioned for these positions?'

As one many-headed creature, they shook their heads.

'Come along now.' He tutted. 'Please don't tell me I've erred and chosen shy, unforthcoming music-makers after all. The world around us may be rapidly slipping into indecorous chaos but it is up to us, indeed up to you, to counteract that decline and smooth the population's way back to a more genteel, civilised way of life through the Genius of Harmony and the Soul of Music.'

He swept his arm behind him to encompass the painted cupola above the stage, his suit jacket splaying open to expose the gold fob chain swinging against his golden embroidered waistcoat. Again, as if their heads were joined and in turn connected to his hand, like puppets to their master, they followed the arc of his elegant fingers. 'You, young man.' He pointed to the sandy-haired boy sitting next to Joan, his soft, pale hands spread with vigilance on his knees. 'How many?'

'Two thousand, perhaps?' the boy stuttered. Joan cringed for him as she felt, rather than saw, the mortified heat rising from his freckled face. There was a moment's silence in which the great man waited. Joan nudged the boy and whispered to him. 'Sir Ralph,' he shouted out with relief, his discomfort coming to an end.

'Thank you, young man,' Ralph conceded, but when he tipped his head it was, Joan was sure, to acknowledge her. 'Now, to put the record straight, there were one hundred and fifty-seven auditions for the places on this very stage.' He stamped his foot lightly then paused to let the resonance abate. 'Some of them I sent back to school, as music masters or mistresses, some I steered to regimental bands and a few lucky applicants I encouraged to try again next year. From you even more fortunate candidates, I expect the following: loyalty to the endeavour of creating superb music, loyalty to the Hall, to each other and to me; punctuality, no excuses; decorum in your speech and manner when on duty here for a performance or rehearsal. You will each receive an invitation in your pigeon-hole to meet with me in my study sometime during the next fortnight. Rehearsals start at nine o'clock Monday morning.'

They watched as he walked down the aisle between them and through a row of red velvet seats towards a door at the back of the Hall, stopping to rub a mark from an armrest. Then he disappeared into the warren of corridors that led to his suite of offices.

'Thanks,' the boy said, delicately running a finger around his collar. 'He's ferocious, don't you think?'

Joan shrugged. 'I thought he was commanding.'

'I'll say. That — and *de*-manding.' He held out his sallow hand and they shook, his touch as insipid as hers. 'What are you?'

'Violin. And it's Joan. How about you?'

'Hello, Joan Violin. I'm Colin Cello. Do you fancy a drink?' He motioned to a group of five or six others standing about talking. 'Some of them mentioned it earlier.' When Joan hesitated, he said, 'No rehearsals until Monday, so the smell will have dissipated by then.'

Joan laughed and pictured Mother's disapproving face when Joan partaking of alcohol was mentioned; Mother, on the other hand, never turned down a drop. She sighed and decided not to chance Mother's indignation. 'I'll have a cordial. I don't drink.' The chance to stay out a bit later pleased her and she could always say the Tube was disrupted or the bus had to take another route because of the bombing. Besides, Mother would only insist she crack on with her practice the minute she got home and there was enough time for all that over the weekend, stranded alone with her in the house.

Every evening and weekend had been the same, as far as Joan could remember, since she had first asked to have a little go on Mother's violin. It was as if Mother was possessed from that moment on:

59

organising lessons, insisting on practice before reading or homework or exploring the garden or skipping rope. Her stomach still tightened into a knot of despondency when she recalled having to turn down an invitation to a friend's birthday tea because Mother said, 'No, Joan has a great musical future ahead of her and can't afford to diverge from her practice schedule.' Of course the friend never asked again.

There were many hilarious impersonations of Sir Ralph and William Benson, who was to be their conductor, that night in the pub. Colin surprised all of them, Joan thought, with his aptitude for the theatrical and the ease with which he laughed at himself, making a comic turn of his earlier humiliation. He even managed to draw Joan into the pantomime by getting her to whisper to him again on cue. 'Next time, though, Joan Violin, I do wish you wouldn't elbow me quite so hard. You managed to get me right in the spot where I snuggle my beloved Cecilia.'

'Aye, aye,' said Edward. 'And when might we get to meet this girl of yours?'

'Monday next. Nine o'clock.' Colin half closed his eyes and feigned rapture. 'Cecilia Cello. My one and only.'

Everyone admitted to the pet names for their instruments, Joan's being the uninspired Violet. By the time they'd had a couple of rounds they had formed quite a little band, comfortable enough with each other to arrange to meet up again after the first rehearsal. Eileen, a tall girl with cornflower blue eyes set off by dark, arched brows suggested they go to see *Top of the World* at the Palladium. 'Let's book seats then,' Colin said.

'I've wanted to see that show for the longest time,' Joan said. She was delighted with the prospect, made more attractive by the fact that Mother, who would never consent, need not know.

The outing to the Palladium went ahead in November, Colin somehow managing to secure five seats together and a sixth just behind. As it turned out, that lone seat wasn't needed. By then Joan was involved with Ralph and they were ensconced together in his dark study. The following morning, Edward and Eileen performed a great take on one of the showstoppers and Joan encouraged Colin to top it, but he shook his head and chastised her for wasting a ticket. He avoided her after that and she was left trying to shake off the touch of shame she felt when he walked away from her, hands in pockets.

Things would have been very different, she supposed, if she'd stuck with Colin and his crowd. She thought they must be wondering how she was recovering from the acute gastroenteritis Mother had alerted the company to in a letter. She'd finished with a postscript, advising that for the sake of their health, they shouldn't visit and none went against her warning. Much to Joan's alarm, that included Ralph.

★   ★   ★

The invitations from Sir Ralph had appeared in their pigeonholes, as promised, the day formal rehearsals began. Joan's slot was the last, Friday

61

week at three o'clock. She would have liked to get it over and done with earlier but at least this way she could grasp the format of the meetings from the others and be prepared. As the fortnight progressed, everyone reported back on the more or less identical fifteen-minute discussion with Sir Ralph. With the exception of Colin, who wiped his brow and contorted himself into a sham fit, everyone came out looking brighter than they had going in.

Having watched all of this take place, Joan was feeling less anxious by the time she knocked on Sir Ralph's door at the allotted time. 'Enter,' he called. Joan closed the door behind her and stood with her back to it, waiting to be summoned forward. Without looking up from what he was reading, Sir Ralph pointed to a hard, straight-backed chair across the desk from him. Hands clasped in her lap and her back as rigid as the unwelcoming chair she perched on, Joan sat and waited. Not daring to move her head in case she distracted him, she looked out the corner of her eye at the certificates on the wall next to her. Then she took in some of the photos on the drinks cabinet to the right, all of them picturing Sir Ralph shaking some dignitary's hand and smiling with reticence, as if he had something more pressing to undertake elsewhere. A woman with sleek hair and sharp features stood behind his right shoulder in two of the photos, wearing a different stylish hat in each shot.

'Don't mind those,' Sir Ralph said. Joan pivoted her eyes back towards him and felt herself start to colour, knowing he'd observed her prying. 'They're nothing. Nothing important, that is.'

'Pardon me, Sir Ralph,' she said, shifting in her chair and looking, she was sure, as awkward as she felt.

'You have nothing to be pardoned for, Miss . . . ' He made a show of rooting amongst his papers for one particular sheet.

'Abbott,' Joan said.

'Yes. Miss Abbott,' he repeated, letting the page drop from his hand. 'Now, tell me a bit about yourself. And please, don't tell me what I already know. All the others did that, spewed out a repetitious reflux of the information on their application forms, or what they told us at audition. You're my last interviewee and I'm bored with it now. Be different. Impress me.'

Joan felt bewildered and could think of nothing to say. This was not going to the plan she'd drawn up based on reports from the others. She half-rose from the chair and said, 'I think perhaps I should come in again and start over.'

It had been a serious suggestion, so she was surprised at the laughter that followed and which went on for some time. Sir Ralph rocked backwards and forwards with delight like the torso of a laughing policeman at the fun fair. Watching him, Joan experienced the same mixture of fear, repulsion and fascination she'd felt as a child, having fed her last penny to the strange marionette.

When his amusement ebbed, he leaned back in his chair and studied Joan for a few uncomfortable moments. 'Well, let me ask you this, perhaps safer, question. What has been the highlight of your career to date?'

Joan felt as though she'd lost her place in a score

and was the only musician playing on the incorrect page. 'I suppose getting my place here, at the Hall, Sir Ralph.'

'And suppose you hadn't. What would your answer have been then?'

Joan thought back through her musical achievements. 'Well, Sir Ralph, it would have to be playing first violin at the RCM Leaving Ceremony.'

'Yes, yes.' He nodded. 'A great honour. We've had more than one first from that particular concert playing here, you know.'

Joan hadn't known that and felt rather shortchanged to be reminded that she was one of many.

'But tell me, when you played in that performance, did you wear your hair as it is now?'

Joan felt she was again sifting through her muddled sheet music with desperation. Her hand went without thinking to her head, to check the pins that held the coiled rolls off her face. Everything was in place, held fast with a dollop of Amami. Sir Ralph watched her agitation, a smile beginning to form on his face. She thought she might have to bolt for the door if his unnerving mirth surfaced again. 'I'm sure I can't remember.'

'I certainly hope you did — it's most becoming.' His voice was softer, more kindly. 'In fact, there is nothing about your aspect that isn't.'

Joan felt compelled to go with the course of the conversation. 'Well, now I think about it, I probably dressed it in a knot, which is much less distracting than having it down when playing.'

He held his hand up to stop her. 'Miss Abbott, I'm paying you a compliment and as I don't do so often, allow me to continue.'

'Pardon me again, Sir Ralph.'

'I don't expect you to be flattered.'

But she wasn't. She was more mystified than anything. She'd always considered herself rather plain. Unlike Eileen, who managed to have every man's eyes on her whenever she walked into a room. Next to her, Joan felt her lack of curves and the thin legs that barely filled her stockings. Her hair was the same shade of brown as stewed tea and she knew her eyes to be small — which was just as well, as their colour was an indistinct grey, like the seaside on a rainy Bank Holiday: nothing to get excited about.

'I have no doubt,' Sir Ralph said with some hesitation, as if he were struggling for the right words, 'that you are admired as a matter of course by every young man you meet. Accolades from a man approaching middle age probably mean nothing to you.'

Joan dismissed the idea with a short laugh, as she hadn't socialised with many young men, Mother saying there was enough time for all that after her career had been established. The young men she did come into contact with never commented on her within hearing, so Joan assumed there was nothing much attractive about her and concentrated on looking neat rather than glamorous. Besides, she told herself, these young men whose compliments were supposed to be so longed for and highly prized were mere boys, gangly and clumsy. Good fun, like Colin and Edward she had to admit, but no more than that.

'You seem so level-headed, too,' Sir Ralph continued, looking down at his folded hands. 'The majority of good-looking women are frivolous and prone to histrionics. You give the impression, however, of judiciousness. That, together with your beguiling demeanour, compels me to ask you to join me from time to time for a sherry and a chat about your burgeoning career. Would there be any chance of that, or am I asking too much?'

Joan didn't know what she had been expecting to find in Sir Ralph's face when he looked up, but it was not the sincerity she saw there. Of course it was Mother's fault that Joan jumped in feet first. Mother with her incessant nagging about strict routines and the future, a future that Joan felt she hadn't had a chance to decide upon for herself. If the idea of seeing *Top of the World* behind Mother's back was exciting, the thought of being with Ralph, and all the furtiveness that went with it, was thrilling. 'I'd like that very much,' she said.

'Good.' Sir Ralph nodded. 'Let's start now. Dry or sweet?' He turned to the cabinet and moved the photos to one side to reach the bottles behind.

She didn't know the difference but plumped for the one she thought would be most palatable. 'Sweet, please. Is that your wife? She's very elegant.'

He hesitated before picking up and studying one of the photos in which Lady Myers stood beside him. When he placed it back, he angled it so Joan couldn't see it with ease. 'Yes. She spends a great deal of time keeping in vogue.'

Joan started to ask whether Ralph's wife was involved in music but Ralph held up his hand to silence her, once more the director. 'I invited you to have a sherry with me, not to discuss my wife.' So she wasn't mentioned again. Joan pushed her and Mother to the back of her mind and relished the time she spent with Ralph, instigating their meetings as often as he did, and feeling more free than she had ever felt before. Besides all that, after the briefest of times, she was in love with Ralph and thought he must feel the same about her.

* * *

Mother was fussing now, having perceived that Joan was shamming sleep, and tried to hoist her up with one arm around her shoulder and the other wedged under her armpit. 'Are you able?' Mother asked. 'I think you should try to sit up now and eat something.'

Joan turned her pillows and punched them into shape, seeking a spot that wasn't slick with sweat. A square on the edge of the top pillowcase brought her some comfort and she bunched it under her head, turning her back on Mother. Beneath the bedclothes, dishevelled and clammy around her legs and arms, she sought out her stomach and stroked its hollows. It was gone. She knew it with fevered clarity. Without the baby, so too were her fragile hopes for a future with Ralph. At very best they would go back to how they were, better than nothing but not enough.

Mother appeared again, carrying a tray around the bed. 'This won't do, Joan dear. At least have a look. There's a lovely bowl of oxtail soup, a bread roll with both our rations of butter, a bit of cake and jelly. It's all very nutritious.'

'Please leave me alone, Mother,' Joan said.

She heard the chink of crockery as Mother

placed the tray on the bedside table, smoothed the bedclothes and sat down next to her. Tentatively, Mother lifted the sheets from Joan's hands where they lay, one on each side of her head, and with gentle strokes began to massage them, starting with the fingers. Joan thought Mother must have mistaken her inertia for compliance, perhaps even solace, because her pummelling became more firm and confident. Joan kept her eyes closed, willing Mother to stop and leave the room.

With a slight movement of impatience, Joan slipped her grip. Mother's hands fumbled for hers again and clung on, the thumbs finding the spaces between the joints and digging down, seeking out sore spots she could worry away at. Something liquid trickled between Joan's legs and she knew she needed to get up and see to herself but felt weighted to the bed. Unable to move from the shape she'd created by her own damp, she felt a fury building up that she hadn't realised she had the energy to release.

In the silence, Joan felt Mother lean towards her and suck in her breath, ready to speak. 'Joan,' she whispered. Joan shuddered when she felt Mother so close and drew herself up on one elbow, intending to make the effort to get up. 'This doesn't have to be the end of everything you've worked for.'

'Move. Please, Mother. Move out of my way.'

'Everything you've always wanted.' Mother's voice was modulated and calm, as if she was trying to hypnotise Joan into agreement.

'Surely you can see you've got that the wrong way round, Mother.' Joan emphasised her words with sarcasm, balling the bed sheets in her fists to keep her composure. 'It's what *you've* always wanted. I haven't had a choice.'

'Release the tension,' Mother said, unclenching Joan's hands.

'I have to get up.' Joan felt feeble and shaky. She prodded Mother's arm, giving her an opportunity to stand and let her pass. Mother wouldn't take the hint and with her last vestige of strength Joan lashed out, slapping the back of her hand against Mother's cheek. Mother let out a cry and protected her face with her arm. Joan went to push her from the bed, shouting for her to get away, but Mother jumped back and stood staring at Joan in horror. The Westminster clock chimed six and rather than distract Joan, it spurred her on and she gained momentum as the first explosion of the night struck. With one swing, Joan swept the tea tray in Mother's direction, making sure that shards of china and bits of food reached her intended target.

'Joan, stop!' Mother screamed. 'Have you gone mad? I don't know you anymore.'

Next Joan tackled the vanity table, throwing bottles and jars at the door Mother scrabbled towards to make her escape. Behind her eyes, bright floating lights were appearing and Mother's voice sounded thin and distant. With one last effort, Joan wrenched the oil painting of a violinist from the wall and hurled it to the floor, catching the side of her hand on a nail that protruded from the frame. 'Your *hand*. Joan, how *could* you?' Mother let out a sob as they watched the blood trail down Joan's arm from the jagged tear.

* * *

A couple of weeks later, as Joan and Mother sat looking at each other over dinner, Mother related the excuses she had given to Dr Thompson when she had called him out after the events of that contentious evening. Joan tried to stop the narrative, embarrassed by the memory of her conduct, but Mother insisted Joan needed to be able to piece things together. Joan let her gabble on. What difference did it make now? The doctor had given her something for the fever as well as a tonic for the long, heavy cycle Mother told him Joan was experiencing.

'You might well look as if you couldn't care less one way or another at the moment, Joan dear. But you'll thank me in time for protecting your reputation, believe me. Father, of course, knows nothing and he never will, will he? I'll tell him what I told the doctor and leave it at that. As for the wreckage in your bedroom, well, the bombing was terrible that night. I wrote and explained that the foundations of the house had been shaken by a particularly nasty raid. We'll stick with that, shall we?'

'Yes, Mother. And what did you tell them about my hand?' she asked, looking down at the bandage.

'I said you slipped and fell on a broken cup.'

Joan nodded. Mother could have told Father that Joan had sliced her hand open shaving her beard. Or that she had been helping a friend train as a knife thrower and had her hand pinned to the rotating board. Or had been scything wheat

70

or disembowelling a partridge. Or she could have told him the truth. It would not have mattered or made any difference. Father would not have come home to enquire about her health. She could not remember him once touching her face or stroking her hair and he would never question Mother about anything, accepting her rules and directions without a murmur.

Sometimes, on the rare occasions he was home, he would look with pity at Joan when Mother started her endless nagging about rehearsals and lessons and her career, but when Joan begged him with her eyes for help or intervention, he just looked the other way. It was a wonder to Joan that he had made it to captain during his career in the RAF. She laughed to herself when she pictured the looks on the faces of his men if they could see him acquiescing to Mother on each and every minor point of their lives.

But, remorse overwhelmed Joan. She tried to hold back the images of her dreadful behaviour but they pushed their way through with harsh persistence. She recoiled away from them into a corner of the chair, but still they came on, making her feel hot with chagrin. She thought about saying something, perhaps asking Mother's forgiveness, but felt that Mother had much to apologise for first and as she, no doubt, felt the same way, neither of them made a move towards the other.

'Well,' Mother said. 'You're looking better these past few days. I believe there's some colour in your face. Are you feeling stronger?'

'A bit,' Joan said, turning her face to the weak sun managing to seep through the clouds, stout with snow.

Mother looked at Joan for a time. 'You must think me awfully heartless.'

Joan was glad when Mother didn't give her time to answer. Mother came to kneel beside her, brushing the serviette from her lap and looking up into Joan's eyes. 'I'm going to show you something now that you have to know about. I hope after you see it, you'll be able to face the truth and get on with things as before.'

'What can you mean?' Joan asked, already imagining a letter from Ralph that perhaps Mother had opened and hidden from her.

Mother unlocked a drawer in the sideboard and took out a folded newspaper. She took a deep breath and placed it on Joan's lap. 'Page twenty-four,' she said. Then she turned and left the room with soft, quick footsteps.

For a moment Joan sat very still. A bird pecked through the wintry garden mire then flew, disappointed, to try its luck in the barren hedge. In the distance a man shouted followed by the loud noise of something heavy falling. Clouds engulfed the sunshine and a few darts of rain gave way to spatterings of snow. Joan turned the paper over and saw that it was dated Friday 30th December 1940; the day after that terrible scene with Mother. *The Second Fire of London*, the headline read.

With controlled movements, she leafed through each sheet until she arrived at the instructed page, in the middle of the Arts and Entertainment section. She peeled the pages apart and there was a photo of Ralph, smiling through the grainy newsprint, his hand lifted as if to fend off the reporters. On his left was his wife, looking sophisticated in a feathery hat that swept low over one eye. *Sir Ralph to be new Musical Director of the ABC SSO*, the headline read. Sydney. He'd never mentioned the possibility.

Joan let the paper fall. Then she scrambled for it again and read through the first paragraph. Ralph had been in negotiations for this post for ages. With a jolt she realised that she would have made no difference to his taking it up, pregnant or not. She couldn't bear to read the rest of the article, learn about his new beginnings and his aspirations for the musical life of Sydney. She crumpled the paper and threw it towards the fire. Mother appeared holding out a handkerchief. Joan snatched it and wiped it around her face as they stood facing each other in the pallid light from the thickening snow.

'I'm sorry for all you've been through, Joan dear,' Mother said, taking a small step in her direction.

Joan turned and looked out over the fence at the end of the garden, across the allotments and as far as possible above the line of trees surrounding the park. There were thousands and thousands of miles between her and Sydney. She imagined what her life might have been if Ralph had asked her to go with him; if in time it would have been her at his side for presentations and opening nights; if the child would have favoured him or her and if there would have been any more. How it would have felt to have an ocean between her and Mother. And that was it, Joan thought, turning back to the gloomy sitting room; that was the

73

real heartbreak. Going back to things exactly as they were before she'd managed to grab something for herself with Ralph.

Mother plucked Joan's violin from its case and, balancing it across her forearms, walked with reverence towards Joan. Without a word, she nudged the instrument across the space between them. Joan took it from her and edged it back, placing it in Mother's hands. Mother pushed it forward again, this time with more force. Again, Joan sent it back. 'Don't be silly, Joan,' Mother said. 'Take it.'

This time Joan put her hand up to stop the violin's progress towards her.

'What else is there now? You're not going to let that Svengali win, are you?'

'Svengali?' Joan snorted. 'I loved every minute of the time I spent with Ralph. It was wonderful. Please don't kid yourself that he had to beg me, Mother.'

'That can't be possible.' Mother looked as though Joan had hit her a second time. 'For some perverse reason you're trying to shield him, but it's too late for all that. He's not coming back and I insist that you get on with your career.'

Joan thrust her hands under her arms. She knew she had to keep her voice steady so she wouldn't stoop to another hideous scene. 'I will never play the violin again,' she said, enunciating each word clearly and looking straight at Mother.

'But Joan . . . ' Mother's voice was pleading. 'I do wish I could understand why.' She let the violin dangle by her side.

Perhaps, Joan thought, *I have never really*

74

explained myself properly. She had huffed and puffed, sighed, sulked and shouted. But, had she ever sat down and told Mother, in plain words, how she felt?

'Mother,' Joan said, softening her voice. 'Let's sit for a minute.' She guided Mother to the couch and sat beside her. 'The violin.' Mother's face furrowed. 'I don't think playing was ever my first choice of hobby or career.'

Mother sat up ramrod straight and her features flattened. 'Then, what was your first choice?'

'Well, that's where the dilemma arises,' Joan said, taking care not to lose control of her patience. 'I was never given the chance to think about anything else I might like to do, or might be good at, as I was always made to concentrate on the violin.'

'That's because, Joan dear, you showed such aptitude when first you picked it up.' Mother's shoulders slumped. 'I thought I was helping you, encouraging you.'

'I would like my own life, Mother. Not yours.' Joan looked away but could feel Mother tense beside her. 'And now, besides all that . . . ' Her voice stuck in her throat. 'It will remind me too much of Ralph. And I couldn't bear it.'

Joan reached out for Mother's hand, but Mother withdrew hers to her own lap.

'So . . . ' Mother tightened her eyes until they tapered. 'It's all my fault, just as it's always been. At least now I can share that burden with Sir Ralph Myers. But, Joan dear, you are worth so much more than him. And I would implore you — ' she produced the violin yet again '— do not give this up for a man like that.'

Joan had tried so hard and she could not believe that Mother was not meeting her at least part of the way. Only just managing to keep her anger in check she said, 'Do whatever you want with it but I don't want to see it or hear about it for the rest of my life. It has brought me nothing but misery.'

Mother held the violin by its neck wishing, no doubt, that it was Joan's throat she could put her hand around and throttle. 'Well,' she said, also making an effort to remain controlled. 'I'm going to leave it here while you consider your other options. You'll have to do something, you know. Now, make yourself useful while I get supper.'

Starting in the sitting room, Joan made her way around the house pulling the blackouts closed. Then she opened the lid of the gramophone and chose a recording without strings.

Mother was right: Joan knew she would have to find something to do and she would have to find it quickly, before Mother wore down her resolve. She watched her hands as she slid the record from its sleeve. She used them gingerly, out of habit, careful not to scrape or chafe them. She unravelled the bandage and looked at her scar. It was healing nicely, but Joan was fascinated by it as the only blemish on the soft, pampered skin. She wondered what it would be like to be a fishmonger's wife, or dig weeds, or throw coal on the fire with bare hands.

She remembered a conversation she'd overheard at the Hall. One of the girls' aunties, or cousin, or maybe it was a sister-in-law, had been rejected from the WAAFs and signed on, instead, to do construction work. Joan clenched and unclenched her fists and studied the sinews and veins that appeared. Then she laughed out loud for the first time in weeks as she imagined Mother's revulsion when she held out her hands, made thick and calloused from the building site, to be massaged. Mother would *have* to believe then, that she meant what she said.

★ ★ ★

As soon as Joan felt able to walk any distance, she donned her mac, rain boots and scarf and left Mother bleating after her from the door. She had never been well covered, but now the half-stone or so she had lost seemed to allow the cold to whirl around her hollows and rattle her bones. Shivering, she waited for the bus into town but when it arrived, late and crowded, she decided to walk. With each stride she felt some of her strength and stamina return. *This*, she thought, *will stand me in good stead.*

In the few months she had been incapacitated, the bombing had been relentless. Now there was not one road on the way into Central London with all of its buildings standing. The closer she marched to the hub of things, the more ruinous the city became. A woman in a green jumper was selling cigarettes and papers from a hole in a boarded corner shop; a young girl stood staring at the shell of a house, her hand on the untouched gate; the centre of a block of flats had fallen in on itself like sand running through an egg timer. She pulled her coat tight, but knew that the chills she felt were not caused by the weather alone.

77

The initial plan she harboured was to stop at any construction site she came upon and ask for a job, but each time she approached a likely-looking situation, her courage dissolved. Some sites were small and manned by one or two older men, who Joan didn't trust not to laugh at her. Many were boarded and fenced and had no semblance of activity she could see or hear. On the corner of Regent Street and Oxford Circus, what looked like a shop and part of a hotel were being worked on by a group of men in navy blue overalls.

Joan stood under the shelter of an overhang opposite the site and watched the comings and goings. Her newfound energy and the orchestrated movements of the workers made her smile. She could imagine herself doing what they were doing. A woman of about her age, in a smart check skirt and carrying a notepad, came out of an office that looked like a caravan and talked to a couple of men, pointing towards parts of the bomb site with her pencil. Joan took a deep breath, smoothed her hair and ran across the road.

'I say,' Joan called. 'Excuse me. Have you a minute?'

The young woman turned. 'Can I help you?'

'I hope so,' Joan said. 'Are you hiring?'

The woman twirled the pencil round in her mouth and looked Joan up and down. 'Who are you enquiring for?' she asked. 'Your brother? Dad? A friend?'

The men had stopped work and were staring at her from behind half-built walls and the rungs of ladders. The image of her being happy here, working and humming and joking amongst these

78

people disappeared as completely as the burnt-out building they were working on. Now she was aware of how they would pry and judge and watch and snigger. But she looked the young woman in the eye and said, 'For me, actually.'

There was a cough behind her, then another and another. 'Well,' the woman said, glancing at her colleagues over Joan's shoulder. 'There are women working on big building sites, but not this one, love. This is a private site. You'll need to sign on and they'll direct you from there.'

'Sign on?' Joan said.

'At the Labour Exchange.' Joan wanted to ask for more information, but the woman turned to resume her discussion with the men and Joan was dismissed.

When she turned the corner towards Tottenham Court Road, she stamped her feet with frustration and cold, but the thought of returning to Mother without definite news of a job spurred her on.

She walked and walked. Piccadilly, Trafalgar Square, Pall Mall, Somerset House, the river. Then she saw an enormous site hidden by wooden screens and sails of tarpaulin. Women were going in and out. This is it, she thought, the project her fellow musician must have been talking about. Her stomach flipped; here she could get on with it and prove her intentions to Mother once and for all. And so many women were crawling all over the works that she would go unnoticed; no interrogations here.

She joined the queue at the enquiries window behind a woman in a rather shabby navy coat and darned stockings. Joan recoiled when she caught sight of the woman's bitten, inflamed nails. 'Any work going?' the woman asked.

'Got plenty, my dear,' the man on duty said. 'But sign on at the Exchange first and tell them you want the Bridge.'

The woman nodded. When she turned, she looked right through dusty spectacles to somewhere in the distance beyond Joan. But she seemed to know what the man was talking about so Joan followed her. To sign on, she supposed.

4

April — July 1941

Evelyn

It was a bright Good Friday morning. The wind was strong and gusty, shepherding clouds together then scattering them into billowing clusters. Up here on the timber the cold had a knack of finding the smallest of gaps, a button left undone or a breach between scarf and collar. Tugging off a gauntlet, Evelyn rubbed under her armpit at the place where her coarse vest scratched and worried, wondering if she'd ever be able to leave it off even in the summer. She pulled her shield aside, pushed the blackened goggles high on her forehead and looked up at the struggling sun through a crisscrossed maze of cranes, buckets swaying gracefully on what looked like well-mannered crooked fingers on the end of lace-gloved arms.

She felt giddy and grasped the side of the workbench. As usual, it would take her a minute or two to get the vastness into perspective after concentrating on her close-up welding job for so long. The Shot Tower rose above the gaffer's hut on the gantry and, never mind the cold, she would much rather be here in the open than stuck inside that narrow, tapering building turning out lead pellets for hunting. St Paul's pierced the clouds; at its base and pockmarking both sides of the river were pitted black bomb sites. In the distance, V-shapes streamed out behind ships and emergency craft patrolling the choppy river.

Leaning back against a load of timber, Evelyn surveyed the activity around her. Gangs of three or four bending close to their flames were dotted along what would eventually be a road crossing. Some sort of machinery sighed and wheezed when it performed its task; concrete churned along the pumping pipes. Lengths of steel reinforcement were lifted and moved.

She had no idea what she was doing. How it all fitted together. She'd never even thought about how bridges held their loads or kept their shape and now that she had, she was no wiser. None of the other girls did either. They simply worked on their little bit — whatever that might be — and at the end of each shift there was more to the bridge than there had been when they started.

'Evelyn.' Her name caught on the wind and trailed off towards Somerset House. The gaffer. Stooping over her work, she covered her face with her shield and lit the flame. A prod on her shoulder. Now she was for it. She turned in time to see Jim catch the stray strand of hair that he combed over his bald spot as it was whipped upwards on a particularly strong gust. He held it down with one hand and slapped his cap on with the other.

'Morning, Gaffer.'

'It's Mr Adams. Or Jim will do.'

Jim was alright. He was the shift manager least likely to have a go at you for stretching. Or take five minutes off your ciggie break for resting your eyes. He had a wife and three daughters of his

82

own and the same bemused look came over his face when he talked about them as it did when he dealt with the women on the bridge. He motioned for her to step aside.

'I wonder if you'd do me a favour. I'm expecting a visitor soon . . .'

'Who?' Evelyn saw herself curtseying in her dirty blue overalls to the queen, who was always out and about. Or maybe it was Churchill. 'Winnie?'

'Steady,' Jim said, clearing his throat and taking a pencil from his top pocket. 'A photographer from the *Daily Herald*.' He checked the timetable on his clipboard. 'He's due in about half an hour and wants to take a couple of pictures up here.'

'Oh.' Not so exciting after all.

'I thought he might snap you at work. Would that be okay?'

Evelyn pulled her shoulders back and brushed crumbs of dried concrete from her bib and braces. 'Of course,' she said.

'Right. I'll have a word with Gwen next.' He pointed his pencil towards Evelyn's partner, her head dangerously close to the sparks spitting from the end of the welding arm clamped in her fist. Gwen never looked up unless it was for a break or dinner. Evelyn had willed her partner to give her the slightest suggestion of wanting a chat or of acknowledging her at the very least. But no, nothing. They'd worked side by side on this section for four weeks, moving their equipment along in a wheelbarrow as their stripe of steel lengthened, but Gwen hadn't exchanged as much as two sentences with her the whole time.

It wasn't as if Evelyn hadn't tried. She talked about the dance halls she visited, she told her about being engaged to Ron and how she'd been glad when he called it off, what Dad had told her and Sylvie about how the old bridge had buckled. There was something so tired about the woman though. Dragged down, dogged and miserable. The skin around her mouth and eyes was flaking and dry and her fingers, when she took her gloves off, were gnawed raw and oozing pus; Evelyn had to look away from them. Her hair was greying from the roots to a straight line above her ears, so she must have looked after herself up until a few months ago.

Evelyn wondered what had happened to her at that point and told her about Mum dying and other ghastly things, like the man around the corner who'd lost a leg and Sylvie's friend who didn't turn up as arranged one evening. When Sylvie took the Tube to where Helen had lived, the house and everyone in it was gone. Evelyn wanted Gwen to know that whatever she'd been through, she wasn't the only one.

During an afternoon break, Evelyn had trailed after Gwen to a cubbyhole and hunkered down beside her. She'd held out her pack of Player's and said, 'Ciggie?'

Gwen turned and stared at her with that faraway, icy look in her eyes.

Perhaps she'd used the wrong word. 'Fag? Go ahead.'

Gwen looked away and took a packet of papers and a tin, which she tapped, from her pocket.

Lighting her own, Evelyn smoked in the silence.

84

'Shall I fetch us both a cuppa?'

Gwen shrugged. 'You go on. I'll help myself in a bit.'

Evelyn wasn't about to give up — they did have to work together after all. Worse luck. She flicked a measure of ash into the wind and made an effort to brighten her voice. 'Well. I've told you all about my family. Dad and Mum. You know Sylvie, anyway.' She laughed. 'Everyone knows Sylvie. How about yours?'

Gwen stopped still, a pinch of tobacco between her fingers. 'I . . . I have a husband.'

'Oooh. What's his name?'

'George.'

'Has he been called up?'

Gwen shook her head. 'He's reserved. On the trains.'

'That's lucky. At least he comes home every night. Any kids?'

With a start, Gwen dropped the brown shards onto her thigh then tried to brush them into a mound to pick up again. 'Three,' she said softly.

Evelyn felt pleased with herself. Everyone she knew with children loved to talk about them. 'Girls? Boys?'

'Two boys and a girl.' Gwen prised the lid off the tin and stuffed the tobacco back inside. Her fingers were trembling. 'Changed my mind.' She mumbled and pushed past Evelyn. 'Tea.'

'Hey,' Evelyn called after her. 'What are their names? Gwen.' But Gwen didn't turn and Evelyn kept her chattering off the subject of kids after that. Problem was, it was getting harder every day to think of what to talk about when there was no

85

response.

'What did she say?' Evelyn asked Jim, now making his way back across the boards.

'She agreed,' he said, looking over his shoulder at Gwen. 'But she won't take her shield off.'

'I will,' Evelyn said. 'Dad'll get some surprise when he opens his paper tomorrow. Will it be in tomorrow?'

'Not sure,' Jim said. 'We'll ask the photographer.'

'Can Sylvie be in it too?'

'Oh, I don't think there's any need.'

'Please. She won't hide behind her shield. She'll do whatever the shutterbug wants. Besides, you know she's got a lovely smile.' Jim had remarked on Sylvie's smile a number of times. Everyone had.

'Go on then.'

Evelyn dodged her way around hammers and jacks, slabs of stone, steel rods and timber to where Sylvie was vibrating the concrete. She signalled with arms above her head and Sylvie held up a finger. One minute. The skip expelled the last of its load, which Sylvie worked on to the last foot. Then she laid the vibrating machine aside.

'I've just had a break,' she said. 'But I might be able to nip off again if I'm careful.'

Evelyn tugged at her sister's hand. 'It's not a break,' she said. 'Take your turban off and come with me. Grab your face shield.'

'Where are we going?'

'To surprise Dad.'

'What?'

Evelyn explained as she pulled Sylvie along.

'We might get discovered yet,' Sylvie said as they

stopped behind a line of hopper cars to touch up their lipstick from the tube she kept in her bib pocket.

'Carry on as normal,' the photographer said. Gwen did as she was told, hunching over her flame. It hadn't even seemed to register with her that anything out of the ordinary was going on. Evelyn removed her shield every time the photographer snapped and Sylvie didn't even manage that pretence, looking straight at the camera and grinning.

'No. Ladies, please.' The photographer shuffled from foot to foot. 'Just get on with what you usually do.' So, Evelyn kept her face covered but stood tall and Sylvie held her mask in her hand, inspecting the next reinforcement rod in line. 'That's a good one. Should be in Tuesday morning.'

But it wasn't. All that appeared was a short article about the bridge that Dad read aloud:

CONSTRUCTION OF NEW WATERLOO BRIDGE
The new crossing at Waterloo Bridge is pressing forward despite the inevitable setback caused by the labour shortage. The men on the bridge are working long hours and are willing to turn their hand to any task that needs to be undertaken in order to complete this vital link between north and south. In addition, the men are taking advantage of green labour to perform unskilled roles. This allows them to utilise their expertise, which is critical to complete what the government terms 'this building work of strategic importance'.

'Is that it?' Sylvie peered over Dad's shoulder.

'That's it. No snap of my girls.'

'Turn over, Dad. There might be something on the back,' Evelyn said.

'No. Nothing there.'

'Well, I'll be blowed. We'll never get in the films now.'

'Perhaps they're saving it for another day. When everyone could do with a cheer-up. Ah.' Dad chuckled. 'Here's something that should interest you.' He spread the pages on the table and pointed to a headline. 'Clothes rationing begins on the first of June.'

'How could they!' Sylvie snatched the paper.

'Let's have a look,' Evelyn said.

Sylvie sat on the arm of the chair so Evelyn could read the article with her.

'Oh, it's not so bad,' Evelyn said.

'Not so bad? Maybe you could manage but I have appearances to keep up. Look, a jacket, one jacket, will cost twelve of your sixty coupons.'

'We only need our overalls during the day so we can spend everything on our going-out clothes. Besides, everyone's in the same boat.'

'I suppose so,' said Sylvie. 'By the way, what's green? Green labour.'

'You,' Dad said.

'Me and Evelyn?'

'All you girls. Never done anything like this before, have you? It'll be a miracle if it stands half as long as the old bridge.'

Evelyn cuffed Dad around his head with the paper. 'Right, you can get your own tea tonight.'

'Not likely,' he said. 'Out of my chair you two

and in the kitchen.'

Whatever she was called, green or otherwise, Evelyn was pleased that she didn't have to queue with the hundreds of women who'd left it to the last minute to register for war work with the Employment Exchange. She supposed they would be asked what kind of work they preferred, but it might not be easy to place them where they wanted to be. She hadn't thought she'd stick this for long. It was only meant to be a stopgap until she found something in an office or teaching in one of the services.

If she did want to change, now might be a good time, but she didn't want to. She loved it. The work was doing wonders for her figure, especially her arms, there was plenty of fun in the dinner break and, although you had to do the same tasks over and over again, it wasn't anything like the soul-destroying monotony of housework. It felt good to see the evidence of what you'd accomplished and the progress that was being made. Wages in your hand on a Thursday afternoon was a good feeling, too; she was pleased to be able to give a few bob to Dad and have a bit left over for herself. But some of the women complained they took home much less than the men and Evelyn did wonder a bit about that, too, from time to time.

★ ★ ★

Sylvie rubbed her eyes and yawned, pushing her plate of savoury mince aside.

'Don't you want that?' Evelyn asked.

Sylvie shook her head. 'You have it.'

89

'You should stay in once in a while. Keep Dad company.'

'Wouldn't have made any difference this weekend. No one managed any shut-eye. You look awful.'

'Take a look in the mirror yourself.'

There was a guffaw, followed by the banging of cutlery from the tables at the back of the canteen. A tall, wiry woman with the curled ends of her hair escaping from her flowery headscarf called out to them. 'Sylvie, Evelyn. Over here. Sit with us.'

'She's such a laugh — Olive. Shall we join them?'

Evelyn nodded. 'I'll get my afters and see you in a minute.'

Olive was in full swing when Evelyn squeezed in on the end of the bench next to a well-built young woman with high cheekbones and a ruddy complexion. Empty plates, smeared with congealing gravy or custard, were all around them; the smell of tepid fat less appetising now their stomachs were full.

'I said to him,' Olive went on, 'I said, "I'll be glad when you're sent to wherever it is you're going. I could do with a bleedin' rest." "Oh, come on," he says. "This might be me last time." So I says, "You've been saying that for the past fortnight," and he comes back with, "You can't say no to a dying wish." "Oh, can't I, you dirty bugger," I says.'

'So did you?' Sylvie asked, her chin on her hands.

'That's a bit too close to the bone,' Olive said, crossing her legs and pursing her mouth. 'Let's

90

just say I'll be leaving me pushbike in the shed for a while.'

The tableful of women burst into laughter again. More knives and forks and plates were pounded on the table. Evelyn joined in with her bowl but could feel the heat reaching her ears. She turned away before anyone could see and point it out to the others. The high colour on the cheeks of the girl next to her — who couldn't have been more than nineteen — spread over her entire face and seemed to be throbbing. Evelyn was mortified for her when she saw Olive glance over and grin, a comment about to take aim.

'Oh look,' someone facing the door whispered. 'Isn't that your partner, Evelyn? What's her name: Gwen?'

Evelyn nodded. Through a hand on her brow, she watched Gwen take what must have been the desecrated remains of the mince, veg, spotted dick and custard and slip into the place closest to the door, her back to their crowded table.

'How do you stand it?' asked the woman next to Olive. 'She never speaks. I tried a couple of times with her but all I got for my trouble was a shrug.'

'And her *hands* . . . ' someone at the other end said with a shudder.

Evelyn felt a knot in her stomach. She didn't like the way this conversation was going and tried to think of how she could bring it back to Olive and her husband's late-night larks. She'd thought the same things herself about Gwen, many times, but now she felt a loyalty towards her. 'Oh, she's not that bad,' she said defensively. 'She's a work-horse.' But no one seemed to hear and if they did,

91

they chose to ignore her.

'I don't know how she manages to hold anything. It's a wonder she hasn't had a nasty accident,' the woman opposite Sylvie said, leaning in and lowering her voice.

'Oh, I hope not.' Olive beat on her chest with an open palm and closed her eyes. 'She's already had something horrible to put up with. So I hear.'

'Haven't we all,' someone sniffed.

Now Evelyn tilted her head forward, eager to hear the story. 'What happened?'

'Her boy ran off one night end of last year. Bad night it was. Got caught in one of Hitler's packets and that was that. His dad found him. Well, so I've been told.'

Evelyn thought about the kids she could have had with Ron and the ones she hoped to have with someone else. She thought about Rosie Harrison and all the other children who'd been in her class. 'That's so sad,' she said. 'What about the others?'

'Two of them left. Boy and girl, I think. Been sent to Wales now.'

'Two?' Evelyn was sure Gwen had said she had three children. 'I thought . . . She told me . . .'

Every face was turned towards her, waiting for another titbit. She shook her head. 'Never mind.'

'Still,' Olive's friend said, nodding towards Gwen's back. 'We could all be like that, couldn't we? No help to herself or anyone else.' That seemed to be the murmuring consensus as chairs were scraped back and cigarettes appeared from pockets. Evelyn took out her pack of three and offered one to the girl next to her, whose face had settled back down to its natural pink flush. As

92

much as she tried, she couldn't stop herself looking towards Gwen, whose shoulders were huddled over what must by now be a stone-cold dinner.

Picking up an ashtray, Evelyn walked across to Gwen's table and sat down opposite her. Evidence of Gwen's good manners, her knife and fork lay together on top of the plate from which only a couple of mouthfuls had been eaten. The bowl of afters Gwen was staring at was untouched, the nose pads of her spectacles green where Evelyn thought salty tears had settled for months on end, her cheeks rough and dry.

But now there was no weeping. Perhaps she was all cried out and left with that blank, faraway expression that Evelyn had come to expect on her partner's face. She wanted to say something, but couldn't think of the right words and, besides, they wouldn't have made it past the lump in her throat. She went to put her hand over Gwen's but hesitated and they both jerked away at the same time. Gwen looked up then, her mouth tight and her eyes narrow, daring Evelyn to come closer. Evelyn cleared her throat. 'Come and sit with us,' she said.

Gwen looked at her as though she was simple, took off her glasses, wiped hard at her face. Then she left without saying a word.

'There's nothing you can do,' Sylvie said, making room next to her. 'Don't be bothered.' But Evelyn was.

★　★　★

93

Three weeks later nothing mattered except they'd somehow lived through the weekend. Dad was a wreck — and for *him* to be alarmed meant things were bad. For the first time he forbade Evelyn and Sylvie to go out. They didn't protest, but followed him down to the Tube where they dozed on and off in a sitting position, squashed into a space that seemed about the size of a packet of rationed tea. When they emerged into the smoky haze the following morning, they stood still for a minute taking in the devastation. There was nothing new. They'd seen it, heard it, smelled it all before, but there was simply much more of it this time. More bulging roads and burst water pipes, a shoe with a torn foot laced into it. Row after row of crushed houses and flats with their sides ripped off, the intimate settings of everyday life laid open to scrutiny. The smell of burning more intense, the moan of sirens unwavering. They hurried along, watching every step.

'We'll make sure everything's okay at home, then see what we can do,' Dad said. His mouth sounded dry.

A warden was walking up and down Mayes Road, jotting notes in his book even though much of the terrace stood solid and upright, proud of making it through the night.

'This one yours?' He pointed to their front door.

'That's the one,' Dad said. 'Everything alright?'

'You're lucky. Very lucky. They took it at both ends but the middle's intact.' He shook his head. 'Funny how it goes. Could have easily been the other way around.'

Dad closed his eyes then forced himself to look

at the blackened houses to the left and the right. Evelyn stepped back to take in the whole road at once and Sylvie joined her, clutching at her arm. 'Number fourteen. Look.'

'Just the walls, hanging there.'

'Who'd have thought they had such poor taste in wallpaper?'

'Sometimes you go too far, Sylvie. That's not funny.'

Sylvie's voice was hoarse. 'It wasn't meant to be,' she said.

There was no gas, no water. They gathered together a few biscuits, a torch and bandages and went along the road where they'd lived all their lives to see which neighbours needed help.

The House of Commons had taken it along with Westminster Abbey, the soap factory, Victoria Station and Big Ben. 'Dear old chap,' Dad said. 'Still chiming though. It'll take more than a few bombs to stop him.' Then, two nights of eerie silence during which the warning sounded a number of times followed immediately by the all-clear. Despite that, Dad was adamant they stick to their routine of bedding down in the underground, waiting for another night like Friday and dreading what they would find when they climbed out of their hole in the ground. But each morning what lay before them was almost unchanged from the night before. Sylvie hoped that was that. Perhaps it was finished and done.

'Or maybe,' Evelyn said, 'we'll just have time to clear this lot up and it'll start all over again.'

By Monday morning they were exhausted. The number 29 took so many detours they didn't recognise where they were most of the time, and the streets that should have been familiar were crumpled and distorted. From Oxford Street they caught the Tube to Waterloo and converged with the swarms of women and a handful of men making their way towards the bridge. Shuffling down to single file past the guards, every head in front of Evelyn turned to stare at a hole in the underside of the temporary bridge, twisted steel and girders hanging from it like entrails from a gaping belly. She took her turn to gawp.

'That'll put us back,' Sylvie said.

'Wonder if the new one's been hit.'

'We might have to start all over again,' someone said. But Evelyn didn't think so; their work was here, above and around them. There might be a minor setback but that was all.

Quickly changing into dungarees and boots, the women shook out an array of coloured scarves and tied them into knots on their heads. One of the ladies, in a blue overall, stuck her head through the door and told them to hurry. 'Jim's called a meeting,' she said. 'And it sounds important.'

Evelyn followed Sylvie to the top, turning her collar up against the fresh breeze. A smouldering residue lingered in the air, but after two nights without bombing, they could clearly smell the tang of the Thames wafting around them. Fumes, mud, silt. It was lovely to smell the river again. For some reason the men stood on the right, the ladies on the left. *How silly*, Evelyn thought. But every meeting was the same.

There'd been some ruckus from the men at the beginning about their jobs, but none of the women could do the skilled work anyway. Fetching and carrying, a bit of welding, that was about it. Some of the senior ladies had a bit of responsibility but they were few and far between. All the women who took a man's job had to sign a piece of paper saying they'd step aside when the men returned, so there was no need for them to worry. Daft buggers.

Evelyn scanned the crowd and nodded to two or three women behind her. Right at the back and standing away from everyone else was Gwen, her gloves under her arm, the tips of her fingers in her mouth. Evelyn caught her eye and waved, but Gwen turned away. *Okay, be like that yet again,* she thought. Despite the rebuff, Evelyn decided to have another go. She excused herself through the crude lines being formed and took up the empty space next to Gwen.

Evelyn nodded at her partner. 'How did you manage the weekend?' she said.

Gwen put her hands behind her back and studied Evelyn for what felt like a long time. Her eyes in their red sockets lost their glare and softened a bit. 'Part of our place took it,' she said.

'Worse luck. Everyone alright?'

Gwen looked down at her boots and nodded.

'What will you do?'

'It's nothing George can't fix. We'll stay with a neighbour till then.'

Jim blew a whistle to get their attention. The men opposite made a point of facing forward, arms folded and lips shut tight. Jim had to blow again in the women's direction, after which the laughter and talking died down. Gwen mumbled what sounded like 'ta'.

'Sorry?' Evelyn leaned closer to Gwen's face.

'Ta. Thanks for asking.'

Evelyn held a wide smile until she got the shadow of one back from Gwen.

Holding a loudhailer and fiddling with his necktie, Jim said, 'As I'm sure you're all aware, the temporary bridge took a hit on Friday night. A bus was caught up in it too, but that's now been cleared.'

'My nephew's wife was on that bus,' a tiny woman said. 'On her way home from town.'

'The damage has been inspected and I've been instructed to tell you about redeployment.' He took in the workforce standing in front of him. 'Unfortunately, most of you will now have to be diverted to implement running repairs on the temporary bridge so that it can be reopened as quickly as possible. I've consulted with the foremen and together we've decided who will be assigned where. For now, carry on with your duties here and I'll make the rounds during the day to tell you who's going to work where, as from tomorrow.'

'I hope we're able to stick together,' Gwen said.

Evelyn started. Coming from Gwen, that degree of sentiment was unnerving. But perhaps there'd been a breakthrough. 'We'll make sure we do,' she said, certain that no one else would be tripping over themselves to work with Gwen.

Evelyn felt her partner inch imperceptibly closer. A cloud scuttled, leaving their stark, inky shadows melded together across the concrete deck.

98

Dad was reluctant to let them loose again, although he did concede that they couldn't stay cooped up with him every evening. The radio and papers told him that the Germans were concentrating their efforts elsewhere: the Atlantic and Soviet Union. 'We saw those Jerries off,' he said. 'They'll never get London.' But still he was wary. The *Bismarck* sank the *Hood*, the Navy sank the *Bismarck*. Dad and Uncle Bert went to the pub to celebrate, Evelyn and Sylvie to the West End. The Strand was buzzing and they were glad to be back, roaming from pub to club and finally settling on the Palace, elegant and airy with a seamless, polished dance floor, throbbing to the resident band's rendition of Judy Garland's 'You Made Me Love You'.

They stood near the curve of the bar, the brass foot-rail reflecting the light from the chandelier as flickering flakes hewn from precious stones. Evelyn looked at her naked ring finger, flanked on the right by a lovely marquisette cocktail ring, which she thought much more attractive than her engagement ring had ever been. Two burly hands, wires of black hair sprouting along their backs and into khaki cuffs, rested on Sylvie's shoulders.

'Hey,' a voice said, drawling and languorous. He twisted Sylvie around and looked into her face. 'Remember me?'

Sylvie examined the man, his hands rubbing her shoulders gently. So did Evelyn. He filled out his tan uniform nicely, his broad shoulders and arms pushing against the sleeves adorned with three insignias: a black flash embroidered with SAS-K.L.I. (M.G.) CANADA in yellow, a red patch, a single striped chevron. His eyes were a pale hazel, striking against his weather-beaten complexion and thick russet hair. Creases appeared around his eyes when he frowned and there were two deep lines framing his grinning mouth, which wore a smile wide enough to challenge Sylvie's.

'No,' Sylvie said, widening her eyes. 'I don't think I do.'

'Oh, come on.' He gave her a little shake. 'Sure you do. It's Alec. We danced together a while back.'

Evelyn giggled and turned away. That wasn't narrowing it down much.

'Well, hey. Never mind,' he said congenially, as if he really didn't. 'Can I get you ladies a drink?'

'Gin and It, please,' Sylvie said. 'Evelyn?'

'The same for me. Thanks.'

'Consider it done. If you take this,' Alec said, producing a folded khaki cap from his pocket and handing it to Sylvie, 'and go sit at that table over there with my buddies, I'll bring you your drinks.'

Evelyn hardly needed the seat she took possession of, twirling and whirling through the evening with anyone who asked. She didn't pay much attention to Sylvie until later in the evening, when she noticed that every time she passed her sister on the dance floor she was with Alec. She'd never known Sylvie to stick with the same fellow for an entire evening. Alec's fingers were splayed territorially across the hollow of Sylvie's back and she played with the place where his starched collar met his neck. Their movements were fluid and relaxed; they looked good together. From then on, Alec turned up wherever they went. Evelyn was reminded of that passage from *A Christmas Carol* that she read to her class before they broke up at the end of the year: *Wherever she went, there went he.*

But Sylvie was having none of it. 'Oh, him,' she said when Evelyn asked how keen she was on Alec. 'He's a bit of a laugh, that's all, with his "Hi, guys" and "You're welcome" chat.'

One warm, clammy Sunday in July, Evelyn took the bus to Holloway to have tea with a friend. As the bus slowed to a stop at the gates to Finsbury Park, Evelyn wiped the window and peered out at the hopeful families — picnics, flasks, bikes and umbrellas in tow — making their way across the swathes of wet grass. She was drawn to a couple sitting on the other side of the iron fence on a tartan blanket. The woman was wearing a dusty pink jacket, very like one of Sylvie's most prized garments.

Evelyn wiped at a fresh layer of mist that had appeared where her breath hit the window. The jacket not only looked like Sylvie's, it *was* Sylvie's, and the man with his arm wrapped around its shoulders was Alec. Evelyn banged on the window to wave. The conductor rang the bell and the bus lurched forward. Alec glanced around, as if aware that someone was trying to get their attention but Sylvie, her head leaning on his expansive chest, looked as though she didn't have a clue what was going on around her, except that she was with him.

Slumping against the back of the seat, Evelyn

101

felt stunned. Not that Sylvie had met someone who made her gaze at him in that spellbound way, but that it had happened so fast. She looked out at the streets she barely recognised on the once-familiar route and wondered at how quickly things could change, in the flare of a bomb or the flash of a smile.

5

August — November 1941

Gwen

George would be furious with her if he knew, having forbidden her from entering the house until it was finished and he'd given the okay. But she needed to dare herself to step over the threshold and test whether the hush of missing children still screeched at her, or if she could feel at peace in the comfort of personal objects and smells and noises in her own home. George was on the late shift, so was spending the day diligently shoring up the hole in the kitchen. She couldn't see him from the front of the house but she could hear the rhythmic scrape of his shovel on concrete. It was like a subdued version of the sounds on the bridge; the harsh clash of hard materials coming together to create something solid and substantial, ready to be knocked down in an instant.

She found her key and turned the chilly piece of metal over in her hand a couple of times, wincing when it caught on a shredded cuticle. Then, with one more glance towards the steady din in the garden, Gwen slipped into the narrow hallway, the echo of her sigh whispering around her.

A coat had fallen from the line of pegs and lay crumpled on the floorboards. They'd talked about repapering the green flowery walls, but that had been months ago. It hardly mattered now. She walked around the sitting room, picking up their wedding photo, fondling the porcelain bell George had surprised her with on her birthday, smoothing the chair backs over the places where their heads rubbed dark, shiny spots onto the fabric. She brushed a few stray cinders into the grate, then sat and closed her eyes, willing some warmth from the past to penetrate the chill.

Even though it was cool for August, she could smell from where she sat the layer of drying mud that George had loosened, releasing with it the earthy scent of turned-over vegetable plots and late summer picnics. She remembered Mudchute Park two years ago when the war was a rumbling undercurrent, unimaginable as they looked out at the heat haze shimmering over their little corner of Cubitt Town, rows of houses and factories safe and intact. Johnny had come racing across the grass, threatening them with his dirt-encrusted palms, Will not far behind. He'd knocked a toddling Ruth off her feet and made straight for Gwen.

Screaming with terror, she'd shouted, 'Help me, Dad, save me from the big, bad, mucky monster!' George had jumped to his feet and grabbed Johnny under his arms, swinging him round and round until they dropped to the ground, exhausted with laughter. Had it really been that easy to be so happy? She hadn't understood it then: simple satisfaction, good fortune, contentment. It was only when she looked back that she knew she'd experienced those things. How sad, to only know happiness in retrospect.

She shivered and wondered if George would be

so intent on his task that she could get away with going into the kitchen. She thought better of that idea, but her eyes were drawn back to the wall separating the hallway from the stairs. She crossed the passage quickly, hoping George wouldn't choose that minute to stretch and look about.

She manoeuvred around the floorboards she knew would creak and groan beneath the red strip of worn carpet. Powdery grime covered the landing, swirling in a vortex as she unsettled it with her movements, taking in the mess: an abandoned slipper, a hairbrush on its side where she'd thrown it the night they took the packet. She'd have her work cut out when they could move back in. There was a clatter beneath her followed by, 'Bugger. Bloody thing.'

Before she could change her mind, she turned right and shoved open the kids' bedroom door. The curtain dividing Ruth's side of the room from the boys' side was pulled back so all three beds were in full view. She remembered washing and ironing Will and Ruth's bedclothes, smoothing them into place and tucking them around the mattresses so they were fresh and crisp, ready for when they came home. But she had no recollection of straightening Johnny's covers or shaking his pillows. Betty had wanted to strip the bed and get rid of it, go through all his things and give them to the WVS for children who'd been bombed out, but Gwen had said she wasn't ready. So Betty must have come up here during a quiet moment and tidied Johnny's bed. She couldn't imagine George would have done such a thing.

Putting her spectacles in her pocket and throwing her coat on the little chair that all the kids had sat in as toddlers, she lay face down on Ruth's bed and breathed in. There was the smell of the copper and boiled linen, a good drying day, a trace of smoke from where the sheets had been finished off around the fire. Will's was the same. She hesitated next to Johnny's bed then threw herself down, clamping his pillow to her face and inhaling until her lungs felt distended. She breathed in and choked and sobbed. Thank goodness Betty hadn't gone ahead in a frenzy, washing away all that was left of her boy; she still had the smell of him.

Rolling over, she grabbed his dressing gown, hanging from a hook. She smothered her face in it, taking in the sweet, boyish smell mingled with the first suggestion of saltier grown-up sweat. Carrying it with her, she found his Christmas book and stroked the pages, feeling for the imprint of his fingers. She brushed a clump of dried mud off his worn football, retrieved countless times from Betty's garden. How she'd nagged him about that and his spellings and taking his shoes off without untying the knots. She couldn't believe she'd ever been so stupid, so petty.

There was a sudden, unnerving quiet from below. Then Betty's voice carried up to her. 'Is she not home yet?'

'Haven't seen her,' George answered.

'Perhaps she's doing a spot of overtime.'

A grunt from George. Gwen imagined him shrugging and looking impatiently at his repair job, waiting to get on.

'Why don't you take her to the pub tonight?' Betty said. 'Or the pictures. It'd be . . . ' Her voice trailed off, as if she'd turned the other way.

George must have moved to face her because, although she strained, Gwen couldn't hear his reply. George took Len to the pub that evening instead, allowing the older man to lean on his arm for support, while she sat in with Betty.

★ ★ ★

Gwen cut through the steel rod on first one edge, then the other. Evelyn caught the discarded ends and threw them into the waste. Each time a length was finished, Evelyn signalled to a banks-man who would signal in turn to a crane driver who swung the load out over the river, then across to where it would be used to bring on the south side of the bridge. She and Evelyn were supposed to swap places every hour, but they rarely both-ered, both of them more content with things this way around. Gwen could keep her goggles and shield over her face and concentrate on the small space in front of her, the cutting flame, the length of steel. Evelyn could chat away to her and she wouldn't be expected to acknowledge or answer. The men preferred Evelyn's quips to her silence, too. Mind you, Evelyn wasn't half the flirt her sis-ter was, although Sylvie herself had calmed down a bit lately.

Gwen was glad the gaffer hadn't separated them when they'd been sent to help patch up the temporary bridge — and he'd kept them together when it was reopened in the middle of September and all hands were back on the tools up here.

The pierce of a whistle cut through the hum of

machinery. The noise ground to a stop and Evelyn put her fingers to her lips and nodded to a crowd of women gathering next to a hut. Gwen waved Evelyn away. 'You go on,' she said. But Evelyn put her arm through Gwen's and almost dragged her along.

Olive was holding court, singing the first verse of 'Roll Out the Barrel' over and over again until there was no fun left in the barrel to bother about. 'Who's for a quick one a bit later?' She was so loud.

'I'd rather have a slow one,' a pretty girl said, blowing smoke out through plump lips.

'Wish I could think that fast,' Evelyn said. 'How about it, Gwen? Do you fancy a drink when we knock off?'

'I didn't think you'd bother with the local,' Gwen said. 'Thought you'd be up town dancing.'

'That's later. There's a crowd who go to The Hero of a Saturday afternoon for one or two.'

Gwen thought about the looks she'd get if she went home with beer on her breath. It was alright for the younger ones, and those like Olive who seemed to do whatever they wanted, but it wasn't for her. 'Ta for asking, but I'll have to be getting home.'

A girl with very red cheeks and her partner, whose name Gwen thought was Joan, joined them. 'I told her it were The Hero and not that other one.'

Everyone laughed, poking fun at the way the girl spoke. It was strange; Gwen had never heard anything like it. She sounded as though she must be from the country and she looked as though she would be at home there, too, milking cows or bringing in the harvest.

'Say it again, Alice,' Joan said, who enunciated each word perfectly as if she'd been born in a bay window. 'What *were* it you told me?'

Alice shook her head. 'No. But I'll try to say it like you does.' And there was more laughter as Alice rolled the words around in her mouth and spilled them out in an upper-crust voice.

Gwen pointed vaguely in the direction of the cloakroom, then scuttled through a canvas-covered doorway and down a sloping tunnel of stifling tarpaulin corridors, held back by crisscrossed planking. When she was level with the river, she made her way across a couple of wooden walkways to a place that she thought of as her own. Here the concrete arches were complete, and she sat under a miniature scaffolding tower that looked as if it had been abandoned. The structure wobbled precariously as if it might topple, leg by leg, rod by rod, into the dirty water that lapped beneath her, and embed itself in all the other junk discarded on the river bed. No one would miss it.

She closed her eyes and felt it sway above her. A good gust of wind and perhaps she'd go over with it. She imagined herself being pulled away from the noise and light, boots dragging her down. Perhaps her head would smash against the pier or her sleeve become entangled in a bit of the scaffolding and she'd thrash around, suspended there like a forgotten item of worn clothing pegged to the line, until her lungs burst. She pictured her spectacles floating away, her turban loosening, the few coppers she had spiralling down, unlucky coins in a mocking well. Sodden fags and matches in her pocket. A grab for the envelope that arrived yesterday.

Voices rose to shouting pitch behind her followed by the grinding of gears, then a lull; indistinct cursing, relieved laughter. They were pouring concrete into the arch that she and Evelyn had been working on. She shivered; it was colder than ever down here, the underside of the bridge untouched by the weak autumn sun. She watched the water slap the pier, a green tidemark already established on the concrete. She took her locker key from her pocket and carved initials in the concrete: GG, GG, JG, WG, RG, encircling them with a chalky heart. Now all of her family was here with her.

Reaching into her bib she pulled out an envelope and took a little postcard from it, turning it over to look at the picture on the front: a puppy outlined in thick black pencil, drawn with diligence and a heavy hand. It looked like a cotton ball with scrawny legs and startled eyes, its tail pointing upwards in a wag. Two figures stood watching, a girl in a pink checked dress clutching a doll who was dressed in identical clothes. She was holding hands with a long-limbed stick-woman. All three had red, crescent-shaped smiles on their round faces. Her first reaction had been that Ruth didn't own a pink dress so the drawing couldn't be of her. Then she read the back:

Dear Mum and Dad,

This is me and Auntie Peggy with my new puppy. Uncle Bryn gave her to me for my

110

own. In the picture I am in my new frock made by Auntie. I am learning my lessons. Here are three kisses, one for Mum one for Dad and one for Betty. XXX

From the start Ruth's cards had been much the same. Nice things seemed to be happening to her: lovely walks, bread-making, bedtime stories. From time to time there was a longer letter from Peggy telling Gwen about Ruth's life in more detail, and although she was pleased to get them she found them difficult to read, part of her jealous that this other woman, kind as she sounded, was enjoying what was rightfully hers.

Next, the letter from Will. Although he and Ruth had been separated, their letters always arrived in the same envelope and his were written on almost transparent paper — to save money on postage, she supposed. His hand was coming on. She could read all of it except the bits where the ink blobbed; she could picture him, gazing intently into the distance searching for the right word, unaware of the stain his pen was making while it rested on the thin paper.

Dear Mum and Dad,
Do you remember the road I told you about that nothing ever goes down except horses and carts? We used to play football there every day after school but now it's dark in the afternoons me and Marty don't have enough time after we finish our chores. Our team, the Vacies, won five games to four over the lads who live here. Vacies is what the boys round

here call us but we just give it them back like Dad told me and Johnny. Don't start it but make sure you give as good as you get. Me and Marty go to bed early and sometimes we can hear Mr and Mrs Morgan talking and laughing downstairs with their David and Jane, but we don't mind because we have an oil lamp and our comics. Please send some more as we have passed the last ones back and forth and they are torn now. Can you send some stamps and another pair of socks as I have put my toe through the ones I've with me? Sorry. I look out for Ruth at school.

Tell Betty I will write to her tomorrow after my homework and chores.

Will XXXXXXXXXXXXXXXXXXXXXX

Gwen folded it over and tucked it away with the postcard. She'd felt uneasy when she'd first read it yesterday but couldn't think why. She had no argument with getting the kids to help out; she and George had always insisted all three of them do their fair share according to their ages. No, it wasn't that or the fact that Will and Marty were sent to their room early. She'd already gathered that Mrs Morgan was no Auntie Peggy, and she told herself that George was right, better off tucked up in bed early than never tucked up in bed again.

And he had his pal with him for company, which must have made things seem a bit more bearable as he and Marty had always been a pair, a right little pair, for as long as she could remember. Sitting on the same bench at school, playing conkers and football and chase, always in and out of each other's houses. But now it struck her. It was the kisses. She'd been pleased to get so many; she'd counted them and pressed her lips to the sheet of paper that many times over. Once there had been three, for her birthday, but other than that, two was his limit. She didn't like it. By the end of the day Gwen had made up her mind. She'd get herself to Llansaint to visit Ruth and Will. Plenty of mothers had made the trip, some of them more than once.

It was dark when Gwen arrived home. Betty's blackouts were drawn as usual, but the familiar clatter of pots and pans, the smell of boiling greens and stewing meat was missing. She turned the back-door knob and put her shoulder to the sticking wood but it jarred against her. She tried harder, then realised it was locked. Gwen couldn't remember Betty ever locking her back door. With shaking fingers she searched for her key and turned the lock.

The kitchen was cold. 'Betty?' she called. 'Bet?' The words echoed back to her. She closed the door and turned on a light. Propped against the brown teapot was a note addressed to her in George's writing telling her that Betty and Len's daughter-in-law was having trouble with the baby. George was helping them to Clapham to be with her. She was a lovely girl, Annie. And their Ray was gentle and quiet, like Len; had his cheeky sense of humour, too. Ray was away with his mob and this was their first little one. When was it due? Gwen wondered.

Shame washed over her for not remembering.

113

Betty would know the expected date to the minute if it had been the other way around. She turned the note over and scribbled a message to George. She would be going to Wales that evening and be home in a few days. She didn't tell him she might have the kids in tow.

★ ★ ★

Somewhere between London and Swansea, during the early hours of the morning, Gwen woke with a start; she could see the icy mist of her breath but her palms and underarms were clammy with sweat. She'd been to Southend on the train but never any further and never by herself. She tucked the ends of her scarf under her collar and glanced into the little mirror above the opposite seats to check on her case in the rack, then nestled her head into the scratchy red seat cover. A woman in the corner, a large brown bag on her lap, was snoring softly through a blocked nose. She peeped around the stiff window blind, hoping that dawn would be breaking, but the sky was as inky as the blackout shade. She closed her eyes again and fell into an agitated sleep.

At Swansea she had almost two hours to wait for the train to Kidwelly. Finding the ladies' waiting room, she bought a cup of tea and a Welsh cake and sat looking at the rain that fell in torrents, as if someone was throwing bucketsful down from a height. She'd never complain about the drizzle in London again. She kept her eye on the station clock, worried she'd miss the train as she couldn't understand a word the station announcer said. As

114

soon as the 6:39 to Kidwelly flipped into view on the departure board she hurried to the platform and heaved her case into the first empty compartment she came across. This part of the journey was an hour and after that, two miles or so to Llansaint.

A woman with dark hair escaping from clips behind her ears opened the compartment door and flopped down next to Gwen. 'Llansaint?' she asked.

Gwen nodded, relieved to hear a London voice.

'Thought so. You look how I feel.'

'Well, it ain't far now.'

'Just the two-mile trek.'

'A trek. Can't we catch a bus?'

The woman chuckled without changing the set of her mouth. 'Is this your first visit?'

'Yeah. You've been before, have you?'

'Twice. And no, there's no such thing as a bus out here. I got a lift on the back of a cart first visit, but the next time I walked.'

Despite being soaked already, they fished out umbrellas and, cowering under them, started down a muddy lane together. Through the curtain of rain Gwen saw rolling fields, trees, stone walls and the odd pinprick of a cottage or barn; no sign of a town. A pungent smell rose up around them, a fresh, green fragrance mixed with a more feral, rotting odour. The quiet was daunting, too. Gwen strained every muscle waiting for the siren, or the screeching of a bomb, or the racket of machinery.

On the outskirts of the town they stopped. 'I'm going this way,' the woman said, pushing her dripping hair off her face. 'Where are yours?'

'My little girl's in Parky Saint,' Gwen answered, having decided it would be better to surprise Auntie Peggy than Mrs Morgan. She held out a bit of paper for the other woman to read.

'Oh,' she said. 'Parc Y Saint. Mine have left the side door open for me. But if yours don't know you're coming you'd be best to wait outside the church.' She indicated a white tower that loomed over the village. 'Everyone'll be in there this morning. If you fancy some company, I'm going home on Wednesday.'

'I'll have to be getting back myself then,' Gwen said. They made plans to meet at the same place in three days' time.

Gwen had expected the town to be as open as the countryside, with space between and around each house. Instead, the terraces were as tightly packed together as they were in London except that they were made from rough, deep blue stone. Coils of black smoke twisted from chimney pots and disappeared into the grey sky. A cat watched her from the steps of The Joiners Arms.

There was a bakery, an ironmonger, a butcher, a little school, the churchyard of All Saints. From behind the graves came the swell of singing, rising to a thunderous crescendo. She opened the gate and sheltered under a yew tree, waiting for the service to finish.

For a second, Ruth didn't know her. Her little girl stared with wide eyes, a frown on her face, then broke away from Auntie Peggy's hand and ran towards her.

'Ruth,' Peggy called. 'Stay with me here, there's a good girl.'

116

Gwen and Ruth clung to each other, muttering each other's names over and over.

'Excuse me.' Peggy strode across the grass with purpose. 'I don't think we know you.'

Gwen produced the postcard from Ruth and said, 'Ruthie's Mum.'

Auntie Peggy's hand covered her mouth, as if to stop herself from calling out. 'Look at you,' she said. 'Why didn't you let us know you were coming to visit?'

'I'm sorry.' Gwen's voice quivered. 'It was spur of the moment.'

'Well. Well, well, well,' Peggy said, her hands on her narrow hips. 'Shall we get Mammy home and get her dry?'

Ruth's head bobbed up and down, the ribbons in her plaits bouncing. Her hair had grown and so had she. A couple of inches taller at least. Ruth put one hand in her mother's, the other in Auntie Peggy's.

'Please,' Gwen said. 'I don't want to be a nuisance, but Will?'

'He's not here, Mum,' Ruth said. 'I looked for him in church.' There was the slightest lilt in Ruth's voice. Endearing and troubling at the same time.

'Ah. Mr and Mrs Morgan.' Peggy shook her head, her thin lips a taut line. 'They don't attend morning service; they wait until the evening.'

'Perhaps I should go there now. I can't wait to see Will, too.'

'Let me send word with Bryn, Mrs Gregson. He'll bring Will round to ours for you. That would be the best idea.'

'Ta,' Gwen said. 'I really am so grateful to you.'

'Now don't be silly. Everyone has to do war work, don't they? And I dare say ours is much more pleasant than most.' She took Gwen's case.

'Please call me Gwen.'

'Gwen? Now, there's a lovely old Welsh name.'

'Yeah I suppose it is. I'd never thought before.'

★ ★ ★

Will burst through the door followed by a stocky man dressed completely in black, limping heavily on his left leg. 'Mum.' He flung himself on her lap and they smothered each other in kisses. 'Is the war over? Have you come to take us home?'

Gwen saw Bryn and Peggy exchange a worried look. 'I've come to visit,' she said. 'See how you're getting on.'

A feeling of warmth cloaked her as both children moulded themselves into her, exactly like they used to. She longed to hold on to the sense of calm they gave her, but within a few short minutes she was more aware of the hollow, empty space that was the size and shape of Johnny, and the comfort slipped away. They gabbled on about school, what they did in the country that they couldn't do at home, their teachers' names, the friends they'd made and the ones they'd fallen out with. Then Ruth remembered her puppy and jumped up. 'Come and see Dot,' she said, pulling on Gwen's sleeve.

'I ain't seen him yet,' Will said.

'Dot's a girl,' Ruth said. 'Ain't she, Uncle Bryn?'

'She certainly is, my lovely,' Bryn answered, turning from the bowl of carrots he was peeling.

'She's still in the yard during the day,' Peggy said, taking them through the cool, flagged pantry. 'We'll bring her in soon, now it's getting colder.'

The puppy jumped up at them, spinning and licking and burying its head in Ruth's lap.

'She's great fun,' Will said, stroking the white spot on the dog's black head. 'I wish we had one. Me and Marty.'

'Well, you can come and see Dot any time you like, can't he, Ruth?'

Ruth nodded.

'I've told him that before,' Peggy said, turning to Gwen. 'And I've mentioned it to Mrs Morgan, but . . . ' She rolled her eyes.

Gwen looked down at the kids standing side by side, passing the puppy backwards and forwards. Ruth was pristine, so clean that the parting in her hair shone pink. Her clothes looked handmade but were neat and serviceable, exactly right for playing. She smelled lovely, too, like fresh air, and while she wasn't plump, she had a good covering on her that boded well for the winter months ahead.

Will was shivering; he was wearing a school jersey, the sleeves two inches shy of his wrists and grey woollen shorts that were stained with ink and gravy. His thin knees were grubby and Gwen could see black in and behind his ears. She raked her hand through his thick hair and he winced when it snagged on a knot. Her fingers came away covered in a sticky film. Auntie Peggy had been watching her and Gwen saw her shudder, either at the dirt or the state of her hands or both.

Gwen squatted between the children and put

her arms around them. 'Will,' she said. 'Why are you playing in your school clothes?'

Will shrugged and threw a rubber ball across the yard. 'Fetch, Dot,' he said.

'Do you have a clean set for tomorrow?'

Will raced across the paving slabs to retrieve the ball from the vegetable patch. 'No,' he said. 'Did you bring the socks I asked for, Mum? And the comics?'

Gwen laughed. 'Yeah,' she said. 'I did. And a few other bits and bobs.'

'Now then,' Peggy said. 'Dinner won't be long.'

Will stopped, the ball in his hands. His eyes looked huge in his pale face. 'It smells good,' he said.

'I'll put up a plate for you, so you can eat with Mam. If Mrs Morgan doesn't mind.'

'She won't care.' Will threw the ball to one side. 'I'll run and tell her.'

'Bring your friend back with you,' Peggy said. 'There's plenty for him.'

'I think,' Gwen said, standing up and straightening her skirt. 'I'll walk round with you, Will. I'd like to meet Mr and Mrs Morgan myself. Say ta for their kindness.'

Peggy set her lips again and nodded.

For a little while Will held her hand. Next he faced her, skipping backwards through narrow lanes and tight alleyways. Then he hugged her and ran ahead, stopping at quite a large stone cottage that seemed to be on the outskirts of the village. 'Come round the back,' he said, winding his way through an obstacle course of broken machinery.

'What does Mr Morgan do?' Gwen asked.

120

'He fixes things.'

Gwen didn't think he could be very successful, judging from the rusting harrows and shears lying about.

Rapping on the door, Will called out. 'Mrs Morgan. It's me.'

'Why's he back so soon?' a thick, deep voice called out.

'Don't ask me,' a woman answered.

The door was pulled open by a small woman in a faded tabard that might once have been pink or mauve or blue. Her greying hair was crossed in two plaits over her head; her arms were crossed over her bulging chest; her face set in cross lines. 'What now?' Her voice trailed off when she saw Gwen.

'How do you do, Mrs Morgan,' Gwen said. 'I'm Will's Mum.'

By the time Gwen found Marty in the chicken coop that he and Will kept in a cleaner state than the house and gathered together their things, she was determined to take them back with her to London. Then she began to doubt her decision. She couldn't take Will and not Ruth, but Ruth was happy and well cared for. If only Auntie Peggy could take the boys, but she hadn't the space. As it was, Gwen had to share a tiny bed with Ruth, Susie squeezed in between them; the boys slept on the sitting-room floor, more comfortable and warm there than they had ever been with the Morgans.

She was desperate for sleep but instead she lay awake most of the night, sweating about what to do for the best. She was up early, helping to organise the kids for school, washing and scrubbing at Will and Marty, dabbing the worst off their uniforms, cutting their bread, checking their copybooks. They were about to leave when there was a knock at the door. Bryn answered it and came into the kitchen with a telegram for Gwen. He handed it to her and said, 'I hope nothing's the matter.'

Gwen stared at it for a minute. It might be alright; it wasn't bordered in black. She tore it open.

DO NOT BRING KIDS HOME STOP BETTY NEEDS YOU HERE STOP GEORGE STOP

'It's from Dad,' Gwen said. 'He wants to make sure I give you a hug from him.' She kissed them both and ruffled Marty's hair.

Surely George would understand if she went against his wishes and took them home with her; he wasn't a cruel man. But he would insist they be sent elsewhere: Cornwall, Scotland, Norfolk. They would be separated from their friends and the school they'd settled into and instead of billeting with an Auntie Peggy they might both get a Mrs Morgan. Or worse. She made up her mind to get Will and Marty moved and be firm about it. She wouldn't take no for an answer.

'Good for you, Mrs Gregson,' Peggy said. 'I'll take you to Jenkins myself.'

For a moment Gwen was puzzled. Then she said, 'He's the billeting officer, ain't he?'

Peggy nodded and marched her through the rain-slick streets, oblivious to the incessant downpour. On the way, she untethered her opinion of Mrs Morgan who, she said, let Wales down with her slapdash approach. 'Trouble is,' she said, 'we

122

have been pushed here. That's no excuse, I know, but every available bed has been taken and at least the boys have been safe from the bombing.'

'That's what George would say.'

Peggy looked at her from under the plaid shawl covering her hair. 'But you're not sure?'

'I used to think . . . ' Gwen hesitated, surprised by how easily she was talking '. . . they could only ever be safe with me. Now I know different.'

Peggy took her arm and squeezed it. 'I think you're doing a grand job,' she said.

By Tuesday bedtime, Will and Marty were ensconced with the Gwilts in their smart cottage near the town green. The two little ones who'd billeted with them had gone to stay with relatives in Herefordshire, so they were delighted with the prospect of having a couple of boys around the place. Gwen left them in the warm kitchen, sitting shyly on benches at the scrubbed table, waiting for Mr Gwilt to come home so they could have their tea. She spent one last evening with Ruth, reading to her, brushing her hair, tucking her up. 'I'll see you soon,' she said, turning down the wick in the oil lamp. She'd said the same thing to Will and hoped that was the case, although she was glad neither of them asked her to promise.

★ ★ ★

She and the other London mum talked a bit on the journey home, but for most of the way Gwen watched the darkening sky, reminded that in another month it would be Christmas and, soon after, a year since that terrible night. She mulled

123

over everything that had happened during the previous few days, satisfied that she'd made the best decision she could for Will and Ruth under the circumstances. She felt different, as if she'd done something she could congratulate herself about, as if she might start to trust herself again. Perhaps.

Betty was scrubbing pans at the sink when Gwen dragged herself into the kitchen. 'Gwen,' she said, drying her hands on her apron and taking the case. 'You look done in. Are the kids alright?'

'They are now,' she said. 'I've sorted things out.'

'First things first. Let me get you a bit of toast and tea. And you get yourself warm.' She made to help Gwen off with her coat, but Gwen pulled her arms free of the sleeves by herself.

'It's okay, Bet,' she said, trying to avoid the guilty feeling she'd had last week, when she realised that she wasn't as good to Betty as Betty was to her. 'You've enough to do. How's Annie?'

'She had a scare when she read something about Ray's battalion.'

'But he's . . . '

Betty raised her hands then let them drop. 'Hope so,' she said.

'Don't say that, Betty.'

They looked away from each other, both of them determined not to set the other off.

'Let me cut some bread,' Betty said. 'I'll have a bit with you. By the way, before I forget, someone named Evelyn called round for you. Lovely girl.'

'What did she want?'

'Not sure, really. To see when you were going back to work, I think.'

124

'I'd spoken to the gaffer about the time off.'

'Anyway, we had a good chat.'

'She stopped for a while?'

'Well, she'd come quite a way.'

'What did you talk about?'

'Usual things. The war, the weather. She talked about dancing. I showed her photos of the kids. She feels for you. You're lucky to work with someone so nice.'

Gwen nodded. 'Yeah,' she said. 'I am.' Now she would have to tell Evelyn the whole story, something she'd been avoiding. She put her fingers in her mouth and started to nibble, something she hadn't done the whole time she was in Wales.

6

December 1941 — March 1942

Joan

For ages Alice had been promising Joan a place in the large, end-of-terrace house where she roomed. Hazel's Hostel, Alice called it. Alice had taken Joan to meet Hazel, who let her spare bedrooms out to single girls working in London. After a couple of wedding dates were cancelled due to suspension of all leave, one of the girls was at last able to get married and vacated her musty but clean and polished room, in which Joan now stood, suitcase in hand.

The life had been beaten out of the square of fringed rug, diminishing rather than reviving its pattern; the floorboards around the faded carpet buffed with a good inch of beeswax. There was a funny, old-fashioned tallboy in one corner freshly painted in a muddy shade of green, the leftover paint used on the frame of the mirror that stood on top. Extra blankets were doubled over on the bottom of the bed, the turned and stitched bed sheet folded across plump pillows. On the wall, a group of smartly dressed picnickers, framed in dark wood, smiled out from their mat on the sand.

Joan opened the embossed doors of the heavy wardrobe that dominated the room and hung the few things she'd brought with her. A navy coat, a black skirt, one white and one fawn blouse, a black jacket, two work shirts, dungarees. In the bottom of the wardrobe she lined up her work boots, lace-ups and black heels. Undergarments and nightclothes went in the drawers that didn't stick. Book, notepad, pencil on the bedside table; soap, hairpins, lipstick, powder on the tallboy.

It was a miserable day, cold and dreary. No sign of snow yet and not much rain, unlike this time last year. Joan unlatched the window and pushed up the sash. The garden was as well organised as the house. Stepping stones led to a vegetable plot along the back wall, resting and waiting for spring; a patch of grass was marked out on both sides of the path, brown shrubs and trees with bare branches around the perimeter. Surveying the room once more, she lay on the bed and closed her eyes. Relief overwhelmed her; she had managed to get out three weeks before Mother could mark the year since that frightful episode with her sighing, her frequent hurt looks, and her nagging about Joan wasting time and talent on that horrid bridge.

Turning on her side, she drew up her knees to her chest. An image of Ralph came into her mind, as it did many times every day. She missed him. It was almost unbearable at times, her yearning for his animal warmth and smell. The feel of his hands skimming over her, grabbing on to her hips, her breasts and thighs, each grasp tighter and firmer than the last. Opening herself to his thrusts and grunts. She had persisted in telling herself that she didn't long for him and tried to make herself admit that she hadn't really known him at all; but none of those ploys worked.

She turned on her back and stared at the papered ceiling. So what was it, she wondered for the umpteenth time, that she had found attractive about Ralph, other than the idea that he wanted her which, she had to admit, was not a force easy to dismiss. She imagined Colin or Edward's eyes looking at her, heavy with lust; their hands roaming her flesh, and she laughed out loud. They could not have ignited the same reactions in her by very dint of their lack of bearing and authority.

Those were some of the qualities that had attracted her to Ralph along with the way he walked, talked, conducted himself, helped her on with her coat and off with her petticoat. His knowledge of politics, food and good wines, the habits he cultivated like coffee and the *Financial Times* at eleven, his deep-seated love of culture and all things cultured, the ardent way he had once or twice corrected the position of her elbow or the slant of her bow. And, she told herself, above everything else, it had been the knowledge that Mother would have found him the epitome of unsuitability.

Climbing out of bed, Joan closed the window then slipped in between the cold sheet and eiderdown. She pressed her hands between her knees to warm them. She had longed for the time and quiet to think and consider, but now that she had it, she was working hard at keeping her most troublesome thoughts at bay. Waves of heat followed the cold. But the truth was she had derived a huge amount of pleasure and satisfaction from knowing that Mother would be disgusted with her

128

choice of man and what she was doing with him. She wondered if spite was a recognised catalyst for passion.

There was also the lightheaded, nascent hopefulness that short period of time had embodied as a possible escape route from Mother, who had been the reason for her wanton behaviour and the cause of all the heartache she had experienced.

Had it been worth the pain, the loneliness, the rejection and humiliation she felt? 'Yes,' she whispered to the happy, innocent young people sipping wine and eating sandwiches in the picture above the chest of drawers, 'it's very sad but the answer is yes.' She flared her nostrils and took in the chilly air of the simple, unheated room. And, she thought, I would do it again if it meant I could make Mother understand that I would no longer allow her to have control over me. And if it meant I could have Ralph back again.

Then she sank into her pillow and felt a familiar sense of defeat. Whenever she thought she had stoked her determination to the point of iron fortitude, the tiniest bit of compassion, or perhaps it was tenderness for Mother, crept into her thoughts and unnerved her. That was the dilemma, and back and forth it went in a repetitive pattern. It had to be stopped — and to do that, Joan knew she had to be strong-willed and rigid in her approach.

She reminded herself of the scene with Mother when she said she was leaving, and recalling it, Joan felt she was justified. 'Moving, then.' Leaving sounded so final. 'It will be easier for work.'

Mother's jaw fell. 'You couldn't have an easier journey to Waterloo.'

'It gets messy sometimes with shifts.'

'You're being pernicious and it doesn't suit you.' Mother looked around the house in astonishment. 'How could you leave this for a shabby little room somewhere?'

'It isn't shabby, Mother,' Joan said, collecting together what she could carry.

Mother followed her around, whimpering and pleading. 'At least wait until Christmas.'

Joan shook her head. 'I don't want to lose the place.'

'After everything you've lost, you're worried about a bedsit.'

Joan made it to the door without saying anything she would regret.

Grabbing a pencil and notepad, Mother said, 'Leave me your address, Joan dear. Please.'

Joan hesitated; she didn't want to be cruel. She scribbled on the paper. 'The street isn't difficult to find, but the house is tucked right up in the corner. A bit isolated even though it's just off Streatham High Road.'

Mother looked as though she was in shock. When Joan kissed her cheek and turned away, she was taken aback to feel tears on her own face. She wiped at them hard with the heel of her hand; she couldn't, after all, have stood it for a day longer.

There was a light rap on the door, the nervous clearing of a throat. 'Have you settled in, sweetheart?'

Joan stood up, straightening her skirt and smoothing her hair. 'Come in, Miss Talbot.'

A woman of about fifty took a couple of steps into the room, as if she thought her presence might cause offence. She was very fair although there was a good scattering of white amongst the pale gold hair that was caught up in a low twist at the nape of her neck. Her skin was almost translucent and every part of it on show — hands, wrists, face, neck — was covered in a faint wash of freckles as if she'd been spattered with tan-coloured paint. She was heavy but moved with light, determined steps; always occupied, always busy. Feathery lines surrounded her mouth and grey eyes, especially when she smiled, like she did now. Joan thought she must have been lovely when she was younger. 'Is everything to your satisfaction?' Her voice sounded forced and formal.

'It's perfect.'

'I'm sure it's not. But I'm glad it suits for now. You'll let me know if you need anything?'

Joan nodded. 'Thank you.'

'Don't forget. You can help yourself to tea and biscuits, if rations allow.'

'What shall I do about my own rations?' Joan looked around and encompassed the room with a sweep of her arm. 'I don't want to keep food up here.'

'Oh no, sweetheart. I'll give you a cupboard in the kitchen, then you must feel free to do for yourself.' She waved for Joan to follow her. 'Or I'll cook for you along with the others if you leave out the rations you want me to use. I'll show you.'

The kitchen was another room as worn by time and vigorous cleaning as the rest of the house. The last glimmer of watery winter sun shone through the spotless windows and fell on the scrubbed wooden table. Joan had thought Mother was house-proud, but not even she could have faulted Hazel's housekeeping, although she would no doubt criticise the lack of ornament. Mother was much prissier in her tastes than Hazel. 'This is your cupboard.' Hazel stretched on her toes to reach above the sink. 'I've washed it out, not that Mary left it dirty, you understand.'

'I could have done that, Miss Talbot. But, thank you. I do appreciate it.'

'You must call me Hazel, everyone does. And this — ' she indicated a small pile of food on the end of the sideboard '— is where you can leave the things you can't use. I'll make a jam tart with the flour and egg and mix the bully beef with some mash and a bit of onion. Then I'll leave it for any of you who's passing and hungry.'

'That's awfully nice of you.'

'Well, we can't have food going to waste, can we?' Hazel said, sounding less diffident now. 'That wouldn't do.'

Furrows appeared in Hazel's forehead as she studied Joan for a moment. She felt sure Hazel wanted to say something more to her, enquire about some aspect of her demeanour. Probably the way she spoke or held herself; she was out of place on the bridge or in this type of accommodation. *Whatever is a girl like her doing here, why ever is she working there?* Joan knew that was what people were wondering. She also knew that the war made it difficult to ask too many questions. Anything was possible now, but people were still fascinated by the improbable. Thank goodness for Alice and her Bristolian dialect, much more puzzling and comment-provoking than her own plummy diction.

Hazel looked away, as if aware she'd been caught staring, and started to fill the kettle. 'Would you like a nice cuppa?' she said. 'Have it with me and Mummy in the parlour. There's to be a special announcement on the wireless from Churchill.'

During her initial visit, Joan had been introduced to Hazel's mother, Ivy, who had been propped up in an overstuffed chair, blankets around her legs, dribbling from her drooping mouth onto a muslin cloth tucked under her chin. The sight had appalled her. Hazel was the last word in patience with her, so kind and thoughtful. If it ever came to it, Joan knew she couldn't care for Mother in the same way, if at all. 'Perhaps I'll go back upstairs. Tidy my things. Alice shouldn't be long, then we might go to the pictures.'

Hazel looked let down. 'Of course, sweetheart. Come and go as you please. But you'd be very welcome. Mummy loves company.'

'Alright then, thank you.' Joan thought she ought to try to get used to Ivy. 'If you're sure it's not any trouble.'

Averting her eyes, Joan threaded her way between the sideboard and footstool and around Ivy's bed to place the tray she carried on a small table next to Ivy's chair. Then she made for a seat out of Ivy's line of vision.

'Look, Mummy.' Hazel pronounced every word with precision. 'It's Joan. Our new girl. She's come to have tea with us. Isn't that lovely?'

'Hello, Mrs Talbot. I'm very pleased to see you again.'

Hazel beckoned for Joan to move closer. 'Bring

133

your chair up here, so Mummy can see and hear you,' Hazel said. 'She's very taken with you.'

Joan wondered how Hazel knew that, as there had been no reaction from Ivy. Not a flutter of a finger in greeting or the slightest inclination of her head. Joan did as she was asked, though, and drew alongside Ivy, slight and squashed in the folds of the huge chair. Hazel perched in front of her mother, daintily putting the teacup to the tremulous lips, breaking off minute pieces of eggless, fatless sultana cake for Ivy to savour.

A scuffed wicker basket overflowing with knitting pins and wool nestled next to the fireplace. When Joan first met her, Hazel had been wearing a lemon cardigan with a yellow brooch pinned to it; today the combination was baby pink. Alice said that Hazel spent every evening sitting with her mother, knitting, and had a whole wardrobe of pastel knitwear. 'She gives one to me,' Alice had said. 'But it were too tight so I gives it back.' Joan supposed that having someone else to talk to was a change for both of them. Not that she was doing much of that.

'This is Mummy's favourite,' Hazel said. 'Isn't it, Mummy? Mind you, she was always partial to a bit of cake, never mind what was or wasn't in it. Isn't that right, Mummy?'

Joan was amazed at how Hazel kept up the banter, as if Ivy was aware of what was being said and was able to join in the conversation. Although when Hazel moved or turned to Joan, Ivy's dull eyes followed her daughter around the room, like the eyes of the *Mona Lisa* she'd read about in an art journal.

134

'Another cup, Joan?' Hazel asked, wiping Ivy's mouth.

'One's plenty. Thank you.'

'And one's enough for you, this late in the afternoon.' Hazel addressed her mother. 'Is that the time? Let's tune the wireless. I'm afraid we've missed it today, Mummy. She does so like *It's that Man Again*. Well, we both do. Do you listen to it?'

Joan had heard it once or twice when Mother was out as she'd never allow it, but she'd found the humour difficult to follow. It was very popular; everyone on the bridge talked about it, so she was able to offer a catchphrase. She lowered her voice to sound like Jack Train. ''Don't mind if I do.''

Hazel laughed. 'She's got it off pat, hasn't she, Mummy?'

'I should have said that when you asked if I wanted a cup of tea.'

'Oh, what's that other one I love? Oh yes.' Hazel's face twitched with mischief. ''Can I do you now, sir?''

Joan knew the character who said that: Mrs Mopp — and she speculated on how apt the idiom was for Hazel.

Hazel played with the tuner until they heard the chimes of Big Ben. A grave voice announced the prime minister and Joan sat forward on her chair, her hands folded in her lap. She imagined the entire nation, like her, still and waiting. Churchill's comforting voice broke through the crepitations. He told them about Japan's attack on Pearl Harbour and the emergency summoning of Parliament. Joan took solace in the fact that

135

Churchill said Parliament had responded quickly to attend to their duties, even though they were given short notice. She looked at Hazel from the corner of her eye and hoped she was thinking the same thing.

A few of Mother's friends had commented, after he was appointed, that Churchill spoke as if he were reciting poetry. Joan could see their point, but said his speeches were more musical than anything and Mother had agreed. During one of their white-flag moments, they had listened together for the staccato breaks, the cadences, the musical phrases, and congratulated themselves on their observations. She took note of them now, seeing before her the oration transposed into a musical score. And wondered if Mother was doing the same.

Churchill was now reminding them of Britain's pledge that, if the United States were to declare war on Japan, a British declaration to the same effect would follow promptly.

'I don't remember that, Mummy. Do you?' Hazel looked puzzled. 'When was that? Joan?'

'I'm sure I haven't a clue,' said Joan. Hazel was solemn and, out of respect, Joan was loath to do anything but mirror the look on her face. Then as if by agreement, they both started to giggle.

'I'm sorry, sweetheart, but I can't keep up sometimes.'

'It's all terribly complicated.'

'The War was enough for us. Who'd ever have thought it would all start up again so soon.' She sighed and her face became sombre again. Alice had told her that Hazel often talked about the War, meaning the Great War and that sometimes it was difficult to get away from her once she started reminiscing.

Together, they once again gave their full attention to Churchill. He had made a transatlantic telephone call to President Roosevelt to discuss the timing of their respective declarations, but had learned soon after that the Japanese had also attacked British territory in Malaya. Then he went on in detail about something complicated to do with the Japanese High Command and the Imperial Japanese Government. The gist of which seemed to be that the United States and Britain were now at war with Japan. In fact, the Cabinet had not waited for the American Congress and had decided to declare war on Japan immediately.

Hazel pressed her hand over her heart. 'Oh, dear,' she said. 'It sounds very bad.'

'Yes,' Joan agreed. 'I'm afraid it is. Not just Germany now. Japan, too.'

With a small scrape, the door opened and Alice tiptoed in. 'Alice.' Hazel jumped up to greet her.

'Shh.' Alice put her finger to her mouth and pointed to the wireless. 'You've heard then?'

Joan and Hazel nodded.

Then Churchill told them that diplomatic relations with Japan had come to an end, which meant the British Ambassador and his staff in Tokyo were being recalled and expulsion of the Japanese Ambassador from London was underway.

The PM's voice trailed off and was lost in a crackle that sounded like distant thunder. Hazel fiddled with the knob but couldn't retrieve the signal so clicked off. Alice kissed Ivy's head with

137

genuine affection and Joan could see why she was such a favourite.

'Sorry I were late,' Alice said, the attack on Pearl Harbour soon forgotten. 'We'll go to the pictures another night this week, alright?'

'Of course. No need to worry.'

'Is your room proper? Come and show me.'

Joan thanked Hazel for the evening and followed Alice who went racing ahead, her unruly, wavy hair working loose from precarious pins. The parlour door was closed behind them and Joan heard Hazel take up her singsong commentary again. That and the muffled click of knitting needles.

★ ★ ★

Mother wrote a clipped note asking Joan to spend Christmas Day with her and Father. Joan replied that she had already accepted an invitation from her landlady, sure the occasion would be jollier with Hazel than it would be at home. On the day, Alice carried Ivy into the kitchen and they sat around the table, four of them with the addition of another lodger named Ethel who worked as a pool typist for the War Office but was waiting to join the ATS. Alice was a big girl, rounded and fleshy, but Joan thought there was nothing soft about Ethel's large frame, flat features, square shoulders leading to a thick waist, with blunt manners to match.

'This is handsome,' Ethel said. She'd slurped her way through two bowls of potato and watercress soup and was attacking the chicken that Hazel had bartered for with a neighbour. In return, Hazel had given up a saucepan full of carrots and sprouts from the garden, the last of which sat on their plates swamped in gravy. There were two dishes of potatoes in the middle of the table: one roasted, the other mashed with parsnip. Suet plum duff was steaming on the stove. Paper crowns cut from old newspapers perched on their heads. Joan and Alice waited for Hazel to take her place next to Ivy but Ethel ploughed ahead. 'You're a marvel with the rations,' she said, talking with a full mouth. 'It's a wonder you never married.'

And it will be a miracle if you ever do, Joan thought. What a topic of conversation for Christmas dinner.

Hazel must have been surprised by the remark, perhaps as embarrassed as Joan was for her. But she didn't falter in her usual mealtime rhythm: a forkful for Ivy, wipe Ivy's chin, a mouthful for herself. 'I would have liked to, but it was all over for me after the War, sweetheart.'

Ethel pulled a face, squashing her nose and flaring her nostrils. 'The war?' she mouthed behind Hazel's back.

'You know, the Great War.'

Joan was interested now, wanting to hear more but afraid to ask when Alice looked so despondent, fixing a sprout to her fork with a morsel of stuffing. With a bit of luck, the fingers of sherry that Hazel refilled for them should help Ethel to blunder on, asking the questions that Joan didn't dare.

'Did you lose anybody?'

Hazel nodded as she held the sticky liquid to

Ivy's lips. 'Daddy and two of my brothers never came back. Nor did Eric. Or the boys down the road.'

'Who was Eric?'

'My intended. I watched him go. Watched all of them go.' She motioned towards the high street beyond the door. 'Marched down the road they did, horses and carts in tow. Everyone was cheering them on, waving little flags and hankies in the air, calling out the names of their husbands or brothers. No one imagined we'd never see them again. I jumped up and down, flapping my gloves when Eric marched past. He turned in my direction and to this day I swear he winked. He could be a one. Then it was as if, as soon as they were out of view, the marching columns simply disappeared, line by line, never to be seen again.'

Hazel's retelling was so vivid that when she stopped, staring into the distance, Joan felt as if she was there amongst the crowd. 'Blimey,' Ethel said. 'So you've carried a torch for him all these years?'

'I would have married someone else, but no one came calling for me again. My sister was lucky, being that bit younger. She got her husband and children, but there was nobody left for me.'

The afternoon was darkening. The garden, through the kitchen window, was obscured by shadows. The five women sat still in the gloom, the atmosphere thick with the biding of time.

'Let's have pudding.' Hazel jumped up. 'And another drink if I can squeeze one out.'

Joan and Alice stacked plates and took them to the sink. 'Take your chances while you can, that's what I say,' Ethel said.

Alice rolled her eyes, a spot of annoyed colour on each cheek. *She must be thinking the same as me*, Joan thought; Ethel would be more than lucky to get *one* chance. But had Ralph been Joan's only opportunity at the life that had eluded Hazel?

'Let me show you something.' Hazel went into the parlour and came back carrying a small blue box. 'I thought I would burst when Eric's mum gave this to me. To think, Eric must have told her we were sweethearts. She passed the medal around and when Joan took it, she read aloud the inscription on the reverse. *1914—1918 The Great War for Civilisation.*

'So-called,' Hazel said. 'Not that you'd know it now. I mean, what did all those boys die for? And Daddy? We've asked ourselves that over and over, haven't we, Mummy?' She shook her head. 'I doubt if any of those men would recognise this as the civilisation they fought for in France. That's why we don't shed a single tear now, do we, Mummy? We've cried ourselves dry.'

There was a truce that night, but they drew the blackouts all the same, as did everyone else; only a fool would trust Hitler. Joan washed and Alice dried. Then they played a few rounds of put-take with buttons for currency and wrung the sherry bottle dry.

★ ★ ★

By the middle of February, it seemed as though they would be able to reach out and touch the women working on the other side of the bridge.

141

The spans being concreted on either side were the last, and when the pre-cast middle piece was lowered into place, the two sides would meet. It was coming together like a symphony, each section doing their ordinary, tedious little bit to create one solid, extraordinary piece of work. Joan worried that the pieces might not fit. An orchestra rehearsed time and again if a part wasn't right, but what would happen if the two sides didn't align? Would some or all of the building work have to be demolished and started again? She had no idea, but none of the supervisors seemed worried, so perhaps she shouldn't be either.

A group of women hung around as close to the edge as they dared, trying to get the attention of their friends on the other side. A risky thing to do, as they were still jumpy after a woman had slipped and drowned last week. That was the eleventh gone the same way. Setting down her wheelbarrow, Joan motioned to Alice to have a look.

'Not me,' Alice said.

'Nor me,' Joan agreed.

They stood to the side of the baying women, clinging on to each other as they gawped over the gap. A gauze of mist whipped across the river, the dirty water beneath it cold and forbidding.

'Ladies, ladies.' Jim bustled out of his hut that served as an office. 'Please.' He put his hands on his hips. 'Come away from there.'

The crowd dispersed and took up their tools again. 'Joan,' he said. 'Come with me a minute, would you?' Alice put down her shovel and made to follow. 'You carry on here, Alice,' he said. 'Joan won't be a minute.'

142

Binders with uninspiring titles like *Testing Shearing Force* and *Concrete Fatigue* lined the shelves surrounding Jim's desk. Account books and an alphabetical list of employees stood next to them. Pinned to the walls and laying across a wooden table were blueprints, charts and drawings. 'This is Mr Ware.' Jim gestured toward a middle-aged man in a dark suit and tie who stood up and shook Joan's hand. 'Mr Ware, Miss Abbott.'

'How do you do,' Joan said, momentarily unnerved at being in such close proximity to a man who was about the same age and height as Ralph. He had his bearing, too, but a less elegant way of dressing to flaunt his station in life.

'Please, sit here.' Mr Ware dusted the seat of his chair with a cambric blue handkerchief.

Jim stood at the window for a minute, surveying the workforce before joining them. 'We're gathering a group of ladies together to train on the cranes. Thought you might be interested, Joan.'

The crane cabs were a male domain. The men who worked them were paid more and everyone thought they were a cut above, or maybe it was the men who created that aura for themselves. 'Aren't those positions filled already?' Joan asked, bemused by the situation.

'The men are joining up and we can't replace them.' His sigh was almost inaudible. 'The decision's been made to promote a few women.'

'Hand-picked.' Mr Ware smiled at her. 'You're well thought of.'

Joan had often thought it would be exhilarating to operate one of the cranes that hovered above

143

them. And, after playing in an orchestra, the concentration and responsibility needed wouldn't be onerous. 'I'd like that very much. Thank you for asking me,' she said.

'Monday morning start, then,' Mr Ware said. 'I'll see you on the South pier.'

'Excuse me?' Joan didn't understand where Mr Ware fitted in.

'I'm so sorry,' Jim said. 'Apologies. Cyril, I mean Mr Ware's, the instructor.'

The two men stood to signal the end of the interview, but Joan hesitated. 'What about Alice?' she asked.

'Not this time,' Jim said. 'But we could shift her to banksman?' He shook his head. 'Sorry. Bankswoman. You know, crane driver's mate.'

Joan bit her lip. 'Yes, that would be good. Can I tell her?'

'Of course.' Jim looked weary as he opened the door for her. Joan supposed he'd never had that sort of request from a man.

★ ★ ★

Joan and Alice sang the theme song from *Woman of the Year* all the way home from the Gaumont Palace. Joan was Allen; Alice was Flanagan. Hazel would get a rendition when they got in; she'd love that. They'd asked her to go to the pictures with them a number of times but she wouldn't leave Ivy, not even when her sister was visiting.

Hazel met them in the hall, her eyes bright and glistening, her hands fluttering. 'Oh what a shame,' she said. 'You've only just missed her, sweetheart.'

144

'Who?' Joan asked, unable to prevent an image of Ralph's wife appearing in her mind.

'Didn't you see her? You must have passed each other within inches.'

'Hazel, who are you talking about?'

'Your mother. Such a well-turned-out woman. You're the image.'

'Whose mother?'

'It weren't mine,' Alice said. 'Not from that description.'

'She brought something for you. Mummy's keeping her eye on it.'

From where Hazel had positioned the violin case, resting against the wall next to the knitting, it did indeed look as if Ivy was watching over it. But when Hazel passed it to Joan, Ivy's lacklustre stare remained glued to the empty space.

Alice sucked in her breath. 'I didn't know you played the fiddle.'

'Violin,' Joan said. She stood clutching the case, knowing they were watching, waiting for her to say something that would reveal more than she wanted to give away.

'You never said,' Alice persisted. 'I'd have said.'

'I'm not much good. Really.' Joan felt she had to offer some explanation. 'Besides, there's not much call for it. You know, on the bridge. I'll take it upstairs.'

'Can't we have a peek?' Hazel asked.

Kneeling on the floor, Joan opened the lid. The strings, taut over the ebony fingerboard, were new. Mother must have changed them; she had probably tuned it, too. The varnished gradations of wood shone as if ready for the spotlight to be

145

turned on them. A piece of rosin, wrapped in cloth, nestled next to the bow.

'I don't think you was telling the whole truth,' Alice said. 'You must be good to have something so proper, even I know that.'

You haven't told me everything about yourself either, Joan thought. *In fact, I hardly know anything about you. Only what you want to tell me about your nagging mum and the dad who drinks too much. What do any of us know about each other but what we choose to tell? Even that poor woman Gwen with the bitten nails, who runs and hides from everyone. What do we know about her?*

Hazel reached out and stroked the polished curves and intricate scroll. 'Play for us. Please. Mummy so enjoys a lovely tune.'

Joan secured the clasps on the case and stood up. 'I don't play any longer,' she said.

'Oh, but surely . . . '

Joan cut Hazel off. 'Did Mother leave a note?'

'No, my sweetheart. But she said she'd write.'

'Thank you, Hazel. Goodnight, everyone.'

Bracing herself to kick the violin under her bed, Joan stopped short of her toe making contact with the lower end of the case. Instead, she pushed it decisively with both hands to where it was hidden from view by the mattress and to where she hoped to be able to forget about its existence entirely.

★ ★ ★

The three weeks' training had been intense. They had learned which levers worked the slewing unit that housed the mechanism allowing the crane to rotate; how to watch the back end as well as the front; how a bell in the cab rang if the load was too far forward; the gears that controlled the horizontal jib and lowered the hook to catch or disgorge its prey. Operating the welding equipment had been different; they dared not look to the left or right but had to stare intently at what they were doing until the electrode ran its course and needed to be changed.

Vibrating the concrete was a matter of too little concentration, although it had to be finished to a satisfactory standard before the concrete started to set. On the cranes it was a case of checking and double-checking every manoeuvre they made, both in the cab and out. They were taught to move deliberately, with studied patience. Each hand on a lever, Joan would focus all her attention on every movement, then survey the surrounding area from the small front and side windows. Of course, when she was fully qualified, she would also have to watch and rely on her bankswoman, Alice, to communicate with her from outside.

During these last couple of training days, there would be a series of tasks to ensure the women were adroit enough to work the cranes on the bridge. Standing in a line, they were taking it in turns to watch each other pick up a bucket of sand, negotiate it through an obstacle course of red conical markers and place it down on a white cross painted on the concrete. Cyril and Jim would also be noting down whether or not the proper procedures had been carried out in the cab before and after the lift.

When it was over, they would probably all go

for a drink together, as they had a few times. On one occasion, as he was going that way, Cyril walked her to the bus stop and asked her to make a date to meet him; they could go to a tea dance, or for a walk, anything she liked. She remained business-like and held her chin at a high angle. 'That would lack propriety,' she'd said. 'Given that you're our instructor.'

'No one need know.' He'd put his hands on her shoulders and bobbed low to look in her eyes. He had a way about him that she liked, easy with himself and everything around him. His light brown hair and moustache were flecked with grey, his eyes never losing their boyish delight. She felt the same rush of mystified attraction she'd experienced with Ralph, followed in an instant by the picture of Mother's face if she knew about Joan's predilection.

She shook her head. 'This training is a good opportunity and I'm taking it very seriously. I don't want to be bothered by distractions.'

'Aha.' Cyril smiled. 'From that I take it you'll agree to meet when the training's complete?'

'Let's talk about it then,' she said, flagging down her bus.

From then on Cyril seemed to take it for granted that something would start up between them when the time was right. Last week, out of sight of the others, he'd given her a tablet of sweet-smelling soap that she put next to the sink in the rooming house. That morning, he'd let his hand linger for a beat between her breasts as he slipped a tiny packet of sugar into her bib pocket. She shared it later with Alice and Hazel, who stirred half a tea-

148

spoon of the precious grains into Ivy's tea. They didn't ask her where the little treats were coming from. For all they knew they might be with the compliments of one of the many Americans swarming around the place. Only last weekend one of them had thrown his arm around a beet-root-faced Alice as a group of them bumped into her and Joan face on in Piccadilly Circus.

She in turn didn't question Cyril; they might have been his own rations he was forgoing or they might be extras he managed to procure. If that was the case, Mother would have found the situation the height of bad taste, but that and the fact he was so like Ralph in some respects, made it all the more enticing for her.

7

April — July 1942

Evelyn

Alec took all his leave in London. Initially he billeted in the Sally Army Servicemen's Hostel in Southampton Row, but it didn't take him long to ingratiate himself with Dad to the extent that he bedded down on the sitting-room floor, a huge bear in a khaki drawstring den.

'No, sir,' he said when Dad told him to kip on the couch. 'Don't spoil me too much, I might get used to it.'

Dad never said, 'Call me Charlie.' The respectful epithet Alec afforded him gave him too much pleasure for that. As a wind-up, Evelyn and Sylvie started addressing Dad as 'sir' and now slipped easily between the two monikers. Dad beamed when he took Alec, smart in battle blouson, a maple leaf insignia pinned on his cap, to the pub for a pint. He saved cuttings from the paper and made a list of points he'd heard on the radio to discuss with Alec; sometimes Uncle Bert joined them, too. Evelyn wondered that Sylvie didn't get impatient to have him to herself, but him being there seemed to be enough to satisfy her and they did always manage to find some time to be together.

That afternoon they were talking about the

Baedeker Raids. Sylvie moved to and fro with tea and morsels of food she'd been saving her rations to buy. Alec never arrived empty-handed either, bringing a small packet of biscuits, a square of chocolate or cocoa powder in a twist of wax paper. Alec let Sylvie hand the cups and plates around, saying a thank you to her that was much lengthier than necessary, his fingers grazing hers and holding her back with a long, deep look until they ended up grinning at each other. But, Evelyn noticed, he would not let her clear up after him. He insisted on piling up as much crockery as he could carry and taking it into the kitchen, where Evelyn could hear him talking and laughing with Sylvie. Sometimes he rolled his sleeves back and washed up as if it was an ordinary everyday occurrence. Perhaps that's how things happened in Canada, but Ron had never done anything like that.

Evelyn was impressed. That's the way it should be, *she thought,* no silly grievances about who does what, more getting on with things together.

Looking in from the kitchen door, Sylvie said, 'Are you coming out with us tonight, Evelyn?'

'Where to?'

'The Paramount.'

Evelyn knew the place on Tottenham Court Road: a favourite haunt of the Canucks. It was a lively place, almost too small to contain the full-bodied laughter and high spirits that filled it. If it wasn't for the uniforms you could almost forget there was a war going on. She hesitated, hearing the music and recalling the party atmosphere. She knew she would kick herself later,

151

but said, 'I promised Gwen I'd spend a couple of hours with her.' She saw Dad, Sylvie and Alec exchange a glance. 'Her husband's on nights and her friend's visiting her daughter-in-law.'

Sylvie put a hand on her hip, emphasising her slim waist for Alec's attention. 'You'd be better off coming with us,' she said. 'You spend every day with Gwen at work and she's still an old misery.'

Although that was the truth, Evelyn hated to hear it. 'And so might you be,' she retorted.

Evelyn waited for remorse to hit Sylvie. When her sister's face dropped, she carried on. 'She's better. *Getting* better, anyway. And I don't mind keeping her company.'

'It's thoughtful of you, love,' Dad said. 'We just don't want you to miss out.'

'Yeah.' Alec felt comfortable enough to add his penny's worth. 'You always have a great time at the club. You've got to have some fun, too.'

Sylvie nodded. 'I don't want to see you back in that rut.'

'No fear of that,' Evelyn said, making her way to the side door. 'You'll be stuck in a pothole long before me, the way things are going.'

Chuckling, Alec said, 'If I have my way.'

'You cheeky mare,' Sylvie said, throwing a tea towel at Evelyn. 'Get out of here,' she yelled. 'And make sure we see you later.'

'You probably will, so save me a seat. Though I don't plan to sit down much.'

★ ★ ★

152

Sometimes, Evelyn's heart sank when Gwen asked her to visit. For one thing it was a trek to Cubitt Town. Tube to King's Cross; change for Whitechapel; walk through to Limehouse for the number 56 to Stebondale Street. For another, Sylvie was right in supposing the evenings there were less than thrilling. Evelyn had never actually said that, always sticking up for Gwen, but Sylvie and Dad had made up their own minds on the two occasions Evelyn had asked Gwen back to Wood Green. Neither visit had gone well. Gwen had seemed overwhelmed by the chat flying backwards and forwards and couldn't muster much to say about anything that was brought up in conversation, not even the bridge. Dad and Alec, who'd been there one of those times, were charming to her, but she sat on the edge of her chair, struggling painfully to keep her fingers away from her mouth.

Of course Gwen knew Sylvie, but that didn't help the situation either. 'What do you think of the dinners in the canteen, Gwen?' Sylvie had asked.

'It's something hot,' Gwen answered, shrugging.

'Were you there when Olive took hers back and complained?'

Gwen shook her head.

'I wouldn't have had the nerve.' Sylvie pursed her lips and looked up through the corner of her eyes. 'Well, maybe I would. But Evelyn wouldn't.'

'No, I would *not*,' Evelyn said.

'I mean one day it's tasty, the next it's like cardboard. I don't know what to make of it, I'm sure.'

Gwen drank half a cup of tea — barely able

153

to lift the thin china to her lips — and managed a piece of toast and jam. It all got too much for her when Sylvie pushed the sitting-room furniture back against the walls, tuned the wireless to the Forces Programme for an hour of swing music, and started practising jive moves with Alec. 'Come on, Gwen,' she'd shouted, jitterbugging with twitching limbs. 'You be the man; Evelyn can be the woman. We'll show you.'

Her eyes wide and looking appalled and awed at the same time, Gwen watched Sylvie then turned an imploring look on Evelyn. 'I think we'd better make a move,' Evelyn said, feeling annoyed about missing out on the dance practice. Gwen mumbled her goodbyes, her hat and coat on in an instant, linking arms with Evelyn as they strode to the underground. Because Gwen found the journey to Wood Green arduous, Evelyn fetched her and took her home, ending up sleeping the night as it was invariably too late to make the trip back. It was wearing and rather puzzling, as Gwen had managed to get to Wales and back by herself.

Feeling cheated about missing out on the fun at home had made her decide to confront Gwen. Keeping her voice even she said, 'I'm not sure if I mentioned how plucky I think you were. You know, going all the way to Llansaint on your own.'

Gwen looked down at her feet, then at that spot in the distance she stared at endlessly. 'I needed to make sure the kids were alright.'

'Yes, I know. But I don't think I could have made that journey on my own. Somewhere I'd never been. So I was wondering. If you can do that, why do you find it so hard to get across London by yourself?'

Evelyn could feel Gwen's arm stiffen in hers.

'And you get to the bridge and back every day. How do you manage that?'

There was a long silence and Evelyn began to wonder if she'd said too much. Or if what she said was unfair and harsh.

'I've never thought about it like that before,' Gwen said. 'But now that I do, I suppose I felt I had to go to Wales. For the kids. And I have to go to work. So I force myself. Just block things out and get on with it.'

Evelyn knew all about that. Perhaps she wasn't doing Gwen any favours, making it easy for her to stand back from some situations and not plough on as everyone else had to. But she wanted Gwen to continue, to talk about herself rather than the kids or Betty or George, so she didn't interrupt.

'It ain't that I don't want to be like I was before.' Gwen's voice rose. 'But journeys around London.' She shook her head. 'Ain't nothing about London is the same. And no one ever knows what's around the corner or what will happen in the next minute. The familiar is unfamiliar.'

'But didn't you feel that on the way to Wales?'

'Not really — I suppose I didn't know what it was like before, and like I said, I was just thinking about the kids. Or maybe the journey used up all my reserves. Perhaps I'll be better when I get my strength back. I don't know. I can't make any more sense of it than that.'

Well, Evelyn thought, *we've been thrown together and I feel an allegiance towards you that I can't fathom either.* They picked their way through a

155

length of broken pavement, a crowd of men working hard to mend it. Evelyn sighed and thought that none of what was happening since the war began made any sense at all. But she did so want to help Gwen all she could and wondered how best to go about that, making sure that it wasn't at the expense of her own fun.

* * *

A rather good-looking gentleman in a grey overcoat and striped tie gave up his seat for her; sinking into it she leaned back and closed her eyes. Even if she spent three hours with Gwen she'd have time for a couple of drinks and a few turns on the dance floor.

It was wicked and she knew it, but she sometimes found it difficult to stop the thought that in many ways this war was the most exciting thing that had ever happened. How else would they ever have had the chance to meet so many different men? Alec's cousin Malcolm, for instance, who pursued her with unabashed, good-natured tenacity. Not like Ron who'd eyed her up for ages before approaching her. Malcolm swung her around the dance floor as if she were a toy who'd lost its stuffing, his own movements casual, almost indolent. He told her stories about Saskatchewan, the vastness of the place overwhelming.

'Oh, that's only one small part of it,' he'd say, amused by her amazement. She loved the place names, too: Maple Creek, Moose Jaw, Regina. She imagined everyone living in log cabins they had to build with their own hands, plotting out acres of land to defend. 'Not anymore,' he said. 'Not in the cities, anyway. Although there's still a hell of a lot of open space. If you want to take a hike, you could go days without seeing another person or a dwelling of any sort.' The picture filled her with fascinated trepidation. She'd shuddered and said, 'The thought of it gives me the jitters.'

But she kept him at arm's length and fended off the others who wanted more than a chat and a twirl. Sylvie asked her if she missed Ron and regretted what had happened to their engagement, despite evidence to the contrary.

'No. Definitely not. I hardly ever think of him now and when I do it's with relief that it's over.'

'Is it Joe then?'

'Joe?'

'You know. The great kisser.' Sylvie hugged herself tight, fingers kneading her arms and back, miming a passionate kiss.

Evelyn smiled. 'He was rather sweet. I do sometimes wonder where he is and what he's doing.'

'Maybe we could find him?'

'I don't think so,' Evelyn said. 'I'm alright as I am. Just because you're no longer free as a bird doesn't mean I can't be.'

Sylvie let it drop but Evelyn knew it wouldn't be for long. There was something missing, though, and it wasn't an Alec or Ron, Malcolm or Joe. Yet despite that thought, she stole another glance at the gallant man who'd offered her his seat, and she admitted to herself that someone to feel special for would indeed be lovely.

But, the true heart of her unrest had something to do with the bridge. And that was another opportunity that wouldn't exist without the war. She would never have had the chance to feel the exhilaration of pouring concrete into formwork that would shape an arch above the river, or cut steel reinforcements, or fix a length of wood into asphalt to mark out the lip of a pavement. Standing on the structure, she felt smaller and meeker as each day went by and the bridge loomed larger and more solid around her. At the same time, she was overcome with a sense of power; she had the ability, the common sense, strength and agility to be part of creating something majestic. No wonder men were so full of themselves; those feelings must be a part of their everyday lives.

A couple of weeks ago, after wetting a pencil on her tongue and checking to make sure no one was watching, she'd written EVELYN DRAPER AGED 23 YEARS BUILT THIS BRIDGE APRIL 1942 on a reinforced concrete beam that would be hidden under the footway.

The whole operation gave her a sense of restlessness that she couldn't quite pinpoint; an impatience and disappointment with herself. She wanted to know more about how it all pieced together from starting point to completion. Why one design was chosen over another. Who chose the materials and for what reasons. How measurements were taken with accuracy. Most of the women didn't care and there were times when she didn't either, when she was out on the dance floor or having a smoke and a gossip over a cup of tea at break. A few of them wondered aloud about the logistics and execution, she'd heard Joan talking to Alice in the changing room along the same lines. But as the months had gone by, she seemed to garner more questions and fewer answers.

Rather than catch the bus, Evelyn decided to walk from the underground. It was a beautiful afternoon, cloudless and fresh. A few daffodils ringed tree trunks and pushed themselves up in random clusters amongst scattered debris. Perhaps she'd haul Gwen out for a walk, see if there was a café in the park where they could get a cup of tea and a bun. She rapped on the door. 'Here I am,' she said when Gwen answered. 'Look at this weather — glorious, isn't it? Grab your coat and we'll go for a stroll. I've not seen much round this way.'

Gwen scraped her hair back and looked down at her slippers. 'I ain't dressed properly. Besides, I've got a few things ready for tea here.'

Evelyn was not going to let her off. 'We'll have them when we get back,' she said. 'Come on, it won't take you a minute to get ready. We're not going to the Palace.'

Gwen stepped out into the sunshine and took a deep breath. 'Yeah. Alright,' she said. 'We'll walk up to the park. Give me one mo.'

There wasn't much left down by the river. Factories and businesses razed to mounds of brick and wood. 'When we finish the bridge, we can start on all of this,' Evelyn said.

'They won't want us,' Gwen said, leading the way through her stamping grounds. 'Not when the men come back.'

'If and when.'

'Don't talk like that. It makes me glum.'

I'll be blowed, Evelyn thought and lifted her

159

eyes skyward behind Gwen's back. How often had Gwen been the gloomy one?

'Besides, it ain't like you.'

'No. I know. Sorry. Anyway, we don't know how long it will be until it's all over.'

'Churchill says we'll win soon.'

'Of course he does. How would we feel if he said there is a real possibility that we could, uh, lose this conflict? And if we do, uh, by any chance, uh, win I predict that it won't be for many, many long years. Chin up, best foot forward, onward we go.'

Gwen chuckled. 'But we have to believe him, don't we?'

'Yes,' Evelyn said. 'We do. But I still think we might have to carry on with what we're doing all over London. Wouldn't you like that?'

'I can't for the life of me think of anything I'd like less.' Gwen spat out each word.

They stopped and looked down the Thames towards Waterloo. 'It's a much different view of the river from here,' Evelyn said.

'Not as nice is what you mean, ain't it? Even without the bombing.'

'Well, I suppose it should be nicer in the middle of town. You know, around all the lovely old buildings.'

'It ain't all that bad here,' Gwen said. 'Especially on a day like today. Everywhere looks better when the sun shines.' She squeezed Evelyn's hand. 'Ta for forcing me out.'

Evelyn wanted to pursue the subject they'd been discussing. 'What would you like to happen then? I mean, we all want the war to end, so don't give me that. What would you rather do than what you're doing now?'

They walked through the park gate and made their way up a gentle incline towards a bench. 'I'd rather be exactly as we were before. George going out to work; me at home cooking, cleaning, mending, taking the kids to school, meeting them when they finish.'

Evelyn stretched out her legs and crossed them at the ankles. 'But don't you want some of what the men have? A bit of responsibility, a feeling of having done something at the end of the day and getting paid for it.'

'I did used to have that feeling. Well-being, Betty calls it. I don't care about the money. George gives me his wages anyway, keeps a bit for his pocket, that's all. No.' She took off her specs and turned her face to the sun. 'I want things to go back to how they were.'

'Well.' Evelyn didn't want to sound thoughtless so hesitated and rehearsed in her mind what to say next. 'Given that we can't go backwards, wouldn't you like to move forward?'

Gwen rubbed at her eyes. When she spoke, her voice caught. 'No, I'll only ever want to go back.'

A couple walked by, each of them holding the hand of a tot, teetering on his feet like a grace-less fawn. Evelyn laughed when they swung him between them and he squealed with delight, then felt guilty for enjoying the moment. 'Can we get tea anywhere?' she asked. 'That pavilion over there?'

'Shall we have it here? They let you bring it out. The day's too lovely to be indoors.'

161

'I'll fetch them,' Evelyn said, not wanting to break the spell that was bringing the first trace of colour to Gwen's pallid face, the first suggestion of brightness to her eyes.

Balancing the cups and saucers on the grass, they broke off pieces of a day-old iced bun and licked the syrupy sugar from their fingers, Gwen flinching when a trace of stickiness seeped into a sore hangnail. She skimmed a tiny fly from her tea and flicked it to the ground. 'George is being posted out of London,' she said.

'Is he?' said Evelyn. 'How long will he be gone?'

'Six to eight weeks at a time.' Gwen seemed nonplussed. 'Moving troops around, I think.'

'Oh,' Evelyn said. 'I thought he'd been allowed to join up at last.'

'No, though he did try again. Must be the tenth time at least he's asked the railway to release him.'

'He's wasting his time then?'

'And everyone else's,' Gwen said. 'They ain't about to let the drivers go. Although George says there's plenty of girls around who could do it and be grateful for the work.'

'Well, he's right there,' Evelyn said.

'There are a lot of ladies on the tracks as it is, cleaning, repairing, taking tickets. I've heard there's to be a couple of women guards, believe it or not.'

'Of course I believe it.'

'But no drivers.'

'Bit like us then.' Evelyn couldn't stay off the topic of the bridge for long.

'I suppose so, but some that wanted to are working the cranes now.'

162

Evelyn sat up and sprinkled the dregs of her lukewarm tea over the ground. Shielding her eyes from the sun, she said, '*I* wanted to.'

'I know,' Gwen said. 'But Jim said you'd be chosen next time, didn't he?'

He had, and that had appeased her a bit, but now it had been brought up again she felt herself bridle. There was always something she couldn't do for one reason or another. Irritation spread through her like a nasty infection. It was the company's prerogative to select who they wanted, she supposed, but surely it would have been fairer to say there were so many places available and ask for those interested to come forward. There was no way of knowing the factors involved in making the decision to ask such a one and not another.

Take Joan; from her speaking voice it would be presumed she was well educated. So was that why she was chosen? Evelyn knew she didn't speak half as nicely as Joan, but she'd been educated; she'd been a teacher for a while, after all. But other women chosen didn't speak like they were reciting Shakespeare, so was the decision based on the grounds of their hard work? If that was the case Gwen should have been asked. Her nose was to the grindstone from the minute she started until leaving-off time.

'Anyway,' Gwen was saying. 'It's all over bar the shouting. We're tarmacking the top.'

'Only two lanes out of six,' Evelyn said. 'There's a fair bit to do yet.' Portland stone facings, the railings, light standards, the steps. Finishing off. 'Then there's the temporary bridge. It'll have to be dismantled, I suppose.'

'Oh well.' Gwen sighed. 'I don't know about all that. I just do what I'm told.'

A tiny sparrow hopped towards the crumbs left on their plate, eyes bulging and dilated with panic, its head twitching from side to side, alert to any danger. 'Looks like a warden on the prowl for a light,' Evelyn said.

'We can't put *that* one out,' said Gwen, pointing to the ball of sun, stark in the deep blue sky. 'Come on, we won't hurt you.' She clicked her tongue softly and edged the plate towards the skittish bird.

Something about the way she did it made Evelyn ask, 'Have you heard from the kids?'

'A letter came from each of them yesterday.'

'Are they getting on alright now?'

Gwen nodded. 'Having a great time. I'm worried they won't want to come home.'

'Don't be daft. Course they will.'

'I've left them out for you. The little notes.'

'Let's go back then,' Evelyn said. 'So I can read them.'

They ate the lovely tea Gwen had prepared. Tongue sandwiches, fudge made with carrots, a baked apple with a splash of condensed milk. All diffidence gone, they talked as if they'd known each other for years until Evelyn took a deep breath and told Gwen she wasn't going to stay. 'I've had another invitation,' she said, not wanting to fib.

'Oh.' Gwen looked interested. 'A date?'

'Not exactly,' Evelyn said. 'She got to her feet to make her point. 'But you never know. It might lead to one.'

164

Evelyn thought Gwen would protest but she looked no more than a little disappointed. 'Well, I have had such a lovely day. That fresh air did me the world of good. I ain't going to be long before I get my head down.' She walked Evelyn to the door. 'Have a good time and mind how you go.'

That was easy, Evelyn thought. Perhaps that's the way to play it from now on, so we have the best of both worlds. Or maybe Gwen is on the mend at last.

★ ★ ★

One evening in June, Sylvie and Alec took Dad to see *Song of the Islands*. 'It was great,' he said. 'Especially that Betty Grable.' He let out a low whistle and fanned his face. 'What a cracking pair of legs. It was a good story, to boot. But I enjoyed the Pathé more.' He went on to explain how the whole newsreel had been about the RAF thousand bomber raids on Cologne. '*On the Chin!* it was called.' With clenched fists, Dad and Alec uppercut the air, swiping short of each other's jutting jaws.

'Watch it, you two,' Sylvie said. 'We don't want an injury.'

'Would that be classed as a war wound?' Alec said, dancing around Dad with his dukes up.

'Maybe in a roundabout way,' Evelyn said, laughing. 'Silly buggers.'

Dad collapsed into his chair, puffing and holding his hands up in defeat. 'That was the catchphrase,' he said. 'Air Marshall Harris kept repeating it. "Let them have it, right on the chin."'

165

'And our guys did,' Alec said. 'There's nothing left of Cologne to talk about.'

'That's right,' Dad said. 'And we'll keep giving it and taking it right here.' He pointed to his lower lip. 'Until there's nothing jerry-rigged left.'

As the weeks went by without any news from Jim, Evelyn remembered that slogan and meant to let Jim have it on the chin the next time an opportunity presented itself. She practised what she would say. One day it was, 'Excuse me, Jim, I thought you were going to get back to me soon about doing something with more responsibility.' The next it was, 'I'm very cross, Jim, about the way this whole crane-driving business has been handled.' And then, 'What about me? When will it be my turn?' Until at last she mustered herself, thought of Air Marshall Harris and the RAF bombers and knocked on his office door.

Lifting his eyes from a mountain of documents he and a circle of men were scrutinising, Jim said, 'I'll be about five minutes, Evelyn. Can you wait?'

Evelyn looked at the wall clock, hanging crooked and covered in dust. She had ten minutes of her break left. 'Yes. Alright,' she said.

The men huddled over the papers, shaking out large transparent sheets covered in an oily sheen and laying them one on top of the other. Turning the drawings upside down, pointing to small smudged sections, they frowned, nodded, grimaced a maybe. Evelyn wondered which part of the bridge was having its fate decided.

She looked out of a grimy window, where muck slowly gathering in the corners of the glass put her in mind of a greasy egg timer. Half of the work-force was on a break, but still there were countless numbers swarming over the site, each a resolute grafting ball of energy. Olive's wiry frame was evident and her voice would probably hit them full force, too, if Evelyn opened the door. Sylvie was scurrying along a walkway with a load of piping on her shoulder.

Books and newspapers were scattered on a small table next to the tea urn, as if they'd been thrown there from a distance. Evelyn picked up a copy of the *Illustrated London News* and looked at the photographs of the Baedeker Raids on Canterbury. She scanned the rest of the pile; nothing interesting until she came to the bottom of the heap and saw a journal from the Institute of Civil Engineers. Flipping through the pages, she started on the articles with relish, but lost heart a couple of paragraphs into each piece. She didn't understand a word.

Sighing, she glanced down the inside cover of the periodical still in her hand. Acknowledgements were made to various people with trailing sequences of letters after their names: CEng, FCIOB, PhD, MSc.Eng, FREng, MCIOB, PEngMSPE. Thanks were also given to The Society of Engineers, The Institute of Structural Engineers and the WES. The Women's Engineering Society. Engineering. It had never been mentioned to Evelyn as a possibility. She'd been thrilled when she came top in her last year in the Juniors, the well-thumbed book she was awarded at prize-giving a treasure on a shelf in the sitting room. When the headmaster said she was able enough for the Seniors and to go on further than that if Dad agreed, the careers she was pointed towards were few and vocational. Nursing, teaching, veterinarian assistant, personal secretary, nursery nurse. That was about it. But the girls who belonged to this society must have been given engineering amongst their choices.

The men were folding their papers along well-creased lines, sharing a joke, shaking hands. Evelyn memorised the address of the WES, then threw the journal down with the others.

'Evelyn,' Jim said, turning towards her. 'What a coincidence. I was about to call you in.'

He scratched the top of his head leaving a pink welt pushing through the few strands of hair he had left. He smiled and pulled up a wooden chair to sit with her. She did so want to believe him, so let him go first.

'I haven't forgotten your query,' he said. 'But at the moment...' His arms floundered and flapped. 'There's nothing on the cranes.'

'But there is still a possibility?'

'There's always that,' he said. 'It depends on which men join up and when. Might you be interested in being foreman, sorry, forewoman, or should it be forelady, of a gang of six? That could be on the cards.'

For a minute, Evelyn balked. Saying yes to something specific was one thing, but agreeing to such a vaguely named position was another. It could be fixing the formwork or some such thing. Something she knew nothing about. But she wasn't about to let an opportunity like this get away. 'Would there be training?'

'Yes,' Jim said. 'We'd make sure of that.'

168

'Alright then, please consider me.'

'Good for you,' he said, looking relieved.

They sat in silence for a couple of seconds, Jim drumming his fingertips on his leg. 'Now,' he said. 'Was there something else?'

'Oh,' Evelyn said. 'No, nothing. That was it.'

'Righto, then,' Jim said, rubbing his hands together. 'I'll get it all sorted.'

★ ★ ★

Over the following month, while she waited for Jim to arrange the training, Evelyn again thought of Dad's new motto and took herself to the WES Reading Room on Regent Street. She'd expected something grand and formidable like the National Gallery or University College Hospital. Instead, number 20 was nothing more than a large shopfront blending in with all the others along the road. The brass plate next to the door told her she was in the right place but she held back, not sure herself why she'd come or what she would say when she ventured in. She could try: I mix concrete, cut girders. Or perhaps: I navvy on a building site. She could explain that she'd read about the society in a journal and wanted to know more, keep it simple and to the point. Taking a deep breath, she pushed the door open and tinkled a polished handbell on the reception desk.

'Can I be of help?' A plump woman in a fitted charcoal suit appeared from a room behind the counter. Evelyn was surprised at how ordinary she looked; she could have been anyone's mother or sister going about ordinary women's business.

169

'I . . . ' Evelyn didn't want to lose her nerve. 'I'm interested in finding out what you do here.'

'We're the WES.' The woman indicated a black and white monogram in a frame on the counter. Inside the octagonal shape, what looked like a leather belt and buckle encircled a monolith entwined with a vine, the lettering WES transposed on top. 'Are you an engineer?'

'No, I'm afraid not.'

'How have you come to hear about us then, my dear?'

'I'm on the tools.'

'Oh, I see. Your war work.'

'Yes, but . . . ' Evelyn wanted to say her job seemed to be more than that now, but didn't want to sound lame.

'Please. Go on,' the woman said, sounding as if she had all the time in the world to listen.

'I'm curious to know more. About the whole procedure. How it all happens.'

'You have an enquiring mind, then. Good.' The woman looked satisfied as if assured she had made a sagacious observation. *I hope she doesn't test that theory*, Evelyn thought.

'What you need is right this way. Sign the visitors' book and follow me.'

They walked through a maze of cubbyholes and archways, writing desks, armchairs and tables, up two narrow flights of stairs to a set of double doors with a sign reading 'Library' above them. Rows of bookcases were packed into the dark, high-ceilinged room, the windows having been replaced with wood for safety. Rests were angled on long tables, books, magazines and drawings propped against them while five or six women took notes, lines of concentration on their faces. 'You can't check any books out today, but do take all the time you like,' the woman whispered. 'I'll give you a copy of our periodical when you leave.' She turned and closed the doors behind her.

Intent on their research, the other women didn't pay any attention to her. Feeling like a complete fraud, she tiptoed to the nearest fusty gangway and hid herself behind the stacks. She plucked random volumes from the shelves, pushing them back into their vacant slots when she came across the same unfathomable vocabulary she'd tried to make sense of in Jim's journal. It might as well have been hieroglyphics or Oriental symbols. She couldn't start somewhere in the middle, it had to be the beginning and these books had gone beyond that point.

Not wanting to have to make excuses to the woman downstairs, who had so much faith in her intellect, she found a chair wedged in an airless corner away from view and fell asleep.

'Did you find that useful?' the woman asked her as she signed out.

'I've never seen anything like it.'

'I'm glad we could help. Will we see you again?'

'It's a bit of a trudge for me,' Evelyn said. 'And then I work shifts.'

'That's a shame.' She handed Evelyn a copy of *The Woman Engineer*, a smiling girl in dungarees and turban holding a spanner on the front cover.

Evelyn chuckled. 'That's me when I'm on the job,' she said. 'We all dress like that.'

'Not very fetching, but wholly practical.'

'I should be honest with you,' Evelyn said, swiping the air over her head. 'That up there was way above me.'

The woman didn't seem too disappointed in her, as Evelyn thought she might be. 'Start with the journal then,' she said. 'It might begin to make some sort of sense if you plough through. Perhaps you'd like to come along to our conference? It's next door in Dorland House in September. With a dinner afterwards at the Forum Club.'

'Wouldn't I have to be a member?'

'You certainly qualify, if you do that.' She pointed to the cover girl. 'Would you like to join? It won't take a minute.'

'Yes, I would. If you're sure.'

'Have a bit of faith in yourself.'

Evelyn filled in the form she was given and thanked the woman for her help.

'Stick with it,' she said. 'An interest's all it takes. This war can't last forever and then we can do whatever we like.'

Evelyn wished she could be so sure on both counts.

172

8

August — November 1942

Gwen

Tuesday 11th August 1942

Dear Will,

Thank you for your newsy letter. I enjoyed reading it and I showed it to Dad, Betty, Len and Evelyn who I've told you about. Do you remember? She works with me and likes to hear all about you and Ruth. We're hoping she'll be able to meet you before too long.

You asked if I would be amazed to hear that your football team won the summer tournament over the local lads and I must tell you that I am not surprised at all. I would have been shocked if you had lost as any team with you playing for them is bound to win. How exciting that Marty scored the deciding goal and you set it up. I could picture the ball being passed to you and you kicking it with all your might to Marty who headed it into the net. Did you hear me cheering from here when I read that bit? Millwall will definitely want a pair of chums like you when we get back to normal. I think it was very good of Mr Gwilt to go along and watch the final match.

So the village boys didn't want to call you by any of the names we thought up for your

173

team? Not even *The London Lads? I* suppose once they got *The Vacies* into their heads they couldn't get it out, but it's good they're not mean to you anymore.

Yes, I did hear about Marty's dad. I know that he must be feeling very sad but it's good he's got you to share a room and play football with. I'm glad you remembered what Betty said about Johnny and that you can now tell Marty that his daddy is a hero, too.

I'm glad you liked the picture card of an engine that Dad sent you. He sent me one with flowers on the front. He likes having to go away because he feels he is doing more to help win the war than when he was stuck here in London.

Today I had the whole morning off to go and watch the first part of a bridge being opened. You know I can't tell you the name of the bridge as I tried to once before and you received my letter with a big hole cut out of the middle of the page. Two lanes of this bridge were ready today and people were very excited because it will be easier for them to get from one side of the river to the other.

A man named Charlie Barnard opened the bridge. I can't for the life of me think why he was chosen — he's only a steel fixer. He lifted seven red flags out of their weights and a load of men pushed aside some barriers. We thought that was that until a race started up without any warning. There was a bus, two taxis, a horse and cart and even an American jeep. But a boy with long, lanky legs was the

174

first to make it to the north side, you know, where all the big buildings are. I've never seen anyone pump so hard on a pushbike. His name is Leonard Mitchell, he is sixteen years of age and I heard someone say he lives in Balham. Everyone clapped and cheered for him. It was great fun. I told my friends that you would have beaten him if you'd been there, as I know you are as fast as lightning. Betty came with me to watch and she agreed.

It's hard to believe that Dot has grown into such a big dog. She was a tiny puppy and I thought she'd stay quite small. Is she eating Auntie Peggy out of house and home?

Ruthie wrote and told me about her knee but said it's getting better now. I'm glad you were with her when it happened so you could take care of her. I told her not to pick the scab as it will leave a scar. Can you remind her when you see her?

Please don't get so carried away with football that you forget your lessons. Mind your manners and say ta to Mrs Gwilt for everything she does for you. You are my good boy.

Lots and lots of love from Mum XXX

Gwen cleared her things away and looked at the clock; she'd give it another fifteen minutes before nipping in to Betty's for an hour or so.

★ ★ ★

They'd strolled along to the bridge together that morning, both of them dressed in smart skirts and low heels. Betty had a paste brooch sparkling on her lapel, a new feather tucked into the band of an old felt hat that she wore tilted over one eyebrow. Gwen had used a tinted colour shampoo on her hair that she'd bought from Joan, who somehow always managed to have a number of bits and bobs to sell from her work bag. *Autumn Chestnut*, the label read. It was either that or *Ebony Night*, which Gwen had thought would be too dramatic a change. What she hadn't reckoned on was the red sheen of the conker shell being more predominant than the brown. Her grey hair was covered and that was the main thing. When she curled the ends under and clipped it at the nape of her neck, the overall effect had given her a lift.

The weather had been glorious. There was a balmy breeze, a trace of river in the air. A knot of ragged kids had set up a game of cricket, upturned bricks for stumps, a plank of rotten wood for a bat. As they passed, one of the lads slammed the poor, misshapen ball with a crack and ran towards a makeshift wicket, wiping a streak of dirt from his nose across his face. Gwen knew when Betty steered her into the road it was not to avoid being hit but to save her from the upset that usually surfaced when she found herself close to children. It was always painful, but this time Gwen didn't turn to stare with longing but looked straight ahead towards where they were going. She could feel Betty studying her.

'I do believe you're looking much better these last few days,' Betty said. 'I'm glad to see it.'

Gwen smoothed a strand of hair behind the arm of her spectacles. 'This tint's done wonders. That and a vinegar rinse. And all for one and six.'

'A bargain.'

'Would you like me to get a tube for you?'

'Me?' Betty laughed aloud. 'I've gone well beyond that,' she said, fingering her mottled silver waves. 'Besides, I try not to get Len too excited.' She pointed to her chest. 'Doesn't do his ticker much good.'

Gwen smiled. Len chasing Betty around the bedroom was an amusing thought, although they'd been together for years so they must have enjoyed their fair share of that side of married life. After they lost their Johnny, Gwen didn't think she'd ever be interested in such things again. They'd slept apart initially — she with the other two children, George on his own — and when they did get back into their own bed together, George made no move towards her. Each of them hugged their side of the mattress, turning away from the other as if there was an invisible line of defence down the middle of the bed. At first Gwen was pleased with the situation, not able to think of anything worse than the crush of him on top of her. But as time went on she began to miss the familiar folds of his skin, slightly slick with effort, the nuzzle of his rough beard on her neck and breasts, the solid outline of his legs and buttocks. But it was too late by then. They'd forgotten how to talk to each other, how to be together. Until last week when George was home for a few days.

'No, it ain't just the hair,' Betty was saying. 'You're beginning to seem more like your old self.'

177

She traced Gwen's features with her eyes as if trying to determine where the changes lay. 'I can't tell how,' she said. 'But you're definitely brighter.'

'It helps to have things like this to look forward to,' Gwen said.

'Oh, I know. Ta for asking me.'

'Don't talk too soon,' Gwen said as they turned off the Embankment. 'It might be as dull as a wet weekend in Bognor.'

But Betty did enjoy the morning. They both had, more for the company than the unceremonious opening lacking in fanfare or flourish. A bobby ushered them towards a queue of onlookers standing behind a barrier. Opposite, a line of cranes stood idle, waiting patiently for this insignificant interruption to pass so they could get on with the important work. Evelyn was standing towards the front with a group of women and when she caught Gwen's eye, she motioned for her and Betty to join them.

'They ain't allowed to have any pomp.' Olive was loud and proud. 'Them Jerries might catch wind of it and — *pouff!*' She snapped her fingers. 'It'd go down like a house of cards. You think this is tough?' She banged on the asphalt with the heel of her shoe. 'It ain't no stronger than cardboard to Fritz.'

'Keep your voice down,' Sylvie said. 'Jerry doesn't need spies when you're broadcasting loud and clear.'

'Your foghorn could be a secret weapon, Olive,' Evelyn joined in. 'Very useful where there's no transmitter signal.'

There were a few others Gwen recognised

amongst the small crowd, but not as many as she thought she might see. She supposed most people had used the opportunity to have a lie-in or catch up with the housework. The thought had occurred to her, but she was pleased she had made the decision to go along and take Betty, who was having a good chat with Evelyn.

Patches of sunlight chequered the smooth, clean roadway that had been undefiled until today when it was handed over to be pounded and trampled. She wondered how long it would stand and what it would see and hear during all those years. Behind her, she could hear the women talking, their voices rising and falling, the occasional burst of laughter. She wasn't listening to what they were saying but felt comfortable to be with them, an accepted part of the crowd she'd shied away from.

She scratched tentatively along the surface of the raw spot deep inside her that was Johnny, the flow of pain emanating from the fresh wound as powerful as ever. That might dull in time, or it might never change. But something was different; a tiny glimmer of appreciation for what she had now. There was a sense of hopefulness about the day; a structure so set in stone being partially opened to the uncertainties of the future.

Traffic trundled past, the race was won, the gathering dispersed. Gwen saw Betty onto the number 15 back to Cubitt Town.

'That Olive really is something,' Betty said, laughing. 'She's much more forward than you described. And Alice, what a sweet little girl.'

'Everyone loves Alice. She's from the country near Bristol. Why she ever left there for London

I'll never know.'

'And Evelyn mentioned a young man who I think she's been seeing a bit of. You never said.'

'You probably know more about him than I do. She's keeping him as close to her chest as a good hand of gin rummy.' Gwen laughed at the thought. 'You'll have to fill me in with what she let on to you.'

'And who was that man with Joan?' Betty went on, excited by what the day, so beyond their usual routine, had dug up. The gossip would keep them going for weeks. 'At least I think he was with her, the way they looked at each other. But then he walked away without saying cheerio.'

'I'll tell you about it later,' Gwen said. 'What I know, anyway, which ain't much.'

'Alright, love,' Betty said, stepping up onto the platform of the bus. 'I'll see you this evening.'

* * *

Turning on the lamp now, Gwen checked the contents of her satchel for the morning: fresh shirt, socks, boots, headscarf, coin purse. The flask was draining in the kitchen. She nestled the letter to Will, ready to post, amongst the clean clothes. Feeling around the bottom and sides of the weather-beaten canvas bag, she fished out a loose fag paper, a boiled sweet Evelyn had given her, the stub of a pencil and the card from George. It had arrived in an envelope three days ago, the first letter she'd ever received from him. On the front was a drawing of pink and lilac wild flowers, held together by a draped blue bow. She couldn't read

180

the Latin name in italic lettering underneath the dewy stems.

As a girl, she'd loved to collect flowers and her father had made a press for her twelfth birthday, the rivets perfectly aligned so the wood met without an overlap. The pungent scent of the bursting blossoms as she squashed them flat made her giddy. She'd related this to George and told him about the book entitled *The Language of Flowers* that she'd read a few years later. When they first married, George would pick a flower from the park or garden and present it to her saying, 'What does this mean, then?'

'I don't know,' she'd say, giggling. 'I can't remember.'

He'd tut and shake his head with mock disappointment. 'I do and I ain't read the book. It means I love you.' Turning the card over, she reread the message on the back: *George X*.

Perhaps it was being apart that had made them tentatively begin to feel closer. On the last night of his leave George had come to bed late, slipping dumbly into the sheets next to her. He lay on his back, then turned over; she fidgeted, loosening the taut bedclothes. Neither of them seemed to make a move towards the other but somehow they touched mouths, tongues, timid fingers sliding over comforting bumps and hollows. She pulled him on top of her and he bellowed like a bull, panting into her hair. They didn't say a word, but cried softly with their arms around each other.

How she wished it had happened on the first day of his leave, then they could have had some time to sit together peacefully like they used to or

181

to say a few words about their worries without fear of argument or blame. She kissed the card and held it to her heart. She'd lost so much. They'd lost so much. She couldn't bear it if they lost each other.

★ ★ ★

For six weeks, Evelyn spent her mornings in Jim's office with three other women and two men, learning how to take charge of a gang of six. She reappeared at dinner time, loose papers and note-pads balanced in the crook of her arm. Gwen couldn't see what the fascination was or why Evelyn took it so seriously. Perhaps it was the extra bob she'd get in her pay packet when she was fully trained. If anyone had told her when she started work that she would miss her partner, she'd have dismissed them without feeling the need to explain herself. As if she could possibly have found anything left inside her to give to a stranger. But now she gazed in the direction of the gaffer's hut and looked forward to the door opening and Evelyn coming towards her to share her news.

Gwen assumed that she'd be one of Evelyn's crew. In the meantime, she'd been instructed to help with unloading the vats of tar. Obnoxious stuff; she hated the blistering globules that burst on the surface of the greasy liquid, so black it was shot through with blue. It reminded her of a heavy pan of treacle left on the stove too long without the advantage of the toffee's cloying sweetness. The stench was vile, coating the lining of her nose and mouth with an invisible viscous film she could

182

feel as it built up, taste on her tongue and the back of her throat, the smell exuding from every inch of her skin. It made her retch and gag, long after knocking-off time.

One of the other girls had given her a hanky to hold over her mouth and told her to bring one of her own in to use. When the weather turned and the washing wouldn't dry, she ran out of hankies so went without for a day. That evening, no matter what she did, she couldn't rid herself of the acid reek of coagulated pitch.

When she went to bed, she lay on her side staring into the blackness that slithered and shifted into a silo of tar that she stirred, from the top of a platform, with a giant, comic-book paddle. She fell in without warning, calling for Evelyn, thrashing around and trying for a foothold until her airways were clogged and she sank, pulled down by the gummy material that clung to her, inside and out.

Waking, she gasped for breath, her heart pounding; she straightened the messy covers, pulling them over her damp and chilly nightgown. The room slipped away again. Hunkering down in the place where she used to go to be alone when she first started on the bridge, the river was at her feet, the scaffolding over her head. The water boiled and fizzed; gas vapours rose and swirled around her. She was trapped as the mild Thames became a rushing tide of ink-coloured goo, one almighty wave engulfing her, dragging her down to the bottom where she stuck fast like a defeated tar baby.

In the morning, her eyelids felt as if they were weighted and she ached all over. Her face was burning, but she had gooseflesh under her nightie. Trying to sit up, she was knocked back by a cough that came from somewhere deep inside where it rasped and bubbled. Betty's face floated above her, the lines between her eyes squeezed together in a frown. The doctor drifted in and out of view, the click of his case too loud to bear, the stethoscope a block of ice on her fiery skin.

Ten days passed until Gwen was able to sit up properly. The day after that, Betty helped her downstairs to the sitting room, George's dressing gown around her shoulders. She felt weak, her wedding band slipping around her thin finger when she took the teacup from Betty with both hands.

'Oh you did give me a fright,' Betty said, cupping Gwen's hands as they held the saucer until she was steady enough to be left with it.

Gwen's mouth felt parched and thick. She worried her tongue over the jagged bits of skin hanging from her lips. 'I'm sorry, Bet,' she said. 'I'm such a nuisance to you.'

'No.' Betty set her mouth in a thin line. 'No, you're not.' She leaned in closer to Gwen. 'You're my dearest friend and I'd do anything for you.'

Gwen took a sip of tea, scalding hot in her furred mouth. 'But it never seems my turn to help you.'

Betty took the cup from her shaking hands and put it on the side table. 'Don't you go worrying about that. You've done your fair share for me.'

Gwen hoped so, but she couldn't remember what she might have done or when. Fatigue caught up with her. Her eyelids drooped and she felt as though she were drifting. 'Was it the tar?'

she asked.

'The what?'

'I was put on the tar and it got into me some-how.'

'No, love,' Betty said. 'You've had flu. The doctor said so.'

Gwen hacked a thick cough that felt easier than it had in days. 'I thought it was choking me.'

'It was, that nasty cough. Not the tar. If you hadn't turned for the better when you did, the doctor was going to put you in Bethnal Green.' Betty stood and started to bustle, checking her apron pockets and turning back the sleeves of her cardigan.

'Has George been home?'

'I wrote and told him you were poorly. He sent a telegram saying he'd come back directly, then I sent another telling him there was no need.'

'Oh.' Gwen opened her eyes, remembering the card she'd been delighted with. 'I've lost track of time. When is his next leave? Do you know, Bet?'

'Should be the day after tomorrow. Now, you stay there. I'll get some powdered egg from my larder. Make us a bit of scrambled. Might have some myself. Alright, love?'

'Ta, Betty. Can I bother you for one more thing? Please pass me my work bag. I think it's in the corner near the back door.' She placed it on her lap and dug around in it until her fingers found the card from George.

★ ★ ★

185

It felt good to be up and dressed, although it was arduous to move her wobbling limbs from room to room. After a few minutes, she flopped gratefully into a chair and waited for the listlessness to pass, then had another go at accomplishing some small task. Betty insisted the doctor call again, although Gwen protested about the cost as her wages had been stopped since she fell ill. But the tonic he prescribed helped right away and he was able to reassure her that she would be back to her old self within weeks, if she was sensible.

What she could really have done with now, the day George was due, was another bottle of *Autumn Chestnut*. When she next saw Joan, she would get two so she had one in reserve. She managed to pin her hair off her face and pinch some colour into her cheeks, tweezer a few wayward eyebrows. Her favourite leaf-print navy dress, the one that had flattered her so well, fell in an almost straight line from shoulders to hem. So often she'd heard Evelyn and Sylvie talking about altering their clothes that she thought she'd have a go with a belt, tucking folds of material in pleats over her slack hips at the back. Betty helped her to set out a cold tea. All Gwen needed to do when George came in was boil the kettle. There was even a bottle of beer for him in the pantry.

George clicked on the lamp and Gwen woke with a start, saliva dripping down her chin and pooling in the wrinkles at the top of her cleavage. He'd pulled the blackouts and set their plates on trays; the kettle was wheezing on the stove. 'I'm sorry, George,' she said, uncurling her legs and making to get up.

186

He smoothed her hair with three long strokes. 'Stay where you are,' he said. 'Everything's under control.'

She lifted her face and he laughed, wiping her mouth with the back of his hand before he kissed her.

They ate off their laps in the dull light of the sitting room. Outside, the rain pinged against the windows, tinkling like glass on glass. There would be another scattering of sad, burnished-coloured leaves to sweep in the morning. George asked Gwen about her illness, saying he thought she still had a way to go until she was back on her feet. They exchanged news they'd had from the kids, reassuring themselves they were happy and cared for.

'What's Swindon like?' Gwen asked.

'You probably know as much about Swindon as I do,' George said. 'All I know is the train station and my digs.'

'How is the guesthouse?'

'It's hardly that. Every room is full of blokes working away from home.'

'I didn't realise you had to share a room.'

'Share a room?' George snorted. 'Bloody hell. That would be luxury. We have to share *beds*. Day shift gets out early morning, night shift gets in and so it goes on. Nice and warm from the last chap. God knows when the sheets get washed.'

Gwen stared at George, her knife and fork motionless in her hands. 'What about the landlady? Can't you complain to her?'

'Oooooh.' George's voice quavered in mock terror. 'You wouldn't want to mess with Mrs Sillery.

Or Mrs Slipshod as we call her.'

'Why? Tell me about her.'

'She stands like this,' George said. He stood, hands on hips, legs wide apart, a gurning scowl on his face. 'Her old pinny is covered in greasy stains.'

'Horrid,' Gwen said.

'Her legs are bare and veins stand out all along the backs of her calves like bruised, bloated earthworms.'

Gwen was doubled over, enjoying the picture so much that her ribs, already sore from coughing, pulled tighter.

'That's not all,' George said. 'She has lank white hair. Strands of it stick to her shiny forehead and sometimes she tries to peel them off.' He brushed some of his own greying hair forward, then pretended to pick it off his skin as if it was glued with solidified fat. 'There's always a rancid smell of stale cooking wafting around her and no matter if you're coming in or going out, she says the same thing, ''You're cutting it a bit fine, ain't cha?''

'Oh dear.' Gwen held her stomach. 'No more, George. Please.'

George sat back down and finished his beer. Gwen put her cutlery together on her plate. *It's good to sit like this*, Gwen thought. But there was something in between them that was keeping them apart. No matter how they tried to skirt around it, or talk over it, push it away long enough to make love under the weight of it, it was there stopping them from reaching each other. She knew what it was. It was Johnny, or rather what had happened to Johnny. And it was more than that: it was the fact that they'd never talked about it, not to the extent the tragedy deserved. She waited, wondering if this was the right time. Probably not, but if not now then she was afraid they would go on behaving in a stiff, courteous manner towards each other, going through the motions but never feeling the depth of each other's hurt, never understanding fully, never clearing that mountain of rubble between them.

She looked over at George and smiled.

'Glad to see some colour in your cheeks,' he said.

A few minutes passed.

'Perhaps when things are back to how they were, we can take a trip to Swindon. Have a look around at the things I've missed. Maybe take the kids.'

'I'd like that.'

Another silence.

'Do you remember that night not long before the kids went to Wales?'

She was sure he did by the startled look in his eyes. 'Which one?' he said, tilting the beer to his lips and straining for one last drop.

'When I came into the kitchen. It was late. And you started to tell me what happened that night. You know, the night Johnny . . .'

'I know which bloody night. I ain't bloody simple.' George staggered to his feet, clenching and unclenching his fists, looking around like a madman searching for something to throw.

'Alright, George,' Gwen said, strangled by a coughing fit. 'Never mind.'

'Just when things were starting to look up.' His

hands relaxed. He sat on the arm of her chair and rubbed her back.

'I'm sorry, George.' Gwen put her hand on his thigh, but he moved away, back to his place.

'It's no good saying never mind. I *do* mind. Twenty-four hours of every single day.' He turned to her, his face etched with lines she hadn't noticed. 'Do you think I've forgotten? How could I?'

'I don't think that. It's just that . . . you never finished telling me what happened after Johnny ran.'

George let out a long, tired sigh. 'I ain't sure . . . I can.'

'Perhaps another time,' Gwen said. By his reaction she thought she might have to get used to living with the obstacles between them.

He looked at the clock. 'I might see if Len wants to walk down for a pint. Shall I get Betty to sit with you?'

Gwen shook her head.

He took the plates into the kitchen and she heard him rinsing his hands and face. He came through with a cup of tea for her, coat on, cap in hand. She took the cup and could feel him watching her trembling hands. Then he sat down with a huff.

'It never leaves me,' he began, looking at the corner above the picture rail. 'Never gives me any peace. On and on it goes. Round and round.'

'I know. It's the same for me.'

'Is it?' he said, looking at her for an instant, his eyes narrowed with misgiving. He found his spot to stare at again. 'It's as if . . . even the smells are still on my skin and up my nose.' He snorted, then sniffed in with a crack. 'Smoke and burning. Blood.' His voice caught. 'The wet wool of his coat.'

Gwen shivered, pulling her cardigan around her. 'That night.' He flinched, as if in pain. 'It was worse than ever. Everything was going up.' He choked on a grunt. 'Except what was falling down. I remember . . .' He hesitated, rubbing his face with his hands. 'That almighty explosion.'

'I heard it, too,' Gwen whispered. 'From Price's.'

'The noise . . . I'd never heard anything like it.' He put his hands to his ears. 'I swear it made the flesh on my face judder and wobble, like I had the palsy. Everyone froze. It wouldn't have been possible to move through it. Then we turned to see the whole of Manchester Road alight. I can't get it out of my mind.' He hit his forehead hard with his fist. 'It's printed there, in my head. Deep inside.'

A dry sob set off Gwen's cough again.

'Let's give it a rest.' George pressed his thumbs on his eyelids. 'It's over. Finished.'

'No.' Gwen breathed steadily, making an effort to calm herself.

'What good will it do?'

'Please. George.'

He shook his head. 'It was hell down there. A bloody hell. I'd never seen anything like it.'

'It was terrible,' Gwen said.

'Someone shouts at me to join the chain reeling hoses from a fire engine. Then I was told to leave that and help with a stretcher. ''Get round the back there,'' someone barks. ''And stop those bloody flames from spreading.'' I grab two buckets of sand and run as close as I can to the edge of

191

the fire. I hear him then, before I see him. He calls to me. ''Dad. Dad.''

Nausea hit Gwen. She wrapped her arms around her stomach.

'I honestly could not . . . I could not believe it. I turn and there he is. Johnny. Our Johnny. Out in the middle of that.' George blew his nose and wiped at his face. 'Ever since I've tried so hard to piece it all together. Why did he run from me?' George shouted, pounding his hands on his knees. 'Why? He must have thought I was cross. That must have been it. In the shadows he must have thought I was angry and he just ran away into that building. I called out and chased after him but he didn't come to me. The whole place was falling in on top of us and he was so little.'

Gwen felt dizzy, as if she was shifting from one world to another. George had his eyes closed, tears pooling in the purple hollows beneath them.

'Oh, George.' Gwen looked around for some comfort. She reached for her tea but couldn't manage to pick it up.

'I should have smiled at him.' George hung his head. 'Stupid, I know. But if only I had. And put my arms out. He would have run straight into them and I could have had him home, told off and safe in bed within a quarter of an hour.'

'You can't blame yourself.' Gwen couldn't believe what she was hearing. 'How could you?'

'If I'd been quicker. I'm so bloody clumsy. Instead of shouting his name, I should have some-how let him know I wasn't cross.'

'George, you mustn't do this to yourself. I'm the one who's to blame. It's all my doing.' Gwen reached for his hand, but he snatched it away, a snarl on his lips.

'You've said that so many times,' he said. 'Especially in the beginning.'

'But it's true. I had him here, in my . . .'

'Over and over again like a scratched record. Then you beg me to tell you my side of things and you don't even bloody well listen. What do you want? Tell me, because I ain't got a clue.'

'I just . . .'

He threw his cap on his head and slammed the door on his way out.

* * *

The bed was divided once more. George talked to her when necessary, other than that he just grunted. There were no more impersonations of the unsavoury landlady who, it seemed, he couldn't wait to get back to. Evelyn came to visit, bringing all the chitchat that Gwen hadn't asked to hear. She said she was sorry Gwen hadn't been well and she should take her time before she started back. The gaffer had picked his gangs of six, but Gwen wouldn't be with Evelyn. She was going to be on something less tiring than dismantling the old temporary bridge.

'But we can still see each other at dinner,' Evelyn said. 'Break times, too, and on our days off. It won't be any different.'

But it *would* be different. Anything good always changed for the worse. 'Never mind,' Gwen said. 'Don't matter.'

After Evelyn left, Betty found Gwen sitting

again, gazing at something far away, her hands locked under her chin. Untouched for weeks, the uneven nails had grown to the top of her finger-tips, the scabs around them ready to reveal pink skin underneath. She didn't have the energy to put them in her mouth and grind.

'Don't go dwelling on things, love,' she said when Gwen told her about the new work arrangements. 'The doctor said you're bound to feel down when you're getting over the flu. You mustn't forget your tonic.'

The day before she started back on the bridge, church bells rang out for the first time since the war began. They pealed with joy for the victory at El Alamein. Churchill spoke on the radio and warned everyone that they must not think of this as the end; it wasn't, according to him, anywhere near the start of the end. But, the nation could be satisfied that just maybe, it was the end of the beginning. Regardless, the bells rang for the brave Allied troops, for the Home Front, the Government, the hospitals, the WVS, the RAF, the children. They rang for everyone, but not for her.

9

December 1942 — March 1943

Joan

'There's a spot here.' Joan pointed to a space next to her that only a waif-like child could slip into. She looked over the shoulders of the other passengers to where Alice slumped, squashed against a handrail near the Tube door. *'Alice,'* she hissed again. Still Alice kept her back turned, but Joan could see her forlorn face thrown back into the carriage from the darkened window. The compressed bodies in their shades of grey and brown shifted, inching themselves into a shape that might be more comfortable. Balancing on her toes, Joan peered through the fissure between two arms and focused on Alice's reflection watching the black walls of the tunnel blur past. Her broad shoulders drooped; her sagging mouth pulled her round cheeks flat against her face. She'd been like this for the best part of a week.

The doors opened with a sigh at the Elephant and Castle and most of the passengers squirmed onto the platform, like worms released from a tin can. Waterloo was the next stop but Joan swung into the nearest seat, put her bag on her lap and patted the space next to her.

'Come along, Alice.' Her voice was pleading. 'Do you intend to stand the entire way?'

Alice turned slowly, moving closer as if she was being forced to do something she loathed. She sat next to Joan without looking at her.

The train lurched forward, hesitated, then glided into a tunnel. Joan said, 'You've hardly spoken a word since you got back.'

'I know,' Alice said, looking into the darkness again.

'I'm getting worried now — it's not like you.'

'Well, today it might be. I'll have to see how I go on.'

Joan felt impatience building up. The age difference between them suddenly seemed huge. Perhaps this petulant Alice was more true to character than the shy, cheerful Alice everyone thought they knew. 'Was it Bristol? Did something dreadful happen that you haven't told me about?'

'Old Sodbury,' Alice said.

'Oh, yes. I beg your pardon.' Alice had put her right a few times before. 'I stand corrected.'

'Just an ordinary Christmas. Norman were home on leave. I told you all about it. More than you told me about your Christmas.'

'There's not much to tell, I'm afraid,' Joan said, crossing her legs away from Alice and smoothing her skirt over her knees. 'Hazel, Ivy and me for lunch. Dinner rather. Very quiet.'

She kept her eyes on the handle of her bag until the train slowed down for Waterloo. Alice jumped over the gap; Joan unfurled down onto the platform primly, keeping her legs as close together as possible. They walked one behind the other up the escalators and stairs and through the gate into the biting wind blowing from the river. Ploughing ahead, Alice stepped over puddles and shattered paving slabs, around lampposts and sacks of potatoes outside a greengrocery, her glistening waves tucked into the upturned collar of her coat. Joan could imagine her clumping around her parents' smallholding, oblivious to the mud and muck, rubber boots and thick green socks on her bare legs, a dog or two running in circles around her, a bunch of carrots in her hand. She did wonder why she was here, when everything about her shouted 'countryside'.

Joan skirted the hazards in her path, not wanting to soak her shoes or ladder her stockings. The steady drip of rain was irritating and when she shook out her hair, she knew it would lie flat and stringy, unlike the riotous mass of flattering curls that would frame Alice's face. She stopped under a baker's awning, fiddling with her umbrella until it flowered above her. Joan hadn't expected Alice to wait, so was surprised when a sturdy hand reached under the brolly and grabbed her arm, pulling her to the side of the works entrance.

'Listen,' Alice said, her breath a mist in the close confines of the waterproof canopy. A spot of saliva curdled in the corner of her mouth. 'I doesn't want to fall out over this.'

'Over what?' Joan said, looking up at Alice.

'And I'm telling you because you're my friend.' Her face softened. 'You are, really, and I want it to stay that way.'

'As do I,' said Joan.

'Well, they're all talking about you.' She indicated the building site behind her with a cocked thumb. 'All of them. Again.'

'They talk about everyone.' Joan felt a flush of defensiveness.

'They says you're still that old fella's bit of stuff. Cyril what's-his-name. Ware.'

Joan shrank from Alice's red, accusing face. 'And is that what you're saying, too?'

'Last summer I told them it weren't true,' said Alice.

'I know. Thank you,' Joan said.

'I said, ''An old geyser like him? And a girl like her? Don't be blad.'' I doesn't say anything this time, though.' Alice drew a rough finger across hard-pressed lips. 'But I'm not daft and I can't keep standing up for you because I know you're still carrying on.'

Joan felt queasy. She thought she'd been so clever. 'Of course I'm not.'

Alice's face told her not to bother with the lie.

'How do you know?' Joan asked.

'It all adds up.' Alice squinted through the anger in her eyes. 'All those times you disappear after work or doesn't show up for a night out. Always with some lame excuse or another.'

'I couldn't tell you, Alice.'

'No, you couldn't. Because you knows it's wrong. And that's why you wouldn't come home with me when I asked.' The high colour in Alice's cheeks shone an offended puce. 'Isn't it?'

'Yes. I'll be honest with you now,' Joan said. 'Yes, it is. I spent part of Christmas Day with Cyril. But,' she said, pulling her shoulders back and mustering herself against Alice's height. 'It's not that easy. Adults who feel strongly about one another find it difficult to be apart. You'll find out for yourself one day when you . . . '

Alice drew back sharply, as if she'd been slapped, exposing half her face and head to the rain and wind. 'I might be from Old Sodbury.' She carefully enunciated each syllable of the place name. 'And I might be five years younger than you, but I know what's what.'

Joan looked down at the rain seeping through the leather toes of her shoes.

'I does.' Alice nodded so hard her features smudged into a blur. 'And I knows right from wrong. And it's not right, what you're up to.'

'I think we should go in now.' Joan tried to manoeuvre around Alice, but Alice moved to bar her way with a firm hand on her arm.

'Well, he's one thing,' Alice said, her face puckering as if she'd eaten a piece of sour fruit. 'Each to their own. I suppose.' Her voice softened a bit. 'Maybe you does love him and all that.'

Joan didn't pass comment. Being in love might be enough to excuse her behaviour in Alice's view of life, but as she was making an attempt at honesty, she couldn't have named the feelings she had for Cyril as love. At least not in the same way she'd been in love with Ralph.

'But those things you sell. For him. You're still at it, aren't you?' Alice folded her arms and leaned back on her hip. 'Gwen and Olive asked me if I were in on it. If I could get this, that and the other for them.'

Joan couldn't meet Alice's eyes. She looked, instead, at her mouth, the moist lips twitching. She'd told the others that it was she alone who could provide them with shampoo, soap, sugar, tea, gravy browning. 'I'm the only one who can help you,' she'd said. 'So don't bother asking anyone else.' The little treats she'd left around Hazel's Hostel had stopped, too, so she'd thought she'd covered her tracks from Alice, who'd been devastated when she'd first found out what Joan was doing.

'Why?' Alice said, so close to her face that Joan could feel droplets of moist, warm spray landing on her cheeks. 'None of us gots everything we want, but we gots enough. Except for you. Why do you need more of them little things than anyone else? Or more lolly?' She stopped and drew her head back to take in more of Joan. Then she nodded. 'Oh, I knows. It's to keep you in good with that Cyril bloke.' She stepped back and took a deep breath. 'I didn't know many fancy words before I met you,' she said. 'But I does now and I think it's *despicable*.' She pushed the umbrella aside and made for the changing rooms.

I should tell her, Joan thought. Tell her everything. About Ralph and how Cyril reminds me of him. Tell her that I throw myself at anything that Mother would hate me for. Make her understand that none of it is my fault. 'Alice, wait.' But Alice didn't, and Joan stood by herself watching fat drops of rain quiver on the rim of her umbrella then slip off into the oily puddles at her feet.

★ ★ ★

A thumbs-up from Alice. Joan pulled the brake in the cab and watched as the planks were released and set down ready for collection. Alice was talking to a couple of women who hovered nearby, lining up lengths of wood. She gesticulated a lot when she talked; perhaps that was why her communications with Joan from below the crane were so accurate — or had the need to talk with her hands for work become part of her essence? Surely everything one experienced changed one in some way, she reasoned with herself. When Alice had first realised Joan was involved with Cyril and his black marketeering, she'd told Joan what she'd thought of her. 'I didn't see it at first,' she'd hurled at her, as if she felt personally betrayed. 'I thoughts you were ever so nice. But you're sly, sneaky and underhand.'

When Joan thought about it, she could see that she might be everything Alice indicted her for, but she could not agree that Cyril or his cheap little business were the causes of her shifty deviousness. That had started a long time ago, with Mother.

One of the women said something that made Alice laugh, her wide smile pushing her cheeks up under her eyes. How lovely to be Alice, Joan thought. Natural, honest, open: a new score of music waiting to be played. No one gossiped about Alice, because there was nothing to blather about. How could anyone find fault with her easy manner, her wonder at whatever she saw, her enthusiasm and energy? Some of the others loved to rib her about her dialect, but it wasn't vindictive and had ingrained itself into the everyday workings of the bridge. Most days, impressions of her Bristolian burr could be heard in passing from workers they hardly knew. Blushing in general had also been attributed to Alice. Whenever anyone reddened out of bashfulness or embarrassment, they were asked if they'd changed their name to Alice.

A hand signal that the crane should be lifted. Another to say the way was clear for grabbing a load of timber. It was a relief that when she was working the controls in the cab, she could not allow herself to think of anything else. When the arm was at its apex, she pulled the lever and raised the hook gracefully, like an inverted question mark, towards the next waiting load. Pedestrians were using the far side of the roadway now and Joan could see them on her periphery, through the windscreen wipers, heads down, hurrying with purpose across the river.

Alice stopped her with the flat of her palm and shifted the lengths of wood onto the hook. She checked the rope for strength and, when she was satisfied, motioned for Joan to lift. Three more loads followed until Alice chopped the air with her hand: break time. They worked well together. When Joan looked back, she felt ashamed to remember that when she'd first met Alice, she thought her no more than a yokel. Unsophisticated and provincial. Quickly she'd added naïve, unworldly and green to that opinion. Now here she was, envious of those same traits she renamed as innocent, sincere, reliable, straightforward. Perceptive and discerning. What she once thought negative characteristics, she now perceived as sterling qualities and wished life had allowed her to develop in the same way.

Following behind Alice and her two companions as they made their way to the canteen, Joan wondered what Alice's mother was like. Ma, Alice called her. Nothing like Mother, Joan assured herself, or else she wouldn't have had a daughter like Alice. A few days after Mother had delivered her violin to Hazel's Hostel, Joan had answered Alice's persistent questions by saying that Mother had been unhappy about her leaving home. Alice looked away, but didn't say anything. Joan wondered if Alice's Ma hadn't wanted her to go away either, but not for the same selfish reasons as her own mother. Probably it was simply that she would miss the girl so much. She would have liked to ask Alice more about her Ma and her life at home, but knew she would then be expected to offer information of her own in exchange.

At knocking-off time, Alice plonked herself down on the bench next to where Joan was changing, putting her belt on a peg, loosening her turban. Patting her fine wisps of hair, Joan could tell that her earlier prediction had been correct: the style had flagged and lay listless against her head. She pulled a comb through it, trying to force a wave or two, and pinned it behind her ears.

Alice smiled across at her. 'It suits you like that,' she said. 'Off your forehead.'

'Thank you, Alice.' The formal tone in her voice made her cringe.

'Are you meeting . . . ?'

'Yes,' Joan said, determined to sound enthusiastic. 'I am.'

'See you sometime later at Hazel's then.'

★ ★ ★

She was going to meet Cyril, but not until later. Somewhere to sit was what she needed, and a bit of time on her own. There was a Lyons on the corner of Tottenham Court Road and Oxford Street where she could probably find a table at the back away from the clatter and chatter.

A square of apple something was on the plate in front of her. She took a bite from the corner and couldn't decide what it was; it remained apple something. At least the tea was good — strong and hot. Her table was crammed into a corner next to the swinging service doors; her view was of a wall, flocked burgundy wallpaper below the picture rail, a photo of the outside of the shop above. This sort of setting was not unusual to her; Cyril would think this secreted spot, with its bleak outlook, perfect for one of their encounters.

Where else did they go besides darkened corners and shabby, deserted clubs frequented by other couples hiding away like them? What else did Cyril do except look over his shoulder and start whenever a door opened or a dark-haired woman came towards them on the street? During the summer, they'd met a few times at some stop along the Green Line and had a drink sitting outside a country pub. They'd wandered across fields and through copses, stopping to eat their picnic on a rough blanket Cyril had squashed into a holdall. Then they'd made love in the open, hidden by trees and foliage. She'd wanted Cyril as much as he'd wanted her, but if it hadn't been for the thrill of imagining Mother's reaction if she knew, each time would have been a disenchanting anti-climax. The way the light dappled through the tree branches, illuminating first the tops, then the undersides of the swaying leaves, was much more interesting than what Cyril was doing, or trying to do to her.

She thought she'd feel the way she had with Ralph: extraordinary, different, the centre of the world. But Cyril hadn't taken the time and trouble that Ralph had; she only knew it was over when he lay still and started to talk about what he would have for her to sell the following week. There was hardly a damp patch to wipe from between her legs.

It was more difficult for them to *be alone,* as Cyril called it, now that winter had set in. Once or twice they'd used his cousin's place in Kenton or taken a B and B as a married couple. Those times had been a little better, Cyril making it plain he felt less rushed or pressurised indoors.

Joan hadn't thought about it this way before, but the same problems would have arisen with Ralph had they not had his offices at the Hall to retreat to. A few times they, also, had found some furtive hidey-hole where they could have a drink and gaze into each other's eyes. Those occasions had been magical to Joan and she had truly believed that Ralph had felt the same.

Lately, she had been listening with what felt like a tinge of envy to some of her co-workers laughing and talking about arranging to meet man friends in public places like cinemas and museums. Having dates with officers in well-lit restaurants, dancing in crowded ballrooms with their arms wrapped around all manner of strong shoulders without having to worry about who might see and report them to unassuming wives. Could Mother have been right? Was Ralph nothing more than a

Svengali? The thought caused her such physical pain that she could not pursue it. She could, perhaps, accept that title for Cyril, but not for Ralph.

She asked a passing Nippy for another cup of tea. When it arrived, she stirred it so vigorously that the spoon, when she let it go, was caught in a vortex and circled the cup a couple of times of its own accord. She was quite sure she didn't love Cyril and probably didn't like him, either. He had reminded her in some vague ways of Ralph and, illogical as it was, she had thought he would prove to be very like him. But then, Mother wouldn't have thought that out of character. Her latest letter to Joan had said as much.

I do firmly believe, Joan dear, that you're not thinking straight. If only you'd come home and let me help you take up the strings again.

Joan couldn't remember the rest verbatim, but it went on and on in the same vein. Draining her tea, she made up her mind about Cyril; tonight she would give him the heave-ho.

Joan looked at her watch; Cyril would be waiting for her in the doorway of the Coach and Horses, squinting occasionally from the shadows to scan the street, not for her, but for anyone who might give him away. She pressed a serviette to her lips, then dropped it on top of the apple something. Peeking in the mirror of her powder compact to refresh her lipstick, she thought she looked less drawn and preoccupied and put the palpable changes down to the decision she'd made.

Cyril's mood was lighter than it had been for ages and Joan found herself enjoying his company. Perhaps, she thought, she had been a bit too hasty. He kept his hand firm around her waist, pulling her close, stroking her hands and ears. Sitting at the end of the bar furthest from the door, they talked about an air raid that had fallen just short of the bridge.

'I do hope it's not starting up again.' Joan winced. 'That horrid bombing, night after night.'

Cyril laughed, touching her hair with a fingertip. 'Don't you worry about that. Jerry's busy elsewhere.'

'How can you be so sure?' she asked.

Tapping the side of his nose, Cyril said, 'Would I lie to you?'

She raised her eyebrows and looked at him from under them. 'Probably,' she said. 'You lie to everyone else.'

He feigned hurt, his bottom lip protruding in a pout. 'You're the exception,' he said, linking his little finger around hers. 'Now, I have some exciting news.'

'Oh?' Joan wondered what it could be. Perhaps his wife was going away for a few days and he was going to invite her to play house, or he'd sniffed out another flat they could use for an hour or two on a Sunday. She could hear herself agreeing to the arrangement despite her better judgement of earlier.

'Spam.' He mouthed the word and then smiled, pleased with himself.

'Pardon me?'

She could see the tiny black hairs on his nose and a brilliantine shine on his moustache as he leaned closer to her and whispered. 'Spam.'

Joan pictured turning the key around the blue tin with yellow lettering, the pale pink slab of meat laced with ashen blobs of lard slithering in pallid aspic onto a plate. She could smell the spitting grease permeating the kitchen, finding its way into wardrobes, hair, cushions, drying laundry. Even so, when she thought of the taste, her mouth watered. 'Spam,' she said, 'is not exciting.'

'To many people,' Cyril said, 'Spam is a banquet. I've seen you tuck in with relish a number of times.'

'Needs must,' she said, remembering the fritter sandwiches they'd shared in the woods last summer.

'Exactly.' Cyril relaxed back. 'If it's needed then it's a must, and musts will always sell.'

'Oh, Cyril.' Joan groaned. 'You're not telling me . . . not Spam.'

'I can start you off with three dozen,' he said, as if he were doing her a favour. 'And there'll be plenty more when that's gone.'

'Cyril.' She withdrew her hand from his tinkering fingers. 'I've been intending to tell you something for ages.'

His arm slipped from around her back; he fiddled with his tie. 'Had enough of me, have you?' He looked into his whisky before putting the glass to his lips.

For a moment, Joan felt pulled in two directions but decided she wasn't quite ready to give

208

up on him yet. 'No, not you,' Joan said. 'This selling business.'

'I thought you were game for it,' he said, lowering his voice and spitting out the words. 'When we first met you said you didn't care what you did or what people thought of you. "Let them talk," you said. "I couldn't care less."'

That was true, Joan thought. She *had* said that, or words to that effect, and at the time she'd meant them. He was staring at her, challenging her. She wouldn't tell him about Alice or her feelings of moral reprehension. He'd laugh at her, never let her forget it. 'Well,' she said, 'that was before there was a fine involved. A monkey, I think I've heard you call it.'

He snorted. 'I know all about that.' He leaned into her again. 'Do you think they'd ever come after a young lady like you?'

'I'm not prepared to take the chance,' she said. 'You don't pay me near enough to cover the fine if it came to it so all in all, it's not worth the bother.'

A few minutes of silence passed. Cyril pointed to his empty glass and the landlord brought him another. 'Yes or no?' he asked Joan, indicating her drink.

'Yes. Please,' Joan said.

After he paid, Cyril went out to 'turn his bike around', as he put it. He lit them both a cigarette when he came back and said, 'I understand, my dear. But do you honestly think I'd put my darling in the way of any danger?'

'I certainly like to think not,' Joan said.

'Whisper in my ear how much of the stuff you have left.'

Joan had to calculate. Her large work bag was full and there was a fair amount stashed away in her bedroom. Cyril nodded when she told him what she could remember being left of each item.

He looked thoughtful, counting on his fingers, his mouth working as he reckoned the numbers. 'I tell you what, Joanie,' he said. 'Sell that lot for me and I'll give you twenty-five per cent. There won't be any need to worry, I'll cover for you as I've done all along anyway. Then that'll be the end of it. What do you say?'

Joan found herself nodding in agreement to what felt like a compromise.

With one swift, calculating look around the pub, Cyril pulled her to him and kissed her hard.

* * *

The tatty treasure seemed to fly out of her hands. She didn't want to say anything to Alice until she'd stopped completely, but let it be known to her regulars that her bag was not bottomless and before long they'd have to look elsewhere for their little extras. The news, she knew, would soon spread to Alice's ears and she would be pacified.

By the middle of February every last item was gone, as was the German 6th Army from Stalingrad. There was a subtle, infectious shift of mood, initiated by newscasters and radio announcers, spread by newspaper reports and Epic Pathé bulletins. Evelyn, whose Dad seemed to know about military strategy, said the turning point had come but he was advising Winnie to keep at it and not get carried away with excitement yet.

The cold was incomprehensible to Joan, watching the news from a cosy cinema seat during one of the warmest Februarys she had ever experienced. No wonder there was no snow in London; by the looks of it, the world's quota for that winter had fallen on Stalingrad. It had crippled soldiers on both sides, that and hunger. How they'd kept going was a mystery to her. But somehow the Red Army had battled through. Running from building to building, defending a pile of bricks to the death. Steel-hearted, the press called them. They never gave up and now they had victory; the Allies had victory in Russia. The poor souls, they stared vacantly at her from the screen until their beleaguered eyes shifted and the wounds from deep within surfaced. She hoped they thought it was worth it.

The Government certainly did, seconding the Albert Hall for a Salute to The Red Army. Eden gave a speech, poems were recited, military formations displayed, Joan's orchestra from the Hall played throughout. No, she corrected herself — it was no longer hers, thank goodness. She and Alice crouched next to their crane sharing a ciggie, listening to Evelyn read aloud a newspaper article about the event.

'They might have got some better music,' Evelyn said. 'You know, something a bit livelier.'

Joan laughed and said, 'Not all classical music is a dirge.'

'Oh well.' Evelyn put on a toff's accent and flicked her finger under her nose. 'I wouldn't know, I'm sure.'

'Have you heard them play then, Joan?' Alice

asked.

'Once or twice. A long time ago,' Joan said.

'I love music.' Alice was watching her carefully. 'Were it good?'

Joan shrugged. 'Yes,' she said. 'Very professional.'

'Let's celebrate ourselves,' Evelyn said, tossing the paper aside.

'It's only Wednesday,' Alice said. 'I don't know if I'm up to it.'

'Oh don't be such an old frosty-knickers,' Evelyn said. 'Let's go and see what the Yanks are up to in Piccadilly. You know you love it there.'

Alice blushed. She did like the GIs and they seemed to think a lot of her. She'd told Joan she could picture herself in a sprawling house in Florida or California, maybe Texas. Joan didn't have the heart to tell her that the Yanks who went for her were from farming states like Idaho and Wisconsin, probably seeing in Alice the physique and fortitude for getting up at the crack of dawn to milk cows or drive a tractor. 'Maybe for a little while,' she said.

'Joan?' Evelyn asked, pulverising her cigarette butt with her boot. 'Or have you got something else on?'

'Yes,' Joan said. 'I have.'

Alice smiled at her behind Evelyn's back. Joan had told her that her business dealings with Cyril were over. Alice had been so pleased that Joan was sure she had made the right decision. She'd got what she wanted, for once: a bit of self-respect, deference from Alice, the freedom to meet Cyril with a clean conscience. And Mother would be horrified with all of it.

212

★ ★ ★

She waited for Cyril in one of their usual back-waters off Trafalgar Square, pressing herself into the dark away from the door of the club, avoiding a patch of sticky beer on the pavement. Big Ben chimed and she checked her watch against the eight tolls. She poked her head out and looked up and down the street; it wasn't like Cyril to be late. G#, F#, E, B for the quarter-hour, variations on a theme for the half-hour and quarter to. She stood motionless and listened to the cycle repeat itself *da capo al fine.*

Groups and couples came out who had noticed her as they went in; a man in a brown trilby said something to the woman he was with as they walked away, then they both turned, looked her up and down and burst into laughter. She waited until the hammer struck the Great Bell ten times before catching the Tube home and creeping into her room; she didn't want to chance Hazel hearing and dragging her into the sitting room for a chat with Mummy. Under the bedclothes, fully dressed, she hugged herself tight.

Joan was sure Alice must have put two and two together and realised Cyril had thrown her over when she'd given his dodgy dealings the push. After all, Alice wasn't daft, as she'd told Joan a few months earlier. The younger girl didn't say anything, though, going along with the vague notion Joan mentioned about her and Cyril tiring of each other. A couple of times Alice made to comfort her by saying, 'I felt the same before I came here when . . .' or 'In Old Sodbury there were . . .'

213

But Joan stopped her short each time. 'No need to feel sorry for me,' she'd say. 'I'm more than glad to be out of that situation.'

Alice would adapt the embrace she'd been aiming for into a pat on the back and say, 'That's proper, then.'

★ ★ ★

During the following weeks, Joan's upset and humiliation turned into anger. She so wanted to give Cyril a piece of her mind, practising what she would say if only she could locate him. His wife, if she opened the door when Joan called at Cyril's unknown address, would hear every dirty detail and Joan would make damned sure she understood that Cyril had been voracious for every bit of her. Cyril, if she could corner him, would be made to hear how contemptible he was and she would threaten him with the police. 'Who do you think they'd believe?' she'd snarl at him. 'A poor, innocent girl or a middle-aged spiv like you?'

She asked questions and found out that he was training crane-handlers on the docks, but she couldn't find him no matter what time of day she wandered past the locks and quays. Hoping to see him, she regularly hung around places she'd heard him mention: betting shops and drinking pubs, Petticoat Lane and Smithfields, but he continued to elude her. She took to skimming faces and heads in crowds, quickly examining shoes and the cut of trousers, glancing over silhouettes in profile. He must be lying low or skirting around the perimeters of human existence like a rat. A few times she thought she spotted him and made to follow, but was thwarted when the suspect showed himself to be an innocent stranger.

At finishing time on a fresh and breezy early spring evening, Joan and Alice surged with a hundred or so other workers onto the south side of the river. Joan was pursuing her habit of scrutinising passers-by while listening to Alice relating something Olive had said about what she wore under her bib and braces. And there, disappearing around a corner, she caught a glimpse of the familiar stride of a straight leg, the confident flapping of an overcoat vent, shoes polished to a lustre.

Cyril's brisk, jaunty walk filled her with rage; she was sure she could hear his thin whistle, spewing out some cheap music-hall number above the noise of the crowd. *How dare he be so sure of himself*, she thought, *so carefree.* Ignoring Alice's shout, she shoved and elbowed her way to the side street he'd disappeared down. Coming out of the dark alleyway, she caught sight of him again and raised her hands to frame a bellow of his name. Then he bounced across the road, waved to a tall woman holding a little girl's hand and bent to kiss both of them.

Joan stared, her hands dropping to her sides. *Don't be wet*, she told herself, *now's your chance.* She watched as he took his child's hand, draped his arm around his wife's shoulder, led them along the street and opened the door of a café for them. *Let him go*, she thought; *he's not worth the effort. And you, Mrs Ware, are welcome to him.*

10

April — July 1943

Evelyn

Dad found it difficult to understand Evelyn's interest in the WES and had no hesitation in telling her what he thought every time she mentioned attending a meeting or a talk. He looked at her with uncharacteristic suspicion and asked, 'What is it again? This thing you're going to?'

'The WES. I've told you so many times already. There's a lecture on technical terms for unqualified building workers.'

'Wes. What does it stand for? Wesley someone?'

Evelyn composed her features into the sort of disappointed glare she might once have turned on a trying child in her classroom.

'It's the Women's Engineering Society,' Sylvie said, sitting next to Dad at the rickety kitchen table.

'Women's.' Dad rubbed his chin. 'That's the bit I don't get,' he said. '*Women's?*'

'I wish now I'd never said anything. I thought you'd be pleased, like you were when I was teaching.'

'Your attitude's a real turn-up for the books,' Sylvie said, tearing a mouldy corner off her slice of toast and waving it in Dad's direction. 'We never thought you were so old-fashioned.'

'Give over, you two.' Dad held his hands up in surrender. 'Stop ganging up on me.'

'How does Alec put it, Sylvie?' Evelyn said. 'You ain't seen nothing yet.' She raised an eyebrow and scraped her chair in Dad's direction.

'No, sir, you haven't,' Sylvie said, following Evelyn's lead and inching her way towards Dad until they'd trapped him between the table and kitchen cupboard, his back against the wall. There they both attacked his armpits with their nails until the three of them were laughing hard and the atmosphere was back to its usual unclouded amiability.

Kissing Dad's forehead, Sylvie picked up the remainder of her toast and said, 'Right. I'm off.'

'See you tonight, love.' Dad mopped his eyes and nose with a handkerchief.

'And I'll see you later on the bridge,' Sylvie said. 'If the ogre allows you out.'

'Oi, enough cheek from you,' Dad called after her.

Evelyn added her dishes to Sylvie's in the sink, leaving them to be washed after tea, when enough had amassed to justify boiling a kettleful of water and using a pinch of their precious three ounces of soap flakes.

When Dad got his breath back, he said, 'I'm sorry, love. I don't want you to think I'm behind the times, but I suppose I am.'

Evelyn sat to face Dad over the table. 'What are you worried about, Dad?'

Dad let out a weary sigh that culminated in a rapid flapping and slapping of his lips. 'I don't know, love. What *don't* I worry about? That might be easier to answer.'

Evelyn grasped Dad's knotted fingers, rubbing the rough spots, caressing the callouses. 'Haven't we done okay, Dad? Aren't we good girls, like Mum wanted us to be?'

Dad nodded. 'So far. But I worry about that sister of yours. I don't want her to get herself, *you know*.' He pointed to his round belly and whispered. '*Pregnant*. Not even by Alec. Not before there's a ring on her finger.'

Evelyn smiled. 'Alec's an honourable man,' she said. 'There, is that old-fashioned enough for you?'

'I know, I know.' Dad scooted a teaspoon across the table, then back again. 'But honour isn't always enough to stop people getting up to a bit of how's your father. Not when there's a war on.' He pinched Evelyn's cheek, brushed a loose curl behind her ear. 'I'm a foolish old bugger,' he said.

'You certainly are,' Evelyn said. 'But we've grown rather fond of you all the same.'

'It's just that ... everything's changing so quickly. I am getting left behind.' Dad worried at a mark on the tablecloth. 'I know I am.'

'Not you, Dad,' Evelyn said. 'You know more about what's going on than men half your age. Whenever we're talking at work about this campaign or that raid, everyone asks what you think and what pointers you'd give Winnie.'

'Do they?' Dad sat up a bit straighter, his eyes widening.

'I can't imagine why, though. Being as you're such a barmy old geyser.'

'That's the side of me I only show to you lot. But this engineering lark you keep on about ... '

218

He shook his head.

'It's just an interest. There's no harm in it. I could be doing a lot worse.'

'But it's all women. However will you meet a husband like that?'

Evelyn laughed aloud, but couldn't bring herself to tell her father that what she found funny was the idea that the only thing to aim for was finding a husband. That and not getting pregnant by your husband-to-be until he *was* your husband.

Dad's fleshy, lined face fell. 'Mum used to say kids and a home were what made women happy. And a good man.'

'Well, she wasn't wrong. And she found one of the best, didn't she?'

'We got along okay,' he said. 'I'd like some of the same for you.'

Now, Evelyn thought, might be the perfect time to tell Dad about Stan. The way things were going between them, she would have to introduce him to her family soon. And it would allay Dad's fears about her missing the boat as far as men and relationships were concerned. But something held her back and instead she said, 'There's plenty of time for all that. And you're right: things are changing. I wouldn't mind betting that before too long women will be able to have a proper job *and* be married both at the same time. Even teachers.'

Dad groaned, his head in his hands. Evelyn covered his tea with a plate and put it on top of a saucepan of water. 'Start it off twenty minutes before you want to eat.' She blew him a kiss. 'See you tonight.'

* ★ ★

Holding tight to the safety pole on the packed bus, Evelyn forced herself to think about Stan rather than the WES and the bridge. Despite herself, she smiled when a picture of him came into her mind.

Of all the glamorous places she could have met someone — a late night club, a bar with dimmed, hazy lighting, a hotel restaurant that served high teas, a shared taxi ride — she had met Stan at a bus stop. It had been late; a cold wind was blowing and her feet hurt from dancing when she tagged onto the queue waiting for the last bus. The catch on her much-loved patent handbag was tricky and she was rather more brutal with it than she should have been.

'Careful,' a deep voice said. 'You'll ruin the whole mechanism going at it like that. Not to mention your good looks by grinding your jaw.'

Evelyn was not in the mood for banter, but when she looked up it was to see the face of a young man in RAF uniform grinning at her. Despite herself, she smiled.

'Stan,' the young man said in a low voice. 'Here, would you like me to have a look at that for you?'

Without missing a beat, Evelyn said, 'Good luck.' And handed over the bag.

Stan studied the intricacies of the catch, looking at it first from one angle, then another. Evelyn studied Stan. 'Ah,' he said, peering at her through long eyelashes. 'Do you see this minute pin here?'

She looked to where he was pointing and their heads almost touched over the open interior of the bag. 'Hmm,' she said, 'I think so.'

220

'Well,' Stan turned the bag so they could see the clasp from the other side. 'The same thing should be here, but it's missing so the two parts won't meet and click together.' With one hand he held the straps and the other he placed with great care underneath the bulging material and handed the bag back to her.

'Oh, I see,' she said and sighed. 'I suppose I shall have to give this one up, more's the pity.'

'A favourite, I'm guessing?'

'Yes, indeed,' she said. 'We've had many a good night out together.'

'Then don't be too hasty,' Stan said, the smile never slipping from his face. 'How about we cut a bargain?'

Evelyn grinned, her eyes wide. 'I'm always on the lookout for a good deal,' she said playfully.

'If you and your handbag agree to meet me for a dance next Friday, I'll bring the small part and fix it for you on the spot.' He held out his hand. 'Shake on it?'

'It's a deal,' she said, and his dry, well-manicured fingers were firm to the touch. 'This is mine.' She pointed to the bus moving towards them and felt an unsettling moment of disappointment to be saying goodbye.

'Friday evening, then,' Stan said. 'Shall we say seven? Outside Tottenham Court Road station?'

'Yes.' Evelyn nodded. 'Thank you. I'll look forward to it.'

'And me,' Stan said.

The bus pulled into the kerb and Stan took her elbow and guided her toward the open door, but her heart sank when she became aware of his limp;

she doubted he'd make a good dance partner. Evelyn wished she hadn't accepted his invitation quite so quickly and wondered what she could offer as an excuse to save his embarrassment.

She thought Stan must have been aware of her quandary because he said, 'Do you like riddles?'

Evelyn tilted her head to one side and was about to ask what he meant when he carried on. 'Most people do, so here's one for you. How does an RAF mechanic with a rather pronounced limp dance?'

Evelyn laughed and repeated the question back to him, like she'd done with riddles as a child.

'Give up?' Stan asked. Then without giving her a chance to answer he said, 'Very well indeed.'

That made Evelyn laugh yet again. 'I think I'm going to hold you to that.'

'Good. I have a feeling I'm going to enjoy being held to things by you.'

As the bus pulled away, they waved to each other and Evelyn watched Stan limp back towards the queue, his half-smile still in place.

They had spent quite a few lovely evenings together since then. Evelyn had been asked to have tea with his mum, dad and younger sister above the ironmonger's shop they owned in Sidcup. It had been very nice and they had made her welcome, but their quiet affability lacked something that she couldn't, at first, describe to herself. Thinking about the afternoon later, she decided that they didn't display the fun that she associated with her own family. Or perhaps she hadn't given them a chance before coming to that conclusion. After all, most families were on their best behaviour when someone new was in their midst. Well,

222

families who didn't have Sylvie amongst their number.

There was also something about their quiet assumption that Stan would take over the running of the shop and that any woman he married would be happy to help in an assistant's capacity, as his mum seemed to have been. That grated on her in the same way as the old, overridden law that women had to give up teaching when they married. And unequal pay. And the fact women couldn't readily take up any career they wanted. It was all so unfair, she wanted to stamp her feet in frustration.

Stan hadn't seen any action, but had been based at RAF Abingdon near Oxford, fixing planes like he'd mended her handbag until some piece of machinery had mangled his foot. When it healed as much as it was going to, he had been sent back to the airfield to work in the stockrooms. So, it had not been difficult to see him when he was home on leave and then to carry on going out with Sylvie and the others when he was posted.

Something inside her had pulled tight and she'd felt a pang of guilt and pity for Stan when she'd introduced him to Sylvie and Alec as her 'friend'. For a split second, she had noticed a look of disbelief pass over his face as when they were alone, they were becoming more and more intimate. When they were next by themselves, Evelyn expected Stan to say something about their 'friendship', but he didn't address the situation, so neither did she.

But Evelyn could not figure out why she had asked Sylvie not to mention Stan to Dad yet or to any of their friends on the bridge other than Gwen in passing. She always looked forward to seeing him. At this very moment, wedged amongst others on the clammy bus with one woman's muddy raincoat brushing her legs and another's shoes dangerously close to her toes, she smiled when she thought about him and wondered which dance hall they would end up in tonight. Perhaps, she thought, she liked him so much that she wanted to keep him all to herself for a little longer, like a secret bar of chocolate you know you should share but can't quite bring yourself to do so. Yes, it wasn't that she didn't think enough of him, it was that she liked him too much. And there was, after all, so much about him to like.

* * *

The same ten girls, including Evelyn, were present at this second talk in a series of six. For the opening lecture, they'd sat in two rows facing the front and listened to a lady architect talk about blueprints — those oily, waxed sheets of paper she'd seen being thrown about and pored over in Jim's hut. She showed them how one page layered over another in a typical house plan: foundations, exterior elevations, detailed floor charts, sewerage, electrics, piping, interior walls, staircases, utilities, roofing. After the break, she ran through a basic list of symbols and abbreviations that accompanied the plans and how to read the scale. All of that in an hour and a half.

This time, the chairs were arranged in a circle around a small wooden table. Evelyn took a seat

224

and opened the notebook she'd brought with her. Lecture notes hadn't been provided last time and she'd felt self-conscious sitting and listening while everyone around her was scribbling furiously. More to the point, the only thing she'd been able to remember when she left the WES Club Room empty-handed and empty-headed was that on a blueprint there is one eighth of an inch to a foot of constructed material. She'd have to do better than that.

Pencil sharpened and ready, Evelyn nodded to a few girls she recognised. None of them were on the bridge, so she wondered where they worked and what they were involved in building. A smart woman, wearing a white coat that gave her the appearance of a doctor, carried the shell of a miniature house into the middle of the room. Her light brown hair was tied back; pencils, pens and a protractor protruded from the top of her breast pocket. Puffing, she placed the model on the table and took it apart into pieces, leaving nothing but the base. 'There. That's that,' she said, clapping the dust off her hands.

She looked younger when she stood tall and smiled around the circle. Pointing to Evelyn and the girl next to her, she asked if they'd fetch the two boxes she'd left by the door. 'Shouldn't be too much for you,' she said, flexing her arm. 'Working on the tools all day.'

The boxes were cumbersome, pieces of what looked like doll's house furniture rattling around inside them. 'Just here, girls.' The woman pointed next to her. 'Well done.' She marched around the room, lifting the heavy curtains away from their ornate hanging poles to check the blackouts were secured, turning up the lamps, talking all the while. 'My name is Cynthia Blackwood. I'm an engineer, or as the chaps like to refer to me, a *lady* engineer. As if the description is necessary. Never mind. There aren't many of us so seeing all of you here this evening is heartening. I'm going to be with you for the next five talks. And this,' she said, pointing to the pieces of replica house, 'will be with us, too. Come.' She beckoned with both hands. 'Move in closer so you can see properly.'

Evelyn carried her chair forward, forming a tight ring with the others. She felt pleased that Cynthia would be their tutor for the remainder of the lecture series, not that there had been anything to complain about with the previous woman, but in comparison she'd seemed aloof, inaccessible. As if her knowledge kept her apart from her audience. No such barriers seemed to exist between Cynthia and the snug circle; she made them feel they had equal standing in a somewhat secretive society.

'We,' Cynthia said, 'are going to build a house. No words allowed like thingamajig, what's-its-name or ask-the-gaffer. We're going to use the correct vocabulary as we go along. Where shall we start?'

'Foundations?' said a girl with fair hair and long red nails.

'All agreed?' Cynthia asked.

Everyone nodded.

'Excellent.' The older woman took a piece from one of the boxes. 'Spread footings extend beyond the frost line. Good enough for shallow foundations. Deep foundations will need reinforced

226

concrete. Just listen and join in for now. I've notes to give you at the end.'

The door was closed, the room warm, the energy fixated on Mrs Blackwood, her facsimile and the information she was so willing to impart. Within that confined, intimate space, Evelyn felt as though she'd chanced into a limitless expanse.

★ ★ ★

No one on the bridge knew about Evelyn's after-hours involvement in the WES and Sylvie had sworn to keep her cakehole closed for once, or twice counting keeping mum about Stan. So during the following week, Evelyn read through her notes, trying to familiarise herself with the technical terms by referring in her mind to things she saw on the bridge using their correct names. The sides became the facings, the gas was now an acetylene flame, sand and gravel were aggregates, concrete cylinders that agitated both ways were reversing or tilting drum mixers. Wherever she moved around the site, Evelyn made a note of what she saw and the way in which it was being used, how each segment fitted with the next.

One afternoon, she let something slip about the beamed deck to Olive and a couple of her cronies, who ribbed her endlessly about it. 'Your training with the gaffer's gone to your head, girl,' Olive said. 'What's a beamed deck when you're at home?'

Evelyn hid her embarrassment by joining in. 'I haven't got a clue. Something I heard one of the blokes say.' She took a deep draw on the end of

227

her cigarette. 'Thought it sounded good.'

'Bloody hell,' Olive said, digging a splinter out of the palm of her hand. 'You're a beamed deck, if you ask me.'

From the north side of the bridge, the grief-stricken moan of a klaxon broke through the constant din of machinery, stopping their banter. Jim tore across the unopened section of the roadway, his unfastened, faded blue work-coat fanning out behind him, three other men with first-aid training joining him on the way to the Somerset end. Hauling equipment and tools from their path, workers flattened themselves out of the way. Traffic noise slowed. In the distance an ambulance sounded, the beating of its bell intensifying before it came to a halt.

Olive scratched the top of one boot with the toe of the other, scuffing the leather. They stood and watched the cigarette butt Evelyn flicked into the wind hover for a second, then spiral away from them and down over the facings to the Thames. Heavy clouds hung so low, that Evelyn thought she would be able to reach up and squeeze the rain out of them. 'Best round my lot up and get on,' Evelyn said.

'Your crew still dismantling?' Olive asked.

Evelyn nodded. 'I swear that old bridge grows bits of itself back overnight. Whatever we take down during the day reappears the next. We'll never get rid of it.'

'Like one of them lizard things,' one of Olive's friends said. 'You know, if you catch hold of it, it sheds its tail and then hides away till it grows another.'

Olive looked at her as if she'd gone mad. 'Where does this happen then?' She nodded towards Evelyn. 'On her beamed deck?'

Olive always had to have the final say and, Evelyn had to admit, it was always witty. 'I came over looking for Gwen, actually,' she said. 'Seen her today?'

'She's in. But she don't seem herself,' Olive said, glancing in the direction of the accident. 'A bit clumsy. You know, away with the fairies.'

'At least she's here. I'll come back across at dinner time to see her. Tell her for me, won't you?'

Evelyn descended to the gantry that connected the new bridge to the partly demolished temporary structure. She'd been backwards and forwards countless times but always ran her hands along the railings, knowing how easy it would be to get cocky and lose her footing. Safety had been one of the facets John covered in his training for the new foremen and women, and Evelyn was so aware of hazards and pitfalls now that she had become a bit of a nag. Sylvie and Gwen, when they were with her, suffered the main brunt of her warnings.

Gwen, in particular, was a worry. Her hands were in a bad way again, ulcerated sores around the cuticles, her nails so bitten back that angry, inflamed patches of skin were exposed to the elements. She was thin and vulnerable, almost scraggy after failing to regain the weight she had lost during her bout of flu. Distracted, too — lifeless and listless. She'd had countless days off: every other day some weeks or two days on, one day off. Jim was doing his best to accommodate her but some of the others were grumbling, wondering why

229

they couldn't come and go as they pleased, even though Gwen had her pay docked every time she was off without a doctor's note.

The girls who worked under Evelyn drained their flasks and stamped on their roll-ups, collected their tools and set to work when she gave them the okay. They were a good bunch: on time most days, easy to talk to, not resentful of Evelyn as she thought they might be. As well as hard work, a lot of singing, swearing and good-humoured teasing went on in Evelyn's gang. The work was nothing new, though. This is what she and Sylvie had been doing when they started, around the time that photographer had snapped their photo that never did appear in the newspaper. Then they were welding reinforcing rods together, nailing lengths of timber; now the men were taking the steelwork apart and the women were cutting the rods into more easily transportable lengths. As for the huge steel girders, Evelyn thought she heard Jim say they would be used somewhere on the front. Good. Double the war effort from the bridge.

Evelyn pulled her shield down and watched what each girl was doing in turn, checking the colour of their flames, ensuring there were plenty of empty flat-bed trolleys on which to load the sets of reinforcements. When she was satisfied, she took up her own station and began to score through a steel rod, the molten metal melting away from either side of a clean slash. She'd got what Jim promised her; she was forewoman of a gang of six, but she'd hoped for something more glamorous, though it seemed a strange, contradictory term to use when it came to building work. Sliding her safety shield onto her head, she did a quick round of her group again, giving a thumbs-up to one of the girls who looked up at the same time.

The job she had wanted was across the temporary bridge, beyond the chasm into the river, over the expanse of the opened half of the new roadway to where gangs of men were working along the far opposite facing of the new structure. At road level, they were fixing reeded cornice bands onto the outer surfaces — a lovely piece of work. Others were setting up fixtures for lighting standards, putting railings in place. Those sorts of jobs required responsibility and the chance to use spirit levels, to read plans, to make decisions. But all of it was being carried out by men. She and the three other girls promoted to forewomen were each given a measuring tape and put here, back where they started.

Dare she complain to Jim again? She pictured trying to explain her gripe to him, heard herself stumbling over the wrong words, could see his hurt, bemused face. If Jim did understand her grievances and transferred her to head a task on the new bridge, there were no qualified women to work under her. Leading a group of men would be impossible. Besides, her condensed training sessions didn't certify her to take on those more intricate, specialised duties. She'd have to be a lady engineer to get in there and even then, that might not be enough. Above her, a crane-load of reinforcements swayed, waiting to be guided down. Taking off her gauntlets, Evelyn signalled the rods perfectly, precisely into place. At least she could guarantee the safe, clean, efficient working of her gang.

★ ★ ★

Two or three stoic birds sang through the rain lashing against the window. Evelyn could hear Dad talking to the milkman, come for his money, at the door. She rolled onto her back, unravelling her arms from the knot she'd made of her fusty bedclothes, and thought it must be about half past ten. Yawning, she stretched her arms above her head and sat up, taking in the familiar set-up of the room she'd slept in since she was a child. Shelves on the wall, one for her, one for Sylvie; the wardrobe with doors that no longer closed; a washstand, jug, basin; half-sized bookcase, shoes, make-up on the dressing table, knickers drying on the back of a chair. A rag rug between two single beds. The disquieting sight of the rounded hump of Sylvie's back huddled deep in her sheets.

It had been Sylvie's habit, before she met Alec, to languish in bed on weekend mornings then potter around the house in her dressing gown and slippers until it was time to get ready again for another evening out. Now she was up first, more often than not, never mind whether the previous night had been a late one. She seemed to be in a fever most of the time, almost unbearably cheerful in whatever she was doing, chattering away about Alec, looking back to when she'd last seen him or forward to when he would next be on leave. The only time she wasn't in a heightened state of agitated happiness was when he was with her; then,

232

she seemed to calm down into a lull of contentment.

There was an exchange of goodbyes from the kitchen below, the banging of a door being closed. Evelyn wondered if she should wake Sylvie and check if she was unwell, but if she was, then she would need to sleep. Leaning over, Evelyn moved the covers away from Sylvie's face with one finger and a thumb but Sylvie's eyes, bloodshot and puffy, were open. She snatched the bedclothes back and up, over her head.

'Are you ill, Sylvie?' Evelyn asked, standing away from her sister's bed.

In response, Sylvie felt under her pillow and pulled out a crumpled piece of paper, tight writing crammed onto every line. Evelyn's heart thumped; she felt sick. She remembered another letter sent from a soldier and hoped this one didn't bear the same sort of news. If it did, she knew it wouldn't be read with the same sense of relief as the one she'd received from Ron.

Evelyn meant to scan through, eager to get to the cause of Sylvie's upset, but the detailed descriptions of exactly how Alec missed Sylvie slowed her down. Supporting herself on an elbow, Sylvie plucked the letter away from Evelyn, turned it over with an indignant huff, then thrust it back into Evelyn's hands.

So Alec was going away. Like thousands of other men. On the first of May he was leaving for training in Scotland. From there, the 1st Canadian Army would be embarking to . . . He couldn't say; wouldn't say. Evelyn smoothed the creases out of the paper, folded it and slipped it

233

back in its hiding place. Her sister would need it to be in good condition for what might be a very long time.

'I know it's hard,' Evelyn said, stroking Sylvie's matted hair off her forehead. 'But he has to go. You know he does. How many times has he said that the Canadians have been stuck here in England for three years doing nothing?'

'They all say that. Those crazy Canucks.' Sylvie put a pillow behind her head, slumping back onto it. 'They think they've been nothing more than an extension of the Home Guard.'

'Well, you're very lucky, you know.'

'How do you make that out?' Sylvie wiped her nose on the sleeve of her nightie.

'You'd never have met otherwise, would you? And you've had him here all this time. On leave more than anything else. Able to take you out, stay downstairs, living it up like he's on his hols.'

Sylvie laughed. 'It's hardly that.'

'Think about all those poor old mares who lost someone right at the start. Olive's friend whose old man took it on his first day in France. Helen. Her whole family gone. Gwen.'

Sylvie played with the binding on her threadbare blanket. 'Oh I know. I'm just feeling sorry for myself.'

'Yes,' Evelyn said. 'You are, and you need to stop it. *Now*. Before Alec starts thinking you're not the girl he fell for.'

'Alright,' Sylvie said. She snivelled again. 'It's just such a shock.'

Evelyn patted her hand. 'Will you see him before he goes?'

'He'll be here for the last three days of April.' Her face brightening, she yanked her fingers through her hair. 'Let's give him some sort of farewell do on the 29th,' she said. 'Something jolly, but not too big. I don't think it would do to shout about it.'

Evelyn thought. The 29th. What was happening that day? It took a while for her to remember it was the date of the next lecture. 'Why not make it the thirtieth?' she suggested casually. 'His last day?'

'I'd rather save the Friday.' Sylvie looked away. 'For the two of us.'

She didn't want to let Sylvie down and although it was disappointing, missing one of the talks wouldn't matter too much. But then, she realised, it did matter — to her. 'Let's think about this a bit more,' Evelyn said.

'What's there to think about?'

'Well, perhaps if the leaving do is early on the Thursday, then you and Alec can have that evening and all of Friday to yourselves.' She tilted her head to one side and hoped she looked encouraging.

'That's a good point,' Sylvie said. 'Although the party might go on and on.'

Evelyn shook her head from side to side. 'I won't let it,' she said. 'It's the WES that night which is sure to put a damper on the evening when I mention it.'

'Yes.' There was nothing like the thought of a party to cheer up Sylvie. 'A tea party, then. Let's start organising it right away.'

★ ★ ★

235

On the Wednesday night, Evelyn joined Alec and Sylvie at the Canuck's favoured club. Loud to the point of being an overbearing distraction, the music began vigorously and ascended to a frenzy. Forced laughter replaced the usual free-flowing guffaws that came so easily and naturally to the Canadians. Fervent couples groped and slobbered over each other well before the lights dimmed. Too many cigarettes were smoked, too much alcohol consumed, too many promises made.

With Stan at his posting, Malcolm pinned Evelyn down for most of the dance numbers, stepping with dexterity between her and any other man who approached to offer her his hand for a spin around the floor. She didn't mind; Malcolm was a great dance partner, and they'd found themselves together so many times when the music started that they were used to how each other moved. They took up their positions for a foxtrot. Evelyn knew where Malcolm's hands would be positioned and how they would feel, one firmly gripping hers, the other on her waist. Gliding together in aligned symmetry, Evelyn glanced at Malcolm, ready for one of his gags or clever observations.

'Hey,' he said, broadening his hand across her back. His eyes were the same transparent hazel as Alec's, but with brows and lashes so fair they seemed to disappear in bright light. He was shorter, too, but had the same muscular build. Always fresh and clean, he looked and smelled as if he'd been out in clear mountain air, under cloudless skies. 'I've been thinking.'

'That, as my dad says, is a very dangerous thing.'

'That's good. I like it,' Malcolm said. He smiled,

his skin pulled tight over his cheekbones. 'I'll have to remember that one.'

Evelyn hoped the flippant exchange would halt what she thought might be some serious admission on Malcolm's part. She didn't want him to ruin things now. They'd had fun together, but as far as she was concerned, that was all. She'd already made it clear there could be nothing between them.

'Would you look at those two?' Malcolm said when they swung around at the corner of the dance floor and faced a different way.

Evelyn looked over her shoulder at Sylvie and Alec, nestled close and unaware of anyone else.

'They're always the same,' she said, keeping her voice casual.

They completed a circuit of the floor before Malcolm sighed and said, 'I sure wish I had a girl to write me.'

'Don't you get letters from home?' Evelyn asked, sure he must.

'Oh, yeah. Of course.' He laughed. 'Don't feel sorry for me, I'm not an orphan or anything. It's just that ... it would mean kind of a lot to get some mail, once in a while, from a special girl. Like lots of the guys do. Look, Evelyn I ... '

Stopping mid-spin, Evelyn kissed him on the tip of his soap-scented nose. 'Let's sit for a bit,' she said.

They found their table, empty now, and downed their drinks. 'I've never led you on, Malcolm, and if I have, then I'm sorry.'

He rubbed her hand and inspected it, as if he was trying to memorise its idiosyncrasies. 'No,' he

237

said. 'Worse luck. I'd have loved to be led on by a girl like you.'

'Are you sure you're not Irish?' Evelyn said. 'You've got enough blarney for it.'

'No, ma'am. Canadian-Scottish through and through. Your king is my king.' He lit each of them a cigarette. 'I know where we stand, Evelyn. And I do know that you're seeing someone else. That Stan guy you introduced to me once? But I was hoping we could write, just while I'm, you know ... away. I'd sure look forward to hearing from you.'

What harm would it do? Evelyn thought. It might even be interesting, give her another perspective on things. 'Of course,' she said, kissing him again. 'I'd love to keep in touch. I'll write once a week.'

The following afternoon was for the family. Sylvie and Evelyn had laid out a high tea, the highlight of which was corned beef sandwiches with a scrape of horseradish sauce on one slice of the bread. The apple jelly was made with the water poured off a saucepan of boiled new potatoes; no one complained or was any the wiser. Uncle Bert brought along his Shove Ha'penny board and they played a raucous game, Evelyn and Sylvie saying they had let Alec win so he wouldn't go away feeling sour. They sang 'Hail, Hail the Gang's All Here' and 'Don't Get Around Much Anymore'. Alec took Sylvie's hand and began a rendition of 'You'll Never Know', but when Sylvie joined in, her strong, animated voice bumped into a sob in her throat and the song came to an abrupt end.

When Evelyn made her excuses to a chorus of

boos and jeers, she heard Dad insist on taking Alec to the pub to have a pint with Uncle Bert and some of the regulars. Pulling the front door closed behind her, she stood and imagined Sylvie's face as their plan threatened to fail. She waited until the three men stepped outside, then grabbed Dad's arm. '*One pint only,*' she hissed in his ear. 'Then you return him to Sylvie.'

'Right you are.' Dad sounded surprised by Evelyn's forcefulness — or his own ready answer — or both.

She didn't see Sylvie or Alec again until early Saturday morning, although Evelyn heard Sylvie slip into the bed next to hers after midnight. There was no butter for Evelyn or Dad at breakfast, no powdered egg, tea so weak it looked as though the leaves had been waved over the pot. Alec protested, but he got all the rations.

Sylvie sat on the stairs while Dad and Evelyn said their goodbyes. 'So long, sir,' Alec said to Dad, his kit bag over his shoulder.

Dad grasped Alec's hand with both of his, holding on tight. 'We don't say goodbye in this country, young man,' he said. 'We say ta-ta, old mate. See you soon.'

Alec nodded, his swollen Adam's apple rising and falling as he swallowed. They clapped each other on the back, circled shoulders with their arms, Dad's head squashing into Alec's chest. Evelyn heard Alec whisper, 'Thank you for . . . .' His eyes turned to the wall that Sylvie was sitting behind.

Dad managed a choking sound in reply. 'We're

very proud of you, son,' he said. Go get 'em.'

A hug and an unsteady smile were all Evelyn could manage, then she turned Alec around and pointed him in the direction of the hallway. He took a deep breath, gathered himself together and strutted smartly towards where Sylvie was waiting.

After a short space of time, the front door closed. A bulky shape passed the sitting-room window, head down, then disappeared. All that energy, the dynamism, the masculinity, the good nature and optimistic outlook — gone. She went to Sylvie and put her arms around her neck.

Sylvie got on with it. She dried her tears, dyed her hair a richer shade of brown, painted her lips and ran a white pencil under her nails. Work on the bridge continued. After a few weeks dancing resumed, although Sylvie refused to partner anyone but Evelyn. Letters began to be delivered, return correspondence posted. Evelyn read Malcolm's letters aloud to Dad and Sylvie, all three of them enjoying his hilarious retelling of arduous training, wet kit, shaving in ice-cold water, lukewarm stodgy rations, card games after lights out.

Evelyn could picture his fresh face, hear him humming through everything. Would you believe I was so beat one night, *he wrote,* that I crashed out on my bunk in full gear? Boots and all still laced. I tell you, there was one mad panic in the morning when I had to be polished and gleaming for parade at six.

Alec's letters were longer and more detailed. Sylvie read parts of them out, but others she kept to herself.

240

It was quite a few weeks before Evelyn could walk past the old dance hall that must be struggling for clientele now the Canadians had been posted. She'd never noticed before how shabby it was from the outside. Dusty and a bit shoddy. A thick residue on the door handle, a flapping flyer stuck to the window by one piece of yellowing sticky tape.

* * *

The third talk at Regent Street was scheduled for a fortnight after the men's departure. But once again there was the possibility she would have to cancel and this time it was because of Gwen. She'd been away from the bridge for a week with no message or doctor's note. Evelyn wrote to her, but didn't receive a reply.

Jim asked Evelyn to check on Gwen, as her confidante and one-time partner, to find out what was going on. One more day, he explained, and he would have to give Gwen the sack. Of course it was right that she should visit, she told herself, the bus to Cubitt Town taking twice as long as it should due to a burst gas pipe. But she didn't want to miss the roof of Mrs Blackwood's little house being put in place, so would try to make the visit short.

Betty answered the door and pulled Evelyn into the kitchen. 'Gwen will be pleased to see you,' she said. '*I'm* pleased to see you. You're a godsend. Tea?'

'Please,' Evelyn answered. 'Where is she?'

'Bed.' Betty pushed her lips together until the

colour drained from them. 'I can hardly get her up.'

'Not flu again?'

Betty shook her head. 'It's her nerves. She's let them get the better of her.'

They drank their tea standing next to the sink. A line of clothes hung in the yard, stiff and dry in the summer sun. 'Do you think she'd come out with me for a bit?' Evelyn asked, remembering the day they'd spent in the park last year, when Gwen's spirits lifted.

'I doubt it, love. She won't even go out with George's arm to lean on when he's home.'

'Why hasn't she been signed off?' Evelyn asked.

Betty sighed. 'The doctor wants her to go to work. Says she'll be better off for it.'

'Do you think she's able? Jim's going to give her the boot if she doesn't come in or produce a sick note.'

'She needs to hear that,' Betty said, putting her cup on the draining board. 'I'll tell her you're here. Get her down.'

Gwen was shaky when she appeared, but kissed the top of Evelyn's head and seemed pleased to see her. She looked hot and sweaty, crusty flakes around her eyes and mouth, her nails a mess. Evelyn could see she was in no fit state for any sort of work, let alone something as treacherous as the tools. When Evelyn mentioned the doctor again, Betty shook her head behind Gwen's back and rubbed her thumb and index finger together. Evelyn bit her lip. It was expensive to keep having the doctor.

Alone with Betty in the hall, Evelyn said, 'I'll

242

have to report back to Jim and hope that's good enough for now. What do you think, Betty?'

'That's the best we can do.' Betty agreed. 'When George gets home, I'm sure ... well I think ... he'll sort it all out.'

Then Betty suggested that perhaps they could work out a schedule between them to help build up Gwen's confidence. Walks, bus rides, shopping, a visit to the baths.

Evelyn said she would be happy to help as much as her shifts allowed. 'But not Wednesday evenings,' she added, unable to look Betty in the eye. 'I have something else I have to do on Wednesday evenings for a few weeks.'

Betty didn't question her, but as she walked to the bus, she felt remorse wash over her. She stopped and was about to turn back and revoke the midweek codicil to their agreement. Then she decided that she would wait and see how things moved along before committing herself and losing out on the lectures she was enjoying so much; she could always step in on a Wednesday evening if push came to shove, and that would assuage her guilt. On the bus to Regent Street, Evelyn thought about Mrs Blackwood. She wondered if while she was training she had felt as though she was being pulled in a hundred different directions, or if she had been ruthless and quashed those thoughts in order to become a lady engineer.

11

August — November 1943

Gwen

She wasn't like this. Not her. The real Gwen was able and sure; strong and confident; up first, last to bed; knew left from right, right from wrong. One mistake, one bad decision, one instance when she didn't have her wits about her, had led to this situation. Betty with her all day, Evelyn popping in and out, jollying her along, keeping her consoling nails from her mouth, arranging outings and little tasks to keep her busy. Gwen wished they would just go away and give her a bit of peace.

The first two weeks were the worst. Every morning Betty stood at Gwen's bedroom door, in irritatingly good spirits, and told her it was time to get up.

'Breakfast's on the table in quarter of an hour,' she'd say. And then go on to list the unappetising choices. Toast and marge with apple jam or stewed tomatoes. Powdered egg on toast. Honey cake or one small sausage with a couple of mushrooms.

It was no use saying, 'I'm not hungry'. Or turning her back and protesting that she'd had a rotten night's sleep but could easily go off now. Betty would wait, making herself busy tidying clothes away or pushing up the windows. Chatting the whole time until Gwen tottered towards the bowl

244

of warm water Betty had brought up and started to wash herself. One morning, without saying a word, Gwen refused to follow orders so Betty hauled her up, wiped her face and dressed her, brushed her hair and, keeping her pressed close for support, managed her down the stairs and into the kitchen. The last time she'd felt so humiliated had been when she wet her knickers in First Year Juniors and was told off by Miss and again by her mother when she got home.

Betty then had her sit until she'd finished whatever was put in front of her even if it was tasteless, hard to swallow and harder to keep down. A chore or two followed. She would be told to tackle the dishes or scour the draining board. Another day she would be directed to the sitting room with a duster. After that, there was a pile of potatoes waiting in a bowl to be peeled. She wasn't allowed to sit, so couldn't attempt to mend or write letters; she had to do things that kept her on her feet to build her stamina, get her strength back.

The shops next, with a list written out by Betty. Queuing was grim, worse than she remembered. Meeting someone while waiting her turn was unbearable. She wanted to run but her trembling legs would have held her back. With heat prickling her armpits and a dry mouth, she stammered her way through conversations that sounded as though they were either taking place in the distance or being shouted through a loudhailer. Betty gave Gwen time to gather her thoughts and talk, taking over when she could see it all got too much. Stroking her wrist all the while with the light touch of an insect's wings that Gwen had to force herself not to swat away.

After dinner, she was exhausted enough to sink into a nap devoid of the intrusive images that had dogged her: George lying twisted on a train track; Will or Ruthie slithering at her feet, their legs in their hands; Evelyn plummeting from the bridge; Betty crushed under the rubble of an Anderson. And Johnny. In the second before she woke, he always appeared, standing and staring at her. Just beyond her reach.

Whenever Evelyn arrived, she looked fresh despite a hard day's work, the journey, the latest war news. Their voices low, she and Betty would have a chat in the kitchen, discussing her, no doubt, but she didn't care to listen at the door to hear what they were saying. Evelyn talked non-stop, too, in what Gwen hadn't noticed before as a rather sickly, girlish voice. A couple of times she mentioned a man named Stan who she'd referred to before in passing. Gwen didn't know they were still seeing each other; she really couldn't keep up. She also read letters aloud from someone called Malcolm who was fighting in Sicily with her sister's boyfriend.

Heroes they were, if the way Evelyn went on about them was anything to go by. She made them sound as brave as Wing Commander Guy Gibson and his crew. They'd go for a walk, a bit further each time. They ventured to the baths where, after completing a number of laps set by Evelyn, Gwen floated on her back with eyes closed, imagining the cold sea caressing her, protecting her in its tidal drift until she reached a warm, sheltered haven where the past three years had never happened.

By the end of the third week, Gwen thought she was no better. But when she recalled how she'd felt and behaved at the start, she realised she was wrong. She was making progress.

Since Johnny passed away, almost all of her energy had gone on thinking about him. Images of him and that night pursued her, hunting her down, clamping into the depths of her with the ferocity of a rat, unable to stop biting until its jaws met. Like rodents gnawing away, leaving waste and debris strewn along the tunnels they carved. Roaming the infinite burrows, her self-reproach for Johnny grew. For George, too, the way she'd spoken to him, how badly she'd treated his attempts at reconciliation. As for Will and Ruth, she couldn't win with them. Her mind would volley disparate thoughts back and forth until she felt she was going mad; she should have sent them away earlier, she shouldn't have let them go at all; she should insist they come home now like so many other kids; or George was right to make them stay in Wales until the war was over; she should write more often — or perhaps less.

Now things were a bit clearer, she added Betty and Evelyn to her list of regrets and was overwhelmed with shame. She hoped she hadn't shown how much she'd resented them helping her, how their trivial chat and masked smiles had wound her up, the catty things she'd thought about them. If they had noticed, neither of them let on.

She grabbed at Betty's hand one morning and wouldn't let go. 'Now, now,' Betty said, prising her fingers loose. 'There ain't time for all that. There's carrots to scrape.'

Evelyn, in her own way, was as dismissive. 'No need for sop,' she said. 'That shower's passed so we can walk to the Island Gardens for a change. Catch the bus back if you can't manage both ways.'

Yet again, she was made to think about what she would do if the tables were turned. In the past, when things had been better, she liked to think she'd been a good friend and neighbour. Often, she'd helped Betty out with bits of shopping, given her an egg or scoop of tea if she ran out. She'd listened to her worries about her son, especially when he was going through his wild days before he settled down. They'd sat together next to the wireless hoping not to hear news that might affect Ray's battalion. She'd been good to other friends, too, that she'd had once. She was sure of it.

But this degree of help? Would she ever have committed herself to anyone other than her children in the same way? Admonishing herself for her mortifying shortcomings, she doubted very much that she would.

As a month of this routine came to a close, thunderstorms broke the dry summer weather. The rotting smell of wet foliage lingered in the cooler autumn air. George had left money for the doctor and Evelyn took her to see him during one of her visits. He was delighted with the evidence of Gwen's recovery.

With a serious look, the doctor took Gwen's wrist and felt her pulse. He scrutinised the hands he placed back on her lap, running his fingertip along the tiny scars and rough edges of her healing nails. She was reminded of the endless tubes of antibiotic cream he'd prescribed to patch up

248

the weeping sores she'd inflicted on herself. Now, a sliver of crescent moon grew white on the end of each nail. Next, he studied her face. 'How do you feel about getting back to your old routine, Mrs Gregson?'

'A bit unnerved,' Gwen answered. But she spent a lot of time worrying about how she would keep paying for the doctor's calls and the medicine he prescribed, so added that she thought she could manage.

The doctor nodded with his eyes closed. 'We don't want you to do too much and set yourself back.' He drummed his fingers one by one on the arm of his chair. 'How about this for a plan? One more bottle of tonic and a final week off.'

'If you think so, doctor,' Gwen said.

'But take the week to fend for yourself,' he said. 'I think you're more than capable now.' He patted Gwen's arm.

Nodding, she said, 'Yeah, ta. I am.'

When Evelyn related the news to Betty, Gwen noticed the flash of relief on both their faces. It would be good for all of them to have their time to themselves again.

* * *

On her own Gwen thrived on things she hadn't realised she'd previously relished. Filling the tea-pot with steady hands; pulling the blackouts at the right time; the way the sun moved across her tiny garden; a clean vest; managing her daily affairs; sending a note to George. She could remember trying to write to him during the dark days, but thought she must have thrown her efforts on the fire with frustration or confusion. She had no recollection of posting anything or of Betty or Evelyn saying they'd done so. Perhaps Betty had kept George informed because one morning, when she arrived home from the shops, there was an envelope from him on the mat.

Picking it up, she turned it over and felt that it was a proper letter this time, not a card. She put her bag on the floor, a couple of parsnips and a tin of pilchards spilling out, and without bothering to take off her outdoor things, tore open the envelope. It was a short letter, one page of thin, white, watermarked paper. Gwen consumed it greedily, her lips moving as she read in her mind. He was proud of her, thought she'd been strong and determined. *Carry on as you have been. I'll be home in a fortnight for a week.* She turned over and read the last sentence twice, holding onto the wall for balance. *After we get over the winter perhaps we can think about visiting the kids together.*

She sat on the bottom stair with a bump. She held the letter to her mouth, then at arm's length, rereading every word. In the spring then, February maybe, when the sheep would be lambing and the first shoots pushing up through the frost. The kids would be waiting for them, washed and scrubbed, jumping up and down with excitement. They'd walk down the lane towards them, she and George, letting go of each other's hands only to put their arms out to Will and Ruth.

She wanted to keep the letter to herself, like a secret treasure, but felt compelled to show it to Betty. Putting the kettle on, she set out two cups,

found a couple of old biscuits in the larder and
went to knock next door.

★ ★ ★

It was good to have something to aim for, a concrete reason to get well and stay strong. Whenever
Gwen felt she might be losing herself again or
could easily slip backwards, she thought about the
spring. Although George reminded her he hadn't
promised, repeating what he'd written in his letter however many times she asked, Gwen couldn't
see any reason other than her health that would
stop them going to Wales. Once there, George
would see what they were missing and agree to
bring Will and Ruth back to London with them.
Most of the other kids around and about had
come back, some months ago.

The weekend before she went back to work
Marty knocked on the door with a letter from Will
in one hand and half a loaf of Mrs Gwilt's home-
made bara brith in the other. He held them out to
her and stood, scratching one ankle with the heel
of his other shoe. Gwen couldn't place him for
a minute; his face was familiar but the height of
him was so different. His hair, too, had changed
from a fine, fair, babyish flop to a coarser head of
brown. 'Oh Marty,' she said, shaking her head in
disbelief. 'Come in. When did you get home?'

'Yesterday, Mrs Gregson,' he said, following
Gwen into the kitchen. The last time he'd sat on
one of her chairs he could pump his little legs in
and out unencumbered. Now his feet were flat on
the floor. Will would more than likely be the same,

251

Gwen thought, and she wondered if he would feel as awkward here as Marty looked.

'Well, I had no idea,' she said. She tried to remember if Marty's mother had told her on one or other of the occasions she'd seen her in the street, but couldn't recall any of their conversations. 'Your mum never said.'

'I think she just decided to fetch me back.' Marty shrugged. 'So she came and got me.'

Gwen couldn't take her eyes off him. Freckles were spread across his cheeks and nose, still tanned from playing outside during the summer. One grey sock was snug on his calf, the other drooping around his ankle. His shorts were too big, his sleeveless pullover too small. She watched him feel around his ear and wipe his finger on his leg. Him being here, back home, made her feel that Will and Ruth were waiting very close by and that their return was imminent. It was as if his mother's snap decision could be contagious and George might go down with the infection. A wonderful sense of calm came over her; Will and Ruthie were coming home, where they belonged.

Marty made to leave and Gwen could see how ill at ease he looked, shuffling around, not knowing what to do with his hands. 'There,' Gwen said. 'How rude of me. I ain't had a visitor for such a long time I forgot to ask if you'd like a cup of tea?'

Marty nodded.

'And a bit of this?' she asked, pointing to the fruity loaf.

'Yeah, ta,' he said, sitting back down. 'We finished our half for tea yesterday and Mam . . . ' He shook his head. 'Mum, I mean, said we had to share with you.'

Gwen lit the gas under the kettle, the cloying smell of it flaring with the flame. 'Well, that's very nice of you. And say ta to your mum, too.' She was aware of him watching her cut through the sticky, tea-infused bread; when she turned to put his slice in front of him, a thin stream of drool trailed from the side of his mouth.

'Mrs Gwilt baked this twice a week. Once on Wednesday and again on Saturday,' he said. He sat very straight at the table, bringing the food to his mouth instead of attacking it in a slouch like he used to. 'We had a piece every day after school, me and Will, sometimes with butter.'

'Well, I'm afraid I ain't even got a scrape of marge for you,' Gwen said, breaking off a corner of the heavy cake and biting into it. It stuck to the roof of her mouth, where she licked it, savouring each flavour as it came to her. Sugar, treacle, fleshy raisins that burst when she prodded them with her tongue. Eggs that had been laid by one of the chickens she'd seen in the Gwilts' yard; none of this powdered rubbish that turned to water when it was cooked. As she broke off a larger piece and chewed with enthusiasm, she caught Marty's eye and he looked away.

'I ain't used to such rich food,' she said, patting her stomach and sliding her slice onto his plate. 'Here, you help me out.'

Marty polished off her piece as quickly as he had his, licking each of his fingers in turn when he'd finished.

'You must be so happy to be back,' Gwen said. 'I'll bet you can't believe it. Back with all your pals

253

in your old school, with Mum and Nan. And your brothers.'

He shrugged again. 'I suppose,' he said. 'Mum says I'll settle down, soon enough.'

'But . . . you missed home, didn't you? Weren't you longing to get back?'

'I did at first,' he said, wetting his finger and picking up the tiniest of crumbs. 'Now I miss them back there.'

'Will, do you mean?'

Marty nodded. 'Especially Will. But Mr and Mrs Gwilt, too. And Miss Preece in Class 5. And some of the lads. We played all sorts with them.' He sighed and Gwen could see now that his eyes weren't wide and bright and his mouth was turned down.

All along she'd worried that Will and Ruth might become too fond of who they were billeted with. Of course it was lovely that Ruth had Auntie Peggy, and Mrs Gwilt was much more favourable than Mrs Morgan. She was grateful to them and could see herself sending them news every Christmas, maybe visit a couple of times throughout the years. But she hadn't liked it one bit when she heard Ruth's funny sing-song way of talking; it grated on her. And the things both kids said from time to time: foreign-sounding phrases like 'isn't it' tagged onto the end of a sentence that wasn't even a question. Jealousy hit her hard at times. Thoughts of someone else sitting and helping her kids with their schoolwork, reminding them of their manners, telling them off, teaching them how to do things around the house and garden, guiding them, cuddling them. She wanted all that for herself. It was hers by rights; she'd earned it and deserved it.

Until now, though, when Marty was here looking gawky and adrift, she hadn't grasped the extent to which the kids might have grown fond of their temporary homes and come to rely on them. And how much real home and family had faded from their minds. The thought of her own kids longing for Wales terrified her; her calm state dissipated and anxiety filled its place.

'I can't for the life of me think what I'll do with this,' she said, handing the wrapped bara brith back to Marty. 'You have it.'

'But Mam said . . .'

'You tell Mum that there's only me here and I'll never finish it before it goes off. That would be a pity.'

'Right then,' he said. '*Lechyd da.*'

'You what, Marty?' Gwen made sure she looked confused, even though she knew full well what the words meant.

'Thanks. Ta very much.'

She nodded her approval. 'Say hello to your mum. Oh, and Marty, let me know if you get a letter from Will, please. Ain't nothing like sharing a letter and a cup of tea.'

After she'd watched him lollop down the road, Gwen found her old notebook and started a list of reasons why Will and Ruth should come home in the spring. Number one read: *If they're away any longer they might think of Llansaint as their actual home.* Same with Auntie Peggy and the Gwilts. They might think of them more fondly than they do us. *They might want to go back to*

255

Wales the minute they get home and never settle with us again.

★ ★ ★

Before it started reminding her of the oncoming winter and that dreadful night, October used to be one of Gwen's favourite months, especially when the weather was like today, the sky an unbroken sheet of pale, glacial blue, the air clean and sharp. She breathed in deeply, trying to get some of the cool expanse past the fluttering in her stomach. Evelyn was meeting her at the works entrance so they could walk into the changing room together, then she'd have to report to Jim for the duty he'd arranged for her.

As she approached, she could see Evelyn leaning against a wall, smoking and chatting to a man and a couple of women. She drew back into the cover of a doorway and waited until she could make out who they all were. The man she didn't recognise, but he soon finished his fag and said his cheerios. Sylvie was next to leave, which left a young girl, Alice maybe, who turned to face Evelyn and continued to talk, flinging her arms around and bobbing her head up and down. Gwen could cope with Alice; it was Olive she dreaded seeing.

Evelyn waved when she saw her and Alice turned, smiling. 'Morning,' Evelyn said.

'Ain't it a lovely one?' Gwen pointed her elbow towards Evelyn for her to grab.

'We'll all have cheeks like Alice's working outdoors today.'

'And mine will look chafed,' Alice said, covering

256

her face with her hands. 'Alright, Gwen? Proper nice to see you.'

'The same.' Gwen nodded towards Alice, surprised that was all the girl had to say. No questions about where she'd been for weeks on end, no prying or poking or looking uncomfortable. She dared not let herself believe it would be the same with everyone.

They moved into the flow of workers jostling their way towards the time clock. 'We were talking about the strike at Hillington,' Evelyn said to Gwen as they joined the queue.

'Where?' Gwen asked.

'At the Rolls Royce in Hillington.'

'I ain't heard about that,' Gwen said. 'But I can't for the life of me find my clocking-in card.'

Evelyn and Alice helped her to search amongst the Gs, letting others move around and past them. 'Perhaps it weren't set up again yet,' Alice said. 'Never mind, tell Jim when you sees him.'

Gwen stood aside while Evelyn and Alice fed their cards into the time recorder that stamped the date and time onto them with a ping. It was amazing, Gwen thought as she watched. A wonderful piece of modern engineering.

'You'll hear a lot of talk about the strike,' Alice said, as if their previous conversation hadn't been interrupted. 'Some thinks it's a good thing. Some don't.'

'You don't get paid if you strike, do you?' Gwen said. 'So it can't be a good thing.'

'Well,' Evelyn said. 'Sometimes you have to suffer for a bit to get fairer pay in the long run.'

'I don't thinks it's the right time for a strike.'

257

Alice directed her remarks to Evelyn over Gwen's head. 'Not when there's a war on. It's taking advantage.'

'Some would say the big gaffers have taken advantage of the war by getting away with paying unfair wages to women workers.' Evelyn pushed opened the changing room door and held it for Gwen. 'Doing exactly the same job as the blokes and all,' she said.

Gwen felt worried for Evelyn; *now* what was she getting herself into?

'I still thinks it's wrong,' Alice said, shuddering. 'Makes them look like traitors to me. Hope it don't spread here.'

The changing room was packed out — hot and fusty. One wall had been painted a dark mustard. Evelyn had told her about that and how, despite the 'wet paint' warning signs, Olive had put a hand on it to steady herself then smeared dirty yellow streaks down anyone within striking distance. The other walls were in a worse state than ever: bubbling, peeling paint; chipped gypsum board. The air was thick with sweat and talc, mildew and wet wool, lily of the valley, fried food, bad teeth, *Evening in Paris*. Shoes and boots cluttered the floor; dresses, coats and hats hung from hooks or lay where they were flung on benches. And the noise. Gwen didn't remember it being this loud before she was ill. She couldn't understand why a girl changing on one side of the room had to shout to her pal at the opposite end instead of moving closer to her, like she did when she wanted to talk to Evelyn.

No one said a word to her as she followed Evelyn and Alice's path to the far corner where there was a postage stamp of space and a couple of empty hooks. Gwen dropped her work bag onto the bench and, turning to face the corner, began to change with quick, adept movements, not wanting to draw attention to herself.

'Oi.' A shout from near the door. It sounded like Olive. 'You.'

Gwen's fingers, working along the buttons on her dress, began to fumble and shake. Her head and neck bobbed with tension. The noise dropped and Gwen could feel dozens of eyes on her back. She was going to get picked on here and now, in front of everyone. The atmosphere pressed in on her, making it difficult to breathe.

'I'm talking to you, Missy.' The screech came again. 'I ain't forgotten that fag.'

Gwen knew she didn't owe Olive — or anyone else — a cigarette, so allowed herself to look across the room over her shoulder. Olive had one hand on her knotted headscarf, the other pointing at Evelyn. Olive glanced at her, then back at her prey.

'Don't worry yourself,' Evelyn said, pulling a tobacco tin out of her pocket. 'Here it is.' She stepped towards Olive and threw the fag towards her as if she was aiming at a dartboard.

'We're quits then,' Olive said, catching it in one hand.

Evelyn moved back to their corner and stepped into her dungarees. 'I'm not sure how you make that out,' she said. 'You owed me two from the week before.'

This remark caused an outburst of laughter and jibes from around the room. 'You'll have to prove it.' Olive laughed louder than anyone, looking from one to another of the women for approval. Her gaze rested on Gwen again for a second, but there was no dig or sarcastic comment.

It was easier after that, when she realised her absence hadn't registered with most of her co-workers. She might have felt offended that she wasn't missed, but to the people who mattered she had been, and now she could go about her business without having to defend herself. Besides, the world had never stood still for her and she'd never expected it to. If by any chance she did have the power to arrange things so it would, this point in time would not be where she wanted her life to pause. That date would be any before 1st September 1939 when this wretched war was declared.

The steady expansion of the bridge hadn't ceased either. All manner of vehicles and pedestrians trundled in an endless flow from one side to the other like ants on the march. To get to this point the work had been immense: colossal slabs of concrete swinging from cranes, huge iron girders slotted into place, enormous vats of tarmacadam stirred and boiled, slabs and spans eased into place. Now crews of workers were bending over, concentrating on small areas of beading, finishing off balustrades and stone steps and the two as yet unopened lanes. The temporary crossing had diminished in size and significance. When Gwen started, she had thought its steel latticework imposing and grand; now it had given up its standing to the permanent bridge.

Evelyn left her at Jim's office, arranging to meet for their break. Jim smiled when he saw her and beckoned her to take a seat. He looked different, too: greyer and more drawn than she recalled. He'd been so good to her, giving her more than a fair number of chances to pull herself together. Not many gaffers would do the same, George had said.

'Good to see you, Gwen,' Jim said.

'Ta, Jim. And thanks for having me back.'

Jim looked down at his hands. 'Wouldn't do us any good to lose one of our best workers, would it?' He clasped his hands behind his head and rocked back on his chair, something she forever nagged the kids about. In her mind she saw them losing their balance and gashing their heads open. She started towards Jim with an outstretched hand but he thumped all four chair legs back on the floor and said, 'I don't want you to take this the wrong way, but now you're here, I don't know what to do with you.'

Gwen was expecting something a bit more sympathetic, but liked his honesty. She shifted in her seat and waited.

'My dilemma is this,' Jim said. 'I could use you out there on any of those crews, but I don't want you to do too much too soon. On the other hand, the only alternative is for you to sit in here with me and tidy up this mess.'

Gwen took in the papers strewn over every surface, cardboard filing boxes stacked in corners, certificates and notices held at an angle on the pinboard by one thumb tack.

Jim followed her gaze. 'My assistants can't keep up with it,' he said, looking sheepish.

Had she been given the same choice when she

261

started, she wouldn't have hesitated. Donning a tabard and wielding a duster, she would have had this tip sorted in no time, then kept on top of it. She would have felt superior to the women playing at a man's game, all of them pressganged into a role they had no business filling.

Now, she looked out through the smudged windows and felt a certain amount of pride bulging in her chest, making her sit taller, tilting back her chin. Out there was where she belonged, even though there was no hope of her ever making sense of it and she didn't have the inclination, like Evelyn did, to find out. But it was a useful thing they were doing. It made her feel good about herself. Besides, why on earth would she want to be cooped up in this office, as constricting and stale as the changing rooms, when she could be out in the open, getting completely well for the spring?

'You've been kind, Jim,' she said. 'But I think I'm ready to go back properly.'

'Good. Alright then.' Jim stood and scratched his head, leaving a strand of hair curling over one ear. 'Report to Evelyn for this week. She said she could do with another pair of hands to bring down the temporary works.'

The day was warmer now. Overhead, squawking gulls looped in a wide circle, dredging for food with their eyes, dive-bombing their targets like Messerschmitts. The din was less forceful and crushing than she imagined it would be, the machinery more of a comforting hum than a grinding, grating racket. Evelyn looked up and smiled when she approached, signalling for her crew to down tools. She introduced Gwen to each of the girls, none

262

of whom she knew. They nodded or said hello in a pleasant enough way then pulled their shields over their faces and carried on.

Evelyn explained what she wanted Gwen to do. 'For now,' she said, speaking firmly, 'I want you to place these cut rods together in half dozens, then a couple of others will lift them onto the back of a lorry and drive them off. Okay with you?'

Gwen nodded, pleased with the task.

'You'll be moved back to the flame after that, I'm sure. We just want to make sure you're acclimatised.'

Gwen smiled to herself at Evelyn's turn of phrase, wondering which course she'd got the word from. Well, if she were younger she might be more ambitious herself, but at this time in her life she was striving for one thing only. The spring.

12

December 1943 — March 1944

Joan

Hazel was assembling some sort of contraption in the middle of the parlour. Spread out around her were large blocks of wood, which she was picking up at random and trying to piece together with the help of a handful of nails and screws.

'Whatever are you up to now?' Joan said, shrugging off her coat and loosening her scarf. 'For goodness' sake, let me help.'

'Oh hello, sweetheart. I didn't see you there.' Hazel sat back on her haunches, looking defeated, pushed back the sleeves of her lavender cardigan, and blew out a puff of air. 'Mummy could do with a cuppa, couldn't you, Mummy? Joan will make it for you.'

Joan glanced at Ivy, barely visible amongst the soft folds of blankets and cushions enveloping her. Every week, more of Ivy seemed to fade away, making the wing chair that was her world appear to swell around her diminutive figure. 'Tea can wait. Let's get this sorted first,' she said. 'What is it?'

Holding her hand out for Joan to hoist her up, Hazel started to sing a verse from the old Jack Buchanan favourite 'Everything Stops for Tea'.

'Mummy used to love that one. Didn't you,

Mummy?' Hazel let go of Joan's hand and tucked the satin edge of a blanket under Ivy's chin. 'You carry on here then, I'll get the tea.'

It took all the patience Joan could rally not to show her frustration. If she'd been dealing with her own mother she would have stormed out long before now. 'But, Hazel,' Joan could hear herself pleading, 'What is it?'

'A shelter.' Hazel mouthed the words, her lips contorting in exaggerated shapes.

'In the house?' Joan asked.

'Come with me a minute.' Hazel made for the kitchen where she washed her hands and filled the kettle. Joan gathered tea things together on the battered George V Silver Jubilee tray that Ivy loved, according to Hazel.

'Churchill,' Hazel started, 'and you know how much I think of him, said, ' "It's quite like old times again." '

'Did he?' Joan asked. 'But I beg your pardon, Hazel, what's that got to do with the shelter in the sitting room?'

'The whole bloody thing's starting up again. That's what,' Hazel said, steam streaming from the water she poured into the pot.

Another series of nightly bombings had everyone living on the edge. The pattern this time seemed to be different: more feeble, less aggressive. Joan sniggered at her cynicism. Was this now the measure of the world they lived in where bombing was ranked on a scale of antagonism? Surely it was all destructive and hostile, no matter the degree of belligerence. Nevertheless, it did seem as though, this time around, the Jerries couldn't muster the same forcefulness and persistence they'd battered London with three and a half years ago.

'It's every night. Again,' Hazel said. 'Regular as clockwork it starts.'

'Yes,' Joan said. 'I know. But it doesn't last until dawn, does it? So, not quite like old times.'

'You are a sensible girl, Joan, but that was last night and the night before. Who can tell what tonight might bring?'

She was right, of course. That was the worst of it and it had everyone scuttling for cover once more. Hoping to revive herself, Joan flicked cold water on her face. The shift had been a hard one, when fog as thick and glutinous as rice pudding made working the crane difficult. Thankfully, no one was hurt when she'd dropped a load too soon — although there was talk of a girl on the far side being taken to hospital with a mangled leg.

Hazel stood close to Joan and lowered her voice, 'I don't want to alarm Mummy.'

'No, of course not,' Joan said.

'But I've got to get her shelter ready to use tonight. I've not slept this past week for worrying she's not safe.'

Picking up the tray, Joan said, 'So that's what you're trying to put together. But how does it work?'

'Wait and I'll tell you. I don't want Mummy to hear.'

Joan turned and looked at her landlady, a fine mixture of strawberry blonde and grey twists of hair corkscrewing from her loose bun, pale eyes almost feverish, high cheekbones pink with exertion. Often when Joan was with Hazel, something inside her seemed to crack open and ooze with

266

pity for the woman whose life had been this and nothing else. That, and a touch of admiration.

'A neighbour made it for me after Mummy had her stroke and wasn't able for getting under the table any longer.'

'Mummy used to . . . I mean, Ivy used to shelter under the table?' Joan remembered the Anderson her father had put up for Mother and kitted out with gramophone, wireless, sherry in a decanter, petit-point frame.

Hazel nodded. 'We both did. Quite happy we were. I had my book so I could read to Mummy, and my knitting, of course. We'd try to make a little party of it, sometimes, when the noise was so loud we couldn't sleep. You know, tea and cake, a round of Old Maid.'

To prevent Hazel from seeing that the irony wasn't lost on her, Joan closed her eyes and nodded purposefully. 'So,' she said, 'how does the neighbour's makeshift shelter work?'

'Well, it was my idea.' Hazel sounded proud. 'But my lovely neighbour made it. When you nail the pieces of wood together — and that's the bit I can't seem to get right — the frame then fits right over the bed. Just the ticket.'

'But what about you? Where do you shelter?'

'I crawl in with Mummy,' Hazel said, looking astounded. 'Like always.'

Joan had never thought about it before, having presumed that after Ivy was tucked up, Hazel made up a bed for herself on a couple of chairs or on the floor.

'Leave it to me and Alice,' Joan said, picking up the tray. 'She'll be back soon. We'll have it done in a flash.'

'You are a couple of sweethearts,' Hazel said. 'Let's see what's left on the sideboard. Oh, a lovely bit of tack. Mummy will enjoy that softened in her tea.'

With another person to hold the boards while they were nailed together, the shelter was constructed without a fuss. In addition to the holes already driven through, Alice and Joan beat in a fresh series to make the crude structure sturdier. They then moved the old, worn furniture around the crowded sitting room so that things were more manageable for Hazel, who was effusive in her thanks.

'We're used to heavy work.' Alice was unfazed. 'We does it every day.'

'Well, I can't thank you enough. We're so lucky to have you two girls here, aren't we, Mummy?'

Joan looked across at Ivy, whose eyes were fixed on Hazel. They'd all get a shock if she answered her daughter one day.

'Oh, in all the excitement I quite forgot.' Hazel stepped over to the sideboard. 'Two letters for you, Joan. One from your mother, not that I peeked but I recognise her writing by now. And another from an unknown sender.' Batting her eyelashes in what she must have thought a coquettish manner, she fanned Joan's face with the envelope.

Grabbing the letter mid-flap Joan said, 'Now, I wonder who that can be from?'

'So did we, didn't we, Mummy?' Hazel said. 'But I'm sure we haven't a clue.'

Joan examined the unfamiliar handwriting. 'That,' she said, 'makes three of us.'

268

Alone in her room, Joan tossed the unread letter from Mother to one side and stared down at the mystery envelope. It could be from Cyril, apologising to her at last. Then again, it looked too neat and well blotted for him. Ralph, perhaps, coming back for her? No, the paper was too WH Smith and not enough Selfridges. But who could the sender possibly be, if not one of them?

She took a deep breath and lifted the flap. *Dear Joan Violin.* It was from Colin. After all this time — she hadn't seen or heard from him since she'd absented herself from the orchestra. She kicked off her shoes and leaned back on the bed, smiling when she remembered how he'd made her laugh.

I don't suppose for a minute you remember me, your old chum Colin Cello? You saved me from what would have been certain death by whispering the correct way to address SIR Ralph Myers. So, as I am forever in your debt, I decided to hunt you down. The last I heard about you, three years or so ago, was that you had a horrid bout of gastroenteritis after which you never returned to the Hall. I do hope you've made a full recovery?

I am still a slave to my first love, the muse of music. But I longed to cut a dash in uniform, so joined the RAF and was immediately assigned to their very own Symphony Orchestra. Somehow, I managed to talk them round to allowing me to fly a plane or two instead of playing it safe with the cello, so I've ratcheted up quite a few hours on the wing.

Perhaps you'd agree to meet up with me for a bit of a chinwag? I expect you're chomping at the bit to find out how and why I traced you. I know I would be. Well, all can be revealed Saturday next, 6:30 p.m., outside the Empire in Leicester Square.
Yours,
Colin

Closing her eyes, Joan thought about Colin. He'd been very entertaining, young and gawky, never afraid to poke fun at himself and everyone else. His face had been so fresh and unlined, he couldn't have shaved more than once or twice a week at the most. She found it hard to imagine a grittier-faced Colin, stubble on his chin and cheeks. During one rehearsal, she'd turned to see him in a rapture, his eyes closed, head waggling from side to side like a puppy listening for the return of his master. She remembered thinking the music must be ingrained in him, living and moving with his every heartbeat. She almost came a cropper then, when his crossed eyes sprang open and his jaw, jutting towards her, pulled his bottom lip up to his nose. He could have won a Cornish gurning competition.

It hadn't all been fun, though, had it? She squirmed when the look of disillusion on Colin's face forced its way past the good memories to the forefront of her mind. He'd known about her and Ralph. Everyone at the Hall must have; she'd been as spectacularly inept at hiding it as she had been at hiding Cyril from the women on the bridge. So, whatever did he want from her now? Folding the

270

letter, she stared at where the smoky sky beyond the blackouts would be camouflaging night-fighters and bombers.

From downstairs came the low grumble of the wooden shelter being shifted into position. Perhaps she should give Hazel a hand; make sure she and Ivy felt safe. It would be interesting to see them lying side by side under their timber canopy, but she lay still and thought about what Colin could want from her now. Bribery, or extortion maybe. But she couldn't imagine the boyish Colin being devious or underhand in any way, even if he was older and wiser now. No, Colin was as readable as a lilting line of music so it was puzzling for her to imagine what he wanted to talk to her about.

A tap on the door, followed by a sturdy hand holding a bottle of sherry. 'A bit of what you fancy?'

Joan threw the letters onto her bedside table. 'Come in, Alice. Where did you get that?'

'Hazel,' she said, placing two minute glasses next to the bottle on the floor and bouncing down on the bed. 'She wanted us to have a drop to say thanks very much for helping, but you hotfooted it upstairs with your secret treasure.'

'Two letters.' Joan tried to sound offhand. 'Hardly a secret. *Or* a treasure.' She inspected the bottle of ruby liquid in the light from the weak bulb. There were a fair few fingers left in it. 'Wonder where she keeps getting this stuff from.'

Alice shrugged. 'No idea. How many times has she said this is the last bottle? Then she finds another one half-full at the back of a cupboard.' Pouring two glasses, she handed one to Joan.

271

'Here's to secrets,' she said. 'And I reckon you has some of those.'

'And I *think* . . .' Joan touched the tip of Alice's nose '. . . you've got a long one of *these*!' Knocking back the sweet, syrupy tipple and filling her glass again, she went on, 'Anyway, don't count on anything mysterious from me. I'm as unexciting as they come.'

Alice raised her glass to her mouth, wet her lips with sherry and licked them. 'Who's the letter from, then?'

'Mother,' Joan said, enjoying the tingling as the alcohol coated her mouth and throat.

'I knows about *that* one. The *other*, with no return sender on the back.'

'Oh.' Joan lingered over the word. 'That one. Nobody important, just the Prince of Wales.'

'Give over. Even I know there's no Prince of Wales. More than likely it's from someone you met at the Prince of Wales. The one in Pimlico that smells of dogs' ends.' They laughed at this until they choked and when one of them stopped, the other took over.

Calming down enough to refill their glasses Alice said, 'Tell us then. What is it you're hiding? I know there's something you doesn't let on about.'

Joan refused to answer. She preferred it when they were being silly.

'I gots something I hide, too,' Alice said. 'Well, not *hide*, exactly. Something that's hard to talk about because of the shame. I tried to tell you a couple of times, but I never got very far.'

'Did you?' Joan asked. She had no recollection of Alice ever attempting to relate anything as traumatic as the experiences she herself had been through.

Alice nodded. 'I think you was busy worrying about that horrible old bugger Cyril.'

Or Ralph, Joan thought. Or Mother. But she couldn't imagine what sort of secret Alice could be harbouring, and was intrigued. Perhaps she'd forgotten to get the chickens in one evening, or had lapped the cream from the top of the milk while everyone else was busy. From the corner of her eye she watched Alice, who was concentrating on the way the last of her sherry clung to the sides of the glass when she swirled it around. Months ago she'd realised that the patronising way she'd initially thought about Alice was inaccurate and unfair, and she didn't want to start the habit again. 'Any more of that left?' she asked, holding her glass out.

'Plenty,' Alice said. 'I'll have a top-up, too.'

'Go on, then. I'm listening now. Tell me.'

'And will you go after me?'

Joan considered and decided she would gauge her response and how much she would or wouldn't tell according to the gravity of Alice's confession.

Alice shook her head, impatient to get started. 'It don't matter one way or another if you does or you don't. That's up to you. I'll tell you anyway.' She took a swig of sherry, a couple of deep breaths, then she began.

'I were an ARP Warden back home and right proud of it. One of the youngest in Gloucestershire, maybe the whole country.' Alice hesitated and ran her finger around the rim of her glass until it played a high, whining note. 'And then because

273

my pa and his friend drunk too much and did a wrong thing, I wrongly thought I was in my rights to do a wrong thing, too and it led to me neglecting my duties.'

Joan frowned and wondered how bad the wrong things could have been.

'I mean because of what I did, or didn't do, people almost died.' She lowered her head and her curls hung over her face. Joan pushed them aside and she could see that Alice's face was burning.

'After the whole sorry mess were finished and done, I suppose you could say I were made to feel so ashamed that I come to London to get away from the stares and wagging tongues.'

Joan looked into the bottom of her own glass. 'I can't imagine you doing anything shameful, Alice.'

'Well, you have to remember. This weren't London, this were Old Sodbury where nothing much good or bad ever happens.'

They were quiet for a moment. Alice sighed, her broad shoulders hitching up and back down. 'It all involved a boy. Now I know he weren't worth my time. After the incident that ended so badly, he never come near me again. But . . .' Alice seemed to brighten. 'The whole thing were a good lesson for me and it's an old one. Two wrongs don't make a right. Just because someone done something bad don't mean you have to follow their lead.' She nodded to emphasise each syllable she spoke. 'I, for one, am determined never to get into the situation again whereby I blame others for what I do. I will make up my own mind about what's right and what's wrong.'

'But you still go back to visit everyone in Old Sodbury?' The concept bemused Joan. 'How could you?'

Alice shrugged. 'It's hard when I'm there, the way they go on about what I did when all the time they've got faults of their own. But they *are* my family. I couldn't let them go altogether.'

The all-clear had sounded an hour or so ago. The sherry bottle was empty and the room was cold and still, icy air clinging to Joan's nostrils as she breathed in. They sat quietly side by side on the bed until Joan took Alice's hand in hers. *So we're all the same*, she thought. *But in so many different ways.*

'It's your turn now,' Alice said. 'Will you tell?'

Joan started at the beginning and didn't leave anything out.

★ ★ ★

It wasn't until the last minute that Joan decided she would meet Colin. He was waiting outside the Empire, stamping his gleaming shoes up and down, blowing into his thick gloves and looking every bit as debonair in his uniform as she had hoped he would. He shook her hand with both of his and skimmed her cheek with his lips. She'd been right to imagine he would look older; his youthful face was more accustomed to a razor now and the lines around his eyes and mouth didn't disappear when he wasn't smiling.

'In here.' He guided her into a lively pub. 'Still a cordial and tonic?' he asked when they'd managed to find a forgotten table and two stools.

275

She laughed aloud, remembering the trip to the pub after their first rehearsal. 'Replace the cordial with gin this time, won't you please?'

When Colin returned with the drinks, Joan crossed her legs and waited for him to launch into his reason for getting in touch with her. He was as charming and animated as ever, talking about news from the orchestra, his eyes bulging to emphasise scandal, narrowing when he whispered behind his hand about some intrigue or another. Edward and Eileen were engaged to be married and had asked Colin to be best man. 'I'll have to stay off the sauce until after the speech,' he said, tongue lolling, eyes flickering. 'Don't want to embarrass them too much.' He sat up and rubbed his chin, looking thoughtful. 'Or do I?' He burst into laughter. 'Well, Joan Violin,' he went on, 'do you want to know why I was so desperate to find you?'

'Yes, please,' Joan said, sipping her drink. 'I'm curious.'

He told her he'd often wondered how she was, what she was doing and whether she still played the violin. 'Your touch was sublime,' he said. 'Other-worldly.'

Joan was surprised but didn't comment.

'I asked the office at the Hall and eventually they gave me your home address. Your mother told me you were working in construction and living in a ladies' hostel. So I wrote to you there. Do you mind awfully, Joan dear, that I ran myself ragged to find you?' Colin batted his eyelashes and went to lay his head on her shoulder. Joan pulled away from him and he let out a sigh that reminded her of a fawning Romeo in the balcony scene.

'But why, Colin?' She remained business-like.

'Do you still play?' he asked.

Joan shook her head with rigid decisiveness.

'Would you again?'

Joan looked him in the eye and said, 'No.'

'Not even for me?' Colin lowered his eyes and feigned bashfulness.

'I've made up my mind,' Joan said. 'And I don't intend to change it. But why are you asking? Unless Mother's put you up to it.'

'No mother involved,' Colin said, sitting back. 'Just me.'

He went on to tell her he had been trying to organise a small jazz combo he had great hopes for and wanted to concentrate his efforts on when the war ended, as he was sure it would any day now. He thought she would suit the set-up perfectly. If she wanted to come along to his mum's house next time he was on leave, they could listen to some of the music he hoped to play and discuss the offer further. Perhaps join him and one or two others on a couple of numbers. Reaching into his pocket, he produced a card on which was printed an address under the heading *Colin's Kats*.

Joan wouldn't take it from him until she sensed he was about to cause a scene, then threw it into the bottom of her bag. She downed her drink and stood to leave. 'Thank you for thinking of me, Colin. But I won't change my mind.'

'As stubborn as ever,' Colin said, his open face hard with disappointment. 'And still intent on cutting off your nose to spite your face.'

The audacity of the remark stung. 'I'll say good-bye,' Joan said, 'before I slap you.'

277

It rankled with Joan the number of times Colin and their conversation came to mind, given that she was so sure of her decision. A whistle off in the distance on the other side of the bridge would make her think of middle C, and that would lead to music, to Colin's compliments, to the group she'd been invited to join. When she had a few moments rest in between lifts with the crane, she wondered about the tunes the trio might play, and what their audience might be like.

Another conundrum was what she would do when the bridge was finished. More of the same, somewhere else? She didn't think so; it wasn't exactly a calling for her like it seemed to have become for Evelyn. Most often, she wondered whether Colin would really have her, if it ever came to it. If her playing was indeed inspired, as he'd intimated.

★ ★ ★

Rain had been scarce during March, until one Thursday when it persisted in falling in sheets. Joan and Alice had planned an outing uptown to a tea dance but the day-long downpour put paid to it. Kicking around in Joan's room for something to do, Alice reached under the bed and dragged out the violin case. 'Play it,' she said.

'Oh, *Alice* . . . ' Joan wished she'd understand. 'We've been through this, haven't we?'

'Alright, then I will.'

'Be my guest.' Joan laughed as Alice opened the case and wedged the voluptuous piece of wood under her chin.

Raising the bow, she scratched it along the

278

strings with all the weight of her hefty hands. 'I can makes it sing,' she said.

'Put it back,' Joan ordered.

Alice pranced around the room, scraping and grating out a caterwauling noise.

'You'll ruin it.' Joan grabbed at Alice as she turned her back.

'What do you care?' Alice said.

'That's not how you do it.' Joan plucked the instrument from Alice and cradled it into her neck. In her hand, the bow stroked and caressed the strings.

Alice smiled at her and nodded. 'Don't stop now,' she whispered.

No, Joan thought, *I won't.* She could not believe how familiar and reassuring the instrument felt in her hands and she realised, with a lurch, how much she had missed playing.

There was a knock on the door. 'Oh, please come down,' said Hazel. 'Mummy's been longing to hear you play for ages.'

13
April — July 1944

Evelyn

The blanched pallor of Dad's face stopped Evelyn short in the doorway. In his lap he turned over a letter, then turned it over again, leaving the imprint of his clammy fingers on the pale, flimsy envelope. 'It's for Sylvie,' he mouthed in a flat whisper that sounded as if all the life had been wrung out of it. 'From Italy.' He shook his head. 'But not Alec's writing.'

'Sorry we're late,' Sylvie shouted from the hallway. 'Anything special happening round here? It'd make a change.'

Their eyes locked, Dad and Evelyn silently begged each other to take charge, to know what to say when they gave the unwelcome and unwanted news, as it couldn't be anything else. But neither of them made a move. At least, Evelyn thought, it's not an envelope edged in black like the one that had arrived last August.

She'd thought that letter from Alec, addressed to all of them, must have been a mistake. Whose death would Alec have been notifying them about? But a letter about a death it was. And so they learned that Malcolm Russell Macoun had been killed on the 12th of September 1943 on the island of Sicily. Alec had thought it right and proper that he should inform the three of them who would, by extension, have become part of Malcolm's family in due course.

They sat together in the kitchen, a dagger of summer sun slicing through the teapot in the middle of the table and cried for Alec's cousin. One final letter from Malcolm, dated the end of July, arrived almost immediately after Alec's. His flippant commentary on what sounded a hot, dusty, hungry conflict was painful to read. Evelyn wondered how he could compare heat exhaustion to all those times he'd had a few too many in the dear old Ship and Shovell. Or how pushing forward hour by hour towards the Bernhardt Line made him feel like a frontiersman trailblazing his way across Canada.

She tried to remember him like that, optimistic and buoyant, jollying the other men along. There were times, though, when she couldn't stop herself imagining him taking the fire that killed him, his face shocked and betrayed, momentarily aged in the instant before death.

There were no more letters after that and she missed them. She missed him being alive, a presence somewhere in the world. And the world would miss out, too, on everything that he could have brought to it.

A very small parcel had arrived that November. Inside was a note from Malcolm's mother in Saskatchewan. As she thought they must have been close, she wanted Evelyn to have Malcolm's ID tag. She would keep the King James Bible he had in his pocket when he died a hero, in his mother's eyes. So despite their chat before he left, Malcolm had been carrying a flame for her all through the Italian campaign. Evelyn had picked up the round, battered, dirt-red disc by its chain and laid it with care in the palm of her hand. The Service Number L124824 was pressed along the top; PREB — for Presbyterian, she supposed — underneath his name; CDN at the bottom. All that it had meant to be Malcolm reduced to those four lines of embossed characters.

Leaving a week or two to pass, Evelyn wrote back to Malcolm's mother telling her what a lovely son she'd had. Evelyn said he'd been a gentleman who danced beautifully and kept everyone entertained with his stories and breezy outlook on life. And although she couldn't recall everything they'd talked about the last time she'd seen Malcolm in London, she told Mrs Macoun that her son had said he was looking forward to getting into the thick of things at last and that he loved his mother very much. There was no harm in that now.

But it did seem wrong to let Malcolm's mother believe they'd been planning a future together, so she finished by saying she'd been fond of Malcolm but they had never made promises to each other and she would understand if, on that basis, Mrs Macoun would like the ID tag back. When there was no reply, Evelyn wrapped the tag in tissue paper and put it in a little box alongside a marcasite brooch that had belonged to her mother.

Now it took Sylvie pushing her way into the sitting room to horrify Dad and Evelyn out of their immobility, but it was too late to hide the letter from view or to prepare Sylvie with an arm to lean on. She stared down at Dad's lap, a puzzled look on her face.

'Sylvie. Love,' Dad said, his lips pale and trembling. 'I think . . .'

Her eyes wide, Sylvie reached out for the envelope.

'Sit down first,' Evelyn said. 'Here. With me on the couch.'

'Or here,' Dad said, levering himself out of his chair.

Sylvie shook her head, raking her hands through her hair. 'He's not dead,' she said. Evelyn saw her sister's chest rise and fall rapidly beneath her blouse. 'I'd know if he was dead and he's not. Nothing else matters. Does it?' She looked up at Dad, a small girl seeking the comfort of rock-solid reassurance.

'That's it, my love,' Dad said.

Evelyn wasn't so sure and hated herself for thinking it, but some of the injured and disfigured men coming home must wish they had been killed; it would have been kinder on them if they had. And on the people who loved them, who had to see and deal with them every day in their dreadful, misshapen states.

The air was heavy and breathless, waiting for the news. A sparrow swooped past the window but didn't make a sound; the pounding pulse in Evelyn's ears muffled the ticking of the clock.

As Sylvie aimed her nail under the corner of the envelope, Evelyn clung to her arm.

'No. No, no.' Sylvie's sobs splintered the hush. She sank to her knees, an empty sack of grief. Evelyn went down with her. 'Alec. No.' She beat

283

her fists on the floor, dormant dust rising from the rug. 'I can't bear it.'

Picking up the letter from where Sylvie had dropped it, Evelyn read it, then handed it to Dad. She heard the words as he read them in a whisper.

23rd May 1944

Dear Miss Draper,

Your intended fiancé, Corporal Alexander Gordon Buchan L124830 Saskatoon Light Infantry (M.G.) R.C.I.C., requested that I write to inform you that he has sustained a serious facial wound in action in the Battle for Liri Valley. After immediate treatment at the Fifth Field Hospital, he has been transferred to the No. 1 Canadian General Hospital here in Andria, Italy.

Corporal Buchan has asked me to tell you that he is otherwise well and in good spirits and will write to you himself when is able. He sends you his love.

Yours sincerely,

Edna Kendall (Nursing Sister R.C.A.M.C.)

'His face,' Sylvie said, her hands playing with the contours of her nose and cheeks, forehead and ears.

Dad leaned into his daughters who were huddled together on the floor. They gripped his legs until the shadows across the yard merged together into nightfall and Evelyn thought she must take charge of tea and food.

Towards dawn, Sylvie fell into a twitching, agitated sleep, Evelyn's arm pinned underneath her.

It had been a long, draining night with Sylvie vacillating wildly between panic and resilience. She paced the room, tormenting herself with thoughts of the hell he must have gone through and what he was experiencing now, this very minute, with Sylvie thousands of miles away from where she should be. At his side. How long had he waited for help? Who had been with him when it happened? The unanswered questions were endless.

Then she'd drop into a chair and reproach herself for not keeping calm. 'Get a grip on yourself, Sylvie,' she'd say. 'Isn't that right, Evelyn? You tell me.'

'It's alright,' Evelyn said. 'Don't worry now. You have a right to be upset.'

Clenching her jaw, Sylvie shook her head. 'You were right before, don't you remember? When Alec was sent away and you said I should try to be the woman he fell for. Besides, am I the only one? No. Not by a long shot. Any woman with a whole fiancé or husband at the end of this war will be the odd one out.'

Then one of them would sniffle or reread the letter, and the cycle would start again.

They picked at a late tea that Evelyn had cobbled together, but none of them could do much more than push it around on their plates.

Desperate to let Sylvie sleep, Evelyn eased her arm from under her sister's weight and folded herself out of bed. She wanted to be washed and dressed with breakfast on the go, ready to help in any way she could before Sylvie woke and reality hit her. And she'd have to scribble and post a quick note to Stan to let him know why she wouldn't be able to meet him for a while. She looked down at Sylvie for a couple of minutes, listening to the whistle of her breathing through swollen nasal passages, tucked the covers around her and crept from the room.

Sylvie seemed to feel better than she looked when she came downstairs with sore eyes set in a pale face. Getting her to eat was difficult; it wasn't that she didn't want the porridge, she said, but it seemed to stick in her throat like concrete and make her gag. Fishing around in his bowl, Dad plopped his lump of jam onto Sylvie's oats, and then she managed the rest.

'Ready?' Sylvie said.

'For what?' Evelyn was at the pantry door, wondering what to cook for dinner.

'Work,' Sylvie said, snubbing her nose with a long wipe of her hand.

'Now then,' Dad said. 'I'm not sure that's a good idea. They'll understand you staying off today. Evelyn won't go in either, will you, love?'

'Of course I won't. Not until Alec writes himself and we know a bit — '

'I can't,' Sylvie said. She was gripping the back of a chair, her knuckles strained and white. 'Don't want to. The letter could take ages. Come on, let's go.'

'Dad?' Evelyn deferred the decision.

Unshaven as yet, Dad's whiskers stood grey and patchy on the loose skin of his chin and neck. He hadn't put on a tie and his braces hung in limp loops at his sides. 'Best you carry on,' he said. 'Do what you have to do. I'll be here waiting for the post.'

286

Sylvie headed straight for Jim's office to tell him why she might not be at her best today, and Evelyn went to prepare for her gang who were inching their way towards the south pier. Gwen was there before her, clapping the previous day's grime out of her gauntlets, minute particles dancing in the sunlight.

'Morning,' Gwen said, waving a hand that boasted white-tipped nails. 'I can't believe the spring we're having.' She breathed deeply, then coughed as the powdery dirt hit the back of her throat. 'Shall I light one for you?' she said, opening her tin of tobacco.

Evelyn nodded. For months on end Gwen had been living for the spring. Building herself up and counting down the days until George would take her to Wales. That time had finally arrived; George was due home on leave and had promised to take Gwen to visit their kids. Evelyn hadn't seen her happier or healthier. A hopeful spring for one; a time of despair for another. Evelyn sat cross-legged on the deck of what was left of the temporary bridge and told Gwen about Alec.

'It's awful,' Evelyn said, tapping ash between the beams beneath her. 'Not knowing's the worst. Bugger, I wish I had a shilling for every time I've heard someone say that since this bloody war started.'

'I'm ever so sorry for Sylvie,' Gwen said. 'I'll look her out during the day and have a word with her. She's a good girl, one of the best.'

'She doesn't deserve this,' Evelyn said, releasing the anger she'd felt since yesterday through

287

snarled lips.

'No one does,' Gwen said. 'But I think you're wrong about one thing. Knowing can be the worst that happens. There ain't no hope after that.'

Determined to keep herself occupied, Sylvie put her name forward for any overtime going and Evelyn, wanting to stay close to her sister, did the same. Whether by instinct or design it was a clever move; Sylvie slept at night and ate at mealtimes and, although she was doing little else, she was taking care of the basics. She didn't miss a day's work until the letter she'd been waiting for arrived five days later.

This time Dad was waiting for them at the bottom of the road, shifting from one hip to the other to give his legs a rest. He waved the envelope above his head when they turned the corner and Sylvie ran towards him and opened it then and there, with a tabby sunning itself on the pavement and a breeze stirring the leaves on the silver birch. Sylvie held the letter at an angle so Dad and Evelyn could read over her shoulder.

28th May 1944

My dearest Sylvie,

I am so sorry if the letter from Nurse Kendall was a shock. I did not mean to alarm you in any way, but all casualties are asked if there is anyone other than their NOK they think should be informed of the incident that has taken place and of course, there was you, my lovely.

A bullet skimmed my cheek and eye, but the area has been patched and stitched by

288

a very clever, careful doctor. I'm not sure if he used blanket, back or cross-stitch but my guess is that he used a combination of all three. I haven't seen the wound as yet, but I'm sure I'm not as pretty as I was, so am beside myself with worry that you will no longer want to be Mrs Alec Buchan. I promise that if you will still have me, I will stay on your left side for as much of our life as possible so you do not have to be repulsed by the change in my appearance.

The fact of the matter is, darling Sylvie, that I have been very lucky. The doctor said another fraction of an inch and I would have been missing my brain as well. That, I told him, would have been difficult as there would have had to be a brain in my thick skull to begin with.

I have not been told where I will be sent next and don't think I will be until I get there. I will keep you informed as best I can, but the news will have to be patchy for obvious reasons.

My thoughts of you are what keep me going.

Give my love to Evelyn and your dad. Take care of each other.

Your Alec X

Sylvie's worn, pallid skin turned to the colour of curds.

'God help us,' Dad said, winding his arm around Sylvie and guiding her home. 'That poor man.'

Revived somewhat by the sweet, weak tea Evelyn made, Sylvie sat under a blanket on Dad's easy chair, the letter next to her. 'I've made up my mind, we're going tomorrow,' Sylvie said, emphasising each word with a jab of her index finger. 'First thing.'

'We can't go to Italy,' Evelyn said with gentle patience, presuming that's where Sylvie meant.

For a moment, Sylvie hesitated then chuckled, the first suggestion of a smile since Nurse Kendall's letter had come. 'I know that, you daft mare,' she said. 'We're going to Canada House.'

★ ★ ★

They linked arms, weaving in and out of the crowds leaving the Tube at Piccadilly Circus. Sylvie had wanted to make an effort with her hair and lipstick that morning and asked Evelyn to do the same so they didn't let Alec down. Wearing heels and a bit of costume jewellery, they looked like any other pair of girls making their way through familiar territory to jobs in an office. But to Evelyn, the West End seemed like a foreign country, even though it had only been a matter of weeks since she and Sylvie last visited a dance hall. Evelyn wondered what everyone could be doing that was so important.

What had she used to do that occupied her mind so fully before this happened to a loved one in her own family? Of course Alec wasn't that yet, but it seemed inevitable he would become so.

They walked straight down the Haymarket towards Trafalgar Square, and it hurt Evelyn to know they were walking parallel to Regent Street where the WES was located, one of the places she'd hurried to, absorbed, before this crisis. She remembered Cynthia Blackwood and how she had made mastering engineering sound easy and within reach for any woman who showed an interest. But, for Evelyn, it seemed at times as if the obstacles were insurmountable.

As they approached Canada House along the bottom end of Cockspur Street, they could see a queue of about thirty people, mostly young women, snaking along the pavement from the steps leading to the heavy, closed doors. Marching past them, Sylvie asked the first girl in line, a toddler clutching her hand, what time the doors opened. The woman shifted the child's fist to the hem of her coat, checked her watch and said, 'Nine. Ten minutes or so to go.'

Sylvie stood where she was and Evelyn was afraid she would cause a scene, saying her need was greater than this young mother's. But looking down at the boy rubbing his eyes and leaning against his mum's leg, Sylvie seemed to come to.

'There's nothing we can do, Sylvie,' Evelyn said. 'Except join the back of the queue and wait like everyone else. Let's go now, before it gets any longer.'

Trailing behind, Sylvie joined her sister at the tail end of the row. She leaned back against the warm bricks of the building, its boarded windows flat and lifeless, and closed her eyes.

Evelyn nodded to a well-rounded girl who joined the queue behind them. The girl smiled back, a crooked eye tooth catching on her upper lip. The top part of her brown curly hair was caught up in one clip, the underneath length in another at the nape of her neck; it looked very fetching and showed off the young woman's round cheeks and pale neck.

'Ain't it annoying?' she said, looking rather cheerful and far from fed up. 'All this waiting around.'

'We had no idea we'd have to queue,' Evelyn said.

'Oh. You always have to queue here.' The girl sounded a bit like Gwen. Definitely from the East End.

'Always? You must be an old hand. Why ever do you have to keep coming back?'

'Trying to find out when I can get to Canada. That's what all the wives are doing.' She swept her dimpled hand in the general direction of the rank and file of waiting women. 'So, which of you is married to a Canuck? Or is it both of you?'

'Neither.' Evelyn shook her head. 'My sister's been told her Canadian boyfriend's been injured in Italy. She wants more information.'

The girl's chubby cheeks slackened a bit. 'That's a shame.' She nodded to the impenetrable facade of the building. 'But they only deal with wives.'

'Really?' Sylvie opened her eyes. 'But I'll be his fiancée soon.'

'Don't matter, I'm afraid,' the girl said, twirling the gold band on her finger. 'They can't offer much help unless it's official.' She turned her attention to a young woman who'd come up behind her. They exchanged a few words, then broke out into peals of laughter.

'What do you want to do?' Evelyn asked. Perhaps it would be better to leave now and save Sylvie

292

the humiliation of standing here for hours, only to be turned away because her lack of marital status rendered her officially insignificant. On the other hand, the podgy girl might not have got her facts right. Or maybe the bureaucracy had changed to meet the dynamic needs of the situation.

Sylvie scanned the street, as if the right answer would magically appear along it. 'What do you think would be best?'

'Let's wait,' Evelyn said. 'You'll never know unless you ask.'

They found themselves in and out of the sun at intervals as the line moved forward at a creeping pace. The first woman in line passed them with her boy in her arms, his head lolling on his mother's shoulder. In her hand she clutched an authoritative buff envelope.

'I am a stupid bint,' Sylvie said, kicking the pavement. 'Daft and stupid.'

The two gossiping women behind looked down at Sylvie's foot, then up at her face. Evelyn smiled at them and they turned back to each other.

'Whatever do you mean?' Evelyn lowered her voice, hoping Sylvie would follow her lead.

'He asked me. He wanted to fix something up in a hurry before he went away but I said no.'

'Didn't you think enough of him?' Evelyn asked. 'I mean, were you still not sure? You had us all fooled if . . .'

Looking maddened, Sylvie ran her fingers over her eyebrows, roughly brushing them into place. 'I wasn't fooling anyone,' she said. 'I think more of Alec than I ever imagined possible. But I told him I wanted to wait until he came back to do things

293

properly.' She was choking up and Evelyn fished a hanky from her pocket. 'Not for the dress, or the cake or the toast and speeches. Not for the ring or the honeymoon. For Dad.'

Evelyn understood. Dad would have agonised about the possible reason for a quick wedding, and when that anxiety was quashed he would have fretted that Sylvie wouldn't have the 'do' Mum would have insisted on. Groaning, she pulled Sylvie towards her and kissed her cheek.

'Now more than anything I wish I was Alec's wife,' Sylvie said. 'Mrs Alexander Gordon Buchan. But we are engaged,' she added, her eyes widening. 'Informally.'

'Alec's fiancée, then.' Evelyn nodded. 'That sounds lovely.'

Sylvie managed a smile. 'Yes it does, doesn't it? And I'd like you to be my bridesmaid.'

'Only if I can have a new frock,' Evelyn said.

Sympathy was all the administrator behind the counter could offer Sylvie. He couldn't say when Alec might be shipped out or to where, although it was unlikely he'd be sent straight back to Canada at this stage. No further information regarding Alec's injury was known, and the best thing Sylvie could do was write to him in Andria.

'Of course I'll write to him,' Sylvie told the man, whose moustache followed the sad, downward contours of his mouth. 'But can't I . . . Oh, I don't know . . . go to him?'

'I'm afraid,' he said, 'that even if by some miracle I could arrange that, your fiancé would be very angry with me for having done so.' Not looking down, he played with the papers in front of him.

294

'I'm sure you agree.'

Sylvie nodded.

'Go home and write a letter,' he said. 'Unless there's something else I can do for you?'

It was too late for dinner, too early for tea when they walked back the way they'd come that morning. Evelyn was worried because they hadn't eaten since breakfast, but Sylvie didn't want to stop; she wanted to get home and start a letter to Alec.

★ ★ ★

The changing room was a hot, stuffy jostle. A few women stopped and spoke softly to Sylvie, including Olive who lowered her voice to a muted honk and told her to keep her end up. Hanging her things on a hook, Evelyn was surprised to see Gwen's navy coat and worn satchel drooping off their usual peg. She spun around, squinting over and through the women in various states of dress and undress, but couldn't see Gwen anywhere, which made sense, as Gwen was on her way to Wales. Would probably be there by now, cuddled up with George and the kids. But she wouldn't have gone far without her coat. And Evelyn knew she hadn't bought herself anything new to go away in; every penny and ration coupon was spent on treats for Will and Ruth.

Evelyn pushed her way through to the fresh air, across the decks and over to the temporary bridge. From a distance, she could make out a figure waiting at her station, hands deep in pockets, sparks of sunlight glinting on spectacle lenses.

'How are you, Gwen?' Evelyn asked, hoping for

an explanation.

'Can I get started?' Gwen asked.

'Let's give it a minute.' Evelyn didn't want to let Gwen loose with a flame in her agitated state. 'Perhaps we'll wait for the others.'

Gwen shrugged.

'Sorry if I've got the days muddled,' Evelyn said. 'But I didn't expect to see you here.'

Sitting on the edge of a waiting beam, Gwen rested her arms on her knees and examined her work boots. When she spoke, the effort she made to sound offhand was pitiful. 'Oh. Well, George wrote that his leave was cancelled. Same for everyone.'

'That's a disappointment,' Evelyn said. 'Still, I suppose there's a good reason for it.'

'Must be,' Gwen said, looking at Evelyn. 'So you're stuck with me again, I'm afraid.'

Evelyn started her daily inspection of the equipment. 'Good job, too,' she said. 'We'd never get this lot done without you.'

'I'm ready whenever you are,' Gwen said, plucking her hands from her pockets and nestling them straight into the waiting gauntlets. Two of her nails, Evelyn saw, were bitten to the quick.

★ ★ ★

A piece of good news, at last. Rome was taken by the Allies and everyone's step seemed lighter, shoulders less hunched, eyes livelier. Sylvie wondered how Alec would be feeling, confined to a hospital bed when he should have been sharing in the victory. He was part of the win, Evelyn told

296

her, as was Malcolm and all the others who'd been prevented from physically being part of the city's overthrow. And she imagined barred trattorias and vibrant oleanders along dusty Italian roads, strewn with broken uniformed bodies.

Eating breakfast two days later while wind and rain assaulted the windows, John Snagge read a special bulletin on the BBC Home Service. Dad turned up the volume with one hand, shushing his daughters with the other. 'D-Day,' Snagge said, 'has come.' Allied armies were landing on the northern coast of France.

The bridge was buzzing. Olive said it was all over and was demanding everyone down tools to celebrate. Gwen squeezed Evelyn's arm and said, 'You were right. There *was* a good reason to cancel leave.' The gaffer did his best to keep the job going, saying this was all the more reason to stick to their schedule. But he sounded a klaxon and as many people as possible gathered in and around his hut to listen to broadcasts by the king, calling for prayer, and Churchill, giving the numbers. Upwards of four thousand ships, plus several thousand smaller vessels. Eleven thousand first-line aircraft. Reports of everything going to plan. And *what* a plan! His voice rose to the occasion. Fighting proceeding at various points. A very valuable first step. But he had a warning: this was no indication of what might be the course of the battle in the next days and weeks. A most serious time was being entered upon.

Both statements were long, and straining to hear in the middle of the jostling crowd, Evelyn was elbowed in the back, her shin scraped by the toe of a boot. Next, she picked up parts of a statement read out by a drawling Eisenhower.

'People of Western Europe. A landing was made this morning on the coast of France by troops of the Allied Expeditionary Force. This landing is part of the concerted United Nations' plan for the liberation of Europe, made in conjunction with our great Russian allies. I have this message for all of you: although the initial assault may not have been made in your own country, the hour of your liberation is approaching ... This landing is but the opening phase of the campaign in Western Europe. Great battles lie ahead. I call upon all who love freedom to stand with us. Keep your faith staunch. Our arms are resolute. Together we shall achieve victory.'

The drizzle dribbling down the back of her neck, a welding iron that wouldn't flame, boiled parsnips for dinner in the canteen again, the WES, the men who got all the best jobs, the filthy river. None of that seemed so awful now if it really was coming to an end. It hardly seemed possible and Evelyn didn't want to get carried away, but perhaps this once, Olive was right.

At knocking-off time, Stan jumped out at her from behind the works entrance, his arms wide and a beckoning look on his face. The surprise caused Evelyn's hands to flutter to her chest, but her next reaction was to throw herself at him and bask in the solidness of his arms, the traces of tobacco and engine oil on his skin, the tickle on her ear when he whispered that he had missed seeing her. She drew back and took his cool face between her hands. 'I've missed you, too, Stanley Philip Richardson.'

And at that moment she could honestly tell herself that she had.

'What news!' Stan said, pulling on her sleeve. 'Come on, shall we get a drink?'

Someone on the bridge had suggested that same thing and a whole crowd, with the exception of Sylvie who wanted to go home, sit with Dad and fill Alec in on the day, was meeting at the pub.

For a split second, Stan's face dropped when she explained where she was heading then it lifted again when she insisted he join her. Tucking her arm under his, he shone with pride as he escorted her along the busy pavement.

★ ★ ★

Kids had to be dragged off the streets by their mothers when they heard the muffled drone of an approaching doodlebug. Jerry's retaliation for D-Day sounded like a motorcycle under water and was, Dad read aloud from his paper, the size of a spitfire, with short, squat wings, a venomous front end, flame for a tail. And no pilot; a bomb with a motor attached. They travelled singly, in pairs, in huge black clouds like furious bees. As long as you could hear them you were alright, but when the buzz stopped the wicked things glided down and exploded on the surface of the ground, the blast rippling out six hundred yards in every direction from where they landed, causing devastation.

If the guards in their chapel across from Buckingham Palace couldn't save themselves from a buzz bomb, then there was nothing for the rest of them but to run for shelter or drop to the ground, hands covering their heads. Many a blouse was ruined or shoes scuffed. One of Evelyn's favourite jackets, a deep burgundy with grey velvet trim, sustained a serious oil stain right below the shoulder. As luck would have it, an ostentatious brooch hid the damage to that item; others weren't so fortunate. They'd been right, Winnie, Ike and King George; it wasn't over yet. Olive got it wrong. And the elation that had bolstered them on D-Day petered out with the incoming whirr of the dreaded V-1s.

★ ★ ★

One by one the white crescent moons on Gwen's nails disappeared; the old, fragile wounds around her cuticles opening up easily. Her skin and hair looked brittle and rough; she was troubled and preoccupied. But, like Sylvie, she didn't miss a day's work.

'Any news on George's leave yet?' Evelyn asked, handing a cup of tea to Gwen during their morning break. She watched Gwen's eyes narrow and cloud over. Her hand, when she reached for the cup, was shaking with the slightest of tremors.

'Oh, he's been home for a couple of days. Gone back now.'

'Not long enough to visit the kids? That's a shame. Might you go again on your own?'

'Could do I suppose.'

Evelyn thought Gwen would be close to tears, but she looked past that, as if she couldn't find it in herself any longer. There was an unsettling air of resignation about her. 'I'll wait and see for a while.'

'Well,' Evelyn said, groping for something to say that might help. 'At least they're out of here already. Hundreds are on the march again, desperate to get their kids somewhere safe. You must have seen them all making their way to the station. Little mites with their suitcases and masks in their hands.'

'Yeah,' Gwen said, misjudging her cup in the depression of the saucer and sending the whole thing rattling around. 'My kids are so lucky, ain't they? Been out of London for years already. Away from home, miles from Mum and Dad, everything they know. Then there's Marty, Will's pal. Don't suppose you remember me telling you about him? Lost his dad a while back? Then his mum, nan and brothers all went the same way when their house took a packet. I suppose you could say he's lucky as he was helping the butcher for a few bob when the bomb hit. Now he's back with the Gwilts in Wales.'

'I didn't mean it like that,' Evelyn said. 'Forget I said anything.'

'It's just that I'd . . . ' Gwen closed her eyes but it didn't stop her looking exhausted. 'I'd convinced myself George would let the kids come home with us.' Gwen snorted with derision at her own naivety. 'But now . . . '

'Maybe it won't be for much longer,' Evelyn said. 'It can't be. Only yesterday Dad was saying . . . '

Scraping her chair back and pocketing her fags, Gwen said, 'Sorry for going off at you.'

301

Watching her scuttle through the door, Evelyn wondered where she would go to hunker down now. Her old hiding place was gone, built into the new contours of the bridge.

14

August — November 1944

Gwen

For the first time in years George had used his pet name for her — but the moment was blighted by the rigid edge of frustration in his voice. 'Don't be ridiculous, Gwennie,' he'd said — and he was right. She was a ridiculous woman. Idiotic even, her base stupidity an embarrassment. There was no visit to Wales and nor would there be. No snug family reunion. No point, George had said. He didn't need to say anything else, but she knew that what could have been a happy occasion had been tainted and spoiled by her mithering. She'd ruined things yet again. Kids who'd never been sent away, and those like Marty, who'd come home to London, were being evacuated again. Another mass exodus was under way, and here she was pleading with George to allow Will and Ruth to come home. Her foolishness beggared belief.

Silently, resentment in his every move, George filled the coal bunker, trimmed the wicks, washed the windows with newspaper soaked in vinegar, tightened a loose catch on the meat-safe. Then he gathered his things together and clicked the door behind him. A minute later he was back, kissing her face without any other contact between them.

'Everything'll be alright,' he said. 'It'll be over

303

soon.'

She couldn't bring herself to respond. If she had, she would have said something rude like, '*Now* who's being stupid.' This was never going to end, not even when it was over.

It had taken Gwen weeks to make the final decision to sort Johnny's things — and what a terrible waste of time that had been, the way it all turned out. Betty had rolled her sleeves up when Gwen announced she was ready for the big clear-out. 'Good on you, love,' she said. 'Len might be able to find a tin of leftover paint somewhere, and we can freshen up the walls. Take that old rug out the back and pretend it's Hitler. Beat the hell out of it.'

It wouldn't have been possible for her to face the job if she hadn't believed Will and Ruth were on their way home soon; it would have been heart-breaking for them to go straight back into a room filled with things that dumbly shouted their dead brother's name.

Carrying a bucket of water, rags, a cake of carbolic and a scrubbing brush, she and Betty pushed the door open together. A layer of dust, the work of the hit three years ago and the passage of time since, flew up and settled back on the surfaces again, unused to the disturbance. The blackouts were pulled closed, so the room was a uniform grey amongst darker shadows. It smelled, too, of unaired clothes, socks, shoes, sleep, and sticky, finger-marked books. And somewhere underneath it all, the musty sweetness of her kids. All three of them. Pulling a face and wafting a hand in front of her nose, Betty pushed the curtains aside and lifted the sash before Gwen could stop her. Air streamed in and the elusive bouquet slipped out.

To start with, they made three piles: Johnny's things that Will could use; Johnny's things that Gwen would allow herself to keep, one small box of mementoes that would fit neatly in the bottom of the wardrobe; a pile of things to be taken to the WVS that would, Gwen was surprised to realise, include Will and Ruth's clothes and games they'd outgrown.

With half of the room still to sort, the crammed box of keepsakes stood in the middle of the floor. Betty, who had been nattering about everything from her grandchildren to the neighbours, from Len to the Landings on the Riviera, the humid weather, the lovely bit of fish she would fry later, sat on Ruth's bed and shook her head. She pulled the box to her feet and took out a pair of worn socks and an imprint of Johnny's hands, the clear-cut, finely chiselled, undefiled fingerprints preserved in flaking green paint. 'I think these,' Betty said, holding up the threadbare socks, 'will have to go. This, though — ' she pointed to the picture '— can stay.'

Gwen looked into her friend's watery blue eyes, a little cloudier than they used to be, her white eyebrows thick and heavy over the folds of her lids. She was being practical, as always, pointing out what should have been obvious. But her voice was gentle.

'Don't you think so, love?' Betty asked, throwing the socks onto the pile to be handed out to some poor bombed-out kid. Another child wearing her Johnny's socks, wriggling pink, blood-filled toes

305

around in the material or scratching at a blister through the wool. An imperceptible scrap of Johnny's skin, caught in a fibre, might adhere itself to another boy's foot and bond with him, allowing a part of Johnny to grow and mature as should have been his right. For a moment the thought consoled her, but any flake that had once been part of Johnny was dead, and had been for a long time.

'Gwen? What do you say?'

'Sorry, Bet. Yeah, you're right. Let's go through this box again, shall we?'

By the time the room was straightened out, the box held a deflated football, an annual plus a dictionary Johnny had won for good spelling, a note he'd written to Will saying sorry for something insignificant, a pared pencil, a comb harbouring a few strands of light, silky hair, a striped jumper knitted by Betty, the picture of his hands, and another showing the five they used to be as stick people, clown-red smiles dominating their faces.

Plumping his pillows, she'd found a white cotton handkerchief, clean and soft, and pocketed it in her pinny before Betty could see. Pressing the spot where it rested, she felt close to her little boy. She promised herself to keep the square of material, something that Johnny had touched and clutched, close to her heart.

'I've some ribbon in my workbox,' Betty said. 'What colour would you like to hold the lid on? We can get it later.'

'Black,' Gwen said.

'I ain't got black.'

Gwen didn't believe her.

'What was Johnny's favourite colour? Blue,

306

wasn't it?'

'That's right,' Gwen said. 'Royal blue. For Millwall.'

'Lovely,' Betty said. 'I'm sure I've a length of that somewhere.'

They stripped the beds and heaped the sheets ready for the wash. Will would go back into his own bed, but Ruth was too old for her cot with the barred side, so she would sleep in Johnny's bed. 'If I move it behind the curtain for her, she probably won't put two and two together and remember it was his.'

Together they lugged the furniture around, washed the window and the skirting boards, dusted surfaces, rearranged the bedding. After dragging the rug downstairs and into the yard, they threw it over the line and took turns bashing it as they shouted the names of everyone they thought would benefit from a good hiding.

Now the room was shut up, gathering dust again. When the kids were allowed to come home she'd have to clean and rummage through a second time. Perhaps by then she would have to get a shaving brush and hair oil for Will, hang a suit behind the door for him. As for Ruth, she'd be in need of women's undergarments and stockings, lipstick, a pot of rouge. That was even supposing they'd want to come back. And why would they? More than likely they'd have Welsh sweethearts and thick accents and be accustomed to the fresh air and open countryside. It didn't bear thinking about, all the lost years, the time that could never be made up.

Gwen was convinced that George stayed away

even when he could be at home. She listened to the wireless, read the paper sometimes; she knew what was going on. Troops were advancing across France and Belgium; Paris was liberated, Antwerp captured. Personnel had to be ferried to and from Portsmouth, Southampton, Dover and Plymouth, and his permanent posting had been shifted to somewhere on the South Coast. So he *said*. She wondered sometimes if he had another woman, maybe the greasy, unkempt landlady he'd aped to make her laugh. Or a blousy, blonde barmaid. It could be a young widow or the wife of one of the uniformed men he drove to the port.

She wouldn't be surprised, looking the way she did. The hair dye she'd used a couple of times was out of circulation and she couldn't be bothered to search out an alternative. Grey roots no longer just showed through at her parting, they covered her entire head of hair. What she glimpsed when she happened to catch herself in a mirror or shop window made her turn away before she could undertake a thorough inspection of her reflection. She preferred not to see what those irreclaimable years had done to her. She told herself she should make an effort, but couldn't get past thinking to doing.

The same lack of energy pertained to George and the affair she'd created for him. It *should* hurt her to imagine him heaving on top of the tart, whoever she might be. Sweating and losing control in his ungainly, boyish, endearing way. The same thoughts that would have driven her to madness five years ago, making her pull George to her by his ears or the hair on his chest until she was satisfied he'd never think of anyone else, now passed through and over her without the slightest change in emotion. Let her have him, this fantasy woman. It saved him from bothering her, which he never did.

Some mornings she woke acutely aware of herself and her place in her surroundings. Colours, sounds, shadows. The piercing shrieks of buzz bombs. The smell of powdered dust, falling plaster mixed with the musty odour of rotting leaves, sharp, crackling air, smouldering wood. The intensity of those things was heightened, reminding her of the time she'd had influenza, but now there wasn't a cough, no fever or chattering chill. So powerfully did she feel her aches and pains that, lying in bed, she thought of herself as nothing but a sack in which to carry them around.

Minor ailments that at one time wouldn't have fazed her stung and throbbed and tortured. The nerves around her fingernails screamed, each fresh tear an electric shock; she could almost see her red, raw chilblains pulsating in rhythmic waves of pain, the bridge of her spectacles digging into the thin skin on her nose, a knife twisted in her lower back, anything she ate scratching its way down her gullet like a shard of glass.

Other times she woke feeling numb — and it was during those days that she felt some relief. The stunned sensation started outside her body and made its way in, surrounding her with a sense of lightness and insensibility. Then she was able to work, tidy up, write to the children, queue for her rations, step calmly into doorways to shelter from doodlebugs, chat to Betty and Evelyn as if through

309

the fine membrane of a bubble. Every part of her that could hurt was blunted and deadened.

But the days when she found respite dwindled, and she longed for the times to return when she'd felt more like her old self. When had that been? She had to sit in a chair, hands in her lap, and concentrate hard to remember. There had been periods when she thought the murk was lifting and that if, like Johnny's coat, she could hold on to them tightly enough, she could see her way forward. But, like the wool in her fist, the feeling of brightness tore away from her grasp. Perhaps this time the bout of melancholy might be less distressing. Or last for less time. After all, she managed to get up every morning and put in a decent day at the bridge.

Betty watched her carefully, but didn't pass comment. Nor did Evelyn or anyone else for that matter. She told herself to keep going, tried to be less scornful, nodding and smiling whenever anyone said it would be over soon. If she kept focused on Will and Ruth getting home instead of picturing their bedroom standing empty, then maybe everything would be alright.

*　*　*

There was no let-up to Hitler's doodlebug onslaught. Through swollen, grey clouds the buzzing bombs droned, without aim, gracefully sashaying down to balance momentarily on a restaurant in Beckenham or the Dulwich Co-op. Hundreds upon hundreds of hits. It felt like a backward step. The wireless reported daily on the

310

advances in France but even so, London was taking it again.

The 6th of September wasn't one of Gwen's few good days. An eerie silence hung heavy, making the softest and most ordinary sounds deafening. Once or twice, the hum of a crane or the hiss of a welding flame made Gwen jump, but when she looked around to see who might be watching her, judging her ability to stay unruffled, no one seemed to have noticed.

Crowds pressed around newsstands on the evening of the 7th, arms reaching out to grab the *Herald*, *Standard* or *News*. Each of the papers had the same gritty, grey photo on the front page of a good-looking young man standing behind a black mouthpiece, one hand in his pocket, the other holding a sheaf of papers. A map covered the wall behind him; uniformed and suited men sat to his left and right. Gwen dropped a threepenny bit into the news-seller's outstretched palm and read the headline: *Duncan Sandys Announces End of Flying Bomb Campaign*. She took the paper in to Betty and Len and started to read it aloud to them.

'I never knew there was such a person as a . . . what does this say?' She pointed a line out to Len.

'Chairman of the War Cabinet Flying Bomb Counter-Measures Committee.'

'Well, I'm glad I'm only a navvy. If I had *his* job the working day'd be finished before I could get that mouthful out.'

Betty chuckled from the kitchen where she was refilling the water steaming a suet pudding. 'You and me both, love,' she called out.

'Well,' Len said, smoothing the paper on his lap. 'Seems like he's done a good job.'

'Is what it says true?' Gwen asked.

'Heard it on the wireless, too. More than once,' Len said. 'What the man said is right here. ''Except possibly for the last few shots the Battle of London is over.'' We'll listen when it comes on again later.'

'How could that happen?' Gwen asked.

'How could that happen?' Len repeated the question, sounding amazed. 'We're better than them Jerries,' he said. 'It's as simple as that. Our lads are kicking down their dirty little launching sites over there, and our barrage balloons and ack-acks are doing their bit over here.'

'Put that paper down,' Betty called from the kitchen. 'Duff's up.'

Gwen took the paper from Len, folded it and put it in her work bag. She might have another read of it later to see if it was as simple as Len said, although she'd be surprised if it was. Nothing else was that easy.

The following day, Duncan Sandys' words were proved true. There were no sirens, no warnings, no rumbling drone or cut-outs before an explosion. There seemed to be a collective intake of breath and then a sigh, as natural and unhurried as the breath of a peaceful, sleeping infant. The lack of bombing was easy to get used to. Taking the void for granted, dinner and break times were filled with chatter about other things, as if Sandys' statement had given them licence to be jolly again.

If only the battering rain could be dealt with in

312

the same way, Gwen thought, hanging her sopping things up to dry in the kitchen. She had tiny bits of leftovers to use up: potato, onion, carrot, bacon rind, flour, powdered milk. It was her turn to get something together for Betty and Len, which would help them as they'd be tired when they came in from visiting their daughter-in-law. She'd settled on a flan, if she could eke out the last crumbs of cheese.

Opening the gas tap, she lit a match and bent over the oven door. From somewhere high above there was a double crack. The flame she was holding shook in her hands and fell, sizzling in a patch of wet from her boots. For a moment she was back in the Anderson, all three children clamouring around her, watching for the candle to be lit. In the whistling roar that followed she managed to stop the gas. Then came the rush of something splitting the sky and a boom that seemed to be reverberating from the surface of the moon.

There were no softer days after that. The V-2 rockets, Churchill assured them, were inaccurate, most of them missing their objective. But that didn't help the people who lived, or used to live, in Staveley Road or Adelaide Avenue. The noise could be heard all over the place as well, whether you were near the hit or not. There was another lull for a few weeks at the end of September, beginning of October, but there were no wild announcements from the Government this time. Gwen thought it was because they knew no one would believe them.

What they did say, though, was that a partial dim-out could replace the blackout, unless of

313

course there was a raid, when the weak haloes of moonshine allowed to glow around streetlamps would have to be switched off again. Evelyn, Betty, Sylvie and even the sensible Jim were beside themselves with excitement about this development, but Gwen couldn't understand why. What difference did it make when you were indoors, the heavy blackouts closed around you?

Nights were getting longer and the wet, grey autumn would merge into a colder, gunmetal shade of winter. The rockets kept coming. Huge craters were scooped out of the earth where they struck, floorboards shuddered and windows shattered miles away from the hits. Once again people were snuffed out, houses were roofless, there was no running water, Andersons were reopened, underground stations sheltered thousands of weary families. No, the Government dare not say it was coming to an end now.

Every day and each sleepless night Gwen waited for a rocket to fall on her. Every day that went by and it didn't, she began to think herself lucky even though the noise, the smell, the open, gaping holes where lives used to be lived, the tension of waiting to be blasted away felt crushing. Olive came in laughing one day, saying a group of women in her street had taken to praying together for the bombs to stop. 'There was loads of them,' she said. 'All going into one old girl's parlour. Asked me to join them, they did.'

'And did you?' Sylvie asked, taking the cigarette Olive offered her.

Olive laughed again, snorting the words out. ''*This*,' I said — ' she pointed to her cigarette

314

"— is what I've got faith in. And a pint of the good stuff in the other hand." Gwen looked at the faces around them, some women joining in the fun, others disgusted.

'And I told them that if I did go in for all that — ' wriggling her hips around in her dungarees '— I'd be begging God for my old man to come home so we could pray together.'

Jeers and catcalls followed them up to their stations. Olive smoked and drank cups of tea off that story for the next two days. That was the last they saw of her. So in the long run, Gwen thought, it didn't matter if or what you prayed for.

★ ★ ★

Flu was making the rounds again. Everyone seemed to be coughing into hankies or hacking in the streets. Gwen could hear shallow, rattling breaths bubbling and gurgling through thin, bony chests. She was relieved that everyone looked like her now: pale, drawn, guarded, worn out. Len came down with something nasty that Betty was treating with poultices. 'Don't come round,' she told Gwen. 'No need for you to catch it. I'll pop in when I can.'

The news from Wales wasn't much better. Peggy wrote to say that every other person there had come down with something nasty and debilitating. Ruth had to have the best part of a week off school with a bad cough, and she'd heard that Will and Marty had missed a few days, too. In the same letter, Peggy reported that Mrs Gwilt had told her, after Sunday service, that she was going to apply to have Marty stay with her as there was no one left in London for him to live with.

Gwen could not fathom it. She knew his dad had died in action and his mum, nan and brothers had all been lost in a blast, but there was an old granny, wasn't there? She thought back to the last time she might have seen old Mrs White and realised it had been months, if not years ago. And even then she'd been frail, hobbling about with a stick. So, Marty was going to be the reality of her worst fears for Will and Ruth: an evacuated child left behind to grow up far from home, either because circumstances had forced him to do so, or because time had passed and he no longer wanted to live anywhere else. And she cringed again when she recalled the easy way he'd spoken to her with a burgeoning Welsh accent.

The numbers on the bridge thinned out, too. Either on sick leave or bombed out like Olive, Gwen supposed. Then she heard Evelyn mention something to another gang leader about letting people go, and asked her about it when they were clocking off.

'Haven't you heard? Evelyn said. 'There's no need to keep everyone on — we're about done now.'

'Are we?' Gwen asked. 'I ain't noticed.'

Evelyn took off her gloves and cupped Gwen's elbow. 'Do you fancy a drink?' she asked. 'We haven't done anything together for ages, except work.'

Gwen thought about Betty nursing Len, the kids' empty room, George doing who-knew-what with some other woman. 'Yeah,' she said. 'I can make time for a half.'

They found a pub occupied by couples and groups of women who looked comfortable being out without men. Gwen had a bitter shandy, Evelyn a vermouth and soda.

'It's been happening for a good few weeks now,' Evelyn said, stirring her drink with a wooden toothpick. 'Girls getting laid off.'

'This is the first I've heard about it,' Gwen said.

'Well, I'm afraid,' Evelyn said, 'that in a week or so it'll be you. And the others in our little gang. The temporary bridge will be gone. Another couple of weeks for finishing off small bits. Then it will be open to traffic both ways.'

'But why me?' Gwen said, her beer glass stopping short of her dry lips. She'd thought that Evelyn could somehow protect her from anything like that.

'It's not up to me,' Evelyn said. 'I don't even think it's Jim's decision. You know, about who goes when. Although, in the end, everyone will be laid off.'

'But,' Gwen started. She felt as if she'd been winded. 'I've managed every day since the doctor sent me to bed that time, ain't I?'

'Everyone thinks the world of you. You're a workhorse. It's not about you or me or Sylvie or anyone. We've finished and good luck to us.' Evelyn raised her glass and nodded at Gwen.

They sat in silence for a few minutes. Gwen felt a fresh grinding in her empty stomach, a thin film of clammy sweat prickled above her top lip. It was hard to imagine the fleeting, wintry days without something to do, someone to look at whose face mirrored her own when a rocket exploded.

317

And the long nights alone — she couldn't be with Betty and Len all the time. No work bag to shake out and get ready for the next day; no exhausted limbs, insisting she sleep. How often she'd thought the work meant nothing to her, that she would give anything to be able to stay at home. But that was before the world changed. 'What will you do?' Gwen asked. 'Spend more time with your bloke, I suppose?'

'I'm not sure.' Evelyn leaned towards Gwen. 'We always have such a lovely time when we're dancing. But . . . '

Evelyn didn't talk much about Stan, so Gwen was eager for her to continue. It was a change from thinking about her own problems. 'But what?'

'The thought of spending another dreary Sunday afternoon with his dull family in Sidcup above their dismal ironmonger's shop makes my heart drop.'

Gwen was flabbergasted at Evelyn's outburst, but before she could think of what to say Evelyn dismissed the conversation with a wave of her hand and said, 'Do you remember I told you that I'd love to stay on the tools? Well, I'm hoping I might be able to do that. I'm trying to take some courses. Get some qualifications. And you — ' Evelyn's smile was broad with genuine happiness ' — I suppose you'll be glad to have the time at home. Get ready for George and the kids, now it's all nearly over.'

'Shall we have another?' was all Gwen said by way of reply.

★ ★ ★

318

Apart from the essentials, Gwen did very little in the house. There didn't seem much point in going to all the bother when there was no one but her to muck things up. She wrote to the kids every day in what read back as a sort of diary. She tried to make it sound exciting, but soon found herself running out of ways to write about going to the shops, boiling a kettle, setting a fire, sitting with Betty.

Betty thought it would do Gwen good to tag along when she helped out at the WVS once or twice a week. So one afternoon, while Len was sitting in his chair, a blanket around his knees, Betty dragged Gwen to the local headquarters. The rain hadn't stopped since the summer. The only difference was that now it was icy instead of warm, and stabbed at their cheeks like cold darts. They sloshed along in the sludge and mud, through streets littered again, as they'd been right at the beginning, with the rack and ruin of bombing raids. No matter that this damage was done by the new doodlebugs and V-2 rockets; the outcome was the same. It looked as though whoever was in charge of clearing the mess couldn't be bothered this time around because it might not be the last. She knew the feeling.

Gwen had heard a lot about the WVS. They were always being praised in the papers or mentioned on the radio, and she'd seen some of the members hurrying about with their canteens and first-aid cases, especially when the bombing was heavy. But she had no idea they were this busy. So much seemed to be left up to them to organise and manage. Steam surged from an urn and

319

row upon row of cups were being set out by the women minding it, a tatty line forming close by.

Behind them, another couple of ladies were washing plates and mugs in a bowl, passing the items to another woman to dry and stack. The pile of unwashed crockery was being replenished from boxes carried in from the street. Saucepans wrapped in teacloths to keep them hot, bowls of potatoes and veg, pudding basins handed over at the door from women in overcoats to women in pinnies.

From underneath a curtained-off area, Gwen could see the legs of beds and nearby a mountain of sheets, probably waiting to be washed and replaced. All manner of seats and chairs dotted the room, all occupied by people who looked shell-shocked. The women were tending to all this and more. Taking down names, wrapping blankets around shivering shoulders, scrubbing, sorting, carrying, fetching, peeling, counting bandages.

The basement hall was lit up like Christmas and Gwen trailed around after Betty, shielding her eyes. She couldn't bear the composed hum; it was abrasive and made her feel on edge, her nerves jangling. The subdued, ordered hubbub jarred; the efficient, confident women irritated. She reminded herself of how uncomfortable she'd felt when she started on the bridge; how strange and looming the machinery had been, the grinding, rasping metallic sounds foreign and menacing. If she could get used to that situation — one she never thought she'd find herself in or miss now she was no longer needed — she must be able to settle down into this more domesticated, familiar environment.

But it was too exhausting to make the effort. When they left, she didn't sign the rota but said she'd take some sheets home to turn, even though she knew sewing with her tender fingers would be painful and time-consuming.

Evelyn called once a week, sometimes with Sylvie, who talked non-stop about Alec. She'd received a number of letters from him, some written by nurses and buddies on his ward saying his eye, or the socket where it used to be, was healing nicely and he would be ready to travel soon. She, too, had been let go from the bridge and was hoping to get her old job back at Lyons. In the meantime, she was taking care of their father and the house. 'In training,' Evelyn said. 'To be Mrs Alec.' The remark must have been some kind of family joke, judging by the way the sisters laughed.

Evelyn was one of the last working on the bridge, but she would finish along with the other stragglers next Tuesday, the day of completion. No ceremony, no dedication, no newspapers or wireless announcements. Open to traffic and pedestrians both ways. That was that.

'But,' Evelyn said, breaking off a bit of flapjack and dunking it in her tea. 'Jim wants as many as possible to meet for a drink. He says we need a bit of a knees-up to mark the occasion.' She glanced at Gwen. 'Shall we meet you on the bridge?'

Gwen imagined the evening; clapping people on the back, dragging up stories about welding irons and Portland Stone cladding. Laughing about niggles like lighting fags in the wind, tying turbans and the canteen food. Then she thought about how she would feel sitting in alone knowing all the old faces were huddled companionably together for the last time.

'Ask Betty to come along,' Evelyn said.

'I will, but she usually has a WVS shift Tuesday evening,' Gwen said. 'Or else she'd be here now.'

'Let's say seven, Gwen, shall we? On the south side.'

★ ★ ★

The rain gave no concession as Gwen stood huddled against the concrete halfway up the steps. She felt miserable and wished she'd made an excuse to stay home, curled in her armchair writing notes to the kids or trying to sew strips of bedclothes together. But instead, she'd brushed down an old, mid-calf forest-green skirt — too long and full now to be fashionable — and pulled on a duck-egg blue blouse that had a faint whiff of tobacco and stale cooking about it. She'd twisted her hair into a coil and flattened down straying strands of grey with a bit of lard warmed between her hands. Adjusting a paste necklace over her blouse, she watched the fake gems twinkle sharply in the mirror as though sending out a distress signal in Morse code. She'd taken off the sparkling strand and replaced it with a cameo brooch pinned to her collar. Twisting this way and that to see if the skirt fell neatly at the back, she noticed she'd gained a bit of weight and the material hung in more flattering folds from her waist.

Shaking a scarf from her pocket and tying it under her chin, Gwen stood back from the people

322

who moved up and down the steps: couples with their arms linked; groups chatting, their voices rising and falling as they climbed up from the shelter of the stairwell to the walkway suspended above the river; women and men on their own, their footsteps clacking as they hurried along. A crowd of women she recognised jostled and bumped their way towards her. One or two put their hands up or nodded, but she let them pass, turning her back and cupping her hands around a match to light a cigarette.

A dim-out replaced the blackout tonight and, for the first time, she was as grateful for that as the others seemed to be. Orbs of yellow moonlight shone from the streetlamps on the bridge and Gwen made her way towards them, curious to see what the structure looked like now it was finished. From the top it was sleek and straight, nothing ornate or fussy about it; all the curves were underneath the roadway. She stopped and gazed at Big Ben, wondering if the clock would ever be lit up again, but it seemed to be encased in a mist. Bloody spectacles, she thought. It was about time they were replaced, if they could afford the cost.

Looking down, she could make out eddies of oily, iridescent water lapping and slapping against one of the piers. It sounded close, like it had when she'd crouched in her retreat of a hidey-hole. It was here, underneath where she was standing, she was sure of it. She'd love to see the spot again and wondered if it would feel as much of a sanctuary as it had done when she first started on the bridge.

Leaning over as far as she could without falling,

she thought she could make out the heart she'd carved into the arch with the initials of all her family at its centre. She squinted. The drawing was there. She was sure of it. And there was something else. Another inch closer and she would be able to see. MW. Who could that be? She shook her head, took off her glasses and wiped them on a corner of Johnny's little white hanky, always nestled in the left-hand side of her vest. When she settled them back on her face, all of the carvings were gone. Or perhaps they had never been there.

But who, she wondered, was MW? Then it came to her. She had to hold on fast to the railings. Of course, Marty White. She'd been thinking about him all day. Every day. Worrying about him to the same extent as she perpetually fretted about Will and Ruth and Johnny. In her mind, the four of them blended in together seamlessly. There was room, surely, in the kids' bedroom and around the table. There was a place for him in their hearts. They would bring Marty home, to them. Where he belonged.

A gust of wind whipped across the river and up, over the bridge. Grabbing the knot of her scarf, she lost her hold on the hanky. In the half-light she lunged for it, but the wind caught it first and sent it tumbling across the roadway and over the far balustrade to where it hovered in mid-air before floating into the river. 'Johnny,' Gwen shouted. Then she whispered his name again as she touched her chest and felt the warmth that radiated from where the hanky had last pressed against her.

15

December 1944 — May 1945

Evelyn

Dad knocked on the girls' bedroom door and said there was a man downstairs to see Evelyn. 'A big bloke. Name's Gregson.' Evelyn pulled on a dress and cardigan, put a couple of combs in her hair and went downstairs. It was then she realised that, although she'd never met Gwen's husband, she had a clear picture of him in her mind from Gwen's descriptions. He was large and lumbering, his movements awkward as if he was embarrassed by his size and had to keep himself from getting in the way or knocking things over. He was good-looking, or had been, but not as handsome as Gwen had thought. The fault of time or circumstances, or the optical illusion of love.

'I'm sorry to bother you, Miss Draper,' he said, standing in the middle of the sitting room, turning the hat in his hand round and round like the pressure gauge on a locomotive. 'Gwen asked me to call.'

Evelyn felt her stomach turn. 'Is she alright?' she asked.

'Yeah.' He put up his meaty hand to stop her thinking the worst. 'Ain't nothing to worry about. For once.'

'Good news then,' Evelyn said, smiling. 'We

325

could all do with some of that. Please, sit down. Can I get you a cup of tea?'

'Someone asked me already.' He looked towards the kitchen. 'Ta very much.'

'Oh, that'll be my sister. I'm sure it won't be a minute.'

Balancing his hat on his lap, George sat on the edge of the armchair. 'The thing is, Miss Draper, I know it's short notice, but the day after tomorrow we're having a bit of a party. Gwen is keen on you and your sister being there but didn't trust the post to get the invitation to you on time.'

'Oh, I love a party. Is it a birthday or anniversary?'

'No,' George said, the beginnings of a grin turning up one corner of his mouth. 'We're welcoming the kids home.'

Evelyn clapped her hands together. 'Gwen must be so pleased. And you.'

'Yeah.' George let the beam take over his face. 'All three of them. Will and Ruth and Marty, who we're taking in as I'm sure Gwen told you.'

'Gwen did mention it,' Evelyn said. 'But I didn't know if you'd made up your minds.'

Sylvie brought in two cups of tea and set one in front of George and handed the other to Evelyn. 'Ta, Miss Draper.' George half stood.

'Call me Evelyn — and my sister's Sylvie.'

George nodded. He tried to force his forefinger through the delicate handle on the teacup, then decided to pinch it hard instead. He took a slurp and the cup rattled when he placed it back on the saucer. Evelyn looked away and waited.

'It ain't been an easy decision,' George said.

'I can imagine.'

His voice caught, but he disguised it with a cough. 'We know we ain't ever going to replace our Johnny. But — ' he opened his hands in a gesture of acceptance '— Marty needs a place and he's a good lad.'

'A very lucky lad,' Evelyn said. 'To have you and Gwen look out for him.'

'We'll do our best.' George drained his tea. 'I wanted to see you, too,' he said, studying the pattern on the hearthrug, 'to tell you that Gwen has never given up saying what a great mate you've been to her.' His eyes met hers. 'And that means a lot to both of us.'

Evelyn swallowed the lump in her throat and went on to tell him how fond she was of Gwen, but he stood, almost knocking over the side table, and wiping the sweat from his forehead. It was as though the simple declaration had taken it out of him.

When she saw him to the door and watched him walk towards the high street, his shoulders back and head up, he seemed self-assured and buoyant. She hoped that Gwen felt the same.

★ ★ ★

Evelyn needn't have worried about that hope coming to fruition. When Gwen answered the door to her and Sylvie, she looked lovelier and more radiant than Evelyn would ever have thought possible. And although some of it was careful grooming, there was a glow about her that could not be put down to hair dye or cosmetics.

327

'Don't stand there. Come in, come in.' Gwen hugged them, beaming with pride at the small party gathered in her sitting room. There was George, much less out of place in his own surroundings, one huge hand on each of Will's and Marty's shoulders. As soon as he greeted Evelyn and Sylvie, Evelyn noticed that he placed his paws back, with a tender touch, around the boys.

Ruth, taller than Evelyn had imagined, was on Betty's lap and Len was chatting to his son and daughter-in-law, their children snuggled up between them. Another few neighbours and friends were introduced; a buffet and drinks were set out and everyone was easy and relaxed with each other. Evelyn smiled at the Welcome Home banner Gwen must have painted and hung above the fireplace.

Balancing a plate of egg and cress sandwiches in one hand, a small glass of sherry in the other, Gwen nudged Evelyn with her knee and tucked herself in next to her.

'You look wonderful, Gwen,' Evelyn said, noticing her friend's perfectly round, healthy nails.

Gwen nodded. 'I feel better than I have done in the longest time. Do you know that this room ain't seen a party since the day before Will and Ruth were going away to Wales?'

'I shouldn't think that was much of a party,' Evelyn said.

'No.' Gwen sniffed. 'It was awful. I so wanted it to be lovely for them. You know, so they could think about it if they were homesick. But try as we might, Betty and I could not make it a jolly occasion.'

'Well, I'm not surprised. It was a terrible time. But . . . ' Evelyn squeezed her friend's hand. 'Look at you now.'

Gwen gazed at each of the children and her eyelids drooped with contentment. 'Yeah. We done the right thing for Marty. And for us. We ain't never going to forget our Johnny, none of us. I ain't going to let that happen. But . . . it does seem that some kind of happiness can still be had.' Gwen glanced back at Evelyn. 'Don't you think?'

At that moment, George called to Gwen to join him and the children who were laughing at a story in a comic. Evelyn watched them huddle together over the page for just long enough not to seem rude. When Gwen broke away to bustle over cutting the cake, she and George mirrored smiles that were for each other alone.

When it was time to leave, Gwen and the children saw Evelyn and Sylvie to the door. Promises were made to keep in touch, which Evelyn knew they had been through too much together not to keep. Pulling Gwen to her, Evelyn whispered in her ear, 'You're right. There is still happiness to be had. And you've found it.'

★ ★ ★

Auschwitz was liberated. She and Sylvie watched the sickening, sorry sight in the cinema and walked out in silence before Vera Lynn and Donald Stewart could start singing and dancing their way through the main feature. The Allies won the Battle of the Bulge, crossed the Rhine and razed Dresden; and Sylvie married Alec in a small, quiet ceremony. She wore a dusty pink suit pinched in at the waist and trimmed in ocelot fur she'd taken from the collar of an old coat, a pair of shiny brown heels, and real silk stockings. Her freshly permed hair was pinned behind one ear, the other side skimming her cheek. Stan had provided a silver horseshoe from his father's shop, which Sylvie decorated with roses and dangled from her wrist with pink ribbon. And her beautiful smile was framed by crimson lips.

Alec wore the uniform he filled out a little less well than before he'd been mobilised to Italy, his hand clutching Sylvie's through the crook of his arm after they said their vows. A photographer took two snaps when the sun shone briefly between downpours outside Wood Green Registry Office; one of the couple with confetti cascading around them, the other of the entire party of eleven. In both of them, Alec turned his head so the eyepatch he wore over an embroidery of crisscrossed scars wasn't on display.

Sylvie hadn't flinched the first time she'd seen him after his injury, too delighted with having him back to bother. And when she spoke about the mutilation, it was with clinical detachment. How the eye couldn't be saved; the damage and immediate treatment he'd had that left it in such a mess; further procedures he might be able to have in Canada.

The patch helped, but one morning Evelyn walked into the kitchen while it was on the side and Alec was bathing the wound. It took everything she had not to show how repulsed she felt, if just for a minute. Alec had fumbled for the black pad

330

but Sylvie said, 'Don't worry, love. Evelyn doesn't mind, do you?'

Evelyn shook her head. 'No, of course I don't,' she said. Although she wasn't so sure.

He replaced it quickly despite the reassurance, but not before she'd seen the inflamed, pink socket as raw and sore and squelchy as an oyster, having rolled sand around in its shell for months. Little puckers and rough stitch marks surrounded the taut, shiny skin, pulled down on the outer edge as if he'd had a bout of dropsy.

There was another thing, too, that was different about Alec. Evelyn had been trying to get to the bottom of it for weeks, concentrating on what else might be missing. Now, in the upstairs room of The Three Compasses, where Dad had arranged the wedding breakfast, it came to her. The difference wasn't in what else he'd lost but what he'd gained. He still laughed in the same joyful way: his shoulders shaking, his hands holding his stomach, rocking down and back with mouth wide open. He was as playful, if not more so, but now he interrupted a little less frequently, content to give others a chance to be witty or have the last say. It no longer seemed that he felt he had to fill every silence or shear off the ends of serious conversations with a clever quip to ease the atmosphere. He listened with interest. There was a tender patience and understanding about him. His empathy was deep and sagacious; his responses more insightful than men much older, but his capacity to accept, dismiss and move on seemed to allow him to view the world as new and enthusing.

For months they had saved ration coupons

and begged, bartered or borrowed from neighbours and friends for handouts so they were able to enjoy pork, crackling, apple sauce, mashed and roast potatoes, carrots, peas, cauliflower and gravy. There was gin and beer. Sherry and port. Speeches inducing all manner of tears. Evelyn thought Alec consumed it all as a man hungry for what could have been denied him.

After a weekend's honeymoon on the Isle of Sheppey, Alec had to report back to Aldershot, where he had a number of medical appointments, before being shipped to Glasgow to wait for his passage home. So Dad and Evelyn took Sylvie to Euston, where she'd told them they would have to say goodbye. In her hand she had a paper with the name of an officer she had to ask for at the enquiry desk and then ... She had no idea where she would be going next, the name of the ship she'd be sailing on, or from which port it would sail. They lingered with Sylvie as long as they could, asking her to check she had her papers, if she had enough money for a meal, her passport, asking her to write soon.

'Yes, there're here. I have. It's in my bag. I will. You too.' Then she threw her arms around both of them and they stood, still and breathless, listening to each other's heartbeats. Evelyn took Dad's arm and they walked away, turning to bat kisses back and forth, waving until the last finger of Sylvie's hand was out of sight.

★ ★ ★

The journey back to Mayes Road was grim. Evelyn and Dad linked arms while they walked to the Underground, pressed themselves tight against each other in the first available seat they could find, interlaced their fingers and squeezed their hands together. Evelyn felt as if she needed to hold fast to Dad, her anchor in a turbulent sea. She supposed Dad was feeling the same. Whenever one or the other of them tried to say something, about Sylvie and Alec and how much they would miss them, mist would film their eyes and the words would stick in their throats.

The minute they let themselves into the house and Evelyn had reached for the kettle, Uncle Bert put his head around the door to find out how the goodbyes had gone and to take Dad to the pub.

'Evelyn won't mind, will you, love,' Uncle Bert stated as if it was fact rather than a question.

Dad looked at Evelyn, his unruly eyebrows raised. There was a lump in Evelyn's stomach, or maybe it was a gaping hole. What she really wanted was Dad to herself for another little while; to sit with him close and have him within her reach. But she shook her head and said, 'Of course I won't.'

While her tea was drawing, Evelyn tidied the sitting room, laid the fire and checked the pantry for dinner. Then she slumped onto the couch and stared at the spot next to her where Sylvie had rested on and off for most of her life, the cushions moulded to the shape of her sister. Evelyn brushed the outlines and curves with her fingertips.

What am I going to do now? Evelyn asked herself. In the short term, she had to pack up the belongings Sylvie had asked her to ship out to

Canada and then sift through the things Sylvie had said she could keep for herself. She would make a start on all that this afternoon. Setting her cup and saucer on a side table, she closed her eyes tight against the pain she felt when she pictured Sylvie, alone and anxious but bubbling with excitement. She looked around the room taking in the furniture, the ornaments, the wallpaper and clock, the newspaper rack and the rug.

The house had a certain smell, which she had never defined before but now recognised as a blend of food on the turn, tobacco, Dad's shaving soap and hers and Sylvie's face powder. Outside the window, she could see the rickety gate and part of the silver birch rooted in the pavement. She sighed; it was all so familiar, which was a comfort but at the same time humdrum, drab and flat.

She asked herself, with a jolt of surprise, if she begrudged Sylvie her adventures and yes, was the conclusion she came to. Of course, not Sylvie as a person. All she wanted for her beloved sister was a happy life and whatever that entailed. But she was envious of all the new things Sylvie was on the brink of experiencing.

To each their lot, she reasoned with herself, but that thought only made her feel worse. She took a deep breath and gently pounded her fists on her knees. Sitting around and brooding would do her no good, she knew that, and there was only one person who could get the life she wanted and that was her. Well, the classroom no longer appealed although, to be fair, if she chose that career again now, she could both teach and get married. At last.

But she'd read recently that a new teacher-training scheme aimed at ex-servicemen and women had been announced for June and it was thought that thousands would apply. And as she'd been out of the profession for a few years she presumed she'd have to reapply and retrain merely to end up where she'd been before the war. The thought of that was difficult to bear.

Biting her lip in determination, she reiterated her certainty that what she really wanted to do was pursue what she had done on the bridge. But the men were coming home now and they would want their jobs back. She heard herself scoff out loud as she recalled that bit of paper they'd had to sign saying that in due course women would have to give up their jobs to men.

And then, of course, there was Stan to consider. If they took their closeness to the next level then her career would be sorted out for her. Or to put it bluntly, she would be stuck behind the counter in that shop full of nails, sieves and shovels wearing nothing more glamorous than a brown smock and pair of flat shoes so she could run up and down the stairs to the living quarters to check on the children or the dinner. She sighed as if ridding herself of the thought.

When she spoke to Stan about her ambitions, he never undermined her. He listened intently and always seemed interested. But, he did not make any concessions to the fact that his future was that little business in that little town and she knew that as a woman, as a wife, she would be duty-bound to fit in with his plans. So the cynic in her said that of course he was interested in her aspirations as he had nothing whatsoever to lose.

One evening before Sylvie left for Canada, Evelyn had asked her if she had ever doubted her feelings for Alec or thought he might have doubted her.

'No.' Sylvie shook her head. 'Not after we had declared ourselves. Why?' She looked at Evelyn with narrowed eyes; she had always been too astute. 'Do you doubt that you love Stan?'

Evelyn had to think carefully about her reply. 'It's more that I'm just not sure how I feel about him,' she said. 'One minute I'm head over heels. The next . . . ' She shrugged her shoulders. 'I can't be bothered. And when I think about the future with him. Well. It seems as if it would be more like going backwards than forwards.'

Sylvie smiled at her with a clamped mouth. 'It doesn't do to compare romances,' she said. 'But all I can say is I would go anywhere with Alec and do anything for him. As long as he was with me it would all be wonderful.'

Evelyn nodded with resignation. 'I know,' she said.

Sylvie picked up Evelyn's hand and held it in hers. Patting it lightly, she said, 'But Alec wouldn't ask me to do anything I didn't want to do. And if I harboured a burning drive? I feel sure he'd do all he could to help me achieve what I wanted to do. Besides all that, I don't think that Alec would want to have a life that was completely to his specifications and nor would I. We want a life that's ours.'

Tears prickled the back of Evelyn's eyes and she wondered when Sylvie had become the sensible one.

Now a sudden downpour made her look up at

the darkening sky; Dad would be back soon and she hadn't sorted his tea out yet. In her mind she made a list of the things she had to do: draw the blackouts, prepare a meal, write and post a letter to Sylvie care of her in-laws, go to the WES on Monday and enquire about how she could move on in construction or engineering. She felt lighter about the chores she had to do now that she had made that decision.

★ ★ ★

When the post fluttered onto the mat, Evelyn stopped still with her toast suspended mid-air; Dad's eyes fixed on hers, his teacup frozen an inch from his waiting lips. Then they both made a dash for the door, Evelyn running in her house slippers with Dad clumping behind.

'Who're these from?' Evelyn said, snatching up the small assortment of envelopes from where they had fanned out on the square of matting.

Dad pointed to a couple as Evelyn shuffled through them. 'That one's the Borough Council. That's from Auntie Lil.'

Evelyn handed them over to Dad without looking at him. 'How about this?' she said, turning over a small, square envelope to look at the back then turning it face up again.

Dad shrugged. 'No idea.' He sounded disappointed. 'It's not from Canada, that's for sure. Postmark says Streatham.'

'You daft bugger.' Evelyn batted the wad of letters in Dad's direction. 'Of course it's not. She only left five days ago.'

'Don't tell me you weren't thinking the same. I can't remember the last time I saw you run so fast.'

Evelyn laughed out loud. 'Well, I was thinking that perhaps she'd posted a letter from wherever it is she's waiting for her ship.' She tried to sound disdainful. 'Not Canada. It wouldn't be possible, and you know it better than anyone.'

Dad turned and Evelyn could tell, by the crestfallen slump of his shoulders, that he had been hoping against logic.

The letter was from Alice. Evelyn tried to remember when she'd last seen her and decided that it must have been about two weeks previously when they'd met in a pub with a crowd of other women. Above the din, she had told Evelyn that the American she'd been dating said she wasn't the girl for him. Alice said she had been upset, but as the days went by, she thought more and more that his decision had been the right one. Then she'd gone on to say she was working in a greengrocer's around the corner from where she was lodging and was using some of her wages to take a Pitman's typing course.

Before she had a chance to stop herself, Evelyn had stared down at Alice's generous hands and fingers, wondering how she would manage the intricacies of a keyboard, then immediately looked away, embarrassed. She coloured again now, thinking about how insensitive she'd been.

Alice seemed a bit lonely, too, perhaps because her pal, Joan, was spending so much time playing in some musical group or another. But she seemed eager to pursue a friendship with Evelyn and the

338

letter was an invitation to meet at the Odeon to see *Give Us the Moon* starring Margaret Lockwood and Vic Oliver. That would be something to look forward to.

When the breakfast things had been cleared and Evelyn had caught up with a few other chores, she pulled the old atlas off the shelf and gave it a good dusting. She handed Dad a thick pencil and they sat close together on the couch. 'Right,' she said. 'Put a ring around Halifax. Good, now another around Saskatoon.'

Dad knew the geography so well it only took him seconds to do as he was told.

'Now, remind me,' Evelyn went on. 'How long does the journey take from here to Halifax?'

'Oh,' Dad rubbed the stubble on his cheek. 'Minimum of five days.'

Evelyn nodded. 'And Sylvie will probably not have set sail yet, will she?'

'We really don't know,' Dad said. 'But maybe not.'

'Well, even if she has and posts a letter the minute she docks, it will take at least another week or two to get to us. Won't it?'

'Yes,' Dad said. 'I know, I know.' He closed his eyes and rested his head on the back of his chair.

Evelyn propped the book under the lamp and put her head on Dad's shoulder. 'Silly sod,' she said.

* * *

When the WES was in sight, Evelyn had to stop herself from breaking into a run. The same woman

339

she had seen on previous occasions was manning the desk and she greeted Evelyn like an old friend. 'Come to join us again, my dear?' she asked, as confident and competent as ever.

'Perhaps,' Evelyn said. 'I actually wanted to have a chat with Cynthia Blackwood. You know, the lady engineer who . . . '

'Of course, Mrs Blackwood.'

Evelyn suddenly felt as if she'd been disrespectful. 'Oh, we always called her Cynthia. She told us to.'

'That's Mrs Blackwood's way,' the woman said. 'She doesn't like to be too formal.'

Evelyn gestured to the area behind the reception desk. 'Does she have an office here and might she be available?'

The receptionist placed both her hands on the desk and shook her head. 'I'm afraid you're out of luck,' she said. 'Mrs Blackwood has been seconded to the University of Kentucky. She'll be back at some stage, but we don't know when.'

Another woman crossing the Atlantic. Evelyn was aware that the same pale green shade of envy was washing over her as it had done when Sylvie left for Canada.

'Can anyone else help?'

Evelyn wasn't sure if she wanted to attend lectures given by anyone other than Cynthia, but told herself that she shouldn't dismiss any opportunity. 'I wondered if there were any other courses going similar to those taught by Cynthia.'

'Ah, well. We're trying to find a replacement but . . . ' The woman's mouth turned down at the corners. 'It's proving to be quite difficult as

340

lady engineers are few and far between.' Then she smiled again. 'We're waiting desperately for the likes of you to step up, my dear.'

Evelyn could feel that the smile she gave in return was thin and, like her projected career, really not worth waiting for.

'There is someone named Mrs Beryl Platt who will be giving a few talks about mechanical engineering. Any good for you?'

'I suppose I could attend one and see.'

The woman nodded her head. 'Mrs Platt is one of only five women to gain a Title of Degree in Mechanical Engineering from Cambridge University and has been working at a test flight department in Bucks.'

Now the veil of jealousy descended on Evelyn in dark, heavy waves and she was tempted to put her forehead on the desk and weep.

'So you see,' the woman went on. 'It is possible. If Cambridge is not for you, the Imperial run a civil engineering course that women can attend and have been able to do so since 1898.'

She expects me to think that's a marvellous achievement, Evelyn thought. But she concluded that the universities, the Government and the institutions that limited half of the workforce should be thoroughly ashamed of themselves.

When she left, she had a new membership card for the year, so she felt as if the journey had not been wasted. But that had put a dent in her dosh for the week, so there was no possibility of paying for either Cambridge or the Imperial if by any chance they would consider her. Perhaps there would be something at the Employment Exchange

341

for an old construction hand like her; if not, she would have to take whatever was going.

But there was nothing on offer in the way of building or engineering and Evelyn thought it beggared belief when every street had taken at least one hit and many were more hits than street. Surely they needed experienced workers like her? The best they could come up with was a job as a relief library assistant working wherever she was needed in London, so she took that.

★ ★ ★

The cinema outing had, in Evelyn's estimation, been much more successful and such a good laugh. The more Evelyn got to know Alice, the more impressed she was with her attitude and good, common sense. She smiled when she recalled Alice telling her about the hostel where she lived and her landlady, who had never married and had devoted her whole life to her elderly mother, who she still called 'Mummy'. Over a drink, Evelyn had said that it all sounded a bit stifling.

'I can see why you thinks that.' Alice nodded. 'But they has been like a family to me.'

Evelyn left it at that. She knew not everyone had a Dad or Sylvie or Uncle Bert to rely on.

Now Alice was expected for tea and Evelyn was setting out bread, butter, a bit of jam roly-poly, thin custard and cups. Churchill was on the wireless talking about how they were pushing forward on all fronts and telling them to keep strong as this was the last little bit. Evelyn looked outside and smiled; blossom was in bloom, daffodils

342

swayed in the warm breeze, a woman walking her dog was wearing a light jacket and no scarf. The weather was reacting to the prime minister's edict by bucking up to a lovely, cheerful spring.

Alice arrived and she was her usual sunny self. She shook her curls and greeted Evelyn with a kiss on the cheek. Two spots of colour shone through the patina of face powder on her cheeks.

'You look lovely,' Evelyn said, taking her coat. 'Are you going on somewhere special afterwards?'

'We are,' Alice said, following Evelyn through to the sitting room.

Evelyn thought she might have forgotten an arrangement they'd made last time they met and hoped that if she had, it was dancing. She and Sylvie had never had that last night out that they'd promised themselves. No — she shook her head — she would have remembered that. 'Are we?' Evelyn asked.

'That's if you doesn't have any other plans,' Alice said.

'No,' Evelyn answered. 'But what were you thinking of?'

'Listening to Joan's jazz group perform.' Alice twisted her hair around her finger and looked hopeful.

'I don't really like jazz,' Evelyn said, thinking about the endless pieces of noise that sounded no more like music to her than cutlery being thrown on the floor.

'I doesn't either,' Alice said. 'But I thought it would be something to do. And not many people go to listen to Joan. You know, just for her.'

Evelyn felt as if she was being bulldozed into

343

something she didn't really want to do, but she couldn't say no now. She cut the roly-poly and poured the tea. 'You're right, Alice,' she said. 'If nothing else it will be something different to do.'

Alice beamed one her smiles that pushed up her already round cheeks and Evelyn could tell that Dad was taken.

★ ★ ★

At last a letter from Sylvie. Dad and Evelyn jostled to tear the envelope open, then both stood back not wanting to ruin the precious letter inside. They read it together in silence, then took it in turns to read it aloud to each other.

7th April 1945

Dear Evelyn and Dad,

I'm writing this sitting in what used to be the lounge area of the Nellie Wallace when she was a cruise liner. That's not what she's actually called, but the crew refer to her by that name with real fondness in their voices, like they're talking about a sweetheart or young child. So it's caught on. The name of the ship is the MS Nea Hellas and we embarked from Glasgow on the 3rd of April bound for Halifax. We were each given a passenger list, along with the number of our berth, and I panicked when I couldn't find my name on it. I was only looking under Draper, wasn't I! Then I found myself as I'll be known from now on: Mrs Alexander G. Buchan. Mr A.G.B.

himself is on a ship full of injured soldiers travelling in convoy with us.

I can hear the squally sea smacking the window, but we're blacked out here, too, in the middle of the Atlantic, so I can't see it. But during drill this morning the froth on the greeny-grey waves was hitting the deck next to me. No point in doing your hair before drill, just pull on a headscarf, bridge-style and try to undo the mess later.

So much has happened already since I said goodbye to you both. It's difficult to describe how much I miss you, although I'm very excited about the journey and starting proper married life. There are hundreds of us all in the same boat (ha ha) on this ship. I've palled up with two or three girls, one of them going all the way to Saskatchewan, like me. Her name is Irene and she's expecting in five months' time. A lot of the girls have babies and children so drying napkins are draped everywhere. There's a nursery on board manned by Red Cross nurses, and I might volunteer my help to give some poor woman a break and to get ready for the houseful Alec wants. (I hope you approve, Dad.)

I can hear the dinner triangle announcing the first sitting so I will write more later.

8th April 1945

We've been told our journey is going to take much longer than the usual five days as we're crisscrossing the Atlantic. So, as there's

345

no way of posting anything until we disembark in Halifax, I'll spin this letter out until then.

I'm not sure where we are as all I can see when on deck is water. Once or twice I've glimpsed another of the convoy ships through the sea mist, but can't make out if it's Alec's or not. I thought travelling in convoy meant staying close together. I do wish I could see him, but I can only imagine him looking out across the waves for me as I look for him.

Thank goodness for Rene. We seem to be almost the only ones left not heaving with seasickness. In the next cabin there are four women, four babies in carrying cots and a two-year-old. All the grown-ups are sick. We can hear them through the thin walls and it's not pleasant. I suppose they were too unwell to attend drill today, but that didn't stop two of the ship's officers rapping on their door and demanding to know why they weren't on port or starboard or wherever for lifeboat practice. Seems we're under army orders and have to comply. I'm sure it's for the best anyway. I carry the tot up the slippery steps now, although she wriggles and squirms looking for her mum. Poor little thing.

10th April 1945

I'm afraid I succumbed to the dreaded motion sickness. All I could manage was to sit up in my bunk, two pillows behind me, and try to hold my pen steady. I wish I could

346

describe it to you; it's nothing like anything I've had before. Serves me right. Rene and I were in the habit of pooh-poohing all the women staggering about with paper bags in their hands, looking as ashen and washed-out as the underside of a boat, even though we could see how ill they were. I felt so bad that instead of going to all the trouble of avoiding torpedoes, I wished the captain would locate a few and steer straight for them. Put us all out of our misery. I felt a bit better after boat drill but came straight back to bed and then felt worse than ever.

Next thing I knew, Rene came to my cabin. I thought I was robust, but she must be made of stern stuff to be up and about on this sea in her condition. She pushed past me and came right in, making herself comfortable on my bunk. 'Put these on,' she ordered, handing me my skirt and jumper. I tried to take them from her but fell back onto the bed instead. She pulled me forward and helped me drag on my clothes. 'The thing about seasickness,' she said, 'is if you give in to it you feel worse. It's the deck for you.'

She steadied me through the corridors and walkways and do you know? She was right. After I'd heaved up my guts over the rail, fodder for King Neptune Rene called it, I did feel better and have spent most of my time up here during the day either walking or sitting on the deck with a blanket around my shoulders. I've been able to keep a bit of food down, but nothing like I could before this sickness set in. And it's heart-breaking — the food is wonderful and there's plenty of it. White bread and lovely jam. And bananas. Yes, Evelyn, we have some bananas today! Do as I say and get yourself a Canuck this very minute. I want you to have some of this handsome nosh, too.

14th April 1945

Yesterday morning was lovely and warm. Someone said we were sailing near the Azores, wherever they are. They do sound exotic though, don't they? I'll ask Alec about them when we're together again and let you know. Today, though, when we came up for drill, icicles were hanging off the rails. No idea where we could be now.

Rene started a lottery for a bit of a laugh. Put in half a bob and guess the time of day we'll dock, not the date as there are too many of us to make that work. I guessed 11:47 a.m. I don't know why, I just thought of it and it stuck.

Books are handed around back and forth among the girls. Nursery World, Woman, Picture Post, Woman's Weekly. And of course, we all have our personal, dog-eared copies of Welcome to War Brides. We play cards sometimes; Rene's teaching me Bridge. That's a bit toffee-nosed for me, love, I told her. We play Newmarket at home. Someone organised a game of Bingo, which was great fun. One of the girls has a first-rate voice and when she sings lullabies to her little ones it puts us all to sleep.

16th April 1945

Rene's got the hang of Newmarket, but I'm still struggling with Bridge. There's a lot of guesswork going on about Canada, especially now we're getting closer. Some say it's hot and humid, others freezing cold with inches of snow on the ground most of the year round. One of the girls said there are a lot of shops and, of course, no rations to worry about. Someone else said if you're not lucky enough to live in one of the big cities then you'd have to find a way of getting the hundreds of miles to the nearest shops as there aren't any buses or Tubes or even roads, in some places. When I'm on deck, I look out over wave after churning, grey wave and think about what's been said. England seems a long way away.

17th April 1945

We're docking tomorrow and everyone is getting very excited but in a rather subdued, relieved kind of way. All the girls are packing up their things, exchanging addresses, pinching their cheeks to put some colour in them, topping and tailing babies with extra care and trying to smooth the creases out of skirts and blouses. I can't wait to see the back of this ship. *When the gangplank is lowered and we're given the okay to disembark, I shall be the first in line off the bloody thing. Five days wouldn't have been too bad, but nearly two weeks feels like a prison sentence. The sailor's life is not for me.*

Between the three of us, I do feel a bit nervy about what's next. I don't think I'll see Alec as he'll probably be put straight on a troop train to his barracks and I'll have to board another for a two-day journey to where Mr and Mrs Buchan will be waiting for me. Fiona and Hugh, they want me to call them, but I think I'll wait until they tell me to do so face to face. Alec always calls Dad Mr Draper, or sir, so I think I should pay his parents the same respect. The thing I'm looking forward to the most about arriving in Saskatoon is reading a letter from you, which I know you will have written and sent by now.

Well, dear Dad and Evelyn, I must try to get some sleep now so I don't look like a ghoul when I first set eyes on Canada. I'm going to seal this letter and as soon as possible tomorrow I will post it. I can picture your faces when you see the Halifax postmark and know it's from me.

With all my love,
Sylvie

'The journey sounds hellish,' Evelyn said. 'I didn't know seasickness could be so awful.'

Dad held his stomach. 'I feel off-balance just thinking about it. But the food . . . Unbelievable.

350

What are we having for tea?'

Evelyn didn't take her eyes off her sister's writing. 'Rabbit and swede stew with dumplings,' she said.

Dad groaned. 'Now I really do feel sick.'

'Afraid it's take it or leave it,' Evelyn said. 'Rene sounds nice. I'm glad Sylvie's found a friend.'

'I hate to think of her lonely, too, love.'

'I know,' Evelyn said. 'Our letters will be waiting for her in Saskatoon, won't they?'

'I'm sure of it, given how long it's taken her to get there. But Bridge?' Dad shook his head. 'I'll stick to Newmarket.'

Evelyn looked at her dad. 'Could you make the sea passage?'

'Not next to a cabin full of crying babies. I've had my fill of all that.'

Evelyn left the letter on the kitchen table so she and Dad could pick it up and reread it any time they wanted to. Later she would throw away all of Ron's letters, something she should have done ages ago, and use Mum's old writing box to store Sylvie's letters in.

She thought continuously about all the things Sylvie had written about and wondered if her own news was enough to hold Sylvie's attention after everything she had experienced already. She wrote about her job in the libraries in and around London; she had been given a season ticket for the bus and Tube and a bit extra in her pay packet for lunch. It was exciting to wonder each morning where she would be posted that day and was surprised at how different from each other areas in London seemed to be. Some libraries were on

351

wide, leafy streets, others crammed in amongst narrow shops and pubs. One was lending from a cordoned-off corner of a newsagent, another from the ground floor foyer of a block of flats.

The people were at odds, too, and spoke with more dialects than Evelyn had heard before; some enunciated their words with clipped tones and some with long vowels. Not to mention the various tastes in clothes, shoes and hats. It was all very interesting, but not something that Evelyn thought she could stick at for long.

★ ★ ★

19th April 1945

Dear Evelyn,

I will try to describe Canada through a train window to you. Big. There's no other word for it. Well, I suppose there are a few. Vast, huge, enormous, gigantic. The list could go on but all the words would mean the same thing. We're puffing away from the coast through what the stewards call the interior, heading towards the prairies.

Halifax was so drab, cold, windy and bleak. It looked as if the sea had battered the town so often it left the houses washed with grey. They were odd, too, like wooden beer crates turned upside down. Some of the girls standing around me on the deck started to cry, I'm not sure whether from tiredness or disappointment. I didn't win the lottery about our arrival time and I wasn't first off the ship, but waited my turn arm in arm with Rene.

The nicest thing about it was a military band playing 'Here Comes the Bride' on the quayside. That made us laugh.

We were ushered through the pier, which looked like a cattle shed (don't say anything about cows), given the once-over by a medical officer, had our papers checked and given an immigration card. Then we were set free, into the arms of waiting husbands or to be directed by the Red Cross to a train or ferry, or to a B and B to wait for a connection this morning.

One poor woman, with two little boys, was handed a telegram by a Red Cross worker who then put her arms around her and led her away. Later, in our overnight hostel, another girl told me and Rene the telegram was from the woman's husband telling her to go home as he'd found someone else. Can you imagine? We were all very quiet for a time after that, feeling sorry for her.

This morning we boarded our train at 8:35 a.m. so we're about four hours into our journey. We've passed through mile after mile without any sign of people, just grey rocks, waves of wheat swaying like the ocean, forests of sea-green trees. The trains are huge, too. You can curve round a bend in the track, look out the window and see the end of the train curling miles behind you. The horns they use have a melancholy wail that sounds so sad. Sometimes I hear it keening to me . . . Nooooo . . . Dooooon't . . . Gooooo. But still we push on.

I must say, though, we're treated very well. Again, lovely food, cups of tea, comfy seats and beds. There are sixty or more of us on board, so we tend to stick together in smaller groups. I'm good enough at Bridge now to play as Rene's partner against other girls. I'll teach you when next we're together. I don't know when that will be, but it can't be soon enough.

Love you,
Sylvie

★　★　★

Stamping books in Bexleyheath Library without looking up at the queue in front of her, Evelyn listened to the tinkle of rain on the window and the whirr of machinery from a site across the road; that was where her heart was and she so wished the rest of her being could join it. She gritted her teeth in frustration and pounded the inky date onto the front pages as if she was using a jack-hammer.

War was cruel, she thought, but most people only thought about the obvious when they agreed on that. There were so many subtle, barely perceptible ways in which the poisonous, far-reaching tentacles of such an almighty conflict grabbed hold of people and dealt them bitter blows. For Alec it was his facial injury, for Stan his limp, for Gwen her Johnny, for Dad the heartbreak of seeing it all again and for her, the introduction to something that she truly loved only to have that avenue denied her.

354

She knew there was no comparison between others' suffering and her disappointment and she would never let on too much about it because she didn't want to offend, but in her heart it felt almost like a bereavement.

★ ★ ★

30th April 1945

Dear Evelyn,
   Well I think I've met everyone at last. Alec has been home on leave for the last week and, do you know, he went to change into his civvies and when he came back into the sitting room I didn't recognise him. My own husband! I thought he was another brother or cousin as I'd never seen him in anything but his uniform. He's going to have an operation, or perhaps a few, to tidy up his face but of course, there's nothing to be done about his eye. He'll have to decide in the long run whether he wants to try a glass eye or stick with the patch.
   Fiona and Hugh and the rest of the clan continue to be as lovely and welcoming to me as possible. I feel very lucky in that respect. Alec's little brothers keep asking me to repeat certain phrases like, 'Yes, my love' and 'Whatever can you mean?' They seem to get a kick out of the way I say 'can't' and 'ask'. Their mum keeps telling them to shush up but I think they're great fun.
   We've been able to get away in Hugh's old heap, as he calls it, to look around the

countryside and meet the family who live even closer to the heart of nowhere than my in-laws. It was a bit slow going at first while Alec got used to driving without his left eye. The car almost came off the road twice but we laughed our way through it. We drove through wheat, around wheat, to the left and right of wheat towards a horizon of wheat for hours before we came to what Alec says is a homestead to spend some time with Malcolm's mum and dad. A shiver ran up my spine when we sat in the parlour with a photo of Malcolm smiling at us from the dresser.

Before I married Alec he told me he lived with his parents on a small farm on the fringe of Saskatoon. So I imagined Cockfosters or somewhere similar, wouldn't you? But the outskirts of town here means no shops. Not one. Except for the general store, which sells flour by the sackful and doesn't count. Saskatoon is a good way away but Alec says he'll teach me to drive so I can go in whenever I like. I find it hard to imagine driving hours through wheat fields, oh and I forgot to mention, acres of rye, canola, lentils, oats and barley to get to the shops, but I might have to get used to it.

Alec and I spent a couple of days in a small hotel in Saskatoon and it's very nice there. Lots to see and do. We had a nice meal in a diner and went to the cinema. We turned up unannounced to visit Rene and her husband who live in an area called Nutana. It was so lovely to see Rene again. Now Alec's talking

356

about trying to get a job in the city selling farm machinery when he's demobbed, which I think would be better for both of us.

Now, Evelyn, there's a university in Saskatoon and we saw girls wandering around with books in their hands. Alec said they take the same courses as the men. Next time we drive in I'm going to enquire about engineering for you. I'm sure you would get on well there and the college would love to have a girl from London with an English accent. You could stay with us and we'd help you out. Dad, too, of course. Please, please, dear sister, say you will at least consider it. I miss you so much.

Love always,
Sylvie

* * *

If only Sylvie were here, Evelyn thought, swishing her blistered feet around in a bowl of warm water. There was no possible way she could capture the atmosphere and the sheer exuberance in a letter to her, but she would try later before she forgot any of the details.

The West End had been crammed with people dancing and singing. 'Where have they all come from?' Alice shouted in her ear.

'No idea,' Evelyn cupped her hands around her mouth and yelled back.

Servicemen jumped in the fountain at Trafalgar Square, soaking anyone within splashing distance. A sopping-wet soldier grabbed two girls at once and pulled them under the foam with him

357

and they'd all come up squealing with laughter. Beer was slopped and shared. Everyone kissed strangers. Evelyn and Alice had tagged onto an endless conga line and an officer carried Evelyn halfway up the Mall in a fireman's lift, with Stan hobbling along behind. Men climbed lamp posts and women tore the obnoxious blackouts to shreds. And the bells, what a heart-warming music they made, answering each other from every corner of London. And standing guard over all of them, as he'd always done, was Big Ben, lit up like a beacon again at long last.

Reaching over to Dad's chair, Evelyn grabbed a cushion and put it behind her head, which was throbbing in rhythm with her feet. The hammering reminded her of vibrating the concrete on the bridge. She closed her eyes and thought of Sylvie, who'd written that where Alec's parents live there was no electricity or running water. How strange, she thought, to have experienced something as profound as VE Day, when Sylvie perhaps hadn't yet read about it in the newspapers or heard any of Churchill's speeches on the wireless.

She, Alice and Stan had caught the one from the balcony of the Ministry of Health.

'God bless you all,' the prime minister had said. And he told them that the victory was theirs.

They'd bellowed back with everyone else, 'No, it's yours.'

Winnie hadn't said anything for a couple of seconds, just growled like he does as if he was trying to find the right words. But Evelyn wondered if he was as choked as they were.

When he was ready he carried on by telling

them that the victory belonged to the cause of freedom all over the world. He said that history had never seen a greater day and that all of them had tried and done their best.

The crowd had been deafening in their agreement. When they'd quietened down a little, Churchill listed all the things that had not weakened their resolve in any way: the long years, the dangers, the fierce attacks of the enemy.

Then that was it from the great man, except for another 'God bless you all' and the roar that followed was more strident than a detachment of V-2 bombers. Everyone jumped up and down with such force that a small child slipped from the shoulders of the man next to her. Some people cried, some laughed, some looked as if they were in shock. And some, like Evelyn, did all three time and again. Then she was swung off her feet by a massive Hokey-Cokey ring and when they couldn't shake it all about any longer, they stumbled into the nearest pub for another drink. No wonder her feet and head ached. She knew she should stay in tonight and rest, but yesterday wasn't the end of it and she didn't want to miss a thing.

She sat up and sloshed her feet around in the tepid water. What she didn't think she could, or perhaps should, describe to Sylvie was how she felt now that reality was sinking in. But she needed to clarify her feelings for herself.

She dried her feet, emptied the bowl into the vegetable patch and put on the kettle. Elation, of course; who wouldn't feel jubilant? It was a wonderful triumph and she agreed with Winnie; they had all been very brave. She hadn't cried much during the last five years, but now tears came to her eyes when she thought about the nights in the Underground, the hours spent queuing for rations, the ear-splitting sirens, the privation, the rounds of flu, the sight of some poor woman's beloved crockery smashed in the street, the missing limbs, the missing people. Already she couldn't comprehend how they'd borne it all and how they would have carried on if they'd had to; it was hard to admit, but they'd been on their knees.

Perhaps she could write all of that down for Sylvie, but she didn't think she could tell her how frightened she felt now that it was over. Anxious about what would happen next. How the independent resolve that Churchill spoke about could be sustained to get them out of the mess that was left. She didn't want to feel down, or entertain a defeatist attitude; she wanted nothing else but yesterday's mood to continue to embrace her and hold her in its power. Yes, there was disorder and disarray everywhere. *But it is* our *chaos*, she thought, our *streets strewn with rubble and rubbish, full of bomb sites and potholes.* Our *lack of flats and houses, want of money, food and fuel.* Our *spoils of the victory and ours to keep.* No one could take it from them now.

Never mind resolving the country's problems, she had her own dilemmas to sort out. Whenever she thought about university in Canada, she pictured herself wandering around with a notebook and pencil looking a bit lost.

Then there was the Imperial to consider and Dad. She couldn't leave him and wasn't sure he

360

would leave Uncle Bert and his mates at the pub.

And she was still interested in Stan. She smiled when she thought about him; he could still make her laugh, he still danced beautifully and he did have good, solid prospects ahead of him. The shop in Sidcup would be, if anything, calm and idyllic. And predictable. Waiting for her tea to cool, Evelyn played with the contours of the cup. She remembered another man in uniform who she'd described as steady and how unshackled and relieved she'd felt when they'd parted company.

The back door opened and Dad came in, his paper tucked under his arm. 'Another of those going by any chance?' He pointed to the tea.

Evelyn nodded and poured him a cup without saying a word.

'Alright, my love?' Dad frowned in concern.

Evelyn nodded again and touched her head.

'And me,' Dad laughed, rubbing his bald spot. 'Out with Stan tonight?'

'Yes,' Evelyn said. Then murmuring with conviction and sadness she added, 'For one last time.'

★ ★ ★

When Evelyn opened the package from Sylvie it contained four Tootsie Rolls and something called a prospectus. She had never seen anything like the colours in some of the photographs and she stroked the pages, half expecting the images to blur. Not wanting to alarm Dad, she took it all up to her room and shut the door behind her. Lying on the childhood bed she'd long outgrown, she read about the university and the engineering course,

361

which sounded daunting, but was also everything she wanted. Then she unfolded the single sheet of writing paper from Sylvie.

16th May 1945

Dear Evelyn,

Just a quick note because I want to get this prospectus in the post to you today. Alec and I took a trip to Saskatoon to look at apartments to rent and we went into the university to make enquiries for you. I told them all about what you did on the bridge and your involvement with the WES. They said they would love to have you in the Engineering Department and would give you all the help you need. The new semester starts in September, which would give you and Dad enough time to pack up there and to sort yourselves out here before you start. Do you want me to mention any of this to Dad when I write to him?

It's a wonderful opportunity, Evelyn, so please don't just dismiss it. Think seriously and I'm keeping everything crossed that you decide to give it a go.

All my love,

Sylvie

P.S. Enjoy the sweets. There are plenty more waiting for you here.

Evelyn closed her eyes and pictured herself again on what was called the campus, but this time in her imagination she looked self-assured

362

and capable.

She knew she would have to broach the subject with Dad. But how? She couldn't demand that he pack up and leave everything he'd ever known for what he perceived to be a silly, whimsical fancy. Besides, if she somehow managed to force him to go to Canada, she knew she would be haunted by her own selfishness and neither the course or being close to Sylvie would make her content. But this was too important to her not to talk to Dad about, even if nothing came of it.

'Evelyn,' Dad's voice carried up the stairs. 'Just popping round to Uncle Bert's.'

She took a deep breath; it was now or never. 'Wait a minute, Dad,' she called. 'I need to talk to you.'

She never dreamed that Dad would come up with such a good solution. He listened and didn't make flippant remarks. But, he said, it would be silly for both of them to leave everything they had here before they were sure that Evelyn would settle. After all, it would be very difficult to have to come back to nothing and start all over again.

That, Evelyn agreed, would put them in a very distressing situation.

'So,' Dad said. 'I want you to go for one, what is it, semester? And see how you get on.'

'And if I like it?' Evelyn asked.

Evelyn counted three beats of her heart before Dad answered, 'I'll join you.'

'Do you promise, Dad?'

'I promise.'

Evelyn put her arms around Dad's neck and held on tight.

When Dad spoke, Evelyn heard the first hint of a catch in his voice. 'When do think you'll leave?'

'Perhaps in the New Year,' she said. 'I need to tie up a few loose ends first. And I'll need to save some lolly for the journey and to pay my way once I get there.'

Dad held Evelyn away from him and looked in her eyes. He nodded and his mouth trembled when he tried to return her smile. Soon he would walk to see Uncle Bert and she would write to Sylvie and give her plenty of notice to have the kettle on for her arrival.

16

June — November 1945

Joan

Joan had no immediate regrets about being laid off the bridge. No teary farewells or last-minute promises to keep in touch. There didn't seem any point in pursuing friendships that hadn't materialised by that stage. She'd remember with fondness some of her time on the tools, others she'd as soon forget. Now she could devote her energy to Colin's Kats. Playing in the, at first, unfamiliar jazz genre was so different from the orchestral music she had been brought up in; it came across to the musician and audience alike as free, easy, relaxed. It evoked images of effortless nonchalance. But the discipline needed to engender that aura was as rigid and structured as that needed to play the music that was considered to be loftier and more highbrow.

Every time she picked up her instrument, she was overwhelmed with a deep sense of what she could only describe as joy: intense happiness at being given this second chance to do something that gave her and others such pleasure. To think, she had almost abandoned it forever. She shook her head, exasperated with herself. Thank goodness for Colin; he had never doubted that she would feel so exhilarated once she had the violin in her hands again.

But the group hadn't, as yet, been able to secure a regular spot in a club, although they played on-off gigs in a number of places and were beginning to recognise a few of the same faces amongst the crowd, looking eager and appreciative.

She advertised for a saxophonist and auditioned seven, leaving the final choice out of her shortlisted three to Colin. He'd gone for Bernie, a short, rather squat man who had a habit of trying to keep his thinning hair behind his ears with the palms of his hands. Joan was pleased, as he'd been her first choice for the way he could hit and hold the high notes. She hadn't been as lucky finding a permanent drummer. They would have loved to keep the session musician they used when possible, but he worked shifts so couldn't be relied on.

Hazel encouraged Joan to practise in the sitting room so she and Ivy could listen, but that set-up wasn't always productive as Hazel kept interrupting with song suggestions or by joining in without knowing the lyrics, dancing around and applauding. From her chair, Ivy moved her eyes to watch her daughter with what Joan sometimes interpreted as a trace of chagrin on her otherwise blank face.

Hazel longed to hear the combo playing together, but refused to ask a neighbour to sit with Ivy and let Alice take her to a club, or to let Alice stay with Ivy while Joan escorted her to Soho and back. 'You are the sweetest girls,' she said. 'But I couldn't leave Mummy, especially not in the evening.' So Alice nagged until Joan arranged for the group to hold a practice in the hostel.

As the blackouts had been taken down, washed and stored away and the afternoon consisted of a sprinkling of showers and sunny patches, Hazel felt justified in leaving the front windows of the house wide open, the white nets billowing in and puffing out. Not that there was anyone passing by, tucked up in the corner of the terrace as they were, to hear when the trio started up.

For the occasion, Hazel wore a turquoise jumper and cardigan with tiny pearl buttons, a matching string around her neck. The skirt she had on must have been at the back of her wardrobe for years; it fell to below the knee, widened at the hip and released a whiff of mothballs every time she moved. Two beautiful mother-of-pearl combs held wiry curls off her face. Her cheeks were rouged, her lips painted. Ivy, too, had been done up. A locket on a chain fell against her lace-collared cream blouse, and the red Hazel had painted on her thin, sliding lips filtered into the delta of lines around her mouth. A syrup loaf had been baked, teacups set out, sherry bottle unstoppered. The sight of the two older women, and the trouble they'd been to, made Joan turn away and concentrate on applying rosin to her bow with vigour.

When Colin arrived, navigating his new double bass down the hall and through the tight sitting-room door, Hazel clapped her hands with delight. He bobbed his head in turn to each of the women, except Joan, and kissed their hands with a brush of his lips. Joan he patted on the back and said, 'Hello there, Joan old girl.' And surprise grated on her like the screech of a flat note when she registered disappointment at being excluded from his show of charm. Reaching for her violin, she fumbled around for something to play and settled on a section of a string quartet by Beethoven.

'Something livelier,' Hazel said.

'Give me a minute, Hazel,' Joan answered. 'I'm just tuning up.'

Colin took off his jacket and put it on the back of Ivy's chair, loosened his tie and rolled up his sleeves to his elbows. 'Hear, hear,' he said. 'I'm with Hazel.'

Joan looked at him, hands on his hips, a loose curve of wavy hair resting on his forehead, egging her on with a smile and a raised eyebrow. 'Alright,' she said. 'How about this?'

She picked out the tune to 'Ac-Cent-Tchu-Ate the Positive' and the bow skimmed over the strings as if it were the wing of a dragonfly, gliding across a still pond.

Hazel squealed, clapping her hands again. 'We know this one, don't we, Mummy?'

Joan stumbled over a few notes, her jaw knocking the chinrest as she laughed out loud, raw and raucous.

'I loves it, too,' Alice said, tapping time on Ivy's delicate, gossamer-fine hand.

'We all do,' Colin said. 'Especially the way Joan plays it.' He bowed from the waist and put his hand out to Hazel. Together they waltzed in circles around the furniture in the crowded front room.

Bernie arrived, was introduced and handed a sherry. The party had begun.

★ ★ ★

Now though, the novelty of waiting for a big break was beginning to wear off and there were long hours, which Joan knew were unhealthy, when she wasn't playing or practising or promoting the combo. She renewed her library pass, ran errands for Hazel, walked, met Alice during her dinner break and tried to untangle the tight knots she'd formed in her mind about her life.

Sitting on a bench in the sun, Joan rested Hazel's shopping next to her and watched children playing with a ball and stick, dogs chasing birds, sunlight sifting through laden trees. Alice had been on her break when Joan called at the greengrocer's. 'Out with another girl,' the shop owner said. Evelyn, Joan supposed.

She had hours until she needed to go back and get her clothes and violin ready for tonight. Breathing in and out slowly, she felt the peace around her. Although there was plenty of evidence lying around to suggest nothing much had changed, Joan sensed a newness, an altered state. Not a new creation; nothing pristine or untouched. More of a make-do-and-mend project. Like the country's vote for Attlee, it was a time for getting rid of what was hackneyed, letting go of the past that was dragging down the present and holding things back.

To begin with she'd felt euphoric, as if everything was happening for her at the right time. Work on the bridge finished, the war ended, she was playing again. She thought that would be enough to allow the way she'd lived and the events that had happened to slip away from her cognisance and bury themselves deep under the rubble. And some of

them she had reconciled: the way she'd demeaned
Alice, the black market, skulking around, hiding
in sly shadows, creating a hardness around herself;
Ralph and Cyril. But there was one person who
refused to be dealt with in the same way: Mother.

Joan was able now to admit, with some reluc-
tance, that Mother had been somewhat right in
her summation of Ralph, but the fact remained
that a large part of the reason Joan took up with
Ralph in the first place was to get away from
Mother. And as far as the violin was concerned,
well perhaps Mother really did want what was
best for her. But why did she think it necessary
to be so single-minded and overbearing about the
whole thing?

Joan shook her head; it kept coming back to
the violin, as it always had. Not to the innoc-
uous lump of wood itself, fashioned to make
exquisite sounds, but to how she'd been forced
into making it her whole life. Or thought she
had. Of course, there was no doubt she'd been
encouraged to the exception of everything else;
pampered and mollycoddled and kept well away
from other influences.

But if that hadn't happened, she wouldn't
be so pleased to have picked up the instrument
again, even if it was to play in an entirely different
fashion. That had been her decision and she was
proud of it. Perhaps Mother and all her nagging
had merely facilitated that conclusion. She began
to wonder if she'd been too cruel. But harshness
had seemed necessary to make her point. Mother
had needed to know her ambition for Joan was
damaging her, but perhaps she had taken it too

370

far and had ended up wounding herself in the pro-
cess. She'd seized on that one injustice to excuse
whatever she did, justify her selfishness and give
credence to her lack of accountability.

Newly available time led her to indulge in a series
of elaborate conversations she held in her mind
with Mother. In these scenes she was enraged but
articulate, calm and to the point. Mother weak
with shock at her eloquent coherence, stunned at
the effect of her actions. Then Mother begged her
forgiveness.

She mentioned to Alice that there were certain
things she'd like to say to a certain person she was
no longer in touch with. 'Write to them,' Alice
said. 'Tell them what you thinks.'

'That's a good idea,' Joan said, but wasn't
convinced she could see it through. 'I'm not so
sure though,' she said. 'It would be so hard, to put
it all down in writing and then imagine the hurt
when she opened it.'

'Or write the letter then reads it to me.'

Joan considered that idea; it sounded as if it
might be cleansing.

'Or say the words aloud in your room then
throw the letters in the bin.' Joan felt Alice watching her. 'Is it your ma? Sorry, your mother?'

Joan nodded her head and left it at that.

It was hard to imagine all of her confused
thoughts coming out in a letter, or face to face.
She and Mother would probably end up tearing
each other apart.

A lady wearing surgical stockings and sturdy
walking shoes strode past, eyes straight ahead,
sidestepping people walking the other way without

varying her pace. Joan followed her progress and thought: *there's a woman with somewhere to go and something to do*. She needed a job; a proper one. One that would take her out every day at the same time, keep her occupied for eight or nine hours and end as the evening was beginning, so she could carry on playing with the group. That's what Colin and Bernie did, and so should she.

The shillings and pence were getting a bit tight, too. The few pounds they made for a night in a club didn't go far when split three ways, and some of that had gone on equipment and advertising. It was lucky she'd put a bit by from her wages on the bridge. But, she could feel the heat rising when she thought of it now, she'd only been able to do so because she'd had that dirty money coming in. Any little job would do now, really, while she kept her eye on the bigger goal. Something like Alice had or — she examined her knuckles, turning her fingers towards her to scrutinise the nails — if she didn't want to get her hands mucky, something in an office.

There was a growling rumble in the distance that a few months ago might have been the start of a bombing raid. No one flinched or started like a spooked rabbit. A man and woman walked past, about the same age as her and Colin, their arms lightly caressing each other's waists, their faces close together. Whispering, giggling, holding their palms up to catch the first drops of rain. She wondered what it would be like to walk with Colin in the same way. But the time when anything good might have happened between them had passed, as it had done with Mother. She collected up her things and ran for home, making it indoors before the first knife of lightning serrated the sky.

The storm was to last all night and into the early hours of the next morning. Hazel was terrified, but her nerves became a bit steadier with someone to talk to and a tumbler of sherry. When Alice came home, she said she would stop in so Joan could get off to her gig.

Is this the way our lives will go, mine and Alice's? thought Joan, changing for the evening in her room. Caring for Hazel and Ivy, and eventually Hazel on her own, as Hazel cared for her mother? It was a revealing yet unsettling notion, and one Joan didn't care to consider too carefully.

'I were telling Hazel,' Alice said when Joan stuck her head around the door to say goodbye, 'that the man from the shop next door poked his head in the greengrocer's this afternoon and said the storm were God showing his displeasure for us pushing Churchill out and voting Attlee in.'

'Oh dear me,' Joan said, laughing. 'What nonsense. We need someone new now, someone with different ideas.'

'I know,' Alice said. 'But he says we did the wrong thing and we'll pay for it.'

'Poor Winnie,' Hazel said. 'He must feel as though he's been put out to meadow like an old nag.'

'This isn't his time,' Joan said. 'He's done his bit.'

As she gathered her outdoor things together in the hallway, she could hear Alice talking to Hazel about Beveridge's Five Giant Evils and how the new Labour Government had pledged to eradicate them with the Welfare State.

373

'Oh, did you hear that, Mummy?' Hazel said. 'Attlee's lot says we're to have no more wickedness. What are the five nasty things he's getting rid of, my sweetheart?'

'I think they was disease, want, ignorance . . . '

Joan sighed and, huddling under her umbrella, made her way through the storm to the Tube.

★ ★ ★

Welfare system or not, no one was going to pay Joan enough to sit around all day waiting for the combo to be discovered. She joined the long queue of women at the Employment Exchange; the window serving men standing empty for most of the time she was there, as they got first grabs at all the jobs going now they were coming home. Holding her head to one side, the woman behind the counter stretched her mouth into a weak, sympathetic smile. Her fleshy bosom rested on the counter while she fiddled with the strap of her watch, trying to ease the pressure points that cut into her wrist.

'Can I sign on for work, please?' Joan asked.

'Of course,' the woman said, picking up a pen and a form. She took down Joan's details. 'Now, experience? Previous employment?'

'My war job was on the Waterloo Bridge. So construction, I suppose. Building. The tools, the girls used to call it. But I . . . '

'Lovely piece of work,' the woman said, twiddling the pen between her stout fingers. 'Made my journey to and from this place much easier. My friend and I were wondering what it's made

374

from. You know, on the sides. It's much lighter than the other crossings.'

'Portland Stone,' Joan said. 'It's self-cleaning. That's why it stays that pale colour.'

'How does that work then?'

Joan shrugged. 'I'm not entirely sure. But I heard someone say it cleans itself every time it rains.'

The woman leaned back and chuckled. 'If only the same could be applied to the house. And the washing. And mending.'

'Yes, if only,' Joan said. 'As I was saying, I really don't want . . .'

'And even if you did, there's nothing going for women at all in that line of work.' She made a few notes. 'What about prior to that?'

Before Joan said a word, she knew how incongruous her answer would sound. 'I played the violin in an orchestra.'

The woman looked at Joan's hands, then added something a line below what she'd already written. 'Two very different occupations,' she said. 'That's happening more frequently now, what with the war having interfered with careers. But I do believe musicians have their own employment office. And union.' She opened a drawer and scoured through the contents. 'I think I have the address here.'

'I'm already playing in a band,' Joan said. 'But I need a day job to keep me going.'

'In that case, we have a number that might suit. Do you have any preference for which service area?'

'One that'll be easy on my hands. If possible.'

'Well, there's catering. Office or shop work. Telephonist?'

Joan decided on breakfast and lunch waitressing at the Strand Palace. The work was hard and she was used to that, but her legs and feet throbbed with fatigue by the end of a shift. She had to wear a black dress, a white apron and a funny little hat.

The crowd she worked with was nice enough, always ready for a laugh or a moan when not in front of the customers. A busboy named Sid had a scathing remark about everyone whose table he cleared, mimicking accents, turns of phrase and gestures with cutting precision. He reminded Joan of Colin, in that respect, although Colin's impersonations were softer. They had to do more with genuine affection and fascination with people than the edge of contempt in Sid's performances. As she watched Sid taking off an elderly Lady Someone-or-Other, wrinkling his nose in distaste and crooking his little finger, she thought about how Colin had her in stitches imitating Bernie. He'd shake his head, rub his hands over his hair, shake his head again, close his eyes, enthralled by the saxophone he tilted towards the ceiling, then open them wide, blinking rapidly as Bernie did at the audience.

The wages from the hotel were reasonable, about the same as the bridge, but with the bonus of pooled tips. All gratuities had to be handed over to the room manager who wrote the amount in a notebook. On Saturday afternoons, after the lunch house was cleared, he sat down and divided it unequally between his staff. He took a clean ten per cent off the top for himself, the two headwaiters were each allotted ten per cent of the remainder, waiters the next cut, waitresses after them, until finally the porters and busboys were tossed the last few pence.

It was usual for a hierarchy to exist; that was the same everywhere. But she was peeved that all the waiting staff didn't get the same reward. It would have been much more reasonable for each individual to pocket what was left on the table by the customers. While she was on the bridge she hadn't thought much about getting paid less for doing the same job as a man. Evelyn had kicked up a fuss about it, or tried to, but it never came to anything. It was more keenly felt now, when hands were held out and she could see the difference between the coins in her palm and those in the gnarly masculine one next to her.

Joan stuck it out for three weeks, and during that time she looked for any excuse to hand in her notice. The unjust division of tips could have sufficed, as could a fear of cutting her fingers on broken crockery, or the dread of developing varicose veins. Those reasons weren't quite enough to substantiate another visit to the Employment Exchange, but one afternoon the perfect pretext presented itself in the form of Mother.

Three-quarters of an hour into the lunch shift and the restaurant was filling up. Nine of Joan's ten tables were occupied by groups of ladies, couples, businessmen, RAF and Army officers, two families with school-age children; some had been handed menus, others had given their orders and were enjoying an early drink. As Joan pushed through the swing doors from the kitchen to the

377

dining room, pad in hand, she looked up to gauge numbers standing in the queue behind the reservations desk. From the middle of a group of immaculately dressed women, Mother caught her eye and reddened. Joan stood inert, ignoring customers' raised fingers, and watched as Mother touched the sleeve of one of her companions, whispered in her ear and turned away.

The colour in Joan's cheeks was a match for Mother's as she swung back into the kitchen, reported sick and never returned. She hoped that her share of that week's tips would help everyone out a bit, Sid in particular.

Filing for a firm in Baker Street was monotonous and repetitive, and — surprisingly — harder on her hands, working with all that paper, than carrying plates and cups. Every morning she was faced with a mountain of paperwork to store away in metal cabinets; by the evening the pile had diminished only to re-materialise the following day. It could have been demoralising, but she didn't mind the work, routine as it was. No one bothered her and she didn't have to kowtow to anyone. She could think or hum to herself while she slotted documents into alphabetical order. Perhaps she was best suited to lying low, secreting herself away.

Sitting alone in the canteen a week after she started, Joan brought a spoonful of lukewarm oxtail soup to her mouth and listened to the discussion at the next table.

'Well,' said a young man. 'They had their chance with the Potsdam Agreement and they wouldn't accept it.'

Another, with tiny eyes behind thick spectacles, said, 'Still, it doesn't seem right. Look, it says here.' He turned the paper around and pushed it towards his colleague. 'That the device was more than two thousand times more powerful than the largest bomb used to date. *Two thousand times.* I ask you. When you think about the capacity of the V-1s and 2s. It makes you wonder.'

'What was the damage? Does it say?'

The man with poor eyesight leaned in close to the newsprint. 'Not really. Only that they can't make an accurate assessment because the bomb, or device as it's being called, left a huge cloud of impenetrable dust covering the target.'

'Well, as I said. They had their chance. What else could the Yanks do?'

They didn't take their paper with them when they got up to leave so Joan pinched it and read the headline. *US Drops Atomic Bomb on Hiroshima.* She tried to take in what was meant by President Truman's statement that the device marked a victory over the Germans in the race to be first to develop a weapon using atomic energy. She hadn't a clue about that. But any sort of triumph over the Germans sounded good as did the warning to Japan that the Allies would completely destroy their capacity to make war. And Hiroshima was one of the chief supply depots for the Japanese army. So all in all, it must have been worthwhile.

But then she was stuck on the same point that had overwhelmed the man in glasses. *Two thousand times* more destructive than any other bomb. If they'd taken a hit from something like that here

379

in London, there'd be no one left to talk about it.

Three days later a larger device was dropped on a place called Nagasaki.

'Have you heard about that other place in Japan?' Alice asked Joan as she took off her coat in The Blue Posts.

Joan nodded. 'I have,' she said. 'Seems to have been the only topic of conversation at work.'

'Strange business,' Evelyn said. 'I feel as though we should be celebrating, but there's something ominous about it.'

Joan was impressed with the astute observation. 'I know what you mean,' she said. 'Almost apocalyptic.'

'Did I tell you what Hazel had to say about last Monday's bomb?' Alice said.

'I don't think you did,' Joan said.

'She listened to Attlee's announcement on the wireless, looked over at me and said, ''I thought he were supposed to be on the side getting rid of evil, sweetheart.'''

Joan snorted; Evelyn's laugh was dispirited.

'And I'll wager a round she says the same thing again tonight.'

★ ★ ★

Colin was jubilant when he secured a regular slot for Colin's Kats every Sunday night at the Jigs in Wardour Street. The drummer they all enjoyed playing with guaranteed he could make the ten o'clock session and if he couldn't, Colin was sure they could borrow a percussionist from another group.

Although the club had a shady reputation it was quite a coup, Joan had to agree. Warming the crowds for the likes of The Caribbean Club Trio or the Harry Parry Band. Fats Waller was said to have frequented the place before he died, and it was supposed to be one of Duke Ellington's favourite hangouts when in town, although Joan had never seen him there.

Their starting date was the third week in September, and they rehearsed as often as they could get together until then. They practised the start and end melody of every song on their playlist over and over again, until they knew their own and each other's parts and moves with absolute accuracy. At each boundary of the piece, Colin impressed upon them, there was no room for error. The audience had to recognise the tune and be able to dance, tap their feet or fingers, nod along to it.

The middle section was much more loose and difficult to judge. What the crowd wanted to hear during the bulk of the number was improvised solos that might or might not have anything to do with the original tune. It was a chance for each band member to develop and interpret the song. Bernie was master at that. But it wasn't as simple as being in your own little world, showing off your musical prowess. During the solos the band still had to interact with each other, read musical signals about how to support the soloist, when to join in, when to back off, the right time to take over. It was a whole new way of playing, so different from orchestral music during which the conductor alone was allowed to indulge his version of the music. More often than not they ended their sessions warm and glowing, laughing with satisfaction at what Colin called their 'sweet sound'.

'Who are you going to invite along?' Colin asked after one rehearsal.

'My sister and her husband, a couple of friends and a girl I've started seeing,' Bernie answered. 'You?'

'Anyone I can bribe or persuade,' Colin said. 'Mum and Dad, uncles, aunts, cousins. Eileen and Ed. You remember them, Joan. Don't you? A few others from the orchestra, friends from school. I think we should try to pack the place out, make it look like we have a fair few followers.'

'Right,' Bernie said. 'I'll see what I can do.' He packed his sax away with obsessive orderliness and ran for his bus.

Colin turned to Joan. 'What about you, old dear?'

'Don't call me that,' Joan said. 'Or if you must, leave off the old.'

'Touchy tonight, aren't we?'

'I wasn't until you started.'

'Alright. I apologise. Well, who's on your opening night invitation list?'

'I intend to ask Alice, Evelyn and Gwen.'

'Gwen?' Colin asked.

'She was on the bridge. But we didn't have too much to do with each other until recently.'

Colin drummed his fingers on the case of his double bass. 'That it?'

Joan nodded, her back to him.

'Listen. Joan. I know you don't want to hear

382

it, but what about your mum? You know, Mother. And your dad?'

'Father's away and Mother . . . ' Joan raised her hands to the ceiling. 'I wouldn't know where to start telling Mother about jazz and dingy late-night clubs. And if by some miracle she did come along, she would probably stand up and shout that I shouldn't be using my hands to play that kind of music.' Joan thought Colin would laugh along with her at the image, but he looked as disappointed in her as he had when she failed to take her seat at the theatre in favour of meeting with Ralph. It was a look she had hoped never to see again, but there it was.

For their first night, Joan wore a full-length, midnight-blue dress that had been passed from Sylvie to Evelyn and from Evelyn to Joan. The material fell in beautiful, soft, unstructured pleats from the waistline, and tiny pin-tucks formed a lovely shape on the shoulders and bodice. With the addition of sequins along the neckline and a sparkling buckle at the hip, Joan felt like she'd stepped out of a magazine.

The club was dark and crowded. Every table was occupied, bodies like shadows dressed in sombre colours pressed together along the walls. Weak candles flickered in empty bottles. Thin, lazy wisps of smoke curled towards the low ceiling and hung there in a haze. Joan could make out the faces of the people sitting almost on top of the stage, but beyond that everyone was a blur. The MC jumped onto the stage and in a low, seductive voice said, 'Ladies and gentlemen. Your new, regular, ten-on-the-dot spot . . . Colin's Kats!'

383

Joan wiped her hands on her dress as he hopped off, clapping. Then they were on, starting their first number.

Joan had never been so nervous when she played with the orchestra, but then she'd been one of many. Here she was exposed and scrutinised; there was no one to hide behind. The first two songs went well; she was grateful Colin had been a stern taskmaster during practice. 'Dig You Later' was next and it was a powerful feeling when the audience joined in with the chorus of *a-hubba-hubba-hubba*. Colin was beaming, a film of sweat shining on his forehead.

Carried away, their solos got a bit rowdy and lasted longer than they'd rehearsed, but it felt like an initiation test. And they were passing it. A trumpet player with the Knights of Rhythm jumped in and improvised with them, and although it threw them initially, they recovered in time to make it work. They finished their last three numbers and enjoyed a good round of applause.

Standing in line for a bow, Joan reached for Colin's hand, but he continued to bend forward with one hand in front of his waist, the other behind his back. She told herself he was ignoring her because he felt he'd be leaving Bernie and the drummer out of the gesture of solidarity. But she felt sure there was something about her that still disappointed him. If there was any chance he wanted to take their relationship further, as she hoped he did, perhaps he thought her refusal to deal with her estrangement from Mother didn't bode well for any future differences they might have.

During the interval before the main act, there were a lot of introductions to be made: Joan to Colin's parents and family, friends and hangers-on. She kissed Eileen, who was expecting a baby, and chatted to Edward, but they seemed distant. Then they met Bernie's girl and his crowd. Joan made sure that her three guests tagged along with her and were included in the handshakes and chit-chat.

The dim lights faded further and the headliners arranged themselves on stage ready to go. She could hear bursts of laughter and the tail end of comments from both her fellow band members' large parties. There didn't seem to be space amongst them for anyone else, but when a tall man in a suit rushed in and clapped Colin on the back, another chair was squeezed in with ease. Joan sat between Alice and Evelyn at a table near the door with plenty of room around them and no one else expected. Looking at each of her friends in turn, she told herself she was lucky to have them — and she meant it. And if she had invited Mother and Father, well, that would have only made two more.

Their technique developed, and every Sunday night the club was full, whether to see them or the leading act didn't matter too much as it gave them the experience and exposure they needed. Friends and family came and went. Alice often showed up, sometimes on her own, sometimes with Evelyn. Gwen never returned, but she had responsibilities at home. Edward put in an appearance from time to time, but Joan didn't see Eileen again, probably too busy with the baby. Colin's mum was their most stalwart and devoted supporter, only absent for other family obligations like grandchildren's birthdays. It was hard to believe she'd given birth to Colin: she was as short and round as he was tall and gangly. Colin's hair was a light strawberry blonde; his mum's bubbly white perm would have been dark when she was younger, if her eyebrows and lashes were anything to go by.

One cold, dank autumn night when Colin wanted to stay on to jam with a few other musicians, he put Joan and his mum in a taxi together and told the driver to drop off Joan first. Their route took them over Waterloo Bridge and Colin's mum said, 'Have you ever noticed that from the Embankment vehicles appear to be gliding across here? I suppose that's how we look now to anyone watching from the walkway below, as if we're drifting along.'

'I drove a crane on this bridge while it was being built,' Joan said.

'Did you?' The older woman looked astonished, her eyes wide, mouth round and puckered. 'How marvellous. Tell me about it.'

'There's not much to tell. It was just a job.' Joan turned to watch the bridge receding behind them as they coasted off it into Waterloo Road. 'It seems like a long time ago now.'

'Well, yes,' Colin's mum said. 'Life's like that when you look back. Broken up into a lot of different chapters or scenes. Changing all the time.'

Neither spoke for a minute or two then Joan said, 'You must really enjoy jazz, to come and listen as often as you do.'

'I much prefer classical.'

386

'Same as my mother.'

'Oh, I didn't know . . . I haven't met her, have I?'

'No,' Joan said. 'I don't think she'd approve of the club. Or the music.'

'What a shame,' Colin's mum said. 'I go anywhere my children invite me, on principle.' She laughed. '*And* to annoy them.'

Joan watched a drop of rain break its hold on the window and spill down the pane of glass. She followed it with her finger. 'It isn't worth inviting her. I know what the answer would be.'

Colin's mum took Joan's chin in her hand and studied her face. 'No wonder you always look so sad,' she said. 'But that might have been her answer during a time that's gone, all but forgotten. Things could be different now.'

Joan brooded on her conversation with Colin's mum for some weeks before she decided to write to Mother. She kept the letter short, asking after her and Father's health and telling her about the filing job and the slot at Jigs. Mother wrote back right away and said she was surprised Joan was playing again. The last she knew, Joan was waitressing at the Strand, or was it the Regent's Palace? She wished Joan luck and signed the letter with love. Although there hadn't been a formal invitation to come along and listen, Joan found herself scrutinising the audience every Sunday night hoping Mother would take the hint.

Then, one evening, she saw a familiar shape in the gloom, head held high, fox fur around her neck, taking a seat at a table right at the back. Joan's mouth was dry, her hands shaky. She turned her back on the audience and whispered to Colin, 'Mother's here.'

'Come on then, old thing,' Colin said. 'Let's give it to her.'

The music took over for Joan that night; she felt light and unencumbered. Mother was here and, whether she approved or not, it seemed she'd been interested enough to turn up. At the end of the set the MC said that Colin's Kats were on fire. Phenomenal. Mother stood, applauding in her gloves, and the crowd followed. Their first standing ovation.

'One more, ladies and gentlemen?' the MC asked.

'Over to you, Joan,' Colin said.

Joan looked straight at Mother, nodded and played the opening bars to 'I'm Beginning to See the Light'. When they finished and took their bows, Colin reached for her hand and held onto it for the rest of the evening.

17

10 December 1945

Dignitaries surrounded Deputy Prime Minister Herbert Morrison as he stood on a makeshift podium in front of a forest of microphones, a pair of scissors in his hand. His wife, standing next to him, had thick waves under a black hat and was pressing an enormous bouquet of red and white flowers to her coat. Morrison alone had his head exposed to the icy wind that whipped an unruly wave into a ripple above his head. Newspaper reporters jostled for a prime spot in front of him as he blinked, like a short-sighted owl, through his round, dark-framed glasses and said, 'Ladies and gentlemen, I am very, very glad this morning to open the new Waterloo Bridge.'

'Did you know,' Joan said to Evelyn, pulling her collar tight around her neck, 'that he's blind in one eye?'

'No,' Evelyn said. 'Poor man. Was that the Great War? Or The War, as your Hazel insists on calling it.'

'Oh,' Joan said. 'I don't know.'

'I does,' Alice said. 'He lost the sight in it through a childhood infection. He were a Conchie in the war before this one.'

Joan turned to Alice and looked her up and down with round eyes. 'You amaze me,' she said. 'How do you know so much?'

389

Alice blushed. 'I listens to what people talk about when they come into the shop. A bit of ear-wigging, I suppose. And I likes to read the papers.'

'He would have been the PM,' Alice continued. 'Except he doesn't have a lot of . . . something . . . charm, I think.'

'No, he doesn't seem to,' Evelyn said.

'Or charisma,' Joan added.

'That's the word.'

They huddled together with a small group of onlookers who had been asked to stand with their backs to Somerset House, behind and away from Morrison who was facing Parliament and Big Ben. They had to strain to hear what was being said.

'The time came when Rennie's bridge became shaky and it had to be propped up. There followed ten years of keen discussion, argument and debate between equally sincere people as to what should be done about the bridge and finally, after these ten or eleven years had passed, it was decided to demolish the old bridge, which was difficult for navigation, and to substitute a new one — and the new one is here.'

Evelyn looked around and wondered what interest the other spectators had in the bridge. 'Do you recognise anyone?' she said. 'I don't.'

'One or two,' Alice answered. 'No one to speak to.'

Gwen shook her head and kept her eyes on her feet as she stamped them in rhythm to keep warm. She could identify those missing more easily than those standing around them. Sylvie, Olive. And of course her Johnny. She touched the spot where her boy's hanky had comforted her. She cleared her throat. 'He must stop talking soon,' she said.

'Time was some girl or another in a turban would have shouted, ''Get snipping or I'll do it for you,'' Evelyn said.

'Go on, then.' Joan laughed. 'I dare you.'

'I'm too much of a nice girl,' Evelyn said. 'Dad will tell you that.'

'Listen,' Alice said. 'I think he's finishing now.'

'The men who built Waterloo Bridge are fortunate men,' Morrison was saying.

Evelyn turned to her friends, her eyebrows fierce and arched, a terrier with her hackles up. 'And ladies,' she mouthed.

'He means mankind,' Joan said.

'No he doesn't, he means men.'

Joan knew she was right.

Morrison paused as a microphone crackled. 'They know that, although their names may be forgotten, their work will be a pride and use to London for many generations to come. To the hundreds of workers in stone, in steel, in timber, in concrete the new bridge is a monument to their skill and craftsmanship. Keep it white. Its whiteness is one of its glories.'

'Cleaning,' Alice said. 'That were his tip of the hat to us.'

'We know everything there is to know about that,' Gwen said.

'I will proceed to cut the tape,' Morrison said. 'And declare the new Waterloo Bridge to be open.' He placed his hat on his head, walked to the ticker-tape and cut it in half, the two ends fluttering for a moment and then drooping to the ground. A trumpet fanfare was sounded by the National Fire

Service band, followed by a round of applause to which Mr Morrison nodded and shook a few hands. Then he and his wife started towards the south side followed by the public figures, reporters, the invited and the bystanders.

They'd seen this view from above the bend in the river every day for years, but Evelyn thought it remained fresh and stunning. All the more startling for being able to enjoy the sight without dread of bombing or attack. The air was crisp and clean around St Paul's to the left; a vapour trail of cloud moving over Big Ben to the right.

'Do you think it's something for London to be proud of?' Evelyn asked. 'You know, like Morrison said?'

'Depends whether it gets shaky or not,' Gwen said.

'Of course it won't.'

'Who knows? The first one did.'

'And if it does,' said Joan. 'It'll be a folly. Not the pride of London.'

'Well, I thinks . . . .'

'What do you think, Alice?'

'I thinks it don't matter either way.'

'Why not?'

'All that matters is it needed to be done and we did it.'

Gwen lagged behind when they reached the spot above her special place. She stood next to the railing, stretching high on her toes and stared into the black, churning river.

'Gwen. Come on,' Evelyn called. 'You won't have time for a drink before you have to get home to the kids.'

'One minute,' Gwen shouted back.

The river lapped against the pier, churning up silt and mud, a length of rusty chain, a skeleton of umbrella spokes, a sheet of shredded tarpaulin. Something light floating on a watery undulation caught her eye. A triangle of flag perhaps, or a page of newspaper. She leaned over as far as she dared and peered down. No, it was a square of white cotton hanky. She watched as a flash of winter sunlight brought the material into stark relief. Then a white-topped swell wrapped it around the concrete where it waved her on towards her friends, her home, her family, her life. She blew a kiss towards it.

'Gwen.'

Gwen turned and put her hand up to the others. When she looked again, the ragged piece of cloth had been released from its old precarious place of refuge and was floating on a swirling eddy before it disappeared from view.

Acknowledgements

From the bottom of my heart I am grateful to my daughter, Kelly Collinwood-Erdinc, and my son, Liam Collinwood, for their love, encouragement and support and for not allowing me to give up. And a big thank you — with much love — to my husband, Don Gilchrist, for his confidence in me and for being my research buddy, especially at the Metropolitan Archives.

To my grandchildren Toby, Kaan, Ayda, Alya and Aleksia I would like to say thank you for being everything and more.

I'm also grateful to Peter and Kathleen Casey, Arie Collinwood, Ozzie Erdinc, Danny and Sonia Gilchrist, Tom Gilchrist and Sue Ward for their love, support and enthusiasm.

I would like to say thank you to the first readers of this novel for their feedback and encouragement: Kelly Collinwood-Erdinc, Liam Collinwood, Johanna Emeney, Steve Farmer, and Jan Hurst.

A thank you, also, to Laura Deitz and Colette Paul, my tutors on the MA in Creative Writing course at Anglia Ruskin University, the Angles Writing Group and The National Centre for Writing, Norwich for awarding me highly-commended in the Escalator Prize for this novel which gave me so much confidence.

Thanks go to my fellow Book Club members Jo Bishop, Kelly Collinwood-Erdinc, Steve Farmer, Don Gilchrist, Maureen John, Nick John, Liz Peadon,

Dave Pountney and Martin Shrosbree who have celebrated every step of the way with me.

I am so grateful to Rhea Kurien at Aria Fiction and my agent, Kiran Kataria at Keane Kataria Literary Agency for choosing me. Thank you also to Vicky Joss, at Aria Fiction, for her help with social media and digital marketing.

I would have been lost without Peter Cross-Rudkin of the Institute of Civil Engineers who gave up his time to sit with me, show me diagrams and photos and explain how bridges were built in the 1940s. Thank you very much.

Thank you to the Women's Engineering Society for information and advice.

And a big thank you to Nick Abendroth, Libby Aitchison, Lizzie Alexander, Helen Chatten, Penny Clarke, Breda Doran, Natalie Farrell, Chris Holmes, Paula Horsfall and Liz Kochprapha for all their support, friendship and love.